37653013849487
Fletcher ▮▮▮▮▮ Fiction
MYSTERY GREER
The mongoose deception

11/07

CENTRAL ARKANSAS LIBRARY SYSTEM

D0966212

The
Mongoose
Deception

Other books by Robert Greer

The Devil's Hatband

The Devil's Red Nickel

The Devil's Backbone

Limited Time

Isolation and other Stories

Heat Shock

Resurrecting Langston Blue

The Fourth Perspective

The Mongoose Deception

ROBERT GREER

Frog, Ltd.
Berkeley, California

Copyright © 2007 by Robert Greer. All rights reserved. No portion of this book, except for brief review, may be reproduced, stored in a retrieval system, or transmitted in any form or by any means—electronic, mechanical, photocopying, recording, or otherwise—without written permission of the publisher. For information contact Frog, Ltd. c/o North Atlantic Books.

Published by Frog, Ltd.
Frog, Ltd. books are distributed
by North Atlantic Books
P.O. Box 12327
Berkeley, California 94712

Cover art by Kevin Bell
Cover and book design by Brad Greene
Printed in the United States of America

North Atlantic Books' publications are available through most bookstores. For further information, call 800-337-2665 or visit our website at www.northatlanticbooks.com.

Substantial discounts on bulk quantities are available to corporations, professional associations, and other organizations. For details and discount information, contact our special sales department.

The Mongoose Deception is sponsored by the Society for the Study of Native Arts and Sciences, a nonprofit educational corporation whose goals are to develop an educational and crosscultural perspective linking various scientific, social, and artistic fields; to nurture a holistic view of arts, sciences, humanities, and healing; and to publish and distribute literature on the relationship of mind, body, and nature.

Library of Congress Cataloging-in-Publication Data

Greer, Robert O.
    The mongoose deception / by Robert Greer.
        p. cm.
    Summary: "A historical thriller that takes streetwise but reluctant investigator CJ Floyd into the bowels of one of the most intriguing assassination cases in world history as he tries to find out how JFK was set up for the kill and who really killed him"—Provided by publisher.
    ISBN-13: 978-1-58394-192-8
    ISBN-10: 1-58394-192-4
    1. Kennedy, John F. (John Fitzgerald), 1917–1963—Assassination—Fiction. 2. Presidents—Assassination—Fiction. 3. Political crimes and offenses—Fiction. 4. Conspiracies—Fiction. I. Title.
    PS3557.R3997M66 2007
    813'.54—dc22
                                                                            2007020042
                                                                            CIP

1 2 3 4 5 6 7 8 9 SHERIDAN 14 13 12 11 10 09 08 07

Dedication

As always, for my beloved, departed wife Phyllis

CENTRAL ARKANSAS LIBRARY SYSTEM
FLETCHER BRANCH LIBRARY
LITTLE ROCK, ARKANSAS

Acknowledgments

Many people assisted the author during the writing of this book. I would especially like to acknowledge the invaluable assistance of Kathy Woodley and Connie Blanchard, who spent endless hours typing and retyping the manuscript for the recalcitrant, computer-challenged author.

I thank John Dunning for his insight into the tribulations surrounding the construction of the Eisenhower Memorial Tunnel and Jane M. H. Bigelow of the Englewood Public Library for providing historical information about the tunnel's construction and the purported fatal 1972 air crash of Congressman Hale Boggs.

Corporal Troy A. Edwards of the Denver Police Department provided police procedural information. Any errors in translating that information to the page lie with the author.

Finally, I wish to acknowledge the continuing support of Connie Oehring for her copyediting skills and the support of my editor, Emily Boyd at North Atlantic Books, and the book savvy of associate publisher Mark Ouimet, always ahead of trends.

Author's Note

The characters, events, and places that are depicted in *The Mongoose Deception* are spawned from the author's imagination. Certain Denver and Western locales are used fictitiously, and any resemblance between the novel's fictional inhabitants and actual persons living or dead is purely coincidental.

We have limitless resources and the people yield themselves with perfect docility to our molding hands.

—Frederick T. Gates, Chairman, John D. Rockefeller
General Education Board

Prologue

Ocean City, Maryland, May 1963

There were eleven of them. Eleven men who had taken a lifetime of instruction unlike any other. They were at once the past, the present, and the future of their kind. Men who sat in the highest, most rarefied circles of power. Men who controlled the very comings and goings of the world. And like their predecessors, these men had pooled their influence and power and fortunes—their cunning and daring—their intellect and their utter ruthlessness in order to amass the unbridled influence that would be passed down from them to theirs, generation to generation.

They were the power behind governments and corporations and organized crime. The hidden face of political corruption, and the might behind the world's military machines. Winston Churchill once called them the High Cabal. And now, after almost two centuries, they were being challenged, questioned by an upstart who would dare to deny them what was theirs. An upstart who would now have to be either eliminated or purged.

The oval table they sat around—a table with a history as stout as that of the eleven men—was three centuries old. The dimly lit utilitarian room they occupied was unseasonably cold. As the man at the head of the table, a man bred of privilege and entitlement, looked up stoically to speak, the room fell silent. His words, matter-of-fact, crisp, and clear, were the words of an anointed royal. "Are we of one mind?" he asked, looking slowly around the table.

"One," came the response of the man to his right.

"One," echoed the next man.

"One," said the man next to him—and so on the answers came until one by one all eleven men had uttered that same fateful word.

After a moment of silence, the man who had first spoken rose and brought his right hand gently to the table and said, "So it will be."

PART I

The Find

Chapter 1

Eisenhower Memorial Tunnel, Interstate 70, Colorado Continental Divide, late August, the Present

Cornelius McPherson loved talking to himself with the rumbling insistence of someone hard-of-hearing, which clearly he was not. He talked to himself in shopping malls, at sporting events, on hiking trails, and in church and once, in a booming voice that startled and unhinged a group of vacationing, camera-laden Japanese onlookers, he held a conversation with himself in the middle of the Colorado capitol rotunda, debating the pros and cons of the Persian Gulf War. More than anything, McPherson loved to talk to himself at work. Talking to himself there, inside a mountain at an elevation of over eleven thousand feet, gave him the in-control, never-alone sense of ease he craved. When you came right down to it—"netted it all out," as McPherson was fond of saying—he didn't really talk to himself so much as he recited, mumbled, and hummed, and not just any convenient piece of trendy prose, scripture, or ditty. What McPherson brought forth in all earnestness, more often than not for no ears but his own, was what he liked to think of as the poetry of life. Hymns, nursery rhymes, poems, famous sayings, quotations, and parables all fought for space, churning effortlessly and endlessly deep inside Cornelius McPherson's head, nudging, sometimes shoving him through the day.

Everybody's got a song or a rhyme that haunts 'em, McPherson loved to say, and no song, poem, rhyme, or hymn gave McPherson more comfort than the song he was currently humming, the old Negro spiritual "Lift Every Voice and Sing."

Just two days from retirement, McPherson was at work and humming that song, doing the same thing he'd been doing for the past three decades and thinking that in less than forty-eight hours he'd be forever free from the cold, dank smells of life inside a tunnel through a mountain. Negotiating his way along a Colorado Department of Transportation tunnel-inspection catwalk inside I-70's Eisenhower Memorial Tunnel, the same catwalk he'd traveled five to six days a week for pretty close to 7,500 days, McPherson found himself smiling and humming to beat the band.

The concrete catwalk, which hugged the tunnel's north wall and stood four feet above I-70's two lanes of westbound traffic, was used for everything from inspecting the tunnel's aging tile walls for cracks to troubleshooting dangerous grout-line water seepage to providing a 1.6-mile-long conveyance along which the tile washers moved their high-powered water-spray equipment once a year.

It was just past 10 a.m., and traffic on the interstate was surprisingly light when McPherson, nodding and swaying to the beat in his head, wrapped up his rendition of "Lift Every Voice and Sing" and cleared his throat in prelude to his always slightly off-key version of "Amazing Grace."

Thirty-nine years earlier, high in the Colorado Rockies sixty miles west of Denver in the spring of 1968, all the elements of a classic duel between man and the earth had been present when McPherson and fifty other miners had gone underground to begin digging one of the largest automobile tunnels in the world, and clearly the highest. The men were on the front end of a bore into the Continental Divide that started at the eleven-thousand-foot level of Colorado's treacherous Loveland Pass. Known back then, in a reference to the creek that ran above it, simply as the Straight Creek tunnel dig, the job entailed blasting through two miles of mountain, a geologic fault, and a nightmare of fractured and crushed rock to run a road across—or, more accurately, through, as McPherson loved to phrase it—the top of the world.

McPherson, a squat, five-foot-nine, 190-pound fireplug of a black man with a skullcap of wiry gray hair and grainy, sandpaper-textured, dark-chocolate skin, had been a 150-pound wisp of a man when he'd begun his days as a member of a Straight Creek tunnel-mucking team that would spend five years battling a mountain and the sometimes eighteen-hundred-foot-wide geologic nightmare of fractured and crushed rock known as the Loveland Fault.

During the early days of the dig, project delays, worker injuries, and an unending flow of cash to nowhere were par for the course, but McPherson had stuck it out, watching the project move from being the Straight Creek tunnel bore to a hole through the Continental Divide that would ultimately become the continent-cresting, automobile-streaking sky window known as the Eisenhower Memorial Tunnel. By the time the dig was finally done in 1973, it had claimed the lives of seven men, and as many as 1,140 people had dug and dynamited their way through a mountain. Along the way, McPherson had worked his way up from tunnel mucker to drift runner to bulk-rock-loader operator, and from there to his present job as the Colorado Department of Transportation's chief Eisenhower Tunnel attendant and troubleshooting walking boss.

Watching the flow of traffic below, McPherson, minus two toes on his left foot that had been there when the Straight Creek dig had begun, broke into a self-congratulatory short-timer's smile. Transitioning from humming "Amazing Grace," McPherson, unmarried, childless, and always a loner, moved quickly into an inner-city skip-rope rhyme: *Once upon a time the goose drank wine, tried to do the shimmy with a monkey on the streetcar line. The streetcar line broke, the monkey got choked, they both went to heaven on a silly billy goat.* After a lifetime of reciting the rhyme, he never missed a word or a beat. Hard hat snugged up and power lamp in hand, he continued walking and scanning the tunnel for burned-out overhead lights, fractured tiles, ventilation problems, and the bane of his existence, eroding grout.

Last night, night before, twenty-four robbers at my door. I got up and let 'em in, hit 'em in the head with a rolling pin. His cadence now on automatic pilot, McPherson scanned the vast catalog of skip rhymes in his head, searching for one that was appropriate for someone just two days away from retirement. Finally he belted out, *The white boys had a rooster, they set him on a fence, the rooster crowed for the colored boys 'cause he had some sense.* He cleared his throat in preparation for a second verse when, without warning, every light in the tunnel blinked out. A fraction of a second later, the five-foot-thick, rebar-reinforced concrete catwalk he was standing on, a 1.6-mile-long virtual seawall, buckled and caved in. Losing his balance as he leapfrogged to a platform of stable concrete a few feet away, McPherson fell to one knee.

"What the shit!" He scanned the darkness with the powerful lamp in his right hand, arcing the light back and forth as warning sirens sounded all around him. Twenty yards ahead of him, a tractor-trailer braked to avoid crashing into a half-dozen pieces of catwalk concrete that had tumbled down onto the roadway. The braking semi jackknifed, and its trailer kissed the tunnel's north wall, sending a Fourth of July celebration of sparks shooting up into the darkness.

A horn blast erupted on the heels of the now steady wail of the sirens. Five seconds later there was a second horn blast, and five seconds later another. McPherson's throat went dry as he recognized the blasts and sirens as the synchronized, coded alarm announcing that the Eisenhower Tunnel had been hit by an earthquake.

The tunnel's walls and the I-70 roadway popped and cracked and buckled as McPherson grabbed a piece of the catwalk's railing and chanted, *Apples, peaches, pumpkin pie, all not ready holler, "I!"* For three lingering additional seconds the tunnel walls and the mountain behind them hissed and snapped and groaned. Boulders and rocks the size of small cars, free from a thirty-four-year encumbrance of concrete, rebar, and tile, dribbled down onto the interstate until finally the horn blasts and sirens stopped and the sound of rushing water and the echo of a lone car horn blaring in the distance were the only things McPherson could hear.

As loudly as he dared, McPherson announced to himself, "I'm still alive!" Still hugging the catwalk's twisted hand railing for dear life, he steadied himself on what was now an undulating platform of concrete rubble and shook his head in disbelief. Before he could screw up the courage to take a step, the backup diesel generators sparked the lights back on. The tunnel was filled with a haze of smoke and dust, but he could see the jackknifed tractor-trailer thirty yards ahead of him, and tunnel lights beyond it to the west. A midsized European SUV had slammed into the trailer, nosing its way beneath the rear end like a rooting terrier. The trapped SUV and squatting trailer sat cockeyed across the interstate, locked together, blocking the lanes in both directions. Recognizing that both the truck driver and the SUV's driver were at least moving, McPherson exhaled a sigh of relief.

With his view of the tunnel to the west blocked by the semi and a particle-filled cloud of smoke, McPherson turned back to see a drunken conga line of pickups, big rigs, and cars tossed hither and yon on an undulating conveyer belt of roadway that stretched a half mile back to the east portal. A dozen or so dazed-looking people who'd escaped their vehicles were moving through the haze, climbing over stalled cars and trucks and rock, making their way toward the east portal and daylight.

McPherson patted himself down, reassured that everything was still in place. Disbelief filling his voice, he said, "A fuckin' earthquake. Who in the hell would've thunk it?" A cave-in was what old-time tunnel muckers and drift runners like Cornelius McPherson worried about. Oh, he'd heard people talk about the risk of a quake, and he knew that the geologists and engineers who'd designed the tunnel were aware that the Loveland Fault and plate of rock were primed for an earthquake. The tunnel design team simply never could judge for certain how powerful an earthquake to engineer for. *Now ya know, now ya know, now ya know,* McPherson chuckled aloud, aware that he'd just lived through the earthquake equivalent of a hundred-year flood.

Gripped by the uncertainty of the moment, he'd almost forgotten about the walkie-talkie clipped to his belt until a voice he recognized as that of his supervisor, Franklin Watts, crackled on a wave of static: "Corny, you all right in there?"

Breathing hard, McPherson answered, "Yeah."

"We just had an earthquake. Golden's already been in touch. They're reporting a 6.7 on the Richter scale."

Aware that the National Earthquake Information Center in Golden, Colorado, forty miles and nearly six thousand feet of elevation back down I-70 and the mountain, was linked directly to the tunnel's command center, McPherson barked, "We got lights in here, and you, Franklin, bless your ever-lovin', pea-pickin' Tennessee heart, have got a bunch of hysterical people headed your way, scramblin' like shit for the east portal. There's a semi with a sport ute pooched up its ass blockin' the roadway just up ahead of me." Barely pausing to take a breath, McPherson added, "We're 'bout four-tenths of a mile in, I'd make it. Most of the cars I can see are bumper to bumper. A few of 'em are kissin' a tunnel wall, but I don't see none over-turned. Can't be certain, though; there's so much haze and smoke in here. Sure as hell can smell gasoline, though."

"I've got paramedics and a disaster team headed your way. Another one's headed in from the west. Can we get past your wreck?"

"Nope. That semi's straddlin' the whole damn road."

"Shit! How many people you think you've still got in there with you?"

McPherson eyed the crumbled concrete that had been a catwalk, then glanced back toward the line of westbound vehicles below. Counting the vehicles off one by one in his head, he said, "I can only see as far back as maybe fifteen vehicles. Figurin' two people to a car, and stretchin' that out a little—not countin' the folks that hauled ass as soon as things started movin' and shakin'—I figure maybe twenty, twenty-five."

"Can you walk any of 'em out?"

"If they don't all run the hell outta here first."

"Then get to it."

"I'm on it." McPherson had started to climb over the catwalk's twisted guard railing when he heard, just barely but perceptibly for an old tunnel rat like him, the unmistakable sound of rushing water. He glanced back toward the tunnel's south wall. "Hey, Franklin, I got water spittin' at me from somewhere. Wait a minute—I see it. There's water gushin' outta a break in the south wall of the tunnel just up ahead of me. Didn't see it before, but I sure as hell can see it now. I better check it out." For the first time since the earthquake had hit, McPherson, iron-willed tunnel rat, miner, and seasoned digger, felt himself shaking. "I think we got a seam break up ahead." Suddenly his whole body turned sweaty.

"How bad?"

"Can't tell."

"Damn! Scratch that victim lead-out we were just talking about," said Watts. McPherson could picture the other man stroking his chin thoughtfully. "I'll send Wilkerson in to handle that. If we've got a crack in the mountain, we've bought ourselves one hell of a problem. See if you can figure out what's goin' on with that stream of water. And Cornelius, better make it fast."

"Is it safe in here, Franklin?"

"The folks who engineered the place claim it is. And she just stood up to a near 7-grade Richter hit, didn't she? I'd say you're pretty safe there for the moment. Long as we don't get another tremor. Take a quick look at our problem. You're the only eyes and ears I got right now. Then haul ass outta there."

"Okay. One quick look and I'm gone." McPherson fumbled with his walkie-talkie, making certain the volume was set on high, clipped it to his belt, took what he hoped wouldn't be his last look through the haze toward the queue of surprisingly orderly people who were making their way over rubble and stalled vehicles toward the east portal, and shouted, pretty certain none of the people could hear him, "Help's on the way!" Hitching up his pants before heading toward what looked to be a gushing waterfall, he swallowed hard as for a fleeting second he brought into focus something he hadn't seen in decades: the unmistakable belly of the mountain he had once cut his way through.

When he got close enough that his legs were being pelted by a shower of ice-cold water, silt, muck, and broken tree roots, he realized that what had seemed to be a massive waterfall from his earlier vantage point was, on closer inspection, simply a fire-hose-sized stream of water spewing from an automobile-sized rhomboid-shaped hole in the south tunnel wall.

Recognizing his mistake, McPherson shook his head. "Shoulda known a real gusher woulda washed my ass outta here by now. Thought you had me, but you didn't," he said boastfully, aiming his words directly at the stream of water and breaking into a chant: "Tried to trick me but you couldn't. I know you did, I know you did. I know you did." With his miner's instincts open full bore, he mumbled, "Goddamn underground spring." Snapping his walkie-talkie off his belt, he barked into it, "Franklin, my water gusher's comin' from an underground spring. I'm sure of it." The sound of water gurgling its way out of the mountain, as if in search of a highway to freedom, had him suddenly recalling the dozens of battles he and other miners had had with underground springs, seepage, and erosion during the first two years on the Straight Creek tunnel dig. "A fuckin' nightmare, and it's back," he mumbled.

Franklin Watts's voice erupted from the walkie-talkie. "Figures." Watts, also a Straight Creek tunnel veteran, hadn't been around for the first year of the tunnel bore—the worst year on the dig, old-timers still claimed—but he'd spent the next four years underground, and the dig's blueprint had been stamped indelibly into his psyche as well.

Confident that the rush of water was subsiding and relieved at having pinpointed the source, McPherson said, "I'm gonna check the far side of the hole I got down here."

"Don't press your luck, man," said Watts. "You've told me what I needed to know. Get the shit outta there."

McPherson shook off his boss's order with a defiant nod. Uttering the words in the same cadence that he and his drift-front mining team had once used to get themselves started every day, he chanted, *Fool me once, shame on me, mishandle the mountain, shame on me, rumble-tumble, rumble-tumble, always on me, always on me, get up and go, digger man, digger man.*

The rhyme's simple meaning, a mantra that every miner kept tucked inside the self-preservation corner of his brain—*run for daylight when you hear the unmistakable rumble-tumble of a cave-in*—wasn't lost on Watts. "I said get the shit out of there, Cornelius! You hear me?"

McPherson smiled, knowing he'd won one more tiny battle with the mountain. "Franklin, Franklin, Franklin. Wasn't but a couple'a minutes ago you told me this ol' tunnel of ours was built to stand every shake, rattle, and roll the man upstairs could deliver. But I hear you talkin'. I'll be outta here and up there with you in that warm supervisor's bunkhouse soakin' up the sunshine in two shakes of a tit. Just gotta check out one more thing." Clipping his walkie-talkie to his belt, McPherson walked through what was now only a limp stream of water spitting out of the mountain. Brushing a shower of muck off his leg, he worked his way to the middle of the truncated hole in the tunnel wall. A river of tile grout, tree roots, and silt swirled around his feet as a blast of freezing air rushed out of the hole in the tunnel's wall to greet him. Shivering and rubbing his hands together, McPherson cupped a hand above his eyes as he strained to see between two pieces of bowed rebar into the dark hole. "Thought you had me," he shouted into the ten-foot-wide cavern. "You thought you did, you thought you did, you thought you did, rumble-tumble, rumble-tumble, digger man, digger man."

The brief resurrection of his mining glory days quickly faded, and the thrill of his tiny new victory over the mountain was short-lived. Reasoning that now wasn't the time to push his luck, he shook a fist at the cavernous hole, shook his head, and turned to leave. Walking off the length of the hole, he counted off the footage: "Eight, nine, ten, eleven, twelve. Twelve foot long, right on the money, damn!"

Eyeing a crumble of concrete at his feet, he noticed what looked like a stubby tree limb lying a few feet beyond his right foot. Deciding he'd take the limb back as a final souvenir of his nearly forty years of wrestling underground with nature, he stooped to pick it up. It wasn't until he took a knee that he realized he wasn't looking at a tree limb, or a broken support timber, or a fractured bearing joist, or even a misshapen piece of steel I-beam. What he found himself staring at, as his eyes expanded and his spine tingled with quixotic numbness, was a frozen, well-preserved, and amazingly intact human forearm.

A rush of curiosity and then disbelief overwhelmed him as he examined the appendage, turning it gently around in his hands, holding it up to the light, rotating it back and forth. The arm, severed at the elbow, was a darker, almost ebony version of what it had been in life, and the remaining skin, patches of it having been stripped away, had the rough, uneven texture of tree bark.

As frigid air continued to rush through the hole in the tunnel wall, the gears in Cornelius McPherson's head ground to a halt, and his whole body suddenly turned numb. It wasn't the air streaming from the belly of an angry mountain that had unnerved him; it was something much more eerie, more unsettling and profound. There was something unmistakably recognizable about the severed arm. Continuing to hold the dark, lifeless form up to the light, he turned it around and around. There was no question about it—it was a forearm he recognized, an appendage stripped from somebody he'd known.

He wanted to say, *No,* wanted to scream at the top of his lungs, *It can't be! It's gotta be some kinda postearthquake mirage.* But there was no mistaking it. The arm bore an immutable and unmistakable signature that told anyone who'd ever seen it before exactly whom the arm belonged to. As dark as it was, and as rough and reptilian as the remaining skin appeared, the red, white, and blue flames that encircled the frozen appendage and the words *breed love* just above the wrist told McPherson that the arm had belonged to one of the five men from his long-disbanded Straight Creek tunnel crew. It was the forearm of the crew's gently spoken, well-mannered rock-hauling truck driver who, in the two years he'd worked with McPherson, had seemed sensitive, secretive, and above all lonely. Cornelius McPherson had known him during that time simply as Ducane. Sad-faced Ducane. And he remembered Ducane telling him in a breathless whisper one night, after they'd spent a weekend drinking and whoring outside the windswept mining town of Hanna, Wyoming—in a voice that had a strange, incisive edge to it—that he knew who had killed President John F. Kennedy.

McPherson knelt and laid the forearm reverently at his feet. Shaken in a way he hadn't been for more than thirty years, he pivoted and stared into the dark cavern in the mountain, wondering whether any more of Ducane's body parts were inside. But more than anything, he found himself wondering just how Ducane had ended up trapped behind a wall of concrete, steel, and tile. He continued asking himself that question as he scooped the arm back up and headed toward the east portal, recalling as he slipped his way over boulders and twisted metal, shattered glass and stalled cars, that the man calling himself Ducane, as far as he could remember, had not been injured even once during the Straight Creek tunnel dig. As he stumbled toward daylight, a cold shiver swept through him, and he found himself thinking about the fact that the man called Ducane, the man who'd told him that he knew who'd killed JFK, had simply turned up missing one day thirty-seven years earlier, never again to show up on the job.

PART II

The Past

Chapter 2

Gary, Indiana, November 1, 1963

Killing never sits easy with compromise, and Antoine "Sugar Sweet" Ducane recognized all too well that that was what he'd been hired to do—suck hind teat, ride shotgun, and grind it out as a compromise, second-string trigger-pulling alternate in a high-stakes game of murder. Murder that had the potential to alter the very course of U.S. history.

Ducane didn't like playing second fiddle, never had. Not six years earlier, when he'd been forced to come off the bench to lead his New Iberia, Louisiana, high school football team to a state championship. Not when he'd given up dreams of being an artist after his high school sweetheart had blasted a hole in the psychological armor he'd always used to hold people at bay, leaving him for a Gulf Coast oil rigger. Not during the three years immediately after high school, when he'd boxed his way up the long-rigged, mob-controlled National Boxing Association ladder to become a middleweight title contender, only to get sponged out of the title picture by the Louisiana mob when it was pointed out that he was Creole, not the great Italian Rocky Marciano hope they'd been trolling for. And finally, not even when, as no more than a tagalong wheelman during the fourth in a series of Baton Rouge bank robberies, he'd been ordered in the midst of a robbery gone sour to kill a man and had done his best to oblige.

As they were racing away from the bank, one of his two cohorts had screamed, "Off the pig!" The man who gave the order had a bullet from the bank guard's .38 police special lodged in his upper thigh. Sugar Sweet Ducane had dutifully pumped two slugs from his mother's .32, a gun he'd stolen from her as an inquisitive, morose teenager, into the security guard's gut. Against the odds, the security guard had lived. The exsanguinating robber hadn't, but more importantly for the man called Sugar Sweet, in the wake of that robbery he never saw the inside of a police station, much less prison or jail. His mother had connections—important ones—the kind that enabled people like Ducane to forever skirt the law. When all was said and done, Ducane, free as the breeze, had garnered $13,000, half of the dead bank robber's take, for staying cool and on point during the shootout, his baptism by fire. His reputation had been made as a solid soldier in the underbelly of Louisiana organized crime, someone who was willing to execute an order under fire.

More importantly, pumping two slugs into an overweight bank security guard who would end up losing half his bowel ultimately earned Sugar Sweet Ducane a shot at being onstage in the American crime of the century.

Now, as he sat in Theodosia's Elbow Room, in the heart of the black community of Gary, Indiana, off center stage for the moment in a spot that afforded him necessary invisibility, all he could think about was the fact that playing second fiddle, no matter the upside, was as thankless and shitty a job as a man could get.

It was a humid, sticky, surprisingly warm Steel City November afternoon. The entry door to the Elbow Room had been propped open, allowing a narrow ribbon of light to dance into the otherwise darkened bar. The burning-coal and sulfur smell of blast furnaces and coke ovens churning out steel wafted into the bar, which was linked by a corridor to a liquor store next door. The family-owned bar and liquor store sat just two blocks west of Broadway, the main drag in this city of 180,000.

Antoine eyed the stream of light arching along the floor, sniffed like a bird dog on point at the intruding, acidic, bitter-smelling Steel City air that carried with it the ground-up human smell of mid-twentieth-century American industry at its zenith, and said to the bartender who was standing a few feet away, "How 'bout hittin' me with another JW Black?"

The barkeep, a long-necked giraffe of a black man with a mis-shapen head and steely gray eyes, grabbed a fifth of Johnnie Walker Black Label from a shelf to his right, half-filled a tumbler on the bar-top without once looking up, plopped a single ice cube into the amber liquid, and slid it down the bar toward Antoine. "You wanna run a tab?" His soft-spoken response was barely a question.

"Nope. Two's my limit." Antoine forced a painful half smile. The pain was courtesy of a barely functional temporomandibular joint that had been crushed in a horseback-riding accident when he was ten. Since then, it had hurt him to smile, chew, or French-kiss a woman. That riding outing had been a birthday gift from his mother, and she'd been so distraught over the accident that she'd had the horse shot and babied Antoine ever since.

Smiling back, the barkeep blinked Sugar Sweet's features into focus, wondering as he did where the man with the light parchment-colored skin, thick, sandy-colored mop of unruly hair who preferred the limes in his drinks on the rot was from. As the barkeep turned and ran a damp, dirty rag down the bar's surface, Antoine asked, "How far's the South Shore Train Station from here?"

"Dead north up Broadway and just past downtown. Twenty-two blocks on the money." The barkeep eyed Antoine quizzically. "You headed for Chi-Town?" Antoine didn't answer, having learned long ago never to share his business with a barkeep. He'd already made three trips to Chicago in the past two days, driving a rented Pontiac, which he'd now returned, the thirty-five miles around the tip of Lake Michigan to the Windy City's predominantly black South Side. There he had met with the people who'd hired him, scoped out the lay of the land, and purchased the things he needed to simplify and carry out his job. At the end of each of the two days, after practicing and refining his part in a much larger mission, he'd made his way back across the Illinois border to disappear into the bowels of the Steel City.

Only four other people besides Antoine and the bartender occupied the dimly lit bar. A pudgy, nervous-looking white woman sat drinking alone at a table against the wall opposite the bar, several feet from Antoine. Three men occupied another table a few feet from her. Two of the men were dressed in bibbed overalls that fit too tightly. The third, a coal-black man with an elongated, rectangular face, was dressed in a pair of faded jeans that looked as if they'd been washed a thousand times. All of the men seemed intent on applying just enough intoxicating lubricant to their minds and bellies to allow them to suffer through one more eight-hour shift at U.S. Steel.

Antoine scooped his floating, dried-out lime from his drink. As he dipped his head to lap the film of bittersweetness from the drink's oil-slick-like surface, a thin, brown-skinned man rushed through the door, shouting in a mix of Spanish and English with his right fist raised skyward. "Bitch!" he screamed. "You're a common whore! Puta! Vete a la chingada! Whore! Whore! Whore!" He'd cocked the opposite arm, prepared to strike the woman, whose eyes flashed fireballs of hate when she tossed the drink she'd been nursing into his face. "Coño!" he screamed, toppling the table over onto her.

The bartender, whose move around the bar was fluid and swift, was on top of the man in a half-hair of a second. Twisting the man's right arm behind him and speaking to him in the calmest of tones, the barkeep said, "I told you not to come back in here today, Arturo." The bartender eyed the woman sympathetically as, wrapping his other arm around Arturo's neck, he ushered the now hammer-locked, inebriated Puerto Rican toward the open doorway. "I told you the next time you came in here drunk, I'd call the cops," said the barkeep, sounding as calm as when he'd given Antoine directions to the South Shore station.

Eyeing the largest of the three unruffled men at the other table, he said, "Willie, how about runnin' next door and gettin' me Speed Scott—saw him go in the liquor store a few minutes ago."

The man responded with a look of bewilderment. "You gonna buy Arturo a pack of trouble, you sic a cop like Scott on him."

The barkeep shook his head. "He brought it on hisself. Now, hurry up," the barkeep ordered as Arturo, wiggling in defiance at the mention of Speed Scott's name, tried to escape his grasp.

The man named Willie lumbered out the door, and within seconds a short, thick, muscle-bound, fair-skinned black cop in plainclothes sauntered into the bar. "Arturo, you drunk again?" Speed Scott shook his head and glanced in the direction of the woman, who'd barely looked up. "Whiskey and women, whiskey and women," Scott lamented as Antoine moved past him, walking very deliberately toward safety and the bar's open door.

Sugar Sweet's exit was soft and imperceptible, the touchdown of a falling leaf. Quickly he was outside, enveloped in daylight and beyond the range of a small-time, small-city cop who could have been his undoing; beyond the battered woman who'd sought out shelter in a bar; and away from detached, intoxicated mill workers and inquisitive bartenders. He'd skirted trouble in less time than it took, as his mother loved to say, for a lecherous Holy Roller preacher to make a date by winking at a woman in the front pew. Striding north up Adams Street, he made his way toward the rancid-smelling rooming house where he was being warehoused, prepared to wait out his date with history or hell.

Santo Trafficante Jr. took a bite of jumbo-sized deep-fried Gulf Coast shrimp and paused to savor the flavor. Then, slapping a fist defiantly into his right palm, he said to one of the men squeezed on each side of him in the back seat of a white Lincoln Continental limo, "Point is, Carlos, you've got us puttin' our future in the hands of some half-breed nigger." Trafficante was a sad-eyed, thin man with a long neck, a flat, prominent forehead, and a gunshot scar on his upper left arm. He controlled all the organized crime in Florida, a state where his long-entrenched family had helped create the language known as Tampan, a cross featuring the Italian and Spanish dialects favored by early-twentieth-century mobsters.

"You're eatin' colored-folks food, ain't you?" countered Carlos Marcello, godfather to the Louisiana and east Texas mafia. Marcello, born in Tunis to Sicilian parents and known in crime circles as "the little man," controlled the lion's share of all gambling in the Pelican State. Leaning back in his seat and smiling, he patted the Cuban cigar in his shirt pocket as he eyed Johnny Rosselli, Chicago's mob boss, who sat on the other side of Trafficante, then popped a shrimp into his mouth and studied the undulating line of black faces that looped from the order window of White's Shrimp House, a Chicago South Side soul food legend, to within fifteen feet of their limo. Extracting another shrimp from the grease-soaked, quart-sized carton sitting on the exhaust hump between his feet, Marcello said softly and politely, "Colored people sure can cook, I'll give you that. Shit, I can't tell this shrimp from the ones they fry up down home in Louisiana. It's like they've got a motherfuckin' worldwide franchise." Marcello licked a dollop of hot-sauce-saturated shrimp batter off his thumb and reached for another deep-fried nugget, eyeing it as if it were a prize at the bottom of a box of Cracker Jack. "Umm, umm, umm."

"Don't come in your pants, Carlos," Trafficante said. "This ain't no meat-beatin' contest." Leaning forward and glancing out the limo's tinted window, Trafficante asked their burly driver, "See anything suspicious?"

Incensed, "Handsome" Johnny Rosselli, a sharp-nosed man with a penchant for expensive sunglasses and equally expensive hats, barked, "Goddamn it, Santo, this is my territory!" He swept his right arm around in a quarter circle, nearly slamming Trafficante in the chest. "Colored, white, gentile, Jew, or Jap, I control these waters. Ain't a chance in hell anybody's peepin' our show. Now, would you sit back in your seat, eat your fuckin' shrimp, and try not to ask Tony about security no more?"

Flashing Rosselli a look that said, *Pipe down,* Marcello asked, "Are we here for a fuckin' sparring match or business? I know it's your turf, Johnny. Santo is just bein' thoughtful, and you gotta be thoughtful when you're usin' an outsider on a job like this. No question, we're pushin' the envelope here." On trial in Louisiana for conspiracy and looking uncustomarily hounded, Marcello took a sip from a twenty-four-ounce container of lemonade. He'd had to work hard to get away for this meeting in Chicago, and he was teetering on the edge, exhausted from trial prep and a two-year jousting match with the feds, but he had as big a stake in the outcome of their project as anyone, so he was there. "I know Ducane," Marcello offered. "Down my way his rep's fuckin' golden. He's done half-a-dozen jobs for me when I couldn't use boys out of Corsica or the East Coast. He's a hungry dog, one I pretty much raised from a pup."

"Okay, okay. So he's your lovable lapdog." Rosselli stroked his chin thoughtfully. "How much does he know about the whole goddamn plan?"

"Yeah. How fuckin' much?" asked Trafficante, riding a new wave of anxiety.

"As much as he's been told." Marcello bit back the urge to lash out. "He knows he's workin' backup detail on a big-time hit, and he knows who the target is. But he don't know nothin' about anywhere else but Chicago. He's aware that he's fallback and a fallback only, and he knows that the lead singer in this deal is somebody else, not him."

"And he's all right with that?" asked Trafficante, flashing a knowing glance Rosselli's way.

"Yeah," Marcello responded, looking puzzled. "Ornasetti's got him under control."

"Ain't what I hear," Trafficante countered. "I hear that little Creole swamp bug of yours likes struttin' center stage. Hear he's into takin' special bows."

"From who?" Marcello shot back.

"Don't matter from who. What matters is, he may be too fuckin' Hollywood for us," said Trafficante.

Marcello's face turned salmon pink. "Goddamn it, Santo! I know where you're headed with this. You still want this whole goddamn thing to play out down your way in Tampa. You've been tryin' your best to nose things that way from the beginning. But you know what? Ain't gonna happen."

Trafficante smiled. It was a self-satisfied *gotcha* kind of smile. "And you can bet I wouldn't use a nigger, or some half-breed Creole, or whatever Ducane claims to be—or for that matter anybody without the same bloodlines as me—as backup on a job like this, especially on my own home ground."

"We both know that," Rosselli said, playing peacemaker once again. "You've told us before, Santo, so move off it. Let's say for the moment we all try and be a little objective. Bottom line is, not one of us should be pushin' for Chicago, or Tampa, or any other city, or for offshore hires, U.S. regulars, Chinamen, niggers, or Jews. You think a dog with a thorn in its paw gives one shit about who takes that fuckin' thorn out? Hell, no! And right now we've got ourselves one hell of a thorn-pokin' problem, gentlemen." Rosselli paused for effect. "Or maybe it's just me who's feelin' the pain, and the two of you ain't hurtin' a bit."

"Oh, I'm feelin' it," said Marcello, licking a tenacious piece of shrimp batter from his thumb. "And what I'm feelin' is more and more like that goddamn lyin', pussy-chasin' asshole and his pissant brother need to be dealt with. They're takin' turns puttin' their dicks up my ass. They've got me in fuckin' court, I'm losin' contracts, lever-age, and, worst of all, I'm losin' money."

"Same for me," Trafficante chimed in. "Word has it they're plan-nin' on prosecutin' my whole damn family. And Hoover's office ain't been one goddamn bit of help. So much for courtin' that sissy."

"So there you are, summed up all over again," Rosselli said with a quick, insightful nod. "It's shit-or-get-off-the-pot time, in case either of you missed it. We've got three shots at solvin' our problem in just under a month, and the first one's here in Chicago. I say we stick with what's been planned. Any discomfort?" Rosselli flashed a quick thumbs-up and turned to Marcello.

Marcello's thumb rose quickly.

"Santo?" Rosselli's tone escalated with the question.

Trafficante, who'd been holding out for weeks to have things play out down his way in Tampa, eyed the limo's plushly carpeted floor, gazed out the tinted window toward the conga line of hungry Negroes still lined up outside the whitewashed cinder-block bunker that was White's Shrimp House, shook his head, raised a thumb, and said hesitantly, "I guess."

Antoine Ducane's trip from Theodosia's Elbow Room to his one-room walk-up flat in a flophouse on the corner of Thirteenth and Adams in Gary's red-light district proved to be uneventful. No cops latched on to his tail, no drunks followed him home, and on the way he encountered not one cheating woman. He settled into his room— a dingy ten-by-ten-foot box that reeked of rancid cabbage and stale cigarette smoke—and watched a couple of sitcoms on TV. Bored with the tube, he doodled in a sketch book for awhile, called home to New Iberia to talk to his mother, assuring her several times during the conversation that he was all right, then went back out and trolled Adams Street for a woman to help him take the edge off a strange, sudden, job-related nervousness. He walked the streets for half an hour, a little disjointed, looking for the right kind of woman—slender, big breasts, all legs, and dark skinned—without any luck before returning to his room.

He sat back on his bed, his head resting against a pillow that smelled of mildew, still uneasy about his assignment, enjoying the last of his favorite snack, a Dad's Old Fashioned Root Beer and a whole-wheat peanut-butter-and-jelly sandwich. He found himself second-guessing his trip north, the entire sketchy Chicago job, and even his loyalty to the two Carlos Marcello contacts back in New Iberia who'd recommended him for the job.

Over the past ten weeks the Chicago plan, a plan that he knew top-level mafia dons had drawn up to rid themselves of ever-increasing government intrusions on their business, had been seared into his brain. To divert attention from themselves, the crime bosses had called in a collaborator—a trusted but unseasoned Rocky Mountain connection. The man was an eager-beaver, twenty-five-year-old, up-bucking would-be don from Colorado who had been recommended to Carlos Marcello, the driving force behind the plan, by a trusted Las Vegas contact.

The three crime bosses, as far as he could tell, had checked out this fourth collaborator, Rolando "Rollie" Ornasetti, to their satisfaction; anointed him their lieutenant on the street, kill coordinator, and mission director; given the job their stamp of approval; and distanced themselves from the action. In the weeks that followed, Ornasetti, a braggart who never let a day pass without sharing the fact with Sugar Sweet or some other underling that he'd graduated from college at nineteen, that his family had roots in the Rocky Mountain mafia that extended back eighty years, and that his member was ten inches long, had managed to rub Antoine the wrong way. Hoping to make points with upper-level movers and shakers of the organized crime world, the brash Ornasetti had choreographed Ducane through six fully orchestrated trial runs of the Chicago job. It had been

Ornasetti who'd suggested that Ducane while away his unoccupied time rotting in Gary, rat-holed forty-five minutes away from the kill zone in a firetrap that smelled of boiled cabbage and piss.

It hadn't taken Antoine but a few minutes into their first meeting to recognize what a kiss-ass Ornasetti would turn out to be and peg him as a little fish trying to swim with the bigs. Despite his instant dislike, $25,000 to play low-risk backup on a kill had proved to be too much of an incentive for him to walk away. Ornasetti's puffed-up, tall-Texan take on the world seemed out of place for a slightly built man from Denver who was barely five-foot-eight, talked with the hint of a lisp, and tended to sound slightly effeminate when he got excited. The fact that he openly coveted the top dog position of his uncle, who was a Denver crime boss, spoke to his lack of loyalty, and that, as much as anything else, rubbed Ducane the wrong way.

It was Ornasetti, not someone above him, who began to refer to their operation as a deception rather than simply calling it what it was—a hit. It was Ornasetti who relished using words and phrases that climbed over the top of what the whole Chicago affair was all about—killing—and Ornasetti who boasted that the job would probably make him.

Antoine complained in one of his frequent late-night calls to his mother, a woman who had worked for decades in the low-tide backwaters of Louisiana petty crime—numbers running, illegal liquor sales, and falsified IDs—that his Chicago job, without detailing the job's specifics, had him dealing with a Rocky Mountain wannabe chickenshit. She assured him that it came with the territory, that some jobs just came with shit-ass bosses.

Sugar Sweet couldn't complain to Carlos Marcello, the man who in effect had okayed him for the job, and he had no way of going up or down a chain of command to which he had no real access. Besides, such a maneuver would have demonstrated that he lacked loyalty and juice. He didn't like the idea that he was playing second fiddle to a man he'd never met, someone from overseas or offshore, as best he could tell—even that information was still under wraps. But he had the sense that there was more to the Ornasetti-orchestrated Windy City job than he was being told, and that, in fact, should things go awry in Chicago, a backup plan for another time and place was already set.

He didn't like the fact that he'd amassed a binder full of information on his mark but only a sheet of information outlining the full blown plan. All he really knew was who his Chicago contacts were, where he would be positioned as a shooter, and that when the job was over he'd be wired $25,000.

Dismissing his concerns with a shrug, his thoughts locked on the money, he dusted the crumbs from his sandwich off his boxer shorts onto the floor. Ignoring the boiled-cabbage smell that seemed to seep from every wall surrounding him, he stretched out, rested his head on the lumpy, musty, poor excuse for a pillow, and drifted off to sleep. Twenty minutes later, an 11:30 phone call jolted him out of a pleasant dream.

"Ducane here," he answered, groggy, fumbling with the receiver.

"R. O.," came Rollie Ornasetti's coded reply. "Our event starts tomorrow, 7 a.m. We just got a package from overseas."

Realizing that the primary shooter had arrived, Ducane said, "I'll be there."

"Good," was the only word Rollie Ornasetti uttered before hanging up.

Ducane sat up, turned on a nightstand lamp next to the bed, and scanned the semidarkness of the foul-smelling room, aware that the next day would involve the real thing, not another trial run. For a fleeting moment, he thought about calling his mother. Instead he simply let out a hollow, lost-child's sigh, turned off the lamp, lay back down, and a few minutes later drifted back off into dreamland.

Chicago, Illinois, November 2, 1963

Scheduled to meet Rollie Ornasetti and their overseas connection in Chicago at the rear of a building on Seventy-ninth and Stony Island at 7 a.m., Sugar Sweet Ducane left Gary for Chicago on the 5 a.m. South Shore train. Standing dutifully in place by 6:30, several blocks up the alley from where he'd stashed the car that had been left for him near the train station, Ducane waited. He was still waiting an hour later. A half-hour grace period, no more, no matter what the job or the connection, was a cardinal rule of his, and Ornasetti certainly hadn't earned even that much leeway. Leaving the appointed meeting spot and stewing, Antoine headed for a pay phone three blocks away to call Ornasetti.

A half block from the pay phone, a Checker cab nudged over to the curb and intercepted him. The rear door opened slowly, and a distraught-looking Rollie Ornasetti waved Antoine inside. A stocky, dark-haired man wearing a stingy brim hat and European-style wraparound sunglasses sat at the other end of the rear seat. As Antoine climbed into the cab's spacious rear, the man barely looked up. Before Antoine could take a seat, Ornasetti announced, "The whole thing's off."

"Why the scrap?" Sugar Sweet asked, disappointed and sounding angry.

Ornasetti shook his head. "Outside forces."

Antoine eyed the man in sunglasses, then looked over at Ornasetti. "Your man from overseas?"

"Not important," Ornasetti said dismissively as the cab's engine shut down.

Antoine nodded, eyed their other passenger from head to toe, and said, "Hello." He got no response. Trapped between a man who was barely talking and another who wouldn't, he had the sudden feeling that there were probably plenty of things about the now scrubbed assignment that he'd never been told. Important things. Things that had him feeling blindsided.

"So what about my equipment?" Ornasetti asked.

"It's in the trunk of the car that was left for me, right where it's supposed to be. You were supposed to be here at seven."

"We'll go back and pick it up. Easy enough."

"Yeah, let's." Antoine shook his head. "Things sure took a quick one-eighty."

"Situations, just like people, sometimes take a turn for the worse." Ornasetti glanced at the man in sunglasses as if expecting an amen, but all he got was silence.

"You wouldn't be holding back on me, would you, Ornasetti?" Antoine asked boldly.

"And if I were?" Ornasetti continued, eyeing the man in the sunglasses.

The man adjusted the glasses on his nose without responding, and for a fleeting moment Sugar Sweet Ducane's mouth went dry. There was something foreboding about the way the man had moved his hand. Something about both the grace and dismissiveness of the motion that suddenly made him feel that if he protested any further,

the man in sunglasses might very well pop him on the spot. Glancing at Ornasetti, Antoine ran the bare-bones framework of the
scrubbed mission through his head. He was to have been the high-post
shooter, the man in sunglasses undoubtedly the shooter in the low
post. He studied the solemn-looking man again, and for a brief
moment he had the eerie, uneasy feeling that even if the aborted
plan had actually played out, things might not have unfolded quite
as they'd been planned.

"I still expect a payday," Antoine said calmly.

Ornasetti smiled. "Of course. It'll simply arrive a little later than
we discussed."

"How much later?" A brewing anger was evident in Antoine's tone.

"A couple of days or so. That's all."

"Don't screw with my money, Ornasetti."

Visibly agitated, Ornasetti sat back in his seat, his upper lip quivering. "You're not dealing with the kind of swamp-rat throwbacks
you normally do business with, Ducane. You'll get paid. Now, let's
go get that rifle."

"Fine by me."

Ornasetti tapped their cab driver, an enormous man with no neck,
on the shoulder and the cab, which Antoine now realized wasn't an
official, city-licensed Checker cab at all, began rolling. "Fine by me,"
Antoine reiterated, aware as the cab gained speed that although he'd
known every tiny nuance of his role as the aborted mission's high-
post shooter, he'd never fully been briefed on the role of the man in
the low post.

Less than fifteen minutes later, Ornasetti, with his .30-06, scope, and
custom-made shooting wedge in hand, had their driver drop Antoine

off at the South Shore train station, leaving him with instructions to return to Gary, retrace his every step, erase any hint that he'd ever been in the Steel City, return to New Iberia, and wait for his money. Sugar Sweet stood on the steps of the train station, bewildered and wondering, though he hated to, if he hadn't stepped into something a level or two over his head.

A half mile from the train station, Ornasetti changed cars and drivers. The new wheelman headed directly for the Calumet Expressway.

The man in sunglasses, who'd remained silent during more than an hour's worth of drop-offs and car exchanges, small talk, bold talk, and innuendoes, finally spoke up. "How much does the Negro know?" His words rode the crest of an unmistakable French accent.

"Enough to make him dangerous if he ever has the sense to sit down and think things through."

"He should be eliminated, then," the man in sunglasses offered matter-of-factly.

"I'm considering it."

The man removed his sunglasses, revealing a broad nose and deep-set eyes. An already evident five o'clock shadow covered most of his face. He looked Ornasetti up and down, suspecting that, like the light skinned Negro, Ornasetti was in over his head. He trained a brief, incisive stare on his American host, drank in his all-too-evident unseasoned youthfulness, and glanced out the window of the car, relieved that things hadn't come to a head in Chicago. He was well aware that the American crime bosses who'd hired him didn't want any fingers pointed their way if the mission Ornasetti was proudly calling the Mongoose Deception, as if he'd thought it up himself, went belly up, but he wasn't certain they fully understood the price they might pay for jumping into bed with people like Ornasetti and the money demanding Louisiana Creole. He wasn't, however, in America to dissect his employer's plans—far from it—and unlike the man called Ducane, he was a seasoned veteran in the killing game. Killing didn't faze him. It never had. He never blinked when it came to killing—even in the face of the worst imaginable kind of storm. He could only hope that in the end, the men who'd hired him were capable of doing that same thing.

The Calumet Expressway rest stop that Handsome Johnny Rosselli had chosen for their scrubbed mission debriefing with Ornasetti, Trafficante, and Marcello, rather than being one of Illinois' roadside bucolic picnic areas, was a glass-enclosed bridge and restaurant that spanned the always clogged expressway. It was in fact a sun-drenched, futuristic, architectural and civil engineering leap of faith designed to give travelers the sense that they were part of some interstate highway brave new world as they dined in the rest stop's restaurant, urinated in its bathrooms, and purchased trinkets to take home from the Windy City. Politicos and a few underworld types, most of them from Chicago, a few from Gary, who wandered in occasionally to bless the place, had carved out a small, private dining room at the far southwest corner of the bridge for private meetings.

Reveling in their anonymity, Rollie Ornasetti and three of America's most influential crime bosses walked into the rest stop dressed in business suits, looking for all the world like the capitalist businessmen they were, and headed for the private dining room. No one took notice as they strolled past the hostess's station—not the balding black man with the overweight wife, or the dairy farmer from Wisconsin with his second wife and an assemblage of five kids, or the two teenage Puerto Rican sisters out on the make, or even the Calumet

City, Illinois, off-duty detective with the telltale gun bulge beneath his leather jacket.

Forty-five minutes after their inconspicuous entry, the three crime bosses and their youthful Colorado connection sat in the private dining room leisurely drinking coffee and espresso and talking after having enjoyed a midafternoon meal, prepared by a chef from a five-star Chicago restaurant who had been whisked out to cook a meal that included shrimp scampi, linguini in wine sauce, and tender baby artichokes flown in from the West Coast.

Dabbing the corners of his mouth with a crisp linen napkin and suppressing a belch, Santo Trafficante shot Rosselli a quizzical glance. "I still don't understand why you like to meet in such a public place."

"It's picturesque," Rosselli offered, sipping his espresso, unperturbed.

"So's the Riviera, and wouldn't you know it? The place crawls night and day with plainclothes French cops."

"This place doesn't. More importantly, I can bring in my own private chef."

"Whatever." Trafficante took a sip of the tar-colored, high-test coffee he preferred to espresso, eyed Marcello, and asked, "Did you put our package from overseas to bed?"

"Sure did."

"Did he look happy?"

"As happy as people like him can be."

Trafficante nodded understandingly. "What's his take on the Chicago scrub?"

Marcello shrugged. "Didn't have one. I don't think it really matters to him one way or the other."

"Well, it sure as hell matters to me," Rosselli interjected, his voice rising. "How the hell do you think the feds got wind of things?"

"Are you fuckin' shittin' me?" Trafficante said, trying his best not to snicker. "We've got a carful of loud-mouthed Cubans flying around the parade route for the whole damn world to see, and you wonder how the feds found out? Not to mention the fact that the local ass-wipes for America's chief G-man and number-one sissy, Hoover, picked up our nutcase who was supposed to be a diversion straight off the bat. And you ask how? We shoulda let Ornasetti's fuckin' Creole boy pop that lunatic diversionary John Bircher like I wanted."

"And quadruple the federal snooping that would follow? The hell we should've," Marcello countered.

"Carlos is right," Rosselli said, taking a sip of espresso. "Beats the hell outta me how the feds sniffed things out. Don't really matter. What matters is, we've got additional shooting arcades lined up, and we don't need to stir the pot."

"Think that Louisiana half-breed Ducane could've been a plant? Maybe he tipped the feds off," Trafficante said, looking squarely at Marcello.

"Not on your life," Marcello countered sharply. "I watched him grow up."

"You sure as hell stick up for him, Carlos," Trafficante said with a smile. "That boy got somethin' on you?"

"No more than he has on you, Santo."

The conversation ground to a halt as the three crime bosses sipped their drinks in silence, recognizing that they were very close to telling tales out of school in front of Ornasetti, who hadn't uttered a peep since the espresso had been brought out.

Helping himself to more coffee, Rosselli broke the silence. "You up for Tampa?" he asked, aiming his question at Marcello.

"Absolutely."

"Could turn out to be another scrub," said Trafficante, turning to face Ornasetti. "You're the logistics whiz—whattaya say about Tampa?"

"Same as I said about Chicago. I'll get the job done as long as there's no interference from local cops or the feds, like we had here."

"Who's your high-position shooter down there?" asked Marcello.

Ornasetti responded quickly, hoping to demonstrate to the three crime bosses that he was on top of every nuance of their plan. "Some dumb-ass Puerto Rican out of Jersey. I promised him a bundle."

Trafficante laughed. "Wonder how he'll spend it?"

"That's his call," Ornasetti said with a quick snort.

Breaking into a pumpkin-faced grin, Rosselli spoke up: "Yeah. His call all the way."

Ornasetti smiled and took a sip of espresso without saying another word, aware that everyone at the table knew that people like Antoine Ducane and the Puerto Rican out of New Jersey were expendable— both of them men who had stepped into water that was way over their heads.

Chapter 4

Northwestern Mississippi, November 14, 1963

Mound Bayou, Mississippi, is a three-hundred-and-fifty-mile drive north and east of New Iberia, Louisiana, most of the drive in the shadow of the Mississippi River. The tiny Mississippi town was founded by former slaves in 1887 and in the seventy-six years since its somewhat ballyhooed founding had subsided into no more than a blink in the highway. Willette Ducane had driven over from New Iberia and taken U.S. 61 out of Baton Rouge early that morning, blazing the old highway for more than four hours, rolling through Natchez and Vicksburg in the fresh-eyed morning sun in a rush to meet her only child. Sugar Sweet had called her ten days earlier to say that his Chicago job was over and he'd be home on November 14. She'd tingled with excitement ever since.

When she pulled her gleaming black, six-month-old Cadillac Coupe de Ville convertible off the highway and onto the dusty gravel driveway of the lone gas station in Mound Bayou and stepped out, a white-haired black man, whittling at a reed that he envisioned becoming a flute, looked up, eyed the solidly built, still curvaceous "redbone" woman who was approaching him, and let out a shrill, staccato whistle.

"You know any other notes?" Willette asked, ignoring the wolf whistle.

The man responded with a second loud whistle.

"Guess not." Willette eyed the doorless lean-to behind the man, scooted around him, stepped through the doorway, and waited for her eyes to adjust to the darkness. Looking back toward the whittler, she asked, "You got any cold soda pop in here?"

The man nodded toward a battered old ice tub sporting an ill-fitting, dingy white lid. "Grab one from inside the tub. Twelve cent for the little 'uns, eighteen for the bigs."

Willette walked over to the tub, extracted a twelve-ounce Coke bottle from the icy water, popped the bottle top on the rusty lip of a wall-mounted opener, and took a long, slow swig. "Ah . . ." Looking back at the man, who hadn't taken his eyes off her since her arrival, she said, "You gonna pump me some gas or sit there whittlin' and dreamin' 'bout yesterday all day?"

"Figured on doin' both," the man offered with a broad grin. Setting aside his half-finished flute and his knife, he rose, looking as if it hurt every bone in his body to do so, and headed for the Caddy.

"High-test," Willette called after him.

"I figured that."

"And wash my windshield while you're at it. It's a mess. Musta hit every bug between Baton Rouge and Mound Bayou on my way up here."

The man glanced back as if he wanted to say something but instead continued toward the gas pumps without uttering a word. Reaching for the high-test nozzle with one hand and twirling the ancient pump's reset handle with the other, he glanced back to drink in the full measure of the big-boned, order-shouting, Caddy-convertible-driving woman before starting to pump gas. She was a raven-haired Louisiana redbone, and Creole, there was no question about that. *Thirty-nine, tops,* he thought. Green-eyed and sultry, she reminded him of a compact, sepia-toned version of some World War II vintage pin-up. She looked as though she might not be wearing a bra, but he couldn't swear to it, and it wasn't until that moment, as he leaned against the Caddy's rear fender and gazed at her nonchalantly, that he realized she was barefoot. As he watched her standing in the doorway, looking more sassy than sexy, sipping a Coke, he felt the hint of an erection. *She must be makin' some lucky son of a bitch happy,* he thought.

He set the gas nozzle's automatic shut-off lever, moved toward the front of the Caddy, and pulled a dry-rotted rubber-tipped squeegee, its business end worn to a nub, from a water-filled bucket, prepared to wash down the windshield. Glancing through the windshield into the front seat, he saw something that made him realize the woman standing in the doorway of what could only loosely be called a store wasn't someone to be trifled with. His penis slumped as, peering through the water-streaked glass, he eyed a holstered long-barreled .38 and box of shells resting on the passenger's side of the front seat.

"You about done out there?" Willette called, tossing her Coke bottle into an empty trash can.

"Yep," the man said, wiping a rivulet of greasy water from the windshield with a shop rag and tossing his squeegee back into the water bucket.

The man was back to within a few feet of Willette when, checking her watch, she asked, "Mind if I wait here for a bit? Won't be for more than fifteen, maybe twenty minutes at the most if the highway gods cooperate. I'm supposed to hook up with my son here in Mound Bayou. He's drivin' in from Chicago, and we're headed back down to Po' Monkey's to take in some blues."

The man smiled, aware that Po' Monkey's, a blues juke joint a few miles up the road in Merigold, was the best-known house of blues—if a former sharecropper's swamp shack could be called that—between Chicago and New Orleans. "In need of a blues fix, I take it?"

"That and a reunion with my son. Boy's been up North for a while."

"Hope he didn't pick up no bad habits up there," the man offered pointedly.

Willette eyed him sternly. "I don't expect he'd do that. He's pretty much like me—independent, if you know what I mean—never been the followin' kind. Whatta I owe you?"

"Seven dollars even for the gas, and eighteen cent for the Coke."

Willette extracted a small coin purse from inside her bra, unzipped it, pulled out a five, two ones, and a half-dollar, and handed it all to the man. As he moved toward the lean-to to get change, Willette held up a hand in protest. "No need for change. I always get to feelin' real generous when I'm about to hook up with my boy."

"Thanks."

Willette nodded and, without making eye contact again, headed toward the Caddy, wondering as she felt the man's eyes track her to the car whether Sugar Sweet would look or act any differently than he had six months earlier.

Po' Monkey's Lounge, a down-home, Southern blues singers' mecca, could rightfully stake a claim to being the best-known backwoods juke joint in the world. People, mostly country and almost always black, had been coming to the desolate-looking tarpaper shack in the middle of a floodplain to dance dirty and suck down the blues for more years than Willette could remember. She had first visited Po' Monkey's as a thirteen-year-old, large-breasted, broad-in-the-hips runaway who at the time looked every bit of eighteen. Now, a month on the downside of forty-four, she still felt like that same wide-eyed teenager whenever she stepped up to the eyesore of a blues edifice with its warped tarpaper skin and weathered hand-painted signs. The signs that directed patrons to refrain from smoking dope, to have their seventy-five-cent cover charge ready at the door, and to leave their personal music in the car or go back home.

Willette and Antoine had walked through the doorway of Po' Monkey's the instant the door swung open at 8:30 p.m. prepared to enjoy a show that started at 9 and planning to be there until closing at 1:45 a.m. Earlier, at a diner in Mound Bayou, they'd shared a feast-sized combo dinner for two that had included three jumbo-sized catfish, a skillet of cornbread and honey, two pints of coleslaw, piping-hot butter beans, and almost a quart of lemonade.

They now sat just a few feet from the famous juke joint's battered contraption of a stage. Willette sprinkled two and a half packets of raw brown sugar on her second rum and Coke of the evening, looked across the table, and drank in her barely twenty-four-year-old son's angular features, features that she'd often thought were far too keen for a black man's, or even a Creole's. He didn't look much different than he had six months earlier. His hair was still unruly and his eyes as penetratingly green as her own. His face seemed a bit fuller, although she couldn't swear to it, and there was a three-inch-long scar above his right eyebrow that hadn't been there before his trip up North.

"Good to have you home," she said, leaning across the table, slipping a hand around Antoine's right hand and the long-necked bottle of beer he was holding, and squeezing tightly.

Antoine forced a smile, not wanting to remind his mother, the woman he'd always simply called "W," that she'd told him that very same thing a half-dozen times in the past hour. He squeezed back affectionately, slipped his hand out of hers, rubbed his slightly painful jaw joint, and regrasped his beer.

Sensing that she might have embarrassed him, and enjoying it, Willette thought it was time to ask, after hours of small talk, a gluttonous meal, and two tumblers of rum and Coke: "What *exactly* did you do up North?"

"Worked."

Willette flashed Antoine a familiar half smile that said, *Don't shit me, son—save that for white folks and fools.* Antoine knew the smile well. It was the self-assured smile of a self-made woman, a smile that announced to anyone looking that it never paid to lie to W. Antoine drew in a thoughtful breath of Po' Monkey's smoke-saturated air. "I did a few jobs for some folks. Straightened out a couple messes."

"Connected folks?"

Antoine nodded without answering.

"Anything go sour?" asked Willette, a woman who'd spent most of her life cooking for, cleaning for, running numbers for, or fornicating with Louisiana's connected people—and lying to the cops about these activities.

"Yes," Antoine said hesitantly.

"Affect any folks I'd know?"

"Come on, W. You know I can't tell you that."

"I know you can't, sweetness. Sorry I asked."

Winding the clock on the conversation and hoping to move it

well past the issue of what he'd done, or not done, in Chicago, Antoine flashed his mother a slightly painful, loving smile. "What time'd you say John Lee's comin' on?"

"Supposed to go on at nine," Willette said with a snicker, aware of Detroit bluesman John Lee Hooker's penchant for arriving at a gig a tad on the late side of late.

"Guess we'll . . ."

"Don't be guessin' nothin'," said Willette, winking across the table at Antoine as she spotted the always trim, dark-skinned John Lee Hooker decked out in an iridescent gold silk shirt and an expensive-looking black hat with a stingy brim. He was standing near the juke joint's entryway, chatting with a man who was bringing in the joint's sidebar necessities—a stash of plastic cups, crushed ice and soda, and a bag of limes. Po' Monkey's rules required that patrons chaperone their own house-bought liquor. Willette glanced at her watch, surprised to see that it was only 9:20. Grinning and fully energized, she said, "We're gonna get a full-blown taste of the blues tonight."

Antoine tapped his beer bottle against Willette's tumbler, thrilled to see the woman who'd always been as much a big sister to him as a mother so excited. "'Til the coon dogs sing," he said, uttering a phrase the two of them had shared over the years whenever times had ascended to their highest or tumbled to their lowest.

"'Til the coon dogs sing." Willette clicked her tumbler against Antoine's beer bottle, sending a shower of rum and Coke over the rim and down onto the table. Watching John Lee Hooker amble toward the stage, she suddenly felt contented and warm inside. Contented enough to no longer be concerned about what Sugar Sweet had done up North in Chicago.

Chapter 5

Miami, Florida, November 18, 1963

The message he'd just been delivered, unwelcome and disturbing, threw Santo Trafficante Jr. off stride, sending him plunging off the treadmill he'd been working out on for the past twenty minutes and into the startled, waiting arms of the thin, cherubic-looking, bulbous-nosed man who'd given it to him.

"Tampa, my own turf—and we can't buy a fuckin' break. Shit. Another fuckin' washout." Regaining his balance, Trafficante adjusted the oversized University of Miami T-shirt that draped him and stepped out of the grasp of the wide-eyed messenger. "Who sent word?"

"Zambredo."

Recognizing that the word was from a twenty-four-carat genuine source, Trafficante shouted, "Damn! And I rode all the way down here to Miami yesterday, flashing my face at every would-be politician, eager-beaver cop, judge, and prosecutor I could throw my body in front of just to establish my whereabouts, and the whole stinkin' thing goes up in smoke." His eyes narrowed in anger. "Ain't that the shits?"

"Zammy says we shouldn't've used no Cubans. Said word leaked out on the street there was somethin' in the wind 'cause of so many of 'em poppin' up everywhere. Tampa's whole two-hundred-seventy-man police force was out patrollin' the streets, and Zammy claims there were another four hundred or so feds millin' around town. Not to mention a shit pot full of air force fuckers. You net it all out, that tight-assed, lyin' SOB we're after had six hundred goddamn people guardin' him."

Trafficante nodded. It was the weight-bearing nod of a man consumed by frustration. "So what about the Cubans? Same problem as Chicago?"

"Nope, a little different from what we had up there. Marcello says— now, this is accordin' to Zammy, mind you—that you shoulda thought the whole Tampa thing out a little more. You and I know that Cubans don't raise the same kinda eyebrows down here as they do up in Chicago," the man, always a messenger and never much more, said with a dismissive sneer. "Four of 'em ridin' 'round town down here don't mean nothin' except they're out for a meal of fried bananas and beans, not lookin' to off somebody. I'm guessin' that not many cops, or for that matter even the feds, gave your Cubans much more than a real short look, if that. And that means that if they weren't locked on to the Cubans as a diversion, they had plenty of time to keep an eye out for your shooter. Least, that's what Marcello claims."

"Marcello claims, Marcello claims. Who the fuck died and made him king? I said the same damn thing two weeks ago in Chicago. We shoulda gone with what worked in Guatemala or the Dominican Republic when we needed to resolve those problems. Eliminate the son of a bitch straight off. But no, instead Marcello and that wet-behind-the-ears cocksucker outta Denver dredge up some diversionary hare-brained 'Let's go home to Cuba' scheme that was originally cooked up by the CIA to support a bunch of fuckin' Cuban carpetbaggers. And to top it off, Ornasetti appropriates the government operation's code name and tries to make it fit for us." Trafficante shook his head. "Stealin' the name of a plan conjured up by the fuckin' CIA. Shit, that shoulda told us everything we needed to know, *from the get-go*, as the shines like to say."

Benny Leopole shook his head, hoping not to rile Trafficante any further. He'd seen the results of Trafficante's fully steamed ire, and he had no intention of being a convenient punching bag. Choosing his words carefully, he said, "We needed somethin' floatin' around out there as a diversion. How else could you have protected your shooter?"

"Yeah, a fuckin' Mongoose Deception," Trafficante blared. "Jesus Christ! Four fuckin' Castro haters ridin' around in a low rider, cruisin' up and down a parade route guarded by an army of feds and cops. And to top it off we cart in some dumb-ass Puerto Rican as a two trigger. Some fuckin' plan." Seething, Trafficante stumbled over to a nearby chair, plopped down in it, took off his left tennis shoe, and rubbed his bare foot. "My foot hurts like hell. Wonder if I'm gettin' arthritis."

"Better go see a doctor."

"Did," said Trafficante. "And a smart one. A Jew boy, no less. And I can guarantee you this. He ain't got one single connection to Cuba. Mongoose Deception, my ass. This whole damn plan's busted flat on its face in two fuckin' states."

"We still got Texas."

"Yeah, we sure do." Trafficante broke into a fully engaged thoughtful grin. "Get me Rosselli on the phone. It's time to cut out the Cubans, and diversionary nutcase right-wingers like the one Ornasetti pulled outta a hat up in Chicago, and Creole half-breeds. Time to go with our original plan, jettison Ornasetti, and put this diversionary shit to bed. Deception, my ass. This ain't a fuckin' war. We might as well have used a carful of spots to direct attention away from the kill zone. At least we'd a known the cops woulda jailed those motherfuckers right off." Massaging the ball of his foot, Trafficante glanced up at Leopole. "Guess it could be arthritis or, God forbid, a blood clot." He paused thoughtfully before reaching for a nearby towel. "But then, if it was a clot, I'd've probably bought it by now." Both eyes suddenly blazing with sincerity, he added, "Maybe that's what we should've ordered up. A blood clot for that fuckin' traitor who promised us hands off. A blood clot right in the middle of his fuckin' highbrow, potato-famine-escapin', woman-chasin', lyin'-ass brain."

New Iberia, Louisiana, November 22, 1963

Antoine Ducane was home. He could feel the warmth and almost reach out and touch the soft amber glow of his mother's kitchen—taste her cinnamony, sugar-frosted sticky rolls, hear the crackle of a late-November, first-of-the-season, cold-snap-breaking, New Iberia sugarcane country fire. But most of all, he could feel the protective blanket of his mother's love.

He watched Willette limp barefoot around the kitchen, suffering through the sixth day of an acute post–Po' Monkey's Lounge onset of gout, her left big toe pulsating in pain, and grimaced. Willette had been hobbling around the clapboard-sided, four-room house for most of the morning, and as he watched her struggle, he wanted to say, *W, no more red meat.* Wanted to shout, *I'm a grown man now, so you can stop the babying!* After all, he was pretty good in the kitchen, and had been for several years. He could fend for himself, and he didn't need her fighting off pain in order to whip him up a four-thousand-calorie, first-light-of-day, cane-field-worker's breakfast, especially since it was now close to 10:30 in the morning. He wanted to tell her all those things, but he couldn't—and wouldn't. Refusing to eat would hurt her too deeply, cause her to think that somehow she wasn't really needed, make her wonder if somewhere up North he hadn't stashed himself a woman.

Leaning against the countertop and smiling through her pain, Willette said, "You want a splash of goat's milk and clover honey to sweeten up your coffee?"

Antoine nodded, preoccupation showing on his face.

"Somethin' hangin' you up, Sugar Sweet?" Willette asked, gingerly making her way across the soft pine flooring toward the refrigerator. Extracting a pitcher of goat's milk from the Kelvinator's top shelf, she wrangled a squeeze tube of clover honey off an adjacent countertop with her thumb and forefinger, limped back across the room, and deposited the milk and honey on the table where Antoine was seated.

"Nothin' I can't fix." Antoine's response had a nervous edge.

"Can't you tell me about it, baby?"

"It's nothin'. My pay's a little late this month, that's all."

Willette winked knowingly. "You gotta expect that when you work for folks up North. Money don't mean the same thing to them that it means to folks down here."

"Guess not." Antoine added a generous pour of goat's milk to his coffee until the drink soon matched the light mocha color of his skin, squeezed in a tablespoon-sized dollop of honey, and stirred the concoction with his middle finger for several seconds before extracting the finger and licking it clean. "What's on the agenda for today, W?" he asked, taking a sip of coffee, unwilling to tell his mother that if he didn't have a resolution to his money problem by that evening, he was headed back up North.

"I gotta run over to Loralene Goodson's to pick up a stash of weed she wants me to dry out for her, and there's my daily numbers run, and I got a few of the boys over in the sheriff's office to fix up with dates."

Holding up his hand, Antoine cut his mother off. "I'd say you've got a full day." He had no idea where W's incandescent energy came from, but for over twenty years she'd managed to be the eyes, ears, and trusted go-between for local organized crime and the people of New Iberia's predominantly black section of parish. He'd never fully understood her true connection to the larger Louisiana crime beast that had swallowed her whole when she was young, and she'd never ever attempted to explain it to him. All he knew was that she had tenacious threads anchoring her to political and criminal movers and shakers all over the state. If it ever came down to it, he knew that W could, at the drop of a pin, seek counsel from the very top echelon of folk who fed and managed organized Louisiana crime. Even knowing what he did about his mother and her friends, he had, regardless of personal need, rarely broached the issue of her under-world connections. It was a hard-and-fast rule and, except for his youthful face-off with the rent-a-cop bank guard he'd almost killed, to his knowledge she'd never sought any special favors.

Shaking his head in awe of her stamina, he said, "You're always on the move, W."

"Keeps me young and supple." Ignoring the screaming pain in her big toe, she flexed into a deep knee bend, floundering momentarily on the way back up.

Rushing to her aid, Antoine said, "No need to prove it. Now, if you don't mind, would you stop with the Radio City showgirl chore-ography and sit down with me for breakfast?"

Willette smiled and limped over to the claw-footed, inlaid walnut kitchen table, a table that had long ago belonged to her mother. As she sat down across from Antoine, she eyed an eight-inch-long gash that radiated from the table's center toward her. The gash, its edges once quite sharp, had rounded off over the years, and the wound in the wood that had been made by a hatchet on the last day she'd ever seen her baby sister, Monique, had become a retracted scar. Willette slowly ran an index finger along the entire length of the gash until her eyes turned misty.

Knowing that if he let his mother's thoughts drift off into the sad, seductive no-man's-land that had swallowed, then devoured, her long-dead sister, the rest of the day would turn predictably morose, Antoine said, "How 'bout some coffee, W?" hoping to skirt certain darkness. "And while you're at it, you better catch those grits. They're steamin'."

Willette's response was a pleading look skyward, a sad, dependent look that asked, *Why?* Forcing herself to smile, she rose and hobbled toward the stove and a pot of steaming grits, telling herself as she did that she had her baby there, her "Sugar Sweet" baby Antoine, and there was no earthly reason once again to walk down a road that always turned her insides into vacuum-filled mush. Stirring the grits, she eyed the rising cloud of steam. "They're just about ready, baby." She winked at Antoine to let him know that the darkness would pass, but for the moment she remained in a pit of sorrow.

Willette had been gone for nearly half an hour and Antoine's belly still growled from overstuffed pleasure when he left the house to walk the quarter mile to Highway 182 to use a roadside pay phone. He didn't want a record of a call to Rollie Ornasetti showing up on his mother's phone bill, and he also didn't want to chance being interrupted by Willette in the midst of a potential long-distance argument with the self-centered Colorado mobster. Antoine knew he certainly wasn't a big enough fish to warrant a wiretap, and although Ornasetti would've liked people to think he was, the Rocky Mountain crime boss wannabe wasn't in that league either, so a pay-phone call was a pretty safe bet.

The sun had slipped out from behind a blanket of high, thin clouds as the warm Gulf Coast air once again asserted its mugginess. A semi loaded with chickens rumbled by on the highway just as Antoine reached the phone booth. The barnyard smell wafting from the truck hung in the air until it crested a rise the locals referred to as a hill. The semi's illegal jake brake backed off loudly, and moments later, except for the hum of a generator far up the road, Antoine's world fell silent.

Extracting a handful of change from the right pocket of his shorts and stepping into the urine-smelling phone booth, he arranged a column of nickels, dimes, and finally quarters on the stainless-steel shelf beneath the phone, dropped a dime into the pay slot, and dialed Rollie Ornasetti's Denver number. When a robotic-sounding operator came on the line and asked for a deposit of seventy-five more cents, Antoine obliged, leaned against one of the phone booth's grimy walls of glass, and waited for an answer on the other end.

The gravelly voiced man who answered wheezed his displeasure. "Ornasetti's." The sound of high-powered blow dryers hummed in the background. It was a signature sound that Antoine, a car-wash-and-buff-and-shine jockey during his early teens, knew well. "Need to speak to Ornasetti. Tell him it's Antoine Ducane callin' from Louisiana," Antoine said in a single quick clip, hoping the man would consider a long-distance call weighty enough to at least try to locate Ornasetti.

"I'll see if he's around," the man said noncommittally before clunking the receiver down and walking away.

Moments later, Ornasetti came on the line. "Antoine, my friend—and all the way from the Pelican State. What can I do for you?" The crystal-clear connection had Ornasetti sounding as if he were standing in the phone booth with Antoine.

"You can pony up my ten grand, for openers," Antoine said forcefully.

Ornasetti squeezed out a weak-sounding snort. Demanding people, and he was clearly one himself, had always irritated him, and a demanding high-yellow, green-eyed, swamp-mucking, third-string Creole hit man rubbed him raw. He'd been traveling in heady company of late, standing shoulder to shoulder with three of America's top crime bosses, and that fact alone had turned his normally inflated ego into a swift tide rising. "Come again?"

"My money from the Chicago transaction. I need it."

"And that transaction would have been?"

Antoine stepped back from the phone, stood ramrod straight, and clenched his teeth, a painful, jaw-joint-popping sure sign that a full head of anger was about to consume him. A queasy feeling shimmered along the wall of his gut, the same undulating bottom dropping out from under him feeling that he'd experienced when, years earlier, he'd pulled the trigger of the .32 that had stopped an overeager bank guard in his tracks. The same hill-cresting, free-fall feeling he'd experienced the first time he'd agreed to kill someone for money. Relaxing his jaw muscles, he said, "Come off it, Ornasetti."

"Okay." Ornasetti's tone was staccato and less than friendly. "You had a Chicago assignment. No question about that. But it didn't come off. Too many technicalities. We agreed on that earlier."

Antoine's voice rose a full octave. "And that's why, like we agreed before I headed back home, I'm settlin' for ten bills instead of the full paycheck."

"Our agreement called for a job to be completed, and as far as I can tell, nothing was ever finished. Tell you what, Antoine. I'll cover all the costs you had out of pocket and pony up for your stay over in Gary. I'll even double up on the expenses you incurred on your way up to the Windy City and back to Louisiana. Let's say we settle on an even fifteen hundred."

"Are you fuckin' crazy?"

"Watch your tone with me, Ducane."

An operator's voice interrupted, "Seventy-five cents for three more minutes, please."

Palms sweating, temples pulsating, Antoine deposited an additional three quarters. Realizing that Antoine was on a pay phone and incensed over the fact, Ornasetti said, "You're on a goddamn pay phone? Are you stupid?"

Antoine rolled his tongue slowly up and down the inside of his right cheek until his mouth suddenly went dry. He gazed out the door of the phone booth into what was now a classic New Iberia misty midday haze, toward the path that led back to his mother's house, and thought about the day five and a half years ago that he'd followed that path, not to some foul-smelling phone booth on the edge of a highway but to a life of no return. "You're playin' with fire, Ornasetti. Hope you understand that, and just for the record, nobody gives one shit about who you're on the phone with."

"You're startin' to sound like you need a lesson, friend." Ornasetti's response was haughty. "I was called in to run the Chicago operation out of respect for the quality and integrity of my services. There's more to this deal than a slow-moving sugarcane country boy like you could ever appreciate. You'll find out quick enough. Take my advice, Ducane. Take the fifteen hundred and vanish."

His eyes still locked on the path that led homeward, Antoine said, "I know the level of the prey, Ornasetti, and country boy or not, I'm really not stupid. So listen up while I'm still in the mood to talk civil. I'm comin' up to get my money, and when I get there you better have it. If you don't, trust me, you'll regret it every day you live afterward."

Ornasetti responded with a truncated bellow: "You're in over your head, bayou boy, and you're gonna end up drowning. Threaten me again and I'll pull the switch on you forever. Peace, brother!" He slammed down the phone.

Enraged and fighting to remain calm, Antoine listened briefly to the insulting hum of a dial tone. He yanked the receiver from its cord, kicked open the phone-booth door, and threw the receiver twenty yards down the path that led to W's. Scooping up his coins and jamming them into his pocket, he glanced at his right arm. A swirling tattoo made up of red, white, and blue flames encircled his right forearm from wrist to elbow. Just above the top of his wrist, the words *breed love* had been scripted in black. He patted the tattoo with an open left hand as if to quell the flames.

Gnawing at his lower lip, he stepped from the phone booth and started down the trail that led back home. He reached the ejected receiver twenty yards into his trek. Kneeling, he picked it up and threw it toward a marsh that was half a football field away. The red, white, and blue flames encircling his forearm sparkled like fireworks in the hazy midmorning sun. "I'll get my money," he muttered, continuing down the path toward home. "Believe me, Ornasetti," he added in a near whisper. "Or there'll be hell to pay."

Chapter 6

Pitching quarters at a wide-mouthed mason jar, Antoine stood in the backyard of the house he'd grown up in, lost his virginity in, and first smoked dope in, looking at once angry and perplexed. The yard, his onetime playground, amounted to just under two acres of rural, largely subirrigated swamp bottom that flooded every spring and smelled of dry rot most of the summer.

Trying his best to control his anger, he continued pitching quarters as he heard a car pull up to the front of the house. The engine noise from W's big-block V-8 and the sound of the car's rear tires skidding to a stop in the front driveway's gravel made him miss his mark with his last quarter by almost a foot. Mumbling "Damn" as he realized he'd missed the jar by his largest margin of the afternoon, he headed across the soft, mushy grass to tally up his hits and misses.

He'd pitched twelve quarters into the jar, or more accurately flicked them in off his thumb and forefinger, launching the coins effortlessly in what had been the final round in ten games of what folks in New Iberia had always simply called pitchin' twenty. He'd played the game endlessly as a child and as a quarter-hustling teenager from the same backyard spot, using the very same mason jar. The jar, its rim and neck scarred and nicked from thousands of encounters with quarters, glistened in the sunlight, a testament to its durability.

As his feet sank into the grass, Antoine silently thanked W for teaching him a game that fostered relaxation. What W, he now realized, had recognized during his sometimes turbulent youth was that a simple game could teach her standoffish, fatherless child, who was trying all too fast to become a man, the elements of eye-hand coordination, the art of depth perception, and, more importantly, a little bit of patience.

Scooping up the errant quarters and dropping them into the jar, he peered beyond the backyard toward a marshy strip of land that paralleled the yard's eastern border. W had always called the cattail-filled strip *the bog*. Antoine remembered W once telling him, when he was a youngster, that the bog stretched all the way from their backyard to the New England cranberry bogs of Massachusetts. He'd even spent time reading up on cranberry bogs, and he'd been devastated to learn, when he'd finally screwed up the courage to venture out and inspect the bog and assess its cranberry-producing capabilities for himself, that the mysterious bog was no more than a mosquito-infested marsh with a three-foot-wide meandering seasonal creek at its center. A virtual foggy bottom that because of the lay of the land and frequent temperature inversions emitted a low-level ground fog that on the most mystical of occasions had the power to engulf their entire backyard.

Mason jar swinging from his right hand, his mind temporarily clear of Ornasetti, Antoine was a few feet from the house's partially screened-in back porch when Willette, looking horrified, arms extended skyward, both hands shaking, hobbled down the three wide-plank steps and screamed, "Kennedy's been shot! Somebody tried to kill the president!"

They nearly collided as Willette, her normally ruddy complected face drained pale from shock, shouted, desperation ringing in each word, "The world's gone stark ravin' crazy!"

Eyes narrowed, Antoine draped an arm over his mother's shoulders and drew her to him. "When did it happen?"

"I . . . I really don't know. Somewhere around noon, I think." A lifelong Democrat and staunch Kennedy supporter, Willette had on more than one occasion felt the painful thud of a policeman's baton during her efforts to register Negro voters in Mississippi three years earlier.

"Where was he when he got shot?" Antoine asked calmly.

"Dallas. He was ridin' around in an open-topped car. Would you believe it?" Willette's eyes glazed over. "Now, who on earth but Jack Kennedy would do somethin' like that?" She uttered the president's nickname as if they'd been lifelong friends. "I can't believe it. Don't wanna believe it."

Antoine walked his mother back up the steps, searching for what to do or say next. They took seats on the top step, the same way they always had when seemingly insurmountable problems had surfaced for one or both of them during their lives. Unmindful of Antoine's less-than-perturbed demeanor, Willette continued to shake. A tear worked its way down one cheek. "The world's a terrible, unforgiving, treacherous place, Sugar Sweet," she muttered. "As long as you live, don't you ever forget that. Things are never exactly what they look like or as peaceful as they seem."

Remaining silent, Antoine swallowed hard. He glanced back toward the bog that he'd once thought was an endless expanse of marshland and said, "Yeah." Nodding and embracing Willette, he added, "Can I get you some water, W? Maybe some whiskey?"

"Nope. Holding me's just fine."

Aware that W was hurting viscerally, Antoine had the strange sudden sense, although he didn't fully understand why, that every mother, father, and child in America must be hurting. Their otherwise substantially predictable lives had suddenly been inverted. He had no way of knowing exactly how people in Natchez or Chicago or Boise or even Iowa City really felt about their president being gunned down. Caring about someone, except of course W, wasn't an emotion he'd ever been much afflicted with. But he could clearly imagine other people's pain, recognize the hurt suffered by faceless strangers, because he could see that pain crushing his mother.

Drying her eyes with a palm, Willette said, "Let's go inside and turn on the TV. I wanna see for myself exactly what happened."

Antoine rose and helped his mother to her feet. "Okay." His response was matter-of-fact and hollow.

As they turned to go inside, Willette said, "You know, Sugar Sweet, I'm almost afraid to turn on the TV."

Antoine nodded without answering as he led W, hobbling and shivering, across the porch and toward the back door.

"It's gonna get worse, Sugar Sweet. I know it. I can feel it in my marrow."

"Things'll be okay, W," Antoine said reassuringly, as his own thoughts galloped miles ahead of America's gathering tragic story.

"Hope so," said Willette nodding, and walked through the open back door, aware for the first time how calm and rock-steady Sugar Sweet, the wellspring of her life, seemed to be.

The world learned two hours later that John F. Kennedy, thirty-fifth president of the United States and America's shining Camelot prince, had died in Dallas, Texas, at Parkland Hospital, at 1 p.m. News about the assassination trickled in slowly as for hours Willette watched Walter Cronkite speak in fatherly tones to a doleful America from the glare of her nineteen-inch black-and-white Philco TV, then switched channels to watch Chet Huntley, in his attempt to dampen the nation's sorrow, talk to the viewing audience as if he were the nation's bereaved and ever-thoughtful eldest son.

By 7 p.m. Eastern time, the whole world knew that Kennedy's probable assassin was a man named Lee Harvey Oswald, and when Huntley introduced the audio portion of an August 21, 1963, Oswald interview with WDSU television in New Orleans, the country had been told by every talking head on television that John F. Kennedy's killer was in custody in Dallas. NBC ran the video portions of the Oswald interview within the hour, and the world watched Oswald, three months before the assassination, meek-looking and pale and appearing as if he were being teleprompted, admit to being a Marxist and a supporter of the pro–Fidel Castro Fair Play for Cuba Committee.

Less than six hours after JFK had been pronounced dead, Lee Harvey Oswald had stepped center stage, there for America and all the world to see him as the lone assassin of John Fitzgerald Kennedy. The bullet that had killed the president, every news channel was reporting, had also wounded Texas governor John Connally, penetrating his back, spiraling around his rib cage, exiting his chest, and striking him in the right wrist before angling down into his left thigh. All told, the world would later learn, the two men had seven bullet wounds between them.

It was almost 10 p.m. in New Iberia and miserably muggy and hot when Willette Ducane, unwilling to watch the television coverage any longer, rose from her uncomfortable kitchen seat, eyed a somber and strangely puzzled-looking Antoine, who'd stayed through the marathon TV watch with her, and, oblivious to the pain in her toe, said, "I can't stomach it anymore. I'm goin' to bed."

"I can turn it off," said Antoine. "We can play cards, or go out for something to eat, or maybe just talk."

"I don't have the strength," Willette said, her tone a deep hollow of sadness. "Keep watchin'. You can tell me what else happens."

"It's already happened," Antoine said, recognizing that his mother, captured by some strange sense of denial, wasn't ready to fully accept the fact that John F. Kennedy was dead and Camelot had ended.

Without responding, Willette moved slowly from the kitchen. Hunched over and burdened with pain, she limped down the short, dim hallway off the kitchen, entered her bedroom, and closed the door.

As the bedroom door clicked shut, Antoine glanced around the kitchen, taking inventory of the seven empty highball glasses that dotted the countertops. Only one of the glasses was his. He'd watched W nervously extract a fresh glass from a cabinet each of the six times she'd mixed herself a rum and Coke during their nine-hour vigil.

Alone and no longer obliged to discuss the sad state of the world, or Cuban dissidents, or Italian rifles, or Dallas police procedure, or the presidential motorcade route with W, Antoine could finally think. The news that Kennedy had been murdered hadn't fazed him; after all, had things gone as planned in Chicago, he would have been the one occupying the high-shooter catbird seat in an abandoned Chicago warehouse, the Windy City's equivalent of the Texas School Book Depository. Aside from having news-speak overload, he was as calm as when he'd first encountered his mother at close to one o'clock. Forcing back a thoughtful smile, he found himself thinking about something an old running buddy, a man who was now serving out his time on Louisiana's death row, had once told him: *News is only news when you don't already know the outcome to a story.* On that score, at least, his friend, ever the loser, had been right. After all, he'd just sat through nine hours of listening to a news story whose outcome he'd known for weeks.

Even so, there was still something that bothered him. Although he probably knew the intricate details of the Kennedy assassination plot better than anyone—the players, the ruses, the planners, and the roles of the diversionary rogues, right down to the well-calculated trigger time and escape plan—he only knew the details for Chicago.

Kennedy, however, had been killed in Dallas, and there were differences. Huge differences. Differences that didn't make sense. The assassination had come down in far different fashion from the way it had been mapped in Chicago, and it was that fact that had kept his insides churning for the better part of nine hours.

In Dallas, everything pointed to there being just one shooter, a nutcase named Oswald. The Chicago configuration, on the other hand, had called for a second, ground-level shooter, and so far— though it was early in the investigative process to be sure—there was no hint of such a person. A chill knifed its way from the base of his neck to the tip of his tailbone as he considered the possibility that in the Chicago assassination model, absent a second shooter, he would have been the world's Lee Harvey Oswald. Breaking into a cold sweat, he rose from his chair, walked over to the sink, turned on the faucet, and drew a glass of water. He drank half the glass before pouring the rest of the water into his palms and splashing it on his face. As water trickled off the tip of his chin and down onto his T-shirt, he had the sudden feeling that he was absolutely, even in his own home, and with W there with him, alone.

He glanced toward his mother's bedroom, knowing that for once it wasn't W he needed to be concerned about, or, for that matter, probing policemen or FBI types or newspapermen or even TV talking heads. Who and what he needed to concern himself with that very second, when all was said and done, was Rollie Ornasetti and the money the half-stepping would-be Denver mobster owed him. In the wake of the Kennedy killing and with a little intervening Texas fate, he found himself holding what some Louisiana country folk would define as a virtually unbeatable high hand. He, Sugar Sweet Ducane, had an insider's knowledge about the crime of the century, and if he played his cards right, he'd milk that knowledge for a lot more than what had started out as a mere $25,000.

November 24, 1963

Antoine Ducane had never met Jack Ruby, small-time thug, wannabe important Dallas nightclub owner, and former Cuban gun runner with loose ties to the mafia and Santo Trafficante Jr., but the two men, eons apart in most ways that mattered, had two important things in common. In their worlds, both liked the limelight and notoriety of being center stage, and, more importantly in their lines of work, both men could be counted on to keep their mouths shut.

Something of a clotheshorse and jewelry hog, Ruby, decked out in a fourteen-carat gold, diamond-studded LeCoultre watch, a flashy silk necktie, and a gold-plated tie clasp, had used his Dallas Police Department connections to worm his way to within a block of Dallas police headquarters some forty-six hours after JFK's death as Lee Harvey Oswald, a man now pegged as the president's killer by nearly everyone in the United States and the world, was being transferred from headquarters to the county jail. It was almost 11 a.m. straight up.

Sugar Sweet Ducane had spent the greater portion of those same forty-six hours comforting his still shaken mother and intermittently jotting pages of notes and sketches into a spiral-bound notebook—notes that capsulized, in a rambling and diagrammatic fashion, his role in the scrubbed JFK assassination plot in Chicago.

After analyzing the composite picture of the Dallas assassination, one that he still couldn't quite match up with the one in Chicago, he'd decided hours earlier to confront Rollie Ornasetti and run a bluff that might earn him double what he should've earned in Chicago. An hour earlier he had grabbed a suitcase out of his closet and packed a week's worth of clothes. He'd decided not to tell W he was leaving until the last minute because he didn't want her to have to deal for too long with the fact that he was leaving so soon again, especially in her grief-stricken stage. But he had to go. Had to come to terms with someone who'd reneged on a promise. In his world, standing center stage, never playing second fiddle, and being flush with money were pretty much equivalent, and Ornasetti had scammed him on all three. Besides, Ornasetti needed to be taught that one never welshes on a contract. Welshing was bad for business all around, and "pulling the juice," as it was referred to in Antoine's circle of independent contractors, simply wasn't done.

He knew he'd be up against a call on his own life if he handled Ornasetti the wrong way. Ornasetti after all was family, and he was just country boy Sugar Sweet Ducane, an outside jobber looking to be reimbursed for a hit that had never gone down. He had a hard sell, any way you sliced it, so he couldn't expect help with getting his money or support from organizational higher ground. He'd simply have to come to terms with Ornasetti on his own.

He did have one hole card. It was a card he wasn't sure he could count on, and he'd never tip that hand to Ornasetti, but W, ever reluctant to admit it, had known Carlos Marcello, some said intimately, for years. He had never mentioned that fact to anyone when he was in Chicago—there would have been no point to it. It never paid for people who weren't family, especially contractors, to try to worm their way uninvited inside a closed circle by dropping names. It was a cardinal rule. Marcello would have mentioned knowing W to Ornasetti if the need had arisen, and he hadn't.

Now, as Antoine sat across the table from W, watching an endless stream of black-and-white, mind-numbing assassination images on the kitchen TV, he paused briefly from jotting notes into the notebook he slipped between the pages of a newspaper and turned his attention to the TV.

"You think that Oswald guy really killed Kennedy?" Willette asked, buttering a slice of toaster-charred Jewish rye.

"Everybody's saying he did."

"I didn't ask you what everyone else is sayin', Sugar Sweet. I asked you if *you* thought he did." Willette studied Antoine curiously. "You've been soundin' real strange all mornin', honey, kinda evasive, if you get my drift. And here you been all mornin' watchin' TV and writin' and drawin' in that notebook." She eyed the notebook and newspaper suspiciously. "I ask you a question about the shootin' and you punt. I ask you how someone could get to the sixth floor of that book depository buildin' reporters keep talking about, totin' a rifle no less, and shoot the president of the United States, and you practically clam up. I say to you, did this guy Oswald pull the trigger or not, and you pass the buck. You got some kinda pipeline on this thing you ain't tellin' me about, Sugar Sweet?"

"No."

"Good." Willette sounded relieved. "So the next time I ask you a question about this assassination thing, you'll fork up your opinion right off?"

Antoine smiled. "Sure will."

Taking a bite of toast and trying her best to curb her suspicion,

Willette said, "Fine. 'Cause I'll have one or two comin' at ya right up."

Jack Ruby entered the basement of the Dallas police headquarters by way of the alley that separated the building from the Western Union building just across from it. Near the alley's midpoint, the door to the first floor of the police building offered ready inside access. Ruby entered the door nonchalantly and, breathing heavily, made his way to the basement via a fire stairway. The stairway door was supposed to be secured, but it wasn't. Jack Ruby had fully expected that.

Willette paused from looking at TV and glanced across the kitchen table at Antoine. Emotionally drained, her voice was sorrowfully deep. "They're moving that bastard, Oswald. Right on television for all the world to see," she said, her eyes glued back on the TV screen.

Seconds later, a gaunt-looking Lee Harvey Oswald, the man purported to have killed John F. Kennedy, appeared on the screen. His left arm was held by a detective later identified as L. C. Graves. To Oswald's right was Detective J. R. Leavelle. A third Dallas police detective walked just behind Oswald. As television cameras showed Oswald moving into the wall of spectators that stood about twelve feet from the jail office door, Jack Ruby stepped out from behind a newsman and a cop, extended his right hand, in which he held a .38-caliber revolver, and fired point-blank at Oswald.

"What the shit?" screamed Willette, watching Oswald grimace and clutch at his stomach. With TV cameras rolling and with the nation watching, the same way as a less-sorrowful nation had been watching two days before, Jack Ruby, with the camera lens of history focused his way, had fired a fatal shot, not at the president this time but at the president's purported assassin. Ruby was immediately wrestled to the floor by Graves, disarmed, and subdued by other officers. "I think somebody shot him!" Willette screamed. "Somebody in the crowd just shot Oswald."

Dumbfounded, Antoine sat forward in his seat, eyes burning, his insides suddenly on fire.

Oswald, lying on the floor, badly wounded and in obvious agony, was asked by someone who appeared out of nowhere with a microphone if he wanted to make a statement. He shook his head *no*.

"They shot him, they shot him!" Willette continued screaming, as if Antoine hadn't just witnessed the very same thing.

"I'll be damned." Antoine's words, rather than being capped with surprise, were words of simple recognition.

"Like I said, the world's gone crazy." Willette slammed a fist down onto her toast.

"Yeah," Antoine muttered, rising from his chair and heading for his bedroom. "It sure has," he called back to W. Thirty seconds earlier the entire JFK assassination puzzle had become crystal clear for Sugar Sweet Ducane. As he reached the door to his bedroom, his jaws clenched in anger, his temples began to throb.

"Where you goin', baby?" Willette called after him.

Antoine didn't answer. He was too busy imagining himself lying on a Chicago police station floor with a bullet in his belly, too busy thinking about playing what people in his line of work called "a dead man's patsy."

"Sugar Sweet!"

Before Willette could utter another word, Antoine stepped into the bedroom, eyed the suitcase on his bed, and slammed the door.

Lee Harvey Oswald was declared dead at Parkland Hospital just after 1 p.m. By 1:30 p.m. television news outlets worldwide were proclaiming his death to the world.

Jack Ruby, who was carrying $2,000 in cash, business cards with the names of several Dallas-area sheriffs, and numerous passes to his nightclub for the Dallas assistant district attorney, was slapped with a charge of assault with intent to kill a little before 3 p.m. Later, several people who were there would report that Ruby, on hearing the charges read, seemed smugly relieved.

Feeling anything but relieved, Antoine Ducane found himself speeding north, heading for Colorado at the same time that Ruby was being charged. He was an hour north of New Iberia, squeezing all the horsepower he could out of his near-showroom-new 1962 Ford Fairlane 500. The car, its trunk loaded down with cinder blocks, its rear bumper hugging the highway, as was the fashion, seemed to glide on air. Upset at having to leave a confused and despondent W behind, and uncertain how best to deal with Ornasetti, he tried to relax, telling himself that he had nearly half the width of a continent to sort things out.

Aware that his bizarre behavior couldn't have done anything but signal to W that he knew something about the assassination, he'd left his mother with a kiss on the forehead, a chilling warning, and a request: *If you don't hear from me in a week, pack up all my stuff and lock it up.* Willette had begged him not to leave, had even cried in an effort to get him to stay, but to no avail.

Antoine had $400 in his pocket, a full tank of gas, a suitcase full of warm clothes, and two long-barreled .38s in his glove compartment as he broke full speed for the Rockies. It wouldn't take him long, driving day and night, to get to Denver, and it wouldn't take but the cost of one bullet, if it came to that, to settle up with Rollie Ornasetti. There were no rules to follow now, and no protocols to attend to. Ornasetti had set him up, sold him a bunch of wolf tickets about making an impact on history, when in fact, if the whole Chicago assassination plot had played out as planned, he would have ended up playing the Lee Harvey Oswald role of a patsy.

He'd kill Ornasetti if he had to, if for no other reason than simply to even the score, but first he'd try to get his money. Ornasetti didn't know him well enough to appreciate his distaste for playing second fiddle. Even better, the pompous Denver native had no way of appreciating the fact that the one thing on earth that made Sugar Sweet Ducane's blood run cold was being made to play the part of a white folks' fool, the very essence of the part he would have played in the Kennedy assassination had things gone as planned in Chicago.

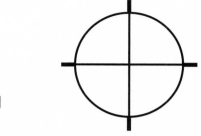

Part III

The Rekindle

Chapter 8

Denver, Colorado,
late August, the Present

Taking a break from sorting through cartons filled with antiques, CJ Floyd stood, stretched with a grunt, and glanced around his friend Mario Satoni's dimly lit basement. Bending to touch his toes, he let out a silent sigh and eyed the dozens of remaining boxes that he still had to dig through. His hair, once jet black, was salt-and-pepper now, and although he felt as strong if not as quick as ever, he had the feeling that, somehow, something he couldn't quite see, touch, smell, or feel was gaining on him.

He'd managed over the past year, with help from his fiancée, Mavis Sundee, to keep his ever upward-trending weight under control by moderating his intake of sweet-potato pie and fried-catfish dinners and restricting the ice-cold Negra Modelo beer he was so fond of to no more than two bottles per week.

His six-foot-three-inch frame hadn't started to slump, his midsection was still firm, and he still wore his trademark riverboat gambler's vest, Stetson, and jeans. Without benefit of a closer inspection, it was next to impossible to distinguish the fifty-three-year-old CJ Floyd from the always-full-tilt bail bondsman and bounty hunter he'd been ten years earlier. But there had been subtle changes that now defined him. His joints ached each morning the instant his feet hit the floor. His eyesight, 20/15 in one eye and 20/10 in the other for as long as he could remember, had faded in both eyes to a less acute level, and although he never felt winded in his rush from being a bail bondsman one minute to being an antiques and collectibles dealer the next, he had the haunting feeling that very soon he would. He knew that after more than thirty years of lighting up a cheroot whenever the urge hit him, one day he'd pay a price. For the moment he was beating back his cheroot addiction and the aging process as best he could, fighting to remain the same CJ Floyd he'd always been—a little older and wiser and still and always navigating a harsh and hard-edged world with a little help from his friends.

It was close to noon, and three hours of unboxing and cataloging inventory had just about stretched the limits of his attention span. Aware that he couldn't possibly finish sorting through all the remaining boxes at his feet and still meet Mavis to take in the final game of a four-game Colorado Rockies home stand, he looked around the suffocating basement and shook his head.

The Rockies had lost two of three games, and he was hoping the team would be lucky enough to get a win and even up the series before they left for a three-game road trip against the Dodgers, the lifelong baseball dream team of Mario Satoni, who was sorting through boxes a few feet away from him.

Mario, once Colorado's most notorious mobster, had turned eighty-two a few weeks earlier. Except for a noticeable loss of hearing in his left ear, an ill-fitting partial denture that had given him fits for years, and the unavoidable shrinking and frailty that came with living for more than eight decades, he was as mentally alert as when he'd controlled most of the organized crime in the state forty years earlier.

Eyeing the frustrated-looking CJ, Mario called out, "You 'bout done with that box, Calvin?" A stickler for formality and a man with an abundance of lingering Old World customs, Mario had called CJ by his given name, Calvin, since the day they'd first met.

"Close. I'd be further along if you'd ever pipe some AC down here."

Ignoring CJ's remark, Mario said, "Well, finish it, man, finish it. That way there'll be one less thing on the agenda for tomorrow."

CJ eyed his longtime friend sternly, looking disenchanted, shook his head, and dug back into the box at his feet.

The bond between the two men, not apparent on the surface, was in fact straightforward and quite simple. CJ's late uncle, Ike Floyd, a bail bondsman, a lifelong alcoholic, and the man who had raised CJ, had saved Mario's life back when he and Mario were in their midtwenties. More importantly, CJ and Mario shared a passion for Western collectibles and antiques that stretched back for years. They had gone into business together after CJ's own short-lived antiques store on Denver's famed Antique Row, named Ike's Spot in affectionate memory of his uncle, had been bombed into oblivion on the orders of CJ's longtime nemesis, Celeste Deepstream. Deepstream was a psychotic Acoma Indian and former Olympic-caliber swimmer who blamed CJ for the death of her twin brother. Luckily for CJ, most of the building's contents had been spared, and Mario, itching to take a stab at a lifelong dream of owning an antiques store, had come calling.

Their new business and the new Ike's Spot became a virtual antiques store that they operated out of Mario's basement with help from Damion Madrid, the computer-savvy college-student son of CJ's former secretary turned lawyer, Julie Madrid. The store had mushroomed into a quick success—a win-win situation for everyone.

Damion Madrid got the opportunity to earn money for college; Mario had what he'd always wanted—although he was disappointed that the store was in fact virtual—and CJ, much to Mavis's delight and relief, now worked only part time as a bail bondsman.

"Less to finish or more, it really doesn't matter, Mario," CJ grumbled. "You've got a lifetime's worth of stuff stored down here." CJ waved an outstretched arm around the dingy, claustrophobic, cinder-block space and mumbled, "Fricking underground bunker."

Recognizing that CJ had reached his limit for the time being, Mario smiled and said, "And it's all ours. Now, go ahead and get outta here. Go watch those lousy Rockies take another butt-whippin'. I'll finish up."

"No need to offer twice." CJ dusted off his hands. Suddenly feeling a twinge of guilt, he asked, "You gonna be okay on your own?"

"Of course," said Mario, a widower for thirty-five years. "What else have I got to do? The Dodgers ain't playin'. And you don't see Angie, my sweet angel, standin' around here waitin' to tickle my fancy, do you?"

CJ didn't answer, aware that other than a Denver-based nephew he detested, Mario had no immediate family. He had walked away from his role as Denver's and the Rocky Mountain region's crime boss forty years earlier, on the day his wife, and more importantly half his soul, had been diagnosed with breast cancer. For the next five years he'd watched Angie Satoni die, and in that time he'd lost the greater part of himself. Now only CJ, his antiques business, and his precious LA Dodgers kept Mario going.

At times Mario's 6 a.m. phone calls to CJ, his late-night requests for CJ to come over and help him recheck inventory, their lengthy business planning chats, and the backyard wiener roasts that never seemed to end made CJ wonder if going into business with Mario had been the right decision. CJ, after all, had his own life to live. But it was Calvin Jefferson Floyd, the nephew of the man who'd once saved his life, whom Mario had come to depend on whenever he needed propping up, and things weren't about to change.

"I'm outta here," CJ said, heading across the basement. He was a few feet from the basement steps when the sound of a thud at the top of the stairs stopped him in his tracks. Aware that Mario had jerry-rigged a motion-detection alarm system that swept the perimeter of the house and that Mario therefore generally left the back door open so he could have quick access to his backyard, a virtual botanical garden, CJ reacted with surprise. "You expectin' company?"

Mario frowned, rose from his seat, pulled a layer of newspaper from around the 1920s-vintage antique cookie jar he'd just unboxed, and tossed the jar to the startled CJ. Taking a half step backward, he popped the top on a vintage Saks Fifth Avenue hatbox that had belonged to Angie, reached inside, and pulled out a silver-plated, long-barreled .44 Magnum. He put a forefinger across his lips, warning CJ to be quiet, and called out, "Who's up there?"

There was no answer except for the sound of footsteps descending the basement steps.

"That you, Boscoe?" Mario yelled, thinking that perhaps the only remaining member of his once large circle of mob-connected friends, Jimmy Boscoe, had decided to pay him a surprise visit.

The normally unarmed CJ slipped a .22 Walther out of a pants pocket. The gun belonged to his partner in the bail-bonding business, Flora Jean Benson. He'd picked it up from her that morning at her office, planning to deliver it to Mavis to give to her father, who refused to move from his house in an increasingly high-crime section of Denver's historically black Five Points community. CJ kept the Walther aimed toward the floor, but Mario, who in all the years since Angie's death had let fewer than a dozen people enter his basement to view the incredible stash of antiques it had taken him a lifetime to gather, had his .44 aimed at the middle of the stairwell.

"You down there, Mario?" a man's voice finally called out.

CJ trained his gun barrel on the empty stairwell, and there was a moment of stand-off silence before the man called out, "Dominico, you there?"

Responding gruffly to his middle name, Mario asked, "Pinkie, that you?"

"Yeah." When Pinkie Niedemeyer stepped into sight, he found himself staring at two gun barrels. His eyes met CJ's, then darted to meet Mario's.

"Damn it, Pinkie! You lookin' to get yourself killed?" Mario lowered his gun barrel and slammed the .44 down on the seat of his chair.

"Shit! I wasn't expectin' to run into the O.K. Corral down here." Niedemeyer watched CJ stow the Walther before curtly saying, "CJ."

"Pinkie."

Incensed by the intrusion, Mario said, "You know I don't let people come down here without an invite. This better be holy-damn-grail important, Pinkie. And when you finish spoutin' off, I wanna know how you managed to get around my alarm system."

"Wouldn't've risked getting my head blown off if it wasn't. And for the record, your alarm system, which any sixth grader could hop scotch, stinks." Niedemeyer smiled, showing off two rows of gleaming white, perfectly aligned dental implants that had recently replaced his aging bridgework. He had lost all his front teeth, top to bottom, eyetooth to eyetooth, and the pinkie finger of his left hand during a 1971 New Year's Eve firefight outside the village of Song Ve three days before he had been scheduled to come home from a year-long tour of duty in Vietnam. He'd received a Purple Heart and earned himself a nickname for doing his duty that day. For the last twenty years he'd been the Rocky Mountain underworld's top "settlement agent"—"hit man," a term Pinkie detested, to the rest of the world. Looking Mario squarely in the eye, he asked, "Read the papers recently?"

Surprised by the question, Mario frowned. "What?"

Niedemeyer shot an uneasy glance at CJ, a glance that shouted, *Damn, I wish you weren't here!* Turning to Mario, he said, "The damn earthquake, Dominico. We need to talk. In private."

Pinkie's insistent tone and the second invocation of his middle name caused Mario to flush. Turning to CJ, he abruptly said, "We're done here for the day, Calvin."

"You sure?" CJ asked, standing his ground, his gaze locked on the intruder.

"Yeah. You go on and meet Mavis. I'll wrap up."

CJ stood his ground. He and Pinkie had had their share of skirmishes during CJ's bail-bonding career, but months earlier, on orders from Mario, Pinkie had derailed Celeste Deepstream's convoluted plan to kill CJ. By virtue of that intervention, CJ had thought that Pinkie had worked off a debt he'd long owed Mario. But the fact that Pinkie was standing there in Mario's basement, primed to discuss an issue that needed to be handled in private, told CJ that Pinkie was still in Mario's debt. Top-level hit men like Andrus Niedemeyer didn't come slinking down basement stairways, hat in hand, peddling information and asking for an audience with a long-retired mobster unless they were looking to erase a heavy debt.

"CJ, weren't you just leavin'?" Mario's tone was insistent.

Recognizing that his continued presence was delaying the resolution of what he and Mario liked to call a Level I problem, CJ said, "Yeah, I'm outta here. I'll call you later."

"Take care." Mario's response was detached, almost hollow.

CJ offered the skinny hit man a departing nod as he headed for the stairwell. Niedemeyer nodded back understandingly, the way two men who'd shared a war experience tend to do. He broke into a knowing half smile as he watched CJ mount the stairs, aware that, given the proper circumstances, CJ Floyd was just as capable of killing as he was.

When Pinkie turned back to Mario, his face was expressionless. Reaching into his pocket, he pulled out a newspaper clipping from that morning's *Rocky Mountain News* and said, "I think that earthquake we had yesterday mighta bought you some problems, Dominico."

Mario Satoni's face slumped as he heard Pinkie use his middle name for the third time that morning. It was a distress code they'd shared for years. Rather than the third time being the legendary charm, Mario knew Pinkie Niedemeyer was more than likely delivering a universe of trouble.

CJ hadn't been able to concentrate on the goings-on on the field for the entire game. Seated in Mavis's father's seats just above the Rockies dugout with Mavis and Damion Madrid, CJ had spent a distracted seven innings watching the Rockies blow a seven-run advantage over the San Francisco Giants. Now, as they rose for the seventh-inning stretch, the game was tied. Oblivious to CJ's agitation, Damion, slim, athletic-looking, six-foot-five and still growing, and as die-hard a fan of the Rockies as Mario Satoni was of the Dodgers, slipped the field binoculars that CJ had carried during Vietnam beneath his seat. As the crowd broke into a sorrowful rendition of "Take Me Out to the Ball Game," he announced, "I'm gonna head up for another Rockie Dog. You want anything?"

CJ shook his head.

"Mavis?" Damion asked.

"Nothing for me," Mavis said, frowning and patting her stomach. "One of those things is my limit."

"Suit yourselves." Squeezing past CJ, Damion stepped into the aisle and headed up the steps to the concourse.

"Youth," said Mavis, watching Damion disappear into the crowd. "And he's an athlete, no less. Julie says he'll be the starting small forward for Colorado State this fall."

"I heard," CJ said, his tone noticeably distracted. "Always figured he'd be a point guard myself. Wouldn't you know it, he grew a half foot."

"You've gotta go with your strengths." Mavis took in the bemused look on CJ's face. "Sort of like splitting your time between being a bail bondsman and an antiques dealer." She hoped she sounded supportive rather than judgmental of the man she'd had a crush on since his junior year in high school. Her father and Ike had thought she'd outgrow that puppy love, expecting that their six-year age difference combined with CJ's obvious lack of interest would solve the problem, but after CJ returned home from two naval tours of Vietnam, the love spark that had always been there for Mavis had ignited in him too.

The road from then to now had been rocky. In spite of their love for one another, they came from vastly different social strata, and CJ had failed until their recent engagement to understand that if he wanted Mavis to be his wife, the excitement and the thrill of the chase that fueled his bail-bonding and bounty-hunting self could no longer be the cord that connected him to life. Similarly, Mavis had had to learn that she couldn't expect to erase every nuance of the very things that made CJ tick. With a December marriage in the offing, they'd finally gotten everything on track after years of false starts.

Mavis took CJ's hand and squeezed it as the crowd capped its rendition of "Take Me Out to the Ball Game." "You're pushing back a problem, CJ. I can see it in your face. You know our deal." She slipped her hand out of his, held up her engagement ring, and rotated her hand in the sun until the diamond sparkled. "Best come clean."

"It's not me with the problem," CJ said hesitantly. "It's Mario."

"His health?"

"Nope. Problems with his past," said CJ, failing to mention that, spurred on by Pinkie Niedemeyer's comment about the newspaper and the recent earthquake, he'd picked up a *Rocky Mountain News* on his way to the game. Scanning it for earthquake stories, he'd found a piece about a man named Cornelius McPherson finding a severed arm in the Eisenhower Tunnel in the aftermath of the recent Colorado earthquake.

Mavis, aware that CJ was bonded to the former Denver mobster in strange ways aside from being his business partner, felt her mouth go dry. She swallowed hard, reminding herself that on the day of their engagement, she'd agreed to living perhaps forever with both sides of CJ's sometimes dangerous and always dichotomous life. Taking a deep breath and letting it out slowly, she asked, "Is someone from his past after him?"

CJ shook his head. "I don't know. But he's in trouble. I know that."

"Bad trouble?"

"More than likely. Pinkie Niedemeyer was at Mario's today when I left."

Well aware of who Niedemeyer was and what he did for a living, Mavis felt a lump rise in her throat. She toyed with her engagement ring and thought about the sleepless nights, the heartache, and the physical pain she'd been forced to endure because of CJ. She'd once been kidnapped and beaten by CJ's nemesis, Celeste Deepstream, and although the physical wounds from that encounter had healed, the psychological scars remained. Recognizing that she was in love with a caring but rough-cut street cowboy who would never change his stripes, she slipped a hand into CJ's and kissed him on the cheek. "If Mario asks, will you help him out?"

CJ nodded and turned to face Mavis. As he watched her naturally curly coal-black hair shimmer in the sun, he couldn't help but think that she'd drawn the short straw in their deal—a deal that would forever force her to acquiesce to his troublesome world. Slipping an arm around her waist, he squeezed her to him tightly as Damion reappeared and the Rockies and the Giants retook the field.

Clearing his throat and blushing, Damion squeezed past CJ into his seat. Hot dog in one hand and lemonade in the other, he picked up the binoculars. "Anything happen while I was gone?" he asked, taking a bite of hot dog.

"Nope," CJ said, winking at Mavis.

"Nothing at all," Mavis added, smiling and winking back.

Chapter

Mining superstition demands that no miner worth his salt ever take up residence on the second-penetration side of a tunnel bore, so for thirty-six years Cornelius McPherson had lived down the mountain on the first-bore side of the Straight Creek tunnel dig in the historic silver-strike town of Georgetown. Miners of his generation liked to call this the "mucker safe" side of the dig.

At an elevation of more than 8,500 feet, with a population of just over a thousand, Georgetown was no longer a rough-and-tumble mining town but a quaint alpine village that, unlike most of its historic gold- and silver-rush counterparts, still had more than two hundred of its original buildings standing. Seemingly every structure in town sported a National Register of Historic Places plaque.

During his Straight Creek tunnel years, McPherson, who was something of an entrepreneur, had rented and later purchased a quaint Queen Anne house in the heart of Georgetown's historic district. He'd paid $7,000 for it more than thirty years earlier and over the years had lovingly restored the house. It served as a testimony to his insight, although when pressed on the subject, he enjoyed telling people who recognized that the house was now probably worth a quarter of a million dollars that his success had been "just a case of dumb miner's luck."

As he sat on his back porch in a wicker rocker, enjoying the late-afternoon mountain breeze and talking with the Clear Creek County sheriff, a man he'd known for more than twenty years, McPherson found himself relishing something that he'd never expected to come in his lifetime. Something the sheriff, who sat in a rocker identical to McPherson's, had just told him every American dreams of: fifteen minutes of fame.

Six copies of the previous day's *Denver Post* sat stacked on an overturned antique milk crate between the two men. Page 2 of one copy had been snipped with scissors from its moorings and rested on top of the pile. The sheriff, a rugged-looking man of fifty, picked up the tear sheet and quoted the headline out loud: "'Tremor Unearths Miner's Remains.'" Handing the sheet to McPherson, he tapped the stack with a stubby finger and said, "You ask me, I think you should've made page 1."

McPherson shook his head. "Hard to overshadow an earthquake, Gunther. Even so, I got myself a three-column story in the state's biggest newspaper—just days before retirement. What more could a man ask for?" Leaning forward in the rocker, McPherson reread the portion of the story that detailed how he'd ridden out an earthquake while trapped inside the Eisenhower Tunnel and how, in the earthquake's aftermath, he'd discovered the arm of Antoine Ducane, a man with whom he'd worked decades earlier. "All in all, I'm pretty satisfied. I was as close as anybody gets to front-page material."

Gunther Tolls nodded and adjusted the brim of his Stetson. "What are you gonna do with all your newspapers?"

McPherson grinned. "Gonna frame one for sure. Guess I'll keep the rest, like they say, for posterity."

Tolls, who'd arrived thirty minutes earlier, hoping to tie up a few investigative loose ends, simply nodded. He took a sip of the syrupy, now tepid coffee McPherson had given him, and, brow furrowed, asked, "Any chance you can add anything to what you told me about that Ducane fellow that you mighta forgot to mention when we talked the other day?"

McPherson stroked his chin, as much for effect as to jog his memory. "Not really. But just for the record, back when I knew Ducane, he was a pretty standoffish sort. Didn't seem to trust nobody. Never did figure out why he took a likin' to me, other than the fact that in spite of him being a Creole and half white, or whatever he woulda been back down South in his neck of the woods, up here in these mountains the both of us was just plain black."

"Good enough reason, I guess," said Tolls. "Now, what was it again that he told you about knowin' who killed Kennedy?"

"I told you that already, Gunther," said McPherson, sounding put-upon. "We got really sloppy drunk one night durin' a weekend over in Hanna, Wyoming. He told me then. I guess for some reason, on that particular night Ducane was feelin' either real confessional or real the hell satisfied. 'Cause it was after one of the women we were with gave him a long, slow blow job that he loosened up."

"So he told you he knew who killed JFK right then?"

Squinting at the sheriff and looking confused, McPherson said, "Shit, man! It's been more than forty years since all that happened. I don't really know if he said he knew who killed Kennedy, or if he said he was in on the killin', or what his exact words were when you really come down to it. Hell, I was pretty near drunk!"

Tolls nodded, reacting calmly to the fire that he'd seemingly lit. "How do you suppose Ducane ever ended up behind that tunnel wall on the wrong side of a mountain?"

"Beats the hell outta me. Like I told you yesterday, after he disappeared off the job, I really didn't think about him that much. But I can tell you this for a fact. Me and Ducane worked together from 1968 through most of 1970, and the south wall of that tunnel with all its fancy-shmancy tile and catwalks and air vents wasn't a done deal 'til close to the end of 1973. That leaves a good year or so after Ducane walked off the job for him to have got hisself stuck behind that wall and inside a mountain."

"A whole year's window when somebody could've killed your friend and stuck him behind that wall, you mean," said Tolls.

"I guess," McPherson said hesitantly.

Tolls fingered the cleft in his chin. "And he was sure enough flat-out murdered. Unless of course he was peekin' back behind that tunnel wall one day on a day trip to the mountains, lookin' for wildflowers and inspectin' the mountain for the quality of its dirt, and a boulder fell on his head."

"Whatta you mean by that?"

"Just this." The look on the sheriff's face turned deadpan serious. "Between the time you found your friend's arm the other day, all nicely frozen, tattooed, and preserved for posterity, and late last night, the boys that do crime-scene investigation and mop-up for me found a few other pieces of him scattered around behind that tunnel wall. Not all of him, mind you, but enough. And wouldn't you know it? The most important piece of Mr. Antoine Ducane they found was pretty much intact. His skull. A skull with a hole the size of a plum punched through the occipital bone." The sheriff tapped the back of his head just above the base of his skull with two fingers. "Right here," he said, looking casually up at the ceiling. "Now, I grant you, a boulder the size of a basketball fallin' from the ceiling would pretty much be guaranteed to open up either one of our heads like ripe summer melons. And first off, I thought about that and said to myself, *Maybe a good-sized rock fell on your friend and took him out accidentally.* But when one of my crime-scene boys had old Doc Withers, who's still a little pissed at me for droppin' a coroner's case in his lap, slip the head of an ordinary, everyday hammer into that hole in Ducane's skull, I found myself thinkin' about the possibility of murder a little harder." Tolls adjusted his rear end in his seat and, looking pleased with himself, said, "The hole in your friend's skull was damn near a perfect match for the head of the hammer, Cornelius."

"So you're thinkin' maybe Ducane got hisself whacked?"

"Whacked, popped, snuffed, the word choice here don't very much matter when you come right down to it. My take is that Ducane was murdered. Especially since when we found your friend's other arm, the one without a tattoo, all frozen and preserved just as pretty as the one you stumbled across, the damn thing had a piece of what Doc Withers and I both think is balin' wire, the kind they used for balin' hay before machines and twine took over, looped—you might even say execution style—around the wrist. And there's some other things the crime-scene boys found I can't even tell you about. I'm thinkin' that somebody killed Ducane all right." Tolls forced a wry smile. "Who knows, maybe it was the same somebody who killed President Kennedy."

McPherson shook his head in disbelief. "You mean you think Ducane was tellin' me the truth all them years ago? Hell, I always figured he was just blowin' hot air."

"Why not? In spite of all the evidence to the contrary, half the folks on the planet have their own pet JFK assassination theory. Might as well include the possibility that Antoine Ducane was in on it."

"No way. All he was, as far as I could see, was some sad sack of a country-boy loner."

"And so was Lee Harvey Oswald." A half-cocked smile formed at the corner of the sheriff's lips. "And so was Oswald."

Richie's Grub Steak Diner, a Denver landmark for more than sixty years, though no longer the dining flagship for mobsters that it had been in the 1950s, nonetheless still warranted emeritus status in that regard.

The forty-five-ton prefabricated club-car-style diner had come to Denver from New Jersey shortly after World War II, secured to two flatbed railroad cars, with its new owner, Toastmaster Richie Dupree, riding in a Pullman sleeper just behind it. Dupree, part French, part Italian, and 100 percent Jersey con, had earned the nickname "Toast-master" by virtue of once having been an MC at Minsky's Burlesque Theater in New York. He'd always considered the term "MC" beneath his dignity, and until the day he died Richie had always referred to himself as "Toastmaster."

The diner's trademark, a forty-foot-high neon cowboy complete with a white hat, silver spurs, purple kerchief, and red kitchen apron, stood on a pedestal in front of the entrance beckoning passersby to drop in for a hearty meal. A full-sized palomino horse feeding at a trough stood atop the diner's roof, Richie's theatrical exclamation mark to the cholesterol-laden delights he served up inside.

Three kinds of people frequented Richie's: North Denver locals who considered the place a historical landmark and knew a feed-bag bargain when they saw one; tourists who had read the weekly North Denver *Tribune*'s popular restaurant insert, "Neighborhood Dining on a Dime"; and descendants of the dozen or so East Coast underworld figures who in 1947 had followed Toastmaster Richie Dupree from New Jersey to the Rocky Mountains to help him organize and fine-tune what until then had been the Wild West stepchild of the organization.

In the years that followed Richie Dupree's death, infighting between competing factions within the Western intermountain crime families eventually resulted in two equally powerful branches of Colorado organized crime: one in Denver, controlled by Mario Satoni, and a second 115 miles to the south in the steel town of Pueblo. Unlike the East, where turf battles could erupt simply because of proximity, Colorado had thousands of square miles of blue sky and wide-open spaces to facilitate peaceful coexistence.

Rollie Ornasetti, who'd come to Richie's to enjoy his favorite dinner—two slices of homemade meatloaf with red sauce, string beans, and mashed potatoes with gravy—was seated in the far southeast corner, snuggled into one of the long, narrow room's 1950s-style ruby-red Naugahyde booths. Between bites, Ornasetti looked up from his plate to eye Randall Maxie, the rotund man seated across from him. Maxie, who'd already wolfed down his meal, barely looked up. He was absorbed in munching on a cookie and drinking hot chocolate while reading the *Denver Post*.

Silver-haired, smooth-talking, and something of a fop, Ornasetti had aged gracefully since his days as a 1960s crime boss wannabe, and he enjoyed boasting that, at sixty-nine, he was like the decanted essence of a fine wine. He'd spent more than four decades climbing the close-knit Rocky Mountain mafia's organizational chart and now reigned as king of the still largely insignificant Rocky Mountain component of America's Italian crime family.

In spite of hop-skipping his way to power ahead of his more

respected, sometimes more ruthless, and certainly more knowledgeable crime family brethren, and in spite of having at one time had a
direct pipeline to men as powerful as Johnny Rosselli, Santo Trafficante Jr., and Carlos Marcello, Rolando "Rollie" Antonias Ornasetti
would never have risen in the organization if his uncle, Mario Satoni,
hadn't vacated that seat. Ornasetti had quickly filled the void left
by his uncle, a void that mafia dons across the country had pleaded
with Satoni not to create. Like a hungry dog with a soup bone,
Ornasetti had devoured the bone and sucked out the marrow. He
had twice as many enemies as friends inside the organization, and
over the years he had used blackmail, threats, and manipulation to
retain power and maintain a significant core of people who were
loyal to him. With Randall Maxie, for whom killing was not a neces-
sity but a delight, and a quorum of other loyalists glued to his side,
Ornasetti had managed to remain in the Rocky Mountain mob's driver's seat for decades.

Dabbing the corner of his mouth with a napkin, Ornasetti eyed his
unusually silent companion and cleared his throat. "How much do
you think the cops can figure out about Ducane?" he asked, waving
for a waiter to remove his plate and the offending sight of food scraps.

"I'm not certain," said Maxie. At five-foot-eleven and 310 pounds,
the cerebral-sounding Maxie had reportedly been key to the elimi-
nation of a half-dozen or more people for Ornasetti over the years.
He was said to drink his own urine in homage to his intellectual
hero, Mahatma Gandhi. "I can tell you this with great conviction,
however. You absolutely and positively do want things to stay bot-
tled up in that yahoo Clear Creek County sheriff's office for as long
as possible."

Ornasetti frowned as he watched Maxie daintily finish off his cookie. "Who the hell would've ever thought that a fuckin' earthquake would out us?"

"Things beyond one's control can and do happen," said Maxie. Despite having spent more than thirty years greasing the skids for or mopping up after Ornasetti, he'd never understood Ornasetti's penchant for crying over spilled milk. To his way of thinking, Ornasetti was too much of a Chicken Little to be a leader, too standoffish to instill loyalty in the troops, and too elitist to fit in with either his lieutenants or the grunts. Nonetheless, he admired Ornasetti's ability to have remained king of the hill in Denver for forty years.

The prevailing explanation of Ornasetti's lengthy tenure at the helm related to the important connection he'd once had to long-dead Midwestern and East Coast mafia kingpins—powerful men who'd reportedly owed him. Men who'd constructed a firewall around him that said *hands off* to those who might topple Ornasetti. Another story had it that Ornasetti hadn't been dethroned or, more importantly, eliminated by factions inside his own organization or those in Las Vegas, where he had powerful and vocal opponents, because of his opponents' remaining loyalty to Mario Satoni. Whatever the case, Ornasetti remained Colorado's top organized crime power broker, and Maxie remained his top gun.

"Maybe you should've never moved the goods," Maxie finally said, his tone calculating and analytical.

"Would you stop with the retrospectives, Max? We've been all through that. I moved Ducane when I had the opportunity and resources."

"And look what that move has bought you: a murder investigation in the offing. At least, according to my contacts that's what you've bought yourself."

Ornasetti smiled knowingly. "Nobody can connect me to Ducane. Hell, I was just a few years out of college when he died, a poor kid working his way through law school, hoping to make myself a better citizen." Ornasetti forced back a snicker. "Now, my uncle, on the other hand, a notorious Denver mobster at the time, might've had a reason to kill Ducane. If I were a cop or a G-man looking to upbuck, and I got wind that Ducane might've had a hand in the killing of a president—which nobody by the way has even a whiff of at the moment as far as I make it—I'd put my money on the bad guy in all this being Mario Satoni." Ornasetti broke into a full-bore snicker.

"So you're planning on laying this at Mario's door?"

"If I have to."

"How, may I ask, do you plan to do that?"

"My worry, Max. My worry. Yours, on the other hand, is to dam up any holes in the dike if we get a water break on this thing."

A roll of loose flesh just above Maxie's barely evident neck undulated as he shrugged and said, "Okay."

"Things could get sticky here, Max. We're not dealing with just any old murder, you know."

"So? Sometimes people get hurt, even killed, years after an assassination. It's a well-documented historical fact."

Ornasetti sat back in his seat and drank in the calm, self-assured look on Randall Maxie's face. It was the look of a man devoid of worries or a conscience. Maxie would do his bidding, no matter what. He knew he could count on that. Smiling contentedly, he said, "I want you to handle that tunnel worker who found Ducane's forearm, McPherson. Looks to me as though he's some kinda publicity hound. Yesterday his face was spread all over the *Denver Post*."

Maxie acknowledged the request with a dutiful nod. "Do you think he knows anything about how Ducane found his way behind that tunnel wall?"

"Nope."

"I see," Maxie said thoughtfully. "But I suspect it doesn't really matter, when you come right down to it, whether the poor man knows anything about Ducane or the Kennedy killing or, for that matter, the power of compound interest. He was simply a man in the wrong position. Do you have a photo of him I can take a look at? Something, as they say, to get me on the scent?"

"Sure do. From a story I tore out of the *Post*."

"Good," said Maxie, salivating at the thought of working a new assignment.

"How soon do you want to start?"

"I've started," said Maxie. "Any restrictions?"

"Not a one. Do what's necessary," Ornasetti said coldly. "Just like always."

Chapter 10

Cornelius McPherson hadn't told Sheriff Gunther Tolls everything he knew about Antoine Ducane. He'd held back two very important pieces of information. First, McPherson still had an index card, stashed in an old traveling salesman's valise, with thirty-seven-year-old emergency contact phone numbers for all the members of his original Straight Creek mining team, including Antoine Ducane. More importantly, he also had the address of a house in Denver's historic Bonnie Brae neighborhood and the name of the home's owner, a woman Ducane had once told McPherson he should contact if anything were to happen to him. He'd never had cause to use any of the phone numbers or search out any contacts. But for some strange reason—a reason he couldn't quite put his finger on—he felt obliged to do so now. So he'd filled up his pickup, polished off a meal of lasagna, steak, and fries, and headed east, making the trip from his house to the outskirts of Denver in just over fifty minutes. As he wound his way out of the Front Range foothills, easing his pickup off I-70 and onto Sixth Avenue, a heavily traveled east-west parkway that knifed its way straight into the heart of the Mile High City, he wasn't quite certain why he hadn't been completely honest with the sheriff other than the fact that his natural curiosity and the exhilaration of seeing his name front and center in both the *Rocky Mountain News* and the *Denver Post* had kindled something that made him want to cling to his flicker of notoriety a little longer.

Cruising along in surprisingly light 8 p.m. traffic, he chuckled at the idea that days before retirement he might have just found a new avocation: private investigation. He couldn't help but laugh at the prospect, aware that he had an insider's knowledge about Ducane that the sheriff couldn't possibly have discovered yet. For example, the fact that Ducane was from New Iberia, Louisiana, and that during a bank robbery he'd once shot a man. He glanced down at an index card that rested on the seat next to him. The card was brown with age. Smiling, he flipped on the overhead light and read down the names of the five other men who'd made up his original Straight Creek crew. Next to Ducane's name and printed in pencil in McPherson's very own hand were the numbers 303-722-2418 and the address 780 S. Elizabeth Street, Denver. Just below the word "Denver" he'd printed the name "Sheila."

In all the years since Ducane's disappearance, he'd never called the phone number in Louisiana, never had reason to go to the address in Bonnie Brae, and never talked to anyone named Sheila. In fact, he'd never thought about his sullen, green-eyed Creole friend much at all—for good reason, in his book. Although Ducane had been family in a sense, he hadn't been the kind of family bound by blood. Ducane and the other men whose names were jotted on the index card had been a different kind of kin, a tumbleweed kind that drifted in and out of his and every other miner's life. They were a drinking-and-carousing-buddy kind of kin that, for a sworn loner like McPherson, faded in and out of his life like ripples in a stream.

At the busy intersection of Sixth and Kalamath, he caught a red light and suddenly found himself deep in thought, unaware that the black BMW that had followed him all the way from Georgetown was just three cars behind him. He knew that men like Ducane sometimes boasted and beat their chests in order to get up the nerve they needed to go back underground the next day. Perhaps Ducane's drunken assertion all those years ago, that he knew who'd killed JFK, had been no more and no less than another frightened miner's tale. Or maybe Ducane had been looking for an extended moment in the sun, just as he was at the moment.

It wasn't until the car behind him honked, breaking his concentration, that McPherson realized just how caught up in the strange mystery of Antoine Ducane he'd become.

He knew the Mile High City well enough to head straight for Bonnie Brae. In fact, he'd spent more than a few weekends drinking at the neighborhood's historic Bonnie Brae Tavern, a watering hole and pizzeria he'd stumbled across years earlier when his mufflerless 1955 Ford pickup had given up the ghost only a few blocks away. Turning off Sixth Avenue, he headed south on University Boulevard, trying his best to remember, as he sped through a yellow light, why on earth he'd been cruising along the northern edge of Bonnie Brae the night his truck had died. Especially since gambling, whores, and endlessly flowing whiskey weren't part and parcel of that section of the city.

It don't really matter now, he told himself, nosing his truck along the northern edge of a neighborhood that he remembered as being made up for the most part of modest single-story brick homes. Even in the twilight, he could now see that many of those homes had morphed into upsized, pregnant-looking two-stories.

"Progress," he mumbled, shaking his head and breaking into rhyme. "Make it big, make it better, two false tits under a sweater. Looks okay but whattaya got? Water-filled balloons ready to pop." Still shaking his head, he slowed his pickup and squinted to make out the name on a poorly lit street sign. "Elizabeth, that's it!" he called out, turning right onto a tree-lined street of rambling ranch homes. "Shit. Ducane must've got lucky," he blurted out, stroking his chin thoughtfully. As the truck crept along slowly, he counted off the addresses on the houses: "720, 740, 760—bingo!"

He eased to the curb, stopped directly in front of 780 S. Elizabeth, and shut down the truck's engine. The home, a blond-brick, single-story 1950s Denver ranch, had been painted white; a three-car garage had been added; the grounds had been landscaped to the hilt; and the house sported a brand-new slate roof. A late-model, full-sized SUV sat in the driveway a few feet from two open garage doors. A couple of mountain bikes rested on the floor in one of the bays. "Upscale," McPherson mumbled, sounding deflated, suspecting from the look of things that Ducane's mystery lady, Sheila—if that was her real name—had more than likely flown the coop years ago.

Turning off the truck's lights and thinking, *Sure hope these white folk are hospitable,* McPherson slipped the index card into his shirt pocket, got out of the truck, and headed for the house. A pigtailed, chubby, rosy-cheeked blond girl who looked to be about six greeted him at the deadbolted, custom-designed, wrought-iron screen door. With her arms folded, looking defiant, the girl said, "You want something, mister?" as McPherson rang the doorbell.

Before he could answer, a stately, square-faced, very pale, and very blond woman stepped into view. "Yes, may I help you?" she asked, trying to look unperturbed by the presence of a strange black man on her front doorstep. Forcing a smile, she edged the girl behind her.

"I hope so, ma'am," said McPherson, looking past the woman into the house and toward the hallway stairs that rose behind her. "I'm tryin' to locate a lady who mighta lived here years back. The only thing I got to go on is her name: Sheila."

Before the woman could answer, a man's voice called out from somewhere beyond the stairs, "Janet, who's at the door?" as the little girl moved back in front of the woman.

With both hands planted firmly on the girl's shoulders, the woman turned and said, "A man who says he's looking for someone named Sheila."

A balding man, slightly shorter than the woman and looking about the same age, early sixties at the most, stepped into view. Holding a half-eaten sandwich in one hand, the man stepped boldly up beside the woman, patted the girl on the head, and placed his sandwich on a nearby entryway table. "No one here by that name," he said adamantly.

"She woulda lived here about thirty years ago, give or take a few years," an unfazed McPherson said, rocking from side to side. Staring down at the slightly nervous-looking man, he decided to drop his bomb. "Sure you don't know her? She may know somethin' about a friend of mine who was murdered."

"What?"

"This woman Sheila may know something about . . ."

"I heard you," the man said curtly.

Glancing at the woman with a hint of guilt, the man said sheepishly, "Could be you're looking for Sheila Lucerne."

"Don't know if that's her last name or not," McPherson said, smiling at the man's quick about-face.

"Was she from Louisiana?"

"Very likely," said McPherson, stroking his chin thoughtfully, the way he'd seen detectives do in the movies. "Did you know her?"

The man's gaze moved from McPherson to the woman standing next to him, then quickly to the floor. "If it's the same person, she owned this house before I bought it back in '72."

"Do you know if she's still living in Denver?"

The man's answer was abrupt. "No. She's dead. Killed in a car crash on the Boulder Turnpike years ago."

"Well, at least you know somethin' about her, mister, ahhh?"

The man looked up from staring at the floor, as if wondering why on earth, other than the fact he didn't want to get caught in a lie in front of his wife, he'd just given information about Sheila Lucerne to some black man he'd never seen before. Without answering McPherson, he eyed the woman whose hand he now held and realized from the look on her face that she was just as interested in learning more about the woman named Sheila Lucerne as the black man. Clearing his throat and looking guilty, the man said, "We should probably clear this up right now. I was engaged to Sheila once."

McPherson watched the woman's jaw drop as she fought to maintain her composure. "Would you like to come in, sir?" she finally said to McPherson.

"It's just plain Cornelius McPherson, ma'am, no 'sir' to it."

Looking not the least bit fearful, the woman unlocked the screen door and swung it open. "We're the Watsons. I'm Janet." Nodding at the embarrassed-looking man, she said, "My husband, Carl, and the lady in pigtails and ballet slippers is our granddaughter, Susan. Come in, Mr. McPherson, and we'll see if we can't straighten this all out for you." She shot her husband a disappointed look as McPherson stepped over the threshold into the foyer. It was a look that also said, *Better come clean.* Slipping her hand out of Carl's and into her granddaughter's, she said, "Susie, I want you to go change and get ready for bed. Grandpa and I need to talk to Mr. McPherson. Would you do that for me?"

"Sure." The girl stared at McPherson, drinking in the essence of his blackness, before pivoting and scooting off around the stairwell.

"We can talk in the living room," Carl Watson offered quickly. "This shouldn't take long." He flipped a nearby light switch and moved toward a suddenly brightly lit, well-appointed sunken living room off the hallway. "Watch your step." His words were directed at McPherson, but his eyes were locked on his wife's.

"I'll do that," said McPherson, catching the look of pent-up rage in Janet Watson's eyes and thinking as he stepped down into the living room, *Nope, my friend, I'm thinking you'd better watch yours.*

Thirty minutes and a round of soft drinks later, Carl Watson had indeed come clean, surprising both McPherson and his wife with his story about the Baton Rouge–born, impetuous, and unabashedly Creole Sheila Lucerne. Carl Watson had admitted that Lucerne had been his fiancée during a stormy on-again, off-again romance that had spanned the early 1970s during the years when he'd been a PhD student in engineering at the University of Denver. Lucerne, several years Watson's senior, and Janet Watson—Janet Highpoint at the time—had known nothing of one another but had shared the nebbishy future mechanical engineer's favors for nearly a year.

According to Watson, he and Lucerne had tried to make the relationship work, even forcing it to the point of their short-term engagement. They'd even lived together briefly in the house that was now his, which Sheila had then owned. But after five months of constant battling over everything from the arrangement of the furniture to their completely opposite takes on politics and tastes in food, movies, and music, they had broken off the engagement. Watson admitted that he'd gotten the house after Sheila had died, largely because he'd been in the right place at the right time and had had the right amount of cash on hand when the house had gone up for sale as part of probate. That revelation caused Janet Watson to gasp, glance around the room, looking betrayed, and fight back tears.

When asked by McPherson whether he'd ever heard Sheila mention a man named Antoine Ducane and whether she might have known any of Ducane's people back in Louisiana, Watson had offered a point-blank "No." The conversation dribbled to a halt after that, but McPherson suspected that after he left, Carl Watson would be offering his wife a much more detailed explanation of his relationship with Sheila Lucerne.

It was nine o'clock when McPherson rose to leave without again mentioning Antoine Ducane's name. As he moved toward the front door, the little girl stepped out from a barely evident recessed telephone nook in the center-hall stairwell and asked, "You gonna leave now, mister?"

"I sure am," said McPherson, surprised by her presence. He patted her gently on the head and cast a final backward glance at the girl's somber-faced grandmother as Carl Watson ushered him to the door.

"Still don't understand all the interest in Sheila," said Watson, looking baffled as they reached the screen door. Swinging the door open and looking as if he were preparing to shoo out a pesky fly, he added, "Do you think she was involved in your friend's murder?"

"Don't know," McPherson said with a shrug.

"Do you think Sheila was involved in something illegal?"

"Don't think so, unless knowin' the wrong man's been made a crime."

"Or the wrong woman." Watson shot a glance over his shoulder toward his wife.

"Thing's'll smooth out, my man. Trust me."

Watson eyed McPherson sternly. "I hope so. But just for the record, don't come back."

McPherson flashed the worried-looking engineer an insightful smile. "I'll make it a point not to. But from now on, if I was you, I'd do like they tell you when you take the witness stand in court."

"How's that?"

"I'd take to tellin' my wife the truth, the whole truth, and nothin' but the truth." McPherson gave Watson a quick wink and headed down the sidewalk toward his truck. He was halfway there when Watson called after him, his tone insistent, "No more surprise appearances, Mr. McPherson, you hear?"

Without answering, McPherson continued walking toward his truck in the semidarkness. When he stopped and turned back to see if Watson was still there, the front door was closed.

"Oh, what a tangled web we weave," McPherson mumbled, stepping off the curb and into the street. He was a few steps from his truck's rear bumper when a black BMW pulled up next to him. The car's interior lights flashed on as the front passenger window eased down smoothly and the driver called out, "Hey, buddy, how far's Colorado Boulevard?"

McPherson raised his left arm to gesture east as the driver, in one fluid motion, raised a 12-gauge, sawed-off, double-barreled shotgun, aimed it squarely at McPherson's chest, and fired two point-blank rounds.

Looking dumbfounded, McPherson stared wide-eyed at the driver, gurgled, "What the fuck?" and stumbled back up onto the sidewalk. He took two truncated steps onto Carl Watson's neatly manicured lawn and dropped. The BMW sped off as Watson, startled by the sound of gunfire, flung open his front door, yelled, "Hey!" and raced toward McPherson.

With a gaping hole in his chest and blood streaming from both sides of his sternum, a near-breathless McPherson wheezed, "Last night, night before, twenty-four robbers at my door. I got up and let 'em in, hit 'em in the head . . ." Cornelius McPherson never finished his favorite skip rhyme. When a hysterical Carl Watson knelt in the dew-covered grass and lifted his head, McPherson was already dead.

Chapter 11

The Denver City and County Coroner's wagon carrying Cornelius McPherson's body pulled away from the curb in front of Carl and Janet Watson's Bonnie Brae home, heading for Denver Health and Hospital and the city morgue, an hour and ten minutes after McPherson died from a shotgun blast to the heart.

Denver homicide Lieutenant Gus Cavalaris, a seventeen-year veteran of the Denver police force who much preferred the title "Detective" to "Lieutenant," had spent almost that same amount of time talking quietly to a visibly shaken Carl Watson and his hysterical wife. Cavalaris's interrogation of the Watsons, although clearly intended not to look like one, had included questions about everything from McPherson's arrival on their doorstep to more penetrating inquiries about the mysterious Sheila Lucerne.

Cavalaris's calm, self-deprecating style of questioning and his thoughtful, easy manner had worn down the shell-shocked couple to the point that anything he now asked them resulted only in a few clipped words and near-catatonic stare. He was about to wrap up the question-and-answer session when the lead crime-scene technician ambled into the Watsons' sunken living room, where the questioning was being conducted, and announced, "We're all done outside, Lieutenant."

"Ga-ga-good," came Cavalaris's reply. A chronic stutterer since childhood, Cavalaris had largely overcome the affliction except for those rare times when he'd nailed some criminal dead to rights, interrogated someone senseless and into a confession, or worked himself up to the point of total frustration over a case. His hour-long tête-à-tête with the Watsons had been a perfect trigger. As the technician pivoted to leave, the seasoned lieutenant slipped a business card out of his pocket and handed it to Carl Watson. "All my phone numbers, my e-mail, and my fax are listed on that card. Get in touch with me if you think you forgot to mention something this evening."

Seated in the middle of one of the room's two overstuffed couches with one arm draped over his wife's shoulder, Watson took the card and laid it face down on the glass-topped coffee table in front of him.

As Cavalaris stood to leave, he couldn't resist the urge to ask a few final questions. "You say y-y-you didn't get a good look at either the car the shots came from or the shooter, am I correct?"

"No, I didn't, but the car was black, just like I told you earlier. And it was real low to the ground. That's all I can tell you," said Watson.

"No license plates that you could see?"

"No." Watson's tone was beleaguered.

"And th-th-the woman who was killed in that automobile accident y-y-you men-men-mentioned, Sheila Lucerne. She was from Louisiana, right?"

Watson frowned and glanced at his pale, exhausted-looking wife. "Why on earth are you asking me the same questions six ways from Sunday, Lieutenant? We've been through all that. I didn't kill that man."

Cavalaris smiled. His front teeth, moist with saliva, glistened. "It's just the way I'm forced to do business I-I-I'm afraid. You do understand that law enforcement is a question-oriented business. And believe me, it's a quirky kind of business sometimes, especially when you're searching for answers to a murder. Answers to questions like, wh-wh-why would a man who told you he was a miner from all the way up in Georgetown—and he did tell you that, you said so yourself—end up shotgunned to death, in the most professional kind of way, right out there on your front lawn?" Cavalaris nodded toward the street.

"I don't know the answer to that, Lieutenant."

"And you know what, sir? I have to believe you," the hovering, lanky, slightly stoop-shouldered Cavalaris said with a nod. "Th-th-that's why I'm fascinated by this whole thing. Purely and simply fascinated by a need to wring a simple answer out of such a complex question." Shaking his head in mock amazement, Cavalaris turned to leave. "I'll be in touch," he said, retrieving a mud-colored Wyoming Cowboys ball cap from the coffee table. He stared thoughtfully into space as he turned to head for the front door. "A miner, and a black miner at that. I'll be damned. And in this pretty much all-white neighborhood. A-a-a black man out there ringing doorbells and asking questions as if he were a cop. Interesting—real interesting—you gotta admit that." Cavalaris donned his cap, pushed the screen door open, and walked out onto the porch without looking back, leaving Carl Watson looking as exhausted as he was bewildered and Janet Watson looking absolutely drained.

Damion Madrid smiled to himself as his fingers darted along the keys of the new laptop he'd unboxed an hour and a half earlier, downloaded software into, and set up to perform pretty much all the functions required in the world of a virtual business, except for the actual delivery of the antiques and collectibles that made up CJ and Mario's Ike's Spot inventory.

Hovering over Damion like an expectant father, his eyes glued to the computer screen, Mario asked, "Sure you got everything in there? It took me and CJ a month of Sundays to catalog all our inventory." Mario reached over Damion's shoulder and tapped the top spread-sheet on a half-inch stack of papers.

"Yeah, I know," said Damion, resisting the urge to sigh as he thought back on all the hours it had taken him to turn CJ and Mario's handwritten list and his own copy and artful photographs into an eye-catching cyberspace antique store. A store with zoom-in close-up color photographs of its rather remarkable inventory. A store, that in addition to detailed descriptions of its merchandise, offered ordering instructions, testimonials, and authenticity guarantees.

Eyeing Mario quizzically, Damion paused and thoughtfully asked, "Why'd you and CJ decide to call the store Ike's Spot, Mario? Don't think I asked before."

Mario smiled. "It's a long story, Damion."

"I've got nothing but time. Clue me in."

Mario forced back a chuckle, aware that the bookish, overly mothered twenty-year-old sitting in front of him, who proclaimed to anyone who asked that, in spite of being a college basketball star on a fast track to the pros, he planned to chuck the game and go to medical school when he finished college, more than likely actually did want to know the history behind the store's unusual name. "Okay, Mister I've-got-nothin'-but-time. Here's why. CJ's Uncle Ike once saved my life. So CJ and me figured that the least we could do was name our store after him."

"When'd he do that?"

"A long time ago."

"Here in Denver?"

"Yeah."

"How'd it happen?"

"You'll have to ask CJ that."

With a smile, Damion said, "Come on, Mario."

When Mario flashed him a stern look that said, *Enough with the questions*, Damion, well schooled in the all-important issues concerning Mario Satoni's past, decided to cut short the question-and-answer session. Looking for a secure place to land, he clicked back to the Ike's Spot home page. "You're in business," he said, trying his best to look unruffled.

Mario rested his hand reassuringly on Damion's shoulder, recognizing that he'd momentarily allowed a tiny piece of his former self, a piece that he normally kept well hidden, to surface. Smiling down at the lanky, dark-haired, self-assured college junior, Mario said, "I'll tell you the whole story one day, kid. Promise."

"No harm, no foul, Mario," said Damion.

Without responding, Mario threaded his way through a gauntlet of boxes and walked over to the 1970s-vintage color TV in the far northeast corner of the cluttered basement. He turned the set on and said, "Let's say we take a gander at the news. Need to see how my Dodgers fared today."

"Hope they did better than the Rockies," said Damion, aware of Mario's passion for his beloved Dodgers.

The TV slowly brightened, and for the next several minutes they halfheartedly watched the news as Damion fine-tuned the Ike's Spot home page and Mario impatiently awaited the eleven o'clock news sports segment. Ten minutes into the broadcast, Mario mumbled, "Get to the damn sports, would ya?"

After a lengthy commercial break, a sportscaster finally appeared. As Mario reached to turn up the volume, the words, "Live late-breaking news" crawled their way across the bottom of the screen, the sportscaster faded into blackness, and in the blink of a satellite feed, an impish-looking reporter, standing on the sidewalk in front of Carl and Janet Watson's house with crime-scene tape flapping in the breeze behind her, announced, "This is Monica Jergens with a Channel 9 late-breaking news exclusive. A man identified by a Denver police spokesman as Cornelius McPherson has apparently been killed in a drive-by shooting in the 700 block of South Elizabeth Street here in Denver. McPherson, you may recall from a story first reported to you here on 9 News just two days ago, survived a mountaintop earthquake that continues to keep the Eisenhower Tunnel and I-70 closed in both directions. In the aftermath of that earthquake, the partial remains of a miner who had worked with McPherson on the I-70 Eisenhower Tunnel project were found. Denver police have not released any further details about this apparent drive-by shooting. Stay tuned for 9 News updates and be sure to watch Channel 9 First News at 6 a.m. for complete details. This is Monica Jergens, reporting from Denver's Bonnie Brae neighborhood."

The Channel 9 sports anchor's face returned to fill the screen as quickly as it had disappeared, and, looking directly into the camera as if his words were meant only for Mario, he announced, "The Colorado Rockies squeezed out an eleventh-inning win over the Padres in a . . ."

Mario clicked off the TV and took two quick breaths, looking as if he'd just been sucker-punched in the gut.

Astonished that Mario had turned off the TV without hearing how the Dodgers had fared, Damion asked, "Something the matter, Mario?"

Staring past Damion into space, Mario didn't answer.

"Mario, you okay?"

"Yeah."

"You're gonna miss the Dodgers score."

"It can wait." Staring around at the basement's whitewashed cinderblock walls, Mario asked, "Is your mom at home?"

"By now, sure. Why?"

"Just need to know," said Mario, aware that in the nine years since she'd left CJ's employ Julie Madrid had finished law school and positioned herself as one of the top criminal defense lawyers in the state.

Looking puzzled, Damion asked, "Want me to call her for you?"

"No, I'll call her myself," Mario said dejectedly, thinking that he hadn't had need of Julie Madrid's kind of counsel in close to thirty years.

"You in trouble, Mario?"

When Mario didn't answer, Damion said timidly, "You're not connected to what happened over in Bonnie Brae, are you?"

"Of course not!" Mario shuffled across the room, wavering from side to side as he moved.

"I think it's time we closed up shop," said Damion. Hoping to leave on a positive note, he added, "Mom stays up to midnight most nights. She works way too hard if you ask me."

"Don't ever second-guess your mother, son," said Mario, who understood Julie Madrid's dogged will to succeed. He was well acquainted with the story of how she had extracted herself from an abusive marriage to Damion's father, who was now dead; worked her way through law school at night while working full time as CJ's secretary during the day; and ultimately earned a stellar reputation as a criminal defense shark.

For the second time in the space of half an hour, Damion caught a glimpse of a sterner, darker side of Mario Satoni—and it unnerved him. "I didn't mean it in that way, Mario."

"We've talked enough this evening, Damion. Time you headed home."

Uncertain what to say, Damion walked quickly toward the basement stairs. "I'll tell Mom you're gonna call her," he said, planting his foot on the bottom step. When Mario didn't answer, he scurried up the stairs. "See you tomorrow," he called back over his shoulder before moving quickly through the kitchen and down a hallway filled with photographs of once powerful politicians, mobsters, and entertainers from Mario's generation.

Moments later he was out the back door and behind the wheel of his SUV. He backed the Jeep, a gift from his mother for maintaining a 3.8 grade point average during his college freshman year, away from Mario's garage and pointed it toward home. As the Jeep gained speed, he couldn't help but think that in the three years he'd known Mario Satoni, he'd never seen him so out of sync, or so reflective and intense.

Weaving his way through Denver's still predominantly Italian northern section of the city toward his own Washington Park neighborhood and home, he had the sudden sense that people like Mario, his mother, and CJ had seen a side of life that he couldn't fully comprehend. Even factoring in his early childhood, defined largely by an absent father and life only a cut above poverty, he would never be able to appreciate how the people closest to him had clawed their way out of life's underbelly. As he turned off Federal Boulevard and onto Speer, he noticed a man who was obviously drunk stumbling

down a sidewalk. For some reason the late-night image of the stupe-
fied man weaving his way to nowhere under the glare of a single
streetlight stuck with him most of the way home.

When he turned onto Downing Street, he had the feeling that
something strange and undefinable was working its way into his psyche—boring its way into that highly competitive and slightly insecure part of him that had made him a star athlete and stellar student
but also a loner. The very same thing that, he suspected, drove his
mother to stay up working far too late on far too many nights.

Long before Damion got home, Mario Satoni had called Pinkie
Niedemeyer to tell him he was probably going to need his kind of
support. He'd then called CJ to schedule an 8 a.m. meeting with him
at CJ's office. He left the issue of how to approach Julie Madrid, someone who'd always been wary of him but whose counsel he desperately needed, to CJ.

Mario had no way of knowing whether his nephew Rollie had
seen the news about the shooting in Bonnie Brae, but if he hadn't, he
was certain one of Rollie's stable of kiss-ass flunkies had—if in fact one
of them hadn't been the trigger man. Whatever the case, it was a
certainty that Rollie was up to his nose hairs in the mess. Rollie,
after all, was the one who'd heeded the siren call to kill a president
forty-four years earlier, jumping at the chance to make a name by
insinuating himself into an assassination plot that was far too big for
him. Now, like it or not, Rollie would have to deal with the fallout
from that decision.

The chickens had finally come home to roost in the form of the
frozen remains of a man named Antoine Ducane. Rollie, already an
insomniac, wouldn't get any sleep at all, Mario told himself—and

unfortunately, because Mario had been captain of Denver's crime family operations when Kennedy had been assassinated, his name would crop up in any police investigation, and that meant he'd miss some sleep too.

Hoping that CJ and Julie could help him extricate himself from a situation that would ultimately reach higher than the mere investigation of the unearthing of some obscure miner's remains, Mario looked skyward and pleadingly said, "Angie," aware that if CJ and Julie couldn't help him, Pinkie Niedemeyer certainly would.

Mario finally drifted off to sleep a little before 2:30 a.m. He'd been asleep for just over an hour when the sixty-year-old Bakelite phone on the nightstand next to his bed rang, jolting him out of his uneasy slumber. Lifting the receiver on the third ring and sounding dazed, he answered, "Mario."

"Mario, my friend. Hope I didn't snatch you away from a good dream."

"Who's this?"

"You mean you don't recognize my voice? Hell, I'm disappointed."

Although Mario recognized something familiar in the caller's tone, something distinctive about the way he'd said *disappointed,* he couldn't place the voice until Randall Maxie said, "Alas, poor Yorick, I thought you knew me."

"Maxie," said Mario, recognizing the quixotic hit man's penchant for rearranging Shakespearean quotations. "What the shit do you want?"

Maxie chuckled. "Not much, old-timer."

Ignoring the insult that would have cost Maxie at least a pistol whipping forty years earlier, Mario said, "You've got one minute to say your piece, Maxie."

"Don't play big shit with me, Satoni. I go back a ways, remember? Maybe you were somebody once, a long, long time ago, but right now you're just a little old man living in a little old house. All bent over with only a little bit of time left on the clock."

Biting his tongue to control his anger, Mario thought back on all the years he'd known Maxie. Maxie had been a pudgy, third-tier, dope-smoking sixteen-year-old North Denver hoodlum when Mario had stepped away from his role as Denver's top don in the mid-1960s. He had missed the army and Vietnam by the skin of his teeth, and while his slightly older counterparts had been getting their heads blown off in Southeast Asia, Maxie had been sucking up to Rollie Ornasetti. As the Vietnam War wound down and most of Maxie's cronies had come home bigger nutcases than when they'd left, Maxie, in an effort to puff himself up and appear their equal, had decided to manufacture a few stateside war stories of his own by taking on the task of providing Ornasetti with highly visible muscle. Soon he was killing people at Rollie's request. "You're down to thirty seconds," Mario said finally. "Get to the point, Maxie."

"Point's this, old man. Rollie's had some recent problems with things from the past popping up. We need to make certain that should any of Denver's boys in blue decide to open old wounds, we don't see you pointing any fingers."

"What makes you think I'd do somethin' like that?"

"Your weakened state of mind, old man, and the fact that you've been away from Rollie's end of the business for a long, long time."

Choking back his anger, Mario said, "Don't question my loyalty, Maxie. I've got more of it in my little toe than you have in your whole damn body."

"Don't get cutesy, old man. Just listen up. Any chance you've read about some guy finding a bunch of loose body parts up at the Eisenhower Tunnel after our recent earthquake?"

"Yeah. And I also heard that the man who found those parts bought it over in Bonnie Brae earlier tonight."

"Good. Real good. You've been listening. So here's the bottom line. Rollie doesn't want you having intestinal distress over, or spewing your guts about, what you might know about the guy they found in the tunnel. Or worse, maybe even running to the cops or even the FBI with a sudden case of diarrhea of the mouth. If you do, it's gonna cost."

"Cost me what, you fuckin' nitwit?"

"Talk to the wrong people when you shouldn't and you'll find out quick enough. Push your luck and you could end up finding out from yet another source. You don't think Rollie set up the framework for what went down in Dallas all those years ago all by his lonesome."

"What the hell are you gettin' at, Maxie?"

Maxie laughed. It was a laugh that quickly escalated to an all-out bellow. "Just this, old man. If you talk to the cops or the feds about what you suspect went down in Dallas, you'll be the goat. Say anything to anyone about that dead man they found up at the Eisenhower Tunnel, even if you're just guessing at what happened, and you'll be a lot more than sorry. Bottom line's this, my friend. Roll over on Rollie and you'll end up lost to the world." Maxie offered Mario a final warning before cradling the phone and leaving Mario staring into space: "Think before you leap, old man."

Left with a dial tone ringing in his ear and aware that he wouldn't get another wink of sleep that night, Mario sat on the edge of his bed, looked skyward, and whispered, "Angie."

Chapter 12

The phone call telling Ron Else that he needed to be on the first nonstop out of LAX the next morning and bound for Denver came in just before 3 a.m. The call, pretty much identical to the scores of similar calls that had interrupted Else's sleep, dinner, poker playing, or lovemaking during his twenty-five years as an FBI agent, had been routine. But before he'd picked up the phone or said hello, he'd known the call would have him once again traipsing after some lead in the John F. Kennedy assassination.

This time he'd been told that he'd be doing follow-up on a possible JFK assassination link initiated by a call from a Denver cop. A cop with a dead man at his door and less than a scintilla of evidence tying the corpse to the Kennedy killing. But in Ron Else's world, a scintilla of evidence was all that was needed to ensure that he'd be bound for Denver.

He'd come to realize that he was no more than a regional public relations man assigned to listen to the stories and hold the hands of hapless JFK conspiracy nuts and fame-seeking lawmen. Not once in the scores of times that he'd caught a Phoenix- or Salt Lake City– or Albuquerque-bound red-eye, driven a rental car across the Mojave Desert, or ridden a train from his home base in LA to Mayberry or Podunk to engage in his specialty, investigating new murders that might possibly be tied to the JFK assassination, had he run across a single case that could be linked to the killing.

More often than not, the excitable cop or sheriff or trembling village constable with the dead man at his doorstep was either misinformed, looking for publicity, kissing the ass of some DA with a political agenda, or just plain stupid. In one instance, it had even turned out that the cop calling for what was known in Else's trade as a "Kennedy linkage investigation" had actually shot the victim, an insurance agent who'd been humping the cop's estranged wife. A year from now it wouldn't matter, Else told himself as he packed his well-traveled carry-on for a 5:30 a.m. flight to Denver. He'd be playing golf in the Caymans.

He didn't yet have all the facts on the Denver fiasco. All he knew was that a Denver homicide lieutenant backed up by some yahoo of a mountaintop sheriff with possible relevant new information about the JFK assassination had requested help. The two Colorado lawmen had no way of knowing that the call would garner a look-see from not just any FBI agent but Ron Else, the West Coast king. A man who'd seen and heard so many JFK assassination stories from so many whacked-out cops, wide-eyed civilians, gullible town marshals, and unschooled sheriffs that he liked to boast that he wasn't sure anymore whether JFK had been killed by Lee Harvey Oswald, Howdy Doody, or the Pope.

"I don't see why Julie couldn't make it," Mario Satoni said, pacing back and forth in the center of the stately drawing room in the old Denver Victorian that housed CJ Floyd's bail-bonding offices. After his Uncle Ike's death, CJ had taken over and operated the business just west of downtown on Delaware Street that Ike Floyd had started in the 1950s. After temporarily declaring himself out of the bail-bonding business, CJ had briefly vacated Bail Bondsman's Row with its string of old Victorian buildings affectionately known as "painted ladies" to enter his failed antique store venture. Though he was still in the antiques business with Mario, he had quickly returned to the world he knew best, linking back up with his bail-bonding partner, Flora Jean Benson. Although he rarely mentioned it to anyone, especially Mavis, the move back to Delaware Street had somehow made him feel whole again.

Fed up with Mario's complaining, Flora Jean, who stood drinking coffee beside the seated CJ, said, "How many times we gotta tell you Julie couldn't come, Mario? She had a court date." Standing just over six feet tall and with the carriage of a Las Vegas showgirl, Flora Jean took guff from no one—including former mafia dons.

"So she should've canceled it."

CJ shook his head. "Mario, come on."

"In my day we would've got the judge to cancel or at least to move the damn thing back."

"It's a new day, Mario," said CJ, surprised that Mario, characteristically tight-lipped about his days as the Colorado mafia's top dog, would mention anything about his time at the helm. That openness, coupled with the fact that Mario had called him at 4 a.m. insisting on an 8 a.m. powwow that had to include Julie Madrid, had CJ worried that Mario was in more than, as Mario had put it earlier, *a little bit of trouble*.

Still pacing the floor, his voice laden with disappointment, Mario said, "Damn it, Calvin. I don't wanna have to say everything twice."

"Julie's gonna be in court 'til at least two." Flora Jean swirled what was left of her coffee around in a large black mug that was stenciled with the U.S. Marine Corps insignia. "Sometimes you just gotta hurry up and wait."

Mario shook his head. "Eighty-two years old, finally livin' my antique-peddlin' dream, and my lyin', connivin', two-faced Napoleonic shit of a nephew starts riggin' things to cave the world in on me." Mario glanced skyward, "You always said he was the kind that would foul the nest, Angie. And you were right."

Unaccustomed to Mario's chats with his dead wife, Flora Jean eyed CJ quizzically. CJ flashed her a reassuring wink, rose from the high-backed leather chair that had once been Ike's, walked around his desk, and draped an arm over Mario's shoulders. "Sooner or later, you're gonna have to explain why you called me at four in the morning sounding like the devil was at your door. Might as well start now."

Looking beleaguered, Mario again glanced skyward and whispered, "Guess I got no choice. But I need to be sittin' in Ike's chair while I'm talkin'. That way I'll be speakin' from the position of an eye for an eye." He eyed CJ pensively. "How about rollin' Ike's chair over here to me?"

CJ rolled the massive chair, its leather stained and cracked from age, out from behind the desk and into the middle of the room. Watching Mario take a seat, CJ realized that he'd never seen the once powerful don look so vulnerable.

"You want somethin' to drink?" Flora Jean asked, sensing the gravity of the situation.

"A shot of somethin', maybe."

Flora Jean left the room to return quickly with a bottle of unopened Jack Daniel's in one hand, and a tumbler and a half-empty bottle of vodka in the other. "Pick your poison."

"Vodka," Mario said weakly.

Setting the Jack Daniel's aside, Flora Jean placed the tumbler on CJ's desk and began filling it with vodka. The tumbler was three-quarters full before Mario said, "That's fine." Turning to CJ, he asked, "You got that special coin I gave you anywhere handy?"

"It's upstairs in my apartment," CJ said, surprised that Mario would ask for a coin that Angie Satoni had given Ike almost sixty years earlier.

"Need you to go get it."

"It's that important?"

"Yeah."

CJ left the room in a rush and hustled up the stairs that led to his second-floor apartment. Moments later he returned clutching the twenty-dollar gold piece that Angie Satoni had given Ike the night Ike had brought Mario home with a bullet in him. CJ knew the story only too well.

It was 1948, and, seated at the bar in Denver's famous Rossonian jazz club, the two men had met for the first time as they both enjoyed a night of jazz. They'd left the club together when the show ended and headed up Welton Street for their cars. Two blocks from the Rossonian, Mario had been ambushed. Ike had subdued the shooter, but hadn't called the cops, at Mario's request—a request Ike thought might be a dying one. Ike had driven Mario across town to his home in North Denver, where he'd been treated by Angie's uncle, a prominent mob physician and Denver socialite. To show her family's gratitude, Angie had given Ike the twenty-dollar gold piece that CJ was now holding. Its fluted edges had been rubbed perfectly smooth, and a tiny boxed "S" had been stamped on the coin's reverse side near the bottom. Angie had given Ike the coin with the following instructions: *This coin represents a lifetime pass out of harm's way from my family to you, Ike Floyd. Use it wisely.*

CJ handed the gold piece to Mario. Clutching it tightly, Mario looked skyward. "I'm breakin' an oath here, Ike, Angie." He mumbled something in Latin that neither CJ nor Flora Jean understood, then stared stoically at CJ. "Back in 1963, when you were still wet behind the ears, my nephew Rollie was involved in the Kennedy assassination," he said in a whisper, handing the coin back to CJ.

When neither CJ nor Flora Jean responded, Mario said, "Did you hear me? Rollie was hooked in to the JFK killin'.'"

"Come on, Mario." CJ stared at Mario in wide-eyed disbelief.

"There's no 'come on' to it. It's the truth," Mario shot back. "Rollie hooked up with some people, real powerful people, who hatched the plan to eliminate Kennedy."

CJ stroked his chin thoughtfully, uncertain why Mario would share such information. Looking concerned, he said, "Maybe you shouldn't take this any further, Mario. Perhaps we should wait for Julie."

Mario smiled. It was the accommodating smile of a man who realized that he was near the end of a very long race. "I appreciate your concern for my health, Calvin. I know the risks. Bottom line is, Pinkie Niedemeyer set me straight the other day when you and I were doin' inventory. That's why I sent you scootin'. Me and Pinkie's little powwow needed to be in private." Mario turned to face Flora Jean. "Either of you hear about them findin' the remains of some guy in the Eisenhower Tunnel in the aftermath of that earthquake we had up in the high country the other day?"

"Yeah," said Flora Jean, taking a seat.

"What about you, Calvin?"

"I heard about it."

Mario took in the astonished looks on CJ's and Flora Jean's faces before continuing. "Well, and I know this for a fact, that guy whose remains they found was tied in to the hit on Kennedy in a real big way. And ..."

CJ cut Mario off midsentence. "You weren't involved, were you?"

Mario swallowed hard, took a long sip of his drink, and glanced skyward. "In a roundabout way, by refusin' to get involved in the assassination plot, I expect I was. And you can bet your last nickel that when the cops and the feds get to diggin' deep enough, my name'll pop up."

Aware now why Mario had been so insistent on Julie being there, CJ asked, "What makes you think that anybody'll start digging that deep?"

"Another murder. One that took place last night over in Bonnie Brae." Mario reached into his pants pocket and pulled out the *Rocky Mountain News* account of Cornelius McPherson's death that he'd clipped from the paper's early edition. He handed the clipping to CJ. "The story's gonna get bigger, Calvin. Trust me."

CJ read the three paragraphs describing the previous night's drive-by shooting of McPherson, handed the clipping to Flora Jean, and turned back to Mario. "So the bottom line in all this is Mr. McPherson found something that he shouldn't have?"

"Sure did."

CJ stroked his chin thoughtfully, reached into his vest pocket for a box of cheroots, tapped one out, and lit up. Watching smoke swirl up into the paddles of the room's vintage ceiling fan, he asked, "So, how much do you know, Mario? About the Kennedy assassination, I mean?"

"This much for sure," Mario said haltingly. "Back when it happened, Rollie was busy tryin' to push his way up what you might call the corporate ranks—and with my help, mind you. Hell, I didn't know the lyin' SOB was a snake." Mario paused and took a sip of his drink. "Shoulda cut his head off then. Shoulda listened to Angie." Mario shook his head in disgust. "Kennedy hadn't been in office but about a year when he started squeezin' folks from both ends, and when he slipped his little brother Bobby in as attorney general, believe me, tom-toms started beatin' coast to coast. Clearances we'd had to do business like always started shuttin' down by the minute, and hands-off agreements we had with the feds, especially the ones we had with that lyin' square-headed sissy Hoover at the FBI, went up in smoke. Most of the pressure was bein' put on operations in Chicago, the East Coast, and the Gulf Coast. I didn't really feel much of a squeeze out here. And that's how Rollie was able to worm his way into the assassination plot. Lots of times people under pressure end up makin' bad choices, and somewhere along the way somebody had the bad sense to choose Rollie."

"What people?"

"You know I can't use no names here, Calvin. You'll just have to listen." He shot Flora Jean a look that said *ditto* before continuing. "I got a call one day from someone in the organization in the spring of 1963. I'm pretty sure it was March 'cause we'd had a huge snowstorm here in Denver a couple of days earlier, and things were just startin' to melt. Anyway, I got asked if I had any interest in solvin' the Kennedy problem. Me and the caller danced around the issue for a while, made small talk, and chatted about friends and his children until I finally came out and said pretty bluntly, as I recall, that Kennedy wasn't causin' me that many problems, but if he really needed help, I'd be happy to send an emissary."

"And you sent Rollie."

Mario nodded. "One of the biggest mistakes I've ever made, but I trusted him back then. After all, even if he was the pampered son of Angie's blockheaded brother, he was my nephew. Never shoulda done it, but I did. Rollie left for Chicago a few weeks later, stayed back there most of the summer. I was never back in the loop after that first call, and it was around that time that Angie started feelin' poorly. It was a whole nine months before we knew what was really wrong with her. By then Kennedy was dead, Angie was dyin', and I was headed for the first stages of the crap-shit life I've been forced to lead ever since. To tell you the truth, with Angie dyin' and all, I didn't give a rat's ass about much of anything, especially some tight-assed meddlin' dead president, or Rollie."

"Did Rollie ever admit to being involved in the assassination?"

"Not to me he didn't, but word bubbled up, and from people who woulda known, that Rollie had a hand in it."

CJ let out a lengthy sigh, uncertain whether he should stop Mario—the man who'd extracted him pretty much single-handedly from the mess that had been his life after Ike's Spot had been bombed by henchmen of Celeste Deepstream into oblivion—from going any further with his story. Turning to Flora Jean, he said, "I think we might end up needing Alden."

Mario shook his head in protest. "I'm all for usin' Julie, Calvin. Odds are, sooner or later I'm gonna need a lawyer. But hookin' up with General Grace, no way." He eyed Flora Jean apologetically. "I know he's your boyfriend, Flora Jean. But he's been involved in intelligence work most of his life, and that means, like it or not, he's been workin' the opposite side of the street from me, and that's dangerous."

Before Flora Jean could respond, CJ said, "But he probably has contacts that can help us out, Mario."

"Don't matter, Calvin. He could roll on me." Mario shook his head. "I appreciate the offer, but I don't need the general's kinda help. Besides, I've already got somebody lined up to do legwork, protection, and cover."

A look of concern arched across CJ's face. "Who?"

"Pinkie."

CJ slapped his forehead. "What?"

"Pinkie Niedemeyer!" Flora Jean said in a near shout. "You can't use him, Mario. He's a hit man."

"Flora Jean's right, Mario. Forget about using Pinkie."

Mario shook his head and held up a hand in protest. "There's a little more to this than I've told you, Calvin."

"Then you better spell it all out if you expect us to help."

"Fine. Rollie knows that if he sends the cops or the FBI, or whoever it is that deals with four-decade-old assassinations, sniffin' my way, they likely won't sniff near as hard in his direction. Besides, everybody knows that when all the Kennedy shit happened, I was in charge of things out here, not Rollie. I don't have one damn thing to prove that I sent Rollie back East as my emissary, then washed my hands of the deal. And I sure as hell don't have anything to prove that after Rollie got to Chicago, he acted on his own. Bottom line is, I've got nothin' to prove that I wasn't in on the Kennedy assassination full-bore from the start."

"So? Where's Rollie's proof that you were involved?"

"Come on, Calvin. He was just some spoiled-brat kid tryin' his best to get into law school back then. How the hell could he have worked his way up to makin' decisions about pullin' the trigger on a president? Besides, all the people who were likely pullin' his strings are long since dead. They can't tell us shit. If you were the cops or the feds, who would you roll on? Me, or somebody who was a wet-behind-the-ears twentysomethin' back then? Anybody with a badge and half a brain would have to think I would've known more about the assassination plot than Rollie. Truth is, all I knew, plain and simple, was that most of my counterparts were sick and tired of Kennedy's shit." Mario crossed his heart. "And as God is my witness, that's it. But, guess when you come right down to it, like it or not, I'm pretty much the last man standin'. Somebody could sure enough make themselves headlines if they could somehow pin JFK's killin' on me."

"There's no need to convince me you weren't involved, Mario. But then, I'm not some congressman looking for headlines, the FBI, or a cop. Sooner or later, if you don't want fingers pointing your way, you're gonna be forced to name names. We'll just have to see what Julie has to say."

"I understand," Mario said haltingly. "But there's one last thing you should know."

"Might as well air it out now."

"I won't call off Pinkie. Can't afford to."

"We'll talk about that later."

"No, we won't," Mario shot back. "Rollie's already sicced that junkyard dog of his, Randall Maxie, on me. Son of a bitch called me at three-thirty this morning with a warnin' and instructions on how I should behave when and if the cops or the feds come callin'. Truth is, it wasn't as much a warnin' as it was a threat. You can be sure Rollie's already given Maxie the okay to dispense with me if need be. So Pinkie's in on this, like it or not. He's the only person I've got who can handle Maxie."

CJ took two steps toward the man who had extracted him from the clutches of bankruptcy, and guaranteed him, by virtue of the coin CJ still clutched in his hand, a lifetime of exclusion from harm at the hands of the Colorado mafia. Looking Mario squarely in the eye, he said, "You're wrong, Mario. You've got me."

The frail-looking former don smiled, rose, and draped an arm over CJ's shoulders. "Sorry, Calvin, but I'd never let you get your hands that dirty. Now, how about us findin' out when we can all hook up with Julie?"

Chapter 13

The letter announcing to Willette Ducane that the remains of her son, Antoine, had been found appeared not in the form of an e-mail or fax, or even as an impersonal telegram in the gut-wrenching form reminiscent of World War II: *Dear Mrs. Ducane, We are sorry to inform you....* Instead the announcement came in a Federal Express envelope that contained a clipping from the *Denver Post* detailing the fact that an earthquake in the mountains of Colorado had unearthed her son's remains. An accompanying note printed on a piece of paper torn from a tablet with a Holiday Inn logo read, *Dear Mrs. Ducane, The enclosed represents my last obligation to your son, Antoine. I am so sorry.*

Seated in the same rocker on the same back porch of the same New Iberia, Louisiana, house she had lived in nearly all her life, Willette read the clipping one final time before glancing out toward the bog that she still thought of as Antoine's, folding the note and the newspaper clipping neatly back into thirds, and slipping them back into the Federal Express envelope.

She had always thought that when this day finally came she would jump to her feet and scream obscenities into the air. She would thrust her arms skyward, take the Lord's name in vain, and shout over and over again until she was hoarse. She'd once thought that she'd do all those things and more the day she learned for certain that her dear Sugar Sweet was dead. But she hadn't—to some extent she couldn't. She was now eighty-eight years old with failing vision and painful arthritis, and on far too many days she simply sat in her rocker, the same chair her grandmother had been sitting in when news that her husband had been killed in World War I had arrived, and rocked. Rocked and thought and silently pleaded with the Lord to take her and walk her up the stairs, away from her past and the prison that had been her life for the past thirty-five years.

The fact that news of Antoine's death had come to her in the form of an impersonal missive in a Federal Express envelope plastered with a badly smudged Federal Express label and a barely readable account number only served to enhance her pain. Her eyes still fixed on the bog, she sighed. It was a sorrowful, oppressed sigh that seemed to go hand in hand with the already stifling heat of the New Iberia morning.

Long ago she'd come to grips with the fact that Antoine had been lost to her forever, and for years she'd tried to subdue her sleepless nights and tormented days with alcohol. Eventually she'd simply outlasted her liquor habit, but she'd never been able to overcome or outrun her simmering guilt, which had robbed her of her robust beauty and turned her sullen. On many days this feeling still caused her to drive slowly around the parish, negotiating Louisiana's lonely back roads in her forty-five-year-old Cadillac, searching for an elixir for her mental suffering. Long ago, at Antoine's urging, she had largely turned her back on her only son. Rocking faster, she tried to push the memories to the back of her mind but couldn't. As always, she found herself looking back.

After the Kennedy killing, Antoine had rushed off to Colorado and stayed there for two months. Long ago she'd come to realize that she never should have let him go. He had come back home to New Iberia a different man—an acquiescent, joyless, pitiful man who seemed to be sidestepping his way through life, hoping to avoid land mines that were visible only to him. After less than a month at home, Antoine had returned to Colorado until 1969. That year he had come home for a two-week stay in the summer, never to return again.

Adjusting herself in her seat and gritting her teeth, Willette tried to keep the rush of memories at bay, but she couldn't. As they flooded her conscience, her stomach turned sour. She'd done all she possibly could have, given the circumstances back then. She'd sent Antoine letters and wires and warnings, but she'd never traveled to Colorado to try to talk to him personally. Instead, Antoine had insisted on always traveling to see her. There'd been reasons for her reluctance to head for the Rockies. Fear and an unending list of excuses that had kept her at home. And now there was lingering guilt that had hollowed her out inside, rendered her less than whole. As she rocked, her left eye, the one the doctors said would soon succumb to blindness, fogged over and began to twitch. Accustomed to the twitching and momentary darkness, she waited for both to pass and in those brief seconds of darkness thought about what she should've done all those years ago.

Massaging her eyelid with her finger, she told herself that there was nothing left for her in life but to rock and stare out at Antoine's bog. She moaned, toying with the envelope in her lap, stroking it and caressing it as if it were the soft, tender skin of her long-dead son, until her eyelid stopped twitching. Then she rose from her rocker and walked down the porch toward her back door. She would put the envelope with the rest of Antoine's things, lock it away forever in the trunk in his room among all his other belongings that even now remained so precious to her. It was all she could do for him now. As she stepped into the house, she glanced back at the bog a final time. It seemed to her that the ever-present thin layer of ground-level fog had lifted, if no more than a hair's breadth, but she couldn't be certain. Judging the rise and fall of the fog had always been something she had left to her precious Sugar Sweet.

There was a look of consternation on Julie Madrid's face as she shook her head and said, "I can't represent him, CJ. I'm sorry."

"But Mario's gonna need help. High-powered legal help. Your kind of help."

Continuing to shake her head, Julie sat back in her seat and scanned the sea of predominantly black faces that filled Mae's Louisiana Kitchen, the landmark Five Points eatery that Mavis Sundee's family had opened more than seventy-five years earlier. A line of people stood at the entry, patiently waiting for a table and their chance to savor a catfish luncheon special or a bowl of red beans and rice, hush puppies, and fried okra.

Julie's fair-skinned, aristocratic Latina looks didn't trigger a second glance from the restaurant's other patrons, and for good reason. She was seated with the owner's fiancé, CJ Floyd, a sure sign that she belonged—and perhaps more importantly, at one time or another she had served as legal counsel for probably a quarter of the people in the place.

Regaining her composure, Julie broke off a piece of sweet-potato pie with her fork and mouthed *No way* to CJ as an elderly black man dressed in coveralls and a dust-covered chambray shirt walked by. Nodding a silent greeting at CJ, the man smiled at Julie and said, "Afternoon, Ms. Madrid."

Julie smiled back. "Afternoon, Homer," she called as two teenagers followed the man to a nearby table.

"Didn't Homer have a heart attack a couple of months ago?" Julie whispered to CJ. "Should he be eating the stuff they serve here at Mae's?"

"Old habits die hard for some folks, Julie. You'd have to kill Homer to get him to quit his ham hocks and butter beans."

Julie shook her head. "Guess so. At least he's out of prison." Julie flashed CJ a *gotcha* kind of grin. "The same could be said for some people when it comes to giving up smoking."

"Not today, Julie. I've already had my daily sermon from Mavis. I'm working at it—just give me some time."

"Hope so."

CJ polished off the last of his sweet-potato pie, the restaurant's signature dessert, set his fork aside, and dusted off his hands. "Now, can we get back to Mario?"

"We can," said Julie. "As long as we're clear on the fact that I won't represent him, but let's go back over what you told me so you can see just how bizarre it sounds. First off, you tell me that Mario's somehow connected to the crime of the century. You follow that up with the fact that Rollie Ornasetti, or at least one of his flunkies, is ready to turn out Mario's lights. And finally, for toppers, you let me in on the fact that Mario's got Pinkie Niedemeyer, the region's top-ranking hit man, covering one of his flanks while you're covering the other."

CJ toyed with his fork. "I owe Mario."

"I understand, CJ, but you want me to stick my head into this oven? We're talking about the John F. Kennedy assassination here. Do you know the kind of trouble nosing around in that can of worms could buy? Besides, the case is closed. In case you haven't heard, a guy named Lee Harvey Oswald did it."

"Mario says that maybe he didn't."

Julie eyed CJ sympathetically. "I know all about Ike and Mario and that twenty-dollar gold piece you carry around, CJ. You're talking to Julie, remember? But the way I see it, you and Mario are pretty much even-Steven in life. Maybe both of you need to start thinking more about today's world and a little less about sixty-year-old debts."

"Could be. But Mario's gonna need a lawyer. Might as well have the best."

"Mario's people have attorneys by the boatload."

"Not like you. Besides, he's been out of that loop for decades."

"Can't do it, CJ. Besides, if what you've said is true, Mario will need a dream team of lawyers. I can do this, though—when I get back to the office, I'll make a call to LA and see if I can get somebody I know out there to help Mario out. Where is he, anyway, in case my contact wants to get in touch with him?"

"When he left my office this morning, he was headed back home to help Damion finish putting the last of our store inventory up on the Internet."

Looking guilty, Julie said, "Damion certainly likes him."

"He's a likable man."

"I know that. I'm just saying . . ."

"There's no need to explain. You're helping out with that LA call. It's just that Mario trusts you. That's all."

Julie eyed the tabletop, unwilling to admit to CJ just why she was reluctant to—no, *wouldn't*—help Mario. She swallowed hard, still not looking up. In all the years they'd known one another, she had never told CJ that she'd fled the close-knit Puerto Rican Jersey City neighborhood where she'd spent the first eighteen years of her life and migrated west because of the mafia. She'd never mentioned to him that the mob had run her father, a small businessman and short-haul trucking company owner, out of business. She had never admitted to CJ that her father had walked off a New York Port Authority wharf to his death after his business had collapsed, or that her mother, until her death three years later, had never recovered from his death or the family's loss of face. Julie's eyes glazed over whenever she talked about her father, so she didn't. But her eyes were glazed over now—not because of her father but because she was thinking about Damion, and the fact that she'd been lucky enough to whisk him away from Jersey City, where he would have likely grown up to be just another wharf rat.

Recognizing that he'd tapped a raw nerve, CJ eyed Julie sympathetically. "We about done here?" He pushed his chair back and stood.

"Yes," Julie said weakly.

"Got one last question for you. Think it would be kosher for me to go talk to that couple over in Bonnie Brae who ended up with the dead man sprawled on their lawn last night? The folks the *Denver Post* ran the story about? I don't want to push the legal envelope too far out of shape, and I sure as hell don't want the cops coming back at me or Mario. Need your take."

"Do you think Mario's connected to that?"

"Nope. But the dead guy's the same man who found that arm in the Eisenhower Tunnel last week in the aftermath of that earthquake, and Mario thinks Rollie and the arm's owner were somehow tied to the JFK assassination."

Julie eyed CJ thoughtfully. "It's not against the law to ask questions."

CJ nodded as his eyes widened in anticipation. Julie recognized the look that he always flashed when he was on the scent of a case. "But harassment and intimidation are. I'd tread lightly if I were you," she added quickly.

CJ nodded again as Julie rose, scooted in front of him, and made a beeline for Mavis, who was standing near the restaurant's entry, greeting customers. A troubled, uneasy look spread across CJ's face as he watched her walk away. Although Julie had never told him about her family's problems with the mafia, locking that information somewhere in the deep reaches of her psyche forever on the day that she buried her mother, Damion had never been party to any binding oath of silence. A few years earlier, after he and Damion had finished an intense game of twenty-one, Damion had told CJ the story of his family's suffering at the hands of the Jersey City mob. Damion had spotted CJ seven points that day, and, like a man on a holy mission, forced by circumstance to absolve a loved one of sin, he'd never missed a shot, soundly thrashing CJ 21 to 7.

Working feverishly to finish inputting Mario and CJ's store inventory data on their website so he could get out of Mario's basement and hit the basketball court, Damion glanced up from his computer screen to watch Mario, down on one knee and sweating a few feet away, finish labeling CJ's collection of 1930s and '40s Colorado and Wyoming license plates with price stickers.

Damion asked, mopping his own moist brow, "Are you ever gonna get any ventilation down here, Mario?" He suspected that the basement, with its blackout enamel-lacquered windows, depressingly low ceilings, heat-generating track lights, and lack of cross-ventilation, was at least 10 degrees warmer than the mid-eighties temperature outside.

Mario barely looked up from what he was doing. "Nobody cares what a virtual store looks or feels like, son. The proof of the puddin's in movin' the merchandise. You're the Internet guru; you should know that. But I'll cool it down for you in a little bit and go get a fan from upstairs as soon as I finish up with this."

"Thanks," said Damion, knowing after having worked for Mario and CJ most of the summer that oppressive heat and poor ventilation weren't about to slow down the former don. Relieved that Mario hadn't asked whether he'd spoken to his mother about helping out with the minor legal problem Mario had mentioned to him earlier, Damion continued working, hoping that if he quickly finished all his entries and cleaned up a couple of spreadsheets, he'd be able to avoid any discussion of the subject. He felt bad for Mario but even worse for his long-suffering mother, who'd told him when he'd asked her about lending a hand that she couldn't help Mario—ever.

Lost in their tasks, they continued quietly working until a noise that sounded to Damion like the clicking of a burned-out automobile starter echoed off the walls at the top of the basement stairwell.

Mario jumped to his feet, suddenly on full alert. Glancing at Damion, he brought a finger to his lips. "It's the alarm system," he whispered. "Somethin' in the backyard's tripped one of my sensors. Think I'd better go have a look," he added, knowing that Pinkie Niedemeyer, the only person besides CJ who should have been anywhere near his backyard, would likely have avoided the Rube Goldberg–style alarm sensors.

Damion looked unperturbed. "Maybe it's the meter reader or some animal."

Mario shook his head in protest. "No way. Just stay put. I'll go upstairs and have a look."

Suspecting that the makeshift alarm system had probably been triggered by a stray dog or cat, Damion was about to shrug off the whole incident when Mario stepped across the room, teased his long-barreled .44 out of Angie's Saks Fifth Avenue hatbox, and slipped it under his belt.

Damion froze in front of his computer screen, dumbfounded.

"You hear a ruckus up there, be prepared to use this." Mario extracted a .38 police special from a nearby gunnysack and tossed it to Damion. "You do know how to use it, don't you?"

"S-sure," Damion stammered. Years earlier he'd been taught by Billy DeLong, a legendary black cowboy and friend of CJ's, to handle everything from a .30-06 to a 9-mm. "But I've never shot at anything but antelope, game birds, and aluminum cans."

Mario frowned and shook his head. "Problem there is, they don't shoot back. Just stay put. If I'm not back down here in forty-five seconds, call CJ." He nodded toward a wall-mounted phone across the room.

"Okay."

Mario tapped the butt of the .44 with his right palm. "And Damion, what's down here in this basement is for my protection. We don't talk about it." Mario started up the basement steps. "Anybody up there? I said ..." A gunshot rang out from the suddenly opened door above before Mario could finish the question. Startled, Mario tumbled back down the steps, still clutching his .44 as the bullet that had missed him ricocheted off the basement floor. His head grazed the edge of the bottom step, opening a three-inch-long gash in his forehead. A second shot sent a bullet thwacking into one of the stairwell's wooden support beams a half foot from his head.

The sound of the shots and the sight of Mario lying dazed and bleeding triggered something primal in Damion. Something that was as much a game on the line, fed by the ball competitive instinct, as it was one of survival. Clutching the .38 tightly with both hands, he raised the barrel, sighted on the open doorway, and squeezed off three quick shots. The sound of footsteps racing across the wooden floorboards above him, melded with the knowledge that someone had just tried to kill Mario, turned Damion suddenly fearless. Gun at the ready, he headed toward the stairs.

Dazed and bleeding, Mario screamed, "Damion, no! Call CJ."

"But they may come back."

"Let 'em," said Mario, shaking his head, his speech noticeably slurred. "See that trunk over there next to the gunnysack?"

"Yeah."

"It ain't locked. Open it up." Gulping air, Mario sat up, pressed his palm to his bleeding forehead, and leaned against the support beam.

Damion rushed over to the steamer-sized wooden trunk, threw back the top, and found himself staring down at two sawed-off, double-barreled shotguns. Beneath the shotguns he could see the muzzle of an M-16, a weapon he recognized as being identical to the one CJ had carried in Vietnam and now kept stowed in a navy foot-locker in his garage.

"Pick your poison," Mario said, watching Damion's startled reaction.

Damion hefted one of the shotguns.

"Be careful—they're loaded." His eyes locked on the doorway above, Mario said, "Now hand me that Vietcong sprayer and call CJ."

Clutching the weapons tightly under each arm, Damion walked

across the room and handed the M-16 to Mario. Mario grabbed the gun one-handed. Leaning against the side of the stairs for support, he raised the muzzle and aimed it at the doorway. Smiling, and with his forehead a bloody mess, he said, "Now if our friend comes back, he'll at least know he's been in a war. Make that call to CJ, son."

Randall Maxie hadn't been prepared for the response he'd gotten after firing off his first round at Mario. Instead of a decrepit old man begging for his life, as Rollie Ornasetti had promised, Maxie had listened to three bullets whiz within inches of his head. Now, as he sped south on Federal Boulevard toward Ornasetti's Lower Downtown law offices, cell phone in hand, with Ornasetti talking to him calmly on the other end of the line, Maxie was fuming. "It was like the dried-up old cocksucker had somebody down there waiting on me," Maxie bellowed.

"Could be Floyd was there with him."

"Maybe—who knows? I didn't get a good look at the shooter. All I know is that whoever was down there with Satoni almost took my head off."

"Could be it was a she," said Ornasetti.

"Whatever. He, she, it. Doesn't really matter. What matters is that the old geezer has turned this into something personal. The first time out of the chute, all I planned to do was scare him. Now I'll very assuredly have to kill him."

"Cool your jets, would you?" Ornasetti said, smiling at how surprisingly proper Maxie tended to sound even under stress. "I've got someone else who can handle my uncle."

"Don't bother with anyone else. Like I said, this has become personal."

"Get off your high horse, Maxie. You know my policies. No petty side wars when it comes to business. Personal vendettas end up causin' too many ancillary problems."

Gritting his teeth, Maxie squeaked out an "Okay."

"Good, because we're flyin' low and easy right now. I haven't had a visit from either the cops or the feds, and you've given Mario a nice little shit-stain-inducin' scare. Our only problem is, he could've made you. And if he did, I'd sure as hell have to put someone else on his case."

"So what's my job going to be? Sit around and feel offended?"

"Your job, my good friend, is to stay put until I make certain America's sterling law enforcement community starts lookin' to drop as many murder raps as they can on my beloved uncle's doorstep. No more scare tactics for the moment. I want the boys in blue smellin' Mario's blood, not ours."

"Is that it?"

"Yeah," Ornasetti said coldly. "You got a problem with where I'm goin' with this?"

"No."

"Then I'll be in touch. And remember, Maxie, no side wars. Later." Ornasetti cradled the phone and sat back in his chair.

Maxie continued on to Lower Downtown and breezed past Ornasetti's law offices without so much as a glance. The fact that someone had come close to killing him had his insides aching. He couldn't stop thinking that the shooting incident at Satoni's could turn out to be bad for business. Whoever had fired the three shots at him might've known who he was. They could've seen the rental car he'd parked a mile away from Satoni's. That very moment, in fact, the shooter could've been laughing his head off, swapping stories about almost offing a big-time hit man, telling friends about how he'd outfoxed Randall Maxie. Those kinds of stories could harm his reputation, hurt his business, devalue stock that had been very hard-earned.

There were, however, a few things working to his advantage. Ornasetti had pulled him back for the moment, and that meant that, regardless of Ornasetti's stance on the issue of personal wars, he had a window of opportunity to settle his score. Whoever had been in Satoni's basement had no way of knowing that he could peg who they were by virtue of the fact that their vehicle had been parked in Satoni's driveway, nuzzled up to the rear of Mario's 1953 Buick Roadmaster classic. There was little chance, he told himself, that the SUV he'd seen belonged to anyone other than his shooter. He'd memorized the car's Colorado license plate number, VXB4570, as he'd fled from Satoni's, angrily reciting it to himself over and over until he'd called Ornasetti. Smiling and repeating the number almost gleefully, he made a U-turn and headed back for Satoni's for a reassessment, hoping that the vehicle and its owner were still there, knowing that if they were, he'd have the opportunity to find out exactly who it was that he was going to have to kill.

The Clear Creek County sheriff's office reeked of mold and must, the consequence of a recent faulty low-bid overhead sprinkler system and the resulting flood after the sprinklers had showered most of the building for nearly an hour. As a result, all but one of Sheriff Gunther Tolls's four Montana-blocked Stetsons had been damaged beyond salvage. The rescued hat now rested, along with a host of other items that had been drenched, as the centerpiece on a ten-foot-long "airing-out" picnic table that occupied the sheriff's department's lone conference room.

Tolls, out of uniform and dressed in street clothes; Lieutenant Gus Cavalaris, outfitted in expensive designer-label jogging attire; and a pensive-looking Franklin Watts were seated in metal folding chairs arranged in a semicircle near the far corner of the room. All three men's eyes were fixed on a burly FBI agent who stood a few feet away, gyrating and talking rapid-fire in front of a classroom-style demonstration easel.

The hazel-eyed agent's face was badly pockmarked; his closely cropped salt-and-pepper crew cut was a lot more salt than pepper. Staring intently at the easel in front of him, he scratched his head thoughtfully before running his left index finger down the paper to where the third of six words was boldly printed in green. "So, here's my point, gentlemen." Ron Else came close to bellowing, wagging the Magic Marker in his right hand at the word. "*Validation*. The word is *validation*. And so far, gentlemen, I don't see any." Eyeing Watts, Else boomed, "All we've got, Mr. Watts, is your very reluctant word that the remains found in the Eisenhower Tunnel belonged to a man named Antoine Ducane." Else frowned and shook his head. "Oh, I almost forgot. And, of course, the word of your friend, Cornelius McPherson, who as it turns out just happens to be dead. Two dead men who can't talk to us ever again, gentlemen." Else fixed a raised-eyebrow stare on Cavalaris and Tolls. "And one of your dead men once claimed that he could've told the world who really killed JFK." Else forced back a chuckle. "No matter how you size it up, Sheriff, Lieutenant, that's not much validation as far as I'm concerned."

Watts, looking every bit the fish out of water, looked to the sheriff for support. Tolls responded with a thoughtful silence.

"Hey, I'm just the messenger here, sir," Watts said finally. "I don't know shit about no assassination or any killing you say took place down in Denver. I'm only here because the sheriff insisted on it, and all I know is that those body parts I was asked to identify along with Cornelius over in the morgue earlier, if somebody didn't doctor 'em, sure enough belonged to Antoine Ducane."

Restless and tired of being lectured by Else, Cavalaris spoke up. "Ducane's not the i-i-issue here, Mr. Watts. My interest is in who killed Cornelius McPherson. If there's a Kennedy assassination link, it's a secondary one a-a-as far as I'm concerned."

Ron Else flashed the other two men a knowing smile before locking eyes with Cavalaris. "Let me fill you in on something, Lieutenant. I've been involved in assassination linkage and follow-up for more than twenty-five years. Some people even call me a JFK assassination expert." He paused to let his words gather steam. "Can you guess the number of Kennedy assassination tie-ins to local killings I've been called on to investigate in that time?" Else rolled his eyes and silently counted off numbers on the fingers of both hands. He held both hands up near his head surrender-style and said, "This many times ten. I've been called out in the blinding rain to listen to a lady peg her son-in-law as the killer because he had a rifle like Lee Harvey Oswald's and the SOB had been abusing her daughter. I've had to listen to white supremacists from Cicero point their fingers at Black Muslims from Detroit, and Black Muslims point their fingers and even their guns right back. I've had to listen to defrocked mobsters, gangland stool pigeons, communists, atheists, born-again Christians, and skin-and-bones once-robust men on their deathbeds with HIV all claim to know who killed JFK. Not to mention my share of political leftists and right-wing nutcases, all with an agenda and JFK assassination information for sale." Else frowned and pursed his lips as if trying to rid himself of a bad taste. "And you know what's pulled me into the thick of things in almost every instance I've alluded to, gentleman? A so-called assassination-associated murder—or what I like to think of as a minor killing on top of a major killing, years after the fact. And you know what? Time after time, investigation after investigation, case after case, I end up wading my way through some time-consuming snipe hunt that in the end more often than not ends up pointing the fickle finger of fate right back at the person who initiated a bureau look-see in the first place."

"Well, at least this time your finger won't end up pointing at poor old Cornelius McPherson," said the sheriff, whose response was punctuated by a vigorous nod from Franklin Watts. "He's dead." The sheriff eyed Watts's bobbing head. "Franklin, think it's time you leave. Everything's gonna be police business from here."

"Yeah, yeah," said Watts, quickly rising from his chair. Before turning to leave, he cast a look at Else that asked, *Can I go?* When Else gave him a quick nod, Watts eyed the sheriff apologetically, grabbed his hat, and slipped out the door.

Else waited for the better part of a minute after the door had slammed before he resumed talking. Tapping the easel with a ballpoint pen he'd taken out of his shirt pocket, he said, "You're right, Sheriff. McPherson is dead, which brings us back to point five on my list: *Other Connections*. Could be McPherson and Ducane had their own sets of enemies."

"Come on," protested Cavalaris. "S-s-some old-time, lost-in-the-shuffle Colorado miner on the eve of retirement suddenly garners the kind of enemies who ride around in h-h-hitmobiles with blacked-out windows, and he just happens to get blown away in the front yard of a house that I later find out once belonged to a woman named Sheila Lucerne, who was originally from Louisiana—Antoine Ducane's home turf? I'm not b-b-buying it."

Ron Else shook his head. "All that's according to your eyewitness. A very nervous eyewitness with total ass pucker. A central casting cookie cutter of a man with an idyllic little wife, a matching little idyllic white house, and an idyllic little pigtailed, rosy-cheeked grandchild. No, you come on, Lieutenant. Your almost too-perfect-to-be-true Mr. Watson has already admitted he knew our mystery woman, Sheila Lucerne. Could be she's the reason Watson wanted McPherson silenced."

"For what?"

"Maybe that house that you said Watson came by so easily after the Lucerne woman died in that car wreck you mentioned presented Watson with a problem. Could be the house was really

Ducane's. Maybe somebody didn't like the idea that Watson ended up with it."

Cavalaris shook his head. "So more than three decades after the fact, that person decides to shoot McPherson? H-h-horseshit! Why not shoot Watson?" Cavalaris eyed the smug-looking FBI agent suspiciously. "I don't like where this is headed, Else. Either you're holding back i-i-information, you're purposely stonewalling, you think we're stupid, or you don't want us involved in this investigation. What the hell's the story here?"

Eyeing Cavalaris and the sheriff as if they were recalcitrant schoolchildren, Else said, "The story's this, Lieutenant. I've outlined the same six things—I like to call them imperatives—that I always outline when I'm pulled back into the Kennedy assassination muck." He aimed an index finger at the easel. "One, *Historical Timelines;* two, *Motive;* three, *Validation;* four, *Witnesses;* five, *Other Connections;* and six, *Coincidence.* And so far I can't link either the Ducane or the McPherson murder to the Kennedy assassination in any way, shape, or form, other than coincidence. Bottom line's this: Ducane was alive and well as late as the early 1970s, as far as I've been able to tell. That's years after the Kennedy assassination." Else slammed a fist into his right palm for effect. "And as far as I can tell, at first blush at least, Ducane had no reason to kill the president that we know of. This whole Ducane-McPherson thing has the smell of coincidence, coincidence nudged to the surface by a once-in-a-century earthquake and a trigger-happy press. Aside from Franklin Watts, I don't have a single person alive who ever knew Antoine Ducane." Else tapped the easel with his other index finger. "We've already discussed *Validation* and *Other Connections,* so I'd say we've come full circle, gentlemen." Else cocked an insipid half smile.

Cavalaris slapped his forehead, flashed Else an acquiescent grin, and sarcastically said, "I get it now. Shit, am I slow? What you w-w-want is for us bumpkins to mosey on off the case and head back into our holes, just in case this time around you hit yourself a home run. Dumb-ass me. And I t-t-thought we were all just a bunch of two-fisted good ol' boys looking for a killer."

"Watch what you say, Lieutenant. You've already said more than you should have in front of Watts."

"No, *you* wait. I don't c-c-care what you do with your Kennedy assassination investigation. And I don't give one shit if you were sent here from LA to cover up, cuddle up, c-c-cogitate, or copulate. Whether you're here to shore up the idea that Oswald killed Kennedy or to close the book on some assassination loose ends that the FBI, the White House, or the CIA are w-w-worried sick about doesn't mean a whole lot to me. What I care about, Agent Else, is that back down in Denver, I have a murder investigation on my hands. And I sure as hell d-d-don't need your permission or anybody else's to pursue it."

Else crossed his arms defiantly. "I'd mind my tongue if I were you, Lieutenant. You could find yourself stepping into extra-heavy muck here."

"Thanks for the advice. I'll t-t-take it to heart." Cavalaris rose, pushed his chair back, and dusted off the seat of his pants.

"And Sheriff Tolls, just so I have a proper head count, what's your position?" asked Else, clearly agitated.

"Afraid I have to stick with Lieutenant Cavalaris. After all, the two dead folks we've got on our hands turned up in our jurisdictions."

Unfolding his arms, Else ran an index finger around the inside of his shirt collar before adjusting his tie. "Guess this really is still the

Wild, Wild West. Have it your way, gentlemen. Just remember, the door swings both ways. We'll talk some more. Count on it."

When Sheriff Tolls stood and pivoted to leave, Else stepped over to the sheriff's Stetson, scooped it up, and handed the hat to him. "'Til we meet again."

Tolls slipped on his hat and adjusted it to his liking as all three men headed for the door. A few steps from the exit, Else stopped and offered the easel a final parting glance. Wrinkling up his nose in protest, he said, "Nice place you've got here, sheriff, except for the smell."

Thin, wispy clouds had blocked out the late-afternoon sun, and the mile-high air had turned late-summer crisp as Damion and his Colorado State University basketball teammate Shandell Bird, affectionately known as Blackbird to his friends and teammates, walked off the basketball court, winded. Damion wiped the sweat from his forehead with the back of his hand before slipping back into his sweatpants.

"You figure we got what it takes?" asked Shandell, moving his basketball from arm to arm.

"What for?"

"The NBA."

"I've told you, Blackbird. I'm not headed there," Damion said emphatically.

"Yeah. I know, you're gonna be a doctor." There was a note of disbelief in Shandell's tone. "You're crazy, man. You got the whole damn package. You got somethin' against money?"

"Nope. Just want to do my thing in life, not what somebody else thinks I oughta do. Got a problem with that?"

Shandell shrugged. Damion had been acting odd ever since they'd hooked up earlier in the day, strangely nervous and his shots had been off, way off. And that wasn't Damion. "Ain't nothin' wrong with that, especially since you been spoutin' off about wantin' to be a doctor since the frickin' fourth grade," he said, unwilling to argue. "But why not a lawyer like your mother? At least that way you'd get the chance to earn yourself 15 percent off one of my big fat contracts."

"One lawyer in the family's enough," Damion said with a shrug. "Besides, I don't have the makeup for it."

"The hell you don't. All it takes is a killer instinct, and you sure as hell got that. Least on the court."

Damion thought back to the three rounds he'd fired at Mario Satoni's would-be assailant a few hours earlier and grimaced. He'd spent nearly every minute since then trying to forget that he'd actually tried to kill someone. The primary reason he'd called Shandell and asked him to hit the courts had been to try to push that reality to the back of his mind. It hadn't worked. "What are you getting at, Shandell?" he finally asked, frowning.

Surprised by Damion's curt response, Shandell's answer came slowly. "Guess I'm just gettin' at the fact that you got a whole lot of shark in you, man. Why else you think I would ever have saddled a New Jersey Puerto Rican transplant like you with a nickname like *Blood?*"

Damion smiled. "Could've been because I'm meant to be a hematologist."

"A what?"

"Nothin', forget it. What time have you got?"

Shandell fished in the pocket of his sweatpants for his watch. "Five past six," he said, rubbing the grease-stained watch face with his thumb.

"Wanta head over to Mae's and grab somethin' to eat?"

"No need to ask me twice. You got any money?"

"Twenty bucks."

"Hell, man. You're flush. Let's hit it."

As they headed toward the bicycle rack where Damion had dropped his gym bag earlier, Shandell glanced toward the side street where cars filled with onlookers often parked to watch the high-powered college basketball players who frequented the court. "I think we mighta had a pro scout watching us," Shandell said as they reached the bike rack. "You know how they hang around here in the summertime lookin' to pluck themselves a gem?"

"What?" Damion's eyes widened with surprise.

"A scout. There was some guy watching us from inside a car the whole time we were scrimmaging."

"From where?" Damion's eyes narrowed into a squint.

"From over there on Kentucky, just north of the stop sign. Where else? You feelin' all right, man?"

"What did the man look like?" Damion's words came out rapid-fire as he found himself thinking about what CJ, who'd earlier rushed to his aid at Mario's, had said to him after the three of them had stood talking and assessing the situation, post shoot-out, in Mario's basement for nearly an hour. *Keep your eyes out for anybody who looks the least bit suspicious to you, Damion, no matter where you are. Call me and tell me about it right off. Whoever you took those shots at more than likely saw your SUV parked outside Mario's, and that means they might be able to peg who you are. Remember, call me about the least little thing, no matter what.*

Looking around in every direction, Damion began to second-guess himself. Maybe he should've called his mother after the shooting incident and filled her in, like CJ and Mario had insisted. Maybe instead of picking up Blackbird and heading for the courts, he should have fled to the safety of his mother's arms. Or maybe he should have simply sat down and thought things out. But he hadn't. He was twenty years old, a fully grown man, and he was tired of being Julie Madrid's baby-faced kid. He couldn't go running to his big-time defense-lawyer mother every time a problem cropped up. Besides, she would've insisted that he call the cops, and that would've put him at odds with Mario and maybe even CJ. So he'd chosen to remain silent and handle things like a man. Now he had the feeling that maybe he'd done the wrong thing. Suddenly he found himself thinking about something his mother had said to him two years earlier when he'd headed off to Colorado State to begin his freshman year. *Book smarts and street smarts aren't polar opposites, Damion. You'll learn one day that most of the survivors in this world have a healthy share of both.*

He shot a glance at Shandell and found himself wondering why Shandell had noticed the man in the car when he hadn't. "What made you spot the guy in the car?" he asked finally.

"What?" Shandell asked, busy reading a text message that had been left on his cell phone.

"The guy in the car—what made you zero in on him?"

Shandell shrugged. "Easy. He was white bread, man. Never seen him around here before. And the whole time we were playin', he never once eased up out of his slouch, took off his hat, or removed his shades."

"So?"

"So that's what you do when you don't want nobody peepin' you, Blood. You don't sit in a car with your lid capped tight, hidin' behind no shades and with most of your windows rolled up in 90-degree heat, unless you don't want people peepin' who you are." Shandell shook his head. "Damn, Blood. For somebody so smart, you sure as hell missed a lot."

"Yeah," said Damion, his mother's words ringing in his ears.

"We still on for Mae's?"

"Yeah."

"Good, 'cause for a second there I thought you were, how do the white kids say it, *lost in space*."

Shrugging off the remark, Damion said, "Come on, let's hit it. My stomach's startin' to talk to me." He slipped his athletic bag over his right shoulder. As they walked along the edge of the court toward Damion's Jeep, Damion asked, "Where was that car with the weirdo parked?"

"Right behind yours, Blood. A couple of feet more and he woulda been kissin' your bumper." Shandell draped his arm over Damion's shoulder and shook his head. "You need to start checkin' out your surroundin's a little closer, man."

Damion nodded without answering, aware that, perhaps for too long, he'd had his eyes glued on too singular a prize.

It hadn't been difficult for Randall Maxie to find out who owned the late-model Jeep that had been parked in Mario Satoni's driveway. The license plate info had been all he needed. He'd only had to make one phone call to run down the vehicle's owner. The name *Damion Madrid* had been passed on to him by a well-placed source in the DMV, a plump little Latina, originally from Chihuahua, Mexico, to whom he slipped a couple of hundred bucks every month to service his many needs.

He'd scored another valuable piece of information when he'd circled back to Satoni's after passing on a face-to-face meeting with Ornasetti. Still fuming at almost having been shot, he'd eased back into Satoni's neighborhood and parked behind a Dumpster that sat in the midst of a mountain of construction debris in the front yard of a house just down the street from Satoni's. He hoped that Satoni or the SUV's driver might telegraph their next move.

Ten minutes into his stakeout, an immaculately restored 1957 drop-top Chevrolet Bel Air sped up to Satoni's. When the driver stepped out, Maxie broke into a round-house grin. Even from a half block away, he had no trouble recognizing CJ Floyd, Satoni's long-time guardian angel.

He'd watched Floyd, Satoni, and a lanky-looking man child, whom he now knew to be Damion Madrid, talk briefly on Satoni's front porch before disappearing inside the house.

A little over an hour later, Floyd and the kid had reappeared. Floyd had scanned the street thoroughly and flashed Satoni a thumbs-up before he and the kid headed for separate vehicles and drove off. Maxie had followed the white SUV, first to a gas station and then to a house in Denver's Washington Park neighborhood. Nervously looking behind him with every step, the kid had gone inside the house and stayed for nearly an hour. He'd reemerged dressed in sweats, carrying a basketball under one arm and toting a gym bag. Maxie had followed him and a black kid he'd picked up to a basketball court in the Denver suburb of Glendale, the court he'd just left.

Maxie now had everything he needed—the entire Damion Madrid–Mario Satoni–CJ Floyd connection. More importantly, he also had Damion Madrid's home base. Now he'd be able to kill Madrid at his leisure. And if it came down to it and Ornasetti gave him the green light, he'd finish up with Satoni. All in all, a day that had started out badly had blossomed with sunshine. *Not a bad turn of events*, he told himself as he turned north on Colorado Boulevard and headed for Shotgun Willy's, a Glendale strip club just west of the Denver city line, to enjoy an end-of-the-day lap dance. Reaching down and stroking his testicles, he smiled and said softly, "Not a bad day at all."

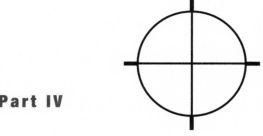

Part IV

The Search

Chapter 15

The word harassment kept ringing in CJ's ears as he walked up the sidewalk to Carl Watson's house. Aside from a windblown strip of yellow crime-scene tape that had partially wrapped itself around the base of a massive ash tree in the front yard, there were no lingering signs to indicate that a murder had taken place on the grounds not quite twenty-four hours earlier—and except for a couple of over-turned trash cans and a tricycle parked in the driveway, the house looked deserted. A stiff, chilly breeze out of the west and a bank of rain clouds capping the Rockies signaled that the weather would soon change. CJ hadn't called ahead to warn the Watsons that he'd be dropping by to talk to them about a murder. He was savvy enough to realize that if they were home, the element of surprise would work to his advantage. If they weren't, he'd keep coming back until they were, because he needed to have at least a half-step lead on the boys in blue when they began sniffing out Mario and scratching the dirt for a link between the onetime Denver don, Antoine Ducane, and Cornelius McPherson. He was surprised that the cops hadn't already pounced, but for the moment, time and the unsuspecting Watsons were on Mario's side.

CJ rang the Watsons' doorbell a little after 7, hoping his visit would be brief because he had an eight o'clock dinner date with Mavis. As he stood at the front door, shaking the bottom of an unruly pant leg off the top of his boot, he caught a glimpse of someone peeking out through a shutter-clad bay window. The silhouette of the person's head disappeared within seconds. Before he could pull his finger back from ringing the doorbell a second time, the front door swung slowly open and he found himself staring through a dead-bolted screen door at a slender, gaunt white man. The man's quick glance over his shoulder and into the hallway behind him told CJ the man wasn't alone.

"Like to speak with Carl Watson, if I could," CJ said politely.

The man in the doorway cleared his throat. "I'm him," he said, sounding unintimidated by the fact that a six-foot-three-inch, 240-pound, Stetson-wearing black man was standing on his doorstep.

"Glad I caught up with you," said CJ. "I'm an antique dealer, and I'm hoping you can help me, ah ... how can I put this ... help out a friend."

"Help them out how?" asked Watson, glancing over CJ's shoulder toward the street.

Thinking that perhaps he should have been better prepared, CJ shot a quick glance back toward the street. "I understand a man was shot on your front lawn last night. I'm hoping to find out if the man might have had a connection to my friend."

"Who the hell are you?" Watson demanded.

"Name's CJ Floyd."

Puzzled, Watson paused to look CJ up and down. As if thinking, *Two black men on my doorstep in as many nights*, he asked hesitantly, "You another friend of Sheila Lucerne's?"

Far better schooled than Watson in the game of gathering information, CJ said, "Yeah, Sheila."

Beads of perspiration broke out on Watson's forehead as he peered past CJ again. "You're lying, buddy. Sheila's dead." Watson almost yelled the words as if he wanted the whole world to hear him. "She died in a wreck on the Boulder Turnpike back in 1973."

Surprised by the absolution-sounding outpouring, CJ glanced again over his shoulder, and asked, "Expecting somebody?"

Before CJ could ask the question a second time, the reason for Watson's repeated glances toward the street became apparent. Two Denver police cruisers appeared from opposite directions and pulled up nose to nose in front of Watson's house. Two uniformed cops burst from the cars and, with 9-mm pistols drawn and aimed directly at CJ, walked slowly toward him.

The taller of the two men shouted, "Stay right where you are, bub. And hands above your head."

CJ slowly extended his arms skyward as the cop screamed, "Above your fuckin' head!"

Looking smug, Carl Watson waved for his wife, Janet, to join him. She had called Lieutenant Gus Cavalaris in near hysteria moments after peering through her shutters and seeing another black man standing on her front porch. The Watsons had done exactly as Cavalaris had instructed them to do if anything suspicious occurred, and their teamwork had landed Cavalaris a second—and very much alive—fish.

The tall cop shouted, "Hands behind you, friend, and I don't wanta see one smidgen of a quiver." He grabbed CJ's wrists with one hand, slipped a set of handcuffs off his belt with the other, and quickly cuffed CJ before patting him down. "No weapons," he called out to the other cop. Then, blowing onion breath in CJ's face, he spun CJ around and shoved him back against the house, never losing his grip on CJ's right arm. "You're trespassing, friend, and as luck would have it, you're trespassing on a crime scene. Now, what are the chances of that happening? Got a name?"

"CJ Floyd."

"Real name, friend," the cop said gruffly. "I don't do initials." He tightened his grip on CJ's arm.

Thinking that ten years earlier he would've jerked his arm out of the insipid patrolman's grip, CJ glanced out into the fading light of day and saw the plainclothes-clad Gus Cavalaris approaching. CJ didn't know Cavalaris, but recognizing him as the ranking officer who would soon be in charge, CJ said to the cop gripping his arm, "First name's Calvin, sonny."

It was almost dark and there was a dampness in the air by the time Gus Cavalaris, after speaking with the Watsons, got into the meat of his interrogation of CJ. He'd already asked CJ about any possible ties he might have had to Antoine Ducane or Cornelius McPherson, but he'd avoided asking CJ about links to the murder of JFK.

The entire interrogation took place with the handcuffed CJ seated in the back seat of Cavalaris's unmarked patrol car, feet dangling out in the street, while Cavalaris hovered curbside on a strip of grass. CJ stonewalled, claiming that he'd never heard of either Ducane or McPherson, and since Cavalaris had no real way of connecting CJ to the two dead men, he found himself trolling unsuccessfully for a lucky connection.

Twenty-five minutes into what he thought of as a no-gain situation, Cavalaris shifted his weight onto one foot, leaned down and forward until he was almost nose to nose with CJ, and said, "I'd love to slap you with a criminal t-t-trespass charge or at least a harassment charge, Floyd, but somehow you've caught yourself a br-br-break." Cavalaris glanced toward the orphaned strip of crime-scene tape in the Watsons' front yard and shook his head. "Looks like either the wind or some ea-ea-eager-beaver crime-scene technician hoping for a quick wrap-up fiddled with our cr-cr-crime-scene tape. A good lawyer might even argue you never saw the tape, and since the Watsons cl-cl-claim that all you did was knock on the door and a-a-ask a couple of questions, I'm afraid I'm going to have to release you. But guess what, friend. Now I know who you are and where you live." Cavalaris smiled, showing off a bottom row of crooked front teeth. "Antique dealer, my ass. Save that for the f-f-funny papers, Floyd."

"That's what I do, Lieutenant," said CJ, realizing that the longer the interrogation lasted, the more the very astute but obviously self-conscious Cavalaris stuttered.

"S-s-sure, Floyd. Strange that when I called in for information on you, the word I got back was that you're more of a bounty hunter and a bail bondsman. Odd background for an antiques peddler." Cavalaris glanced back toward the house, where the Watsons were taking turns peeking through half-opened shutters. "You sc-sc-scared the shit out of the people who live here, Floyd."

"Didn't intend to."

"Well, you did. So here's a little food for thought. I don't want to hear of you setting foot within twenty square blocks of this neighborhood for a long, long time. If you're d-d-driving down University and you get hungry, keep on going and f-f-find yourself somewhere else to eat. If you've suddenly gotta go to the b-b-bathroom and you're in the area, hold it. 'Cause guaranteed, if you come back and try to talk to the Watsons again, I'll consider that harassment, and even in this golden age of criminal-coddling, I'll make sure that you spend at least a couple of nights in jail. Got it?"

CJ responded with a nod.

"Last question, Floyd. What's your c-c-connection to Sheila Lucerne? Carl Watson says you knew her."

"Yeah," said CJ, hoping the look on his face didn't telegraph the fact he was lying.

"Old girlfriend?"

"Nope. Just a friend," said CJ, keeping a straight face.

"Well, try not to end up like her. You just m-m-might if you keep nosing around people's houses late at night uninvited."

"Yeah," said CJ, aware that a new first priority would be to find out all he could about a woman named Sheila Lucerne.

"Gonna let you go, Floyd. You've got your instructions. Don't come within twenty blocks of this place. Get on up, and I'll uncuff you."

Cavalaris unlocked the handcuffs, slipped them into the pocket of his sport coat, took two steps backward into the mushy grass, and looked down the street. "Vehicle down the street yours?" he asked, eyeing CJ's showroom-mint drop-top 1957 Chevy Bel Air.

"Sure is."

Cavalaris whistled. "I guess you really do deal in antiques—at least on some le-le-level. Makes me wonder what else you're into. Best get outta here, Floyd, before I do some more dig-dig-digging."

Massaging his wrists, CJ pivoted and, without a word, walked down the street to the Bel Air and slipped behind the wheel. Eyes glued to the road, he cranked the engine and slowly drove away. When he reached the end of the block, he glanced back over his shoulder. Cavalaris had disappeared into the darkness. As he made a quick left turn onto Exposition Avenue, and what was now going to be a very late dinner date with Mavis, he couldn't get the mystery woman, Sheila Lucerne, out of his mind.

Thirty minutes after he'd watched the taillights of CJ Floyd's Bel Air disappear into the night, Gus Cavalaris, seated in his newly appointed office in Denver's recently constructed, surprisingly non-institutional-looking District 3 police station, called his longtime friend Otis Billups, a Five Points–based black cop whom he knew from their days together at the Denver Police Academy. When Billups, who he knew would be at home studying for the police lieutenant's test, answered, Cavalaris said, "Gus here, man. How's the cr-cr-cramming going?"

Billups, sweating bullets over a set of sample tests, said, "Fuckin' peachy, Gus. How 'bout you?"

"Just fine, j-j-just fine. I know you're doing the lieutenant drill, so I'll be brief. You can make my day peachy too if you'll give me the lowdown on a guy named CJ Floyd. I had a run-in with him tonight. Operates out of your p-p-part of town, from what I've been able to gather. What's his story?"

Billups laughed and picked up a spoon to stir the half-eaten contents of a bowl of chili that was sitting on the kitchen countertop where he was studying. "Surprised Floyd would be over in your high-brow neck of the woods, Gus, unless maybe he's workin' a case."

"I think he is," said Cavalaris.

"Um," said Billups. "Well, here's the lowdown. Floyd's your basic tough-ass old-school brother with plenty of street smarts. He was born and bred down here on the Points. He's a bail bondsman, and he does a little bounty huntin' on the side. Did two tours of Vietnam and brought himself home a Navy Cross. He has an office down on Bondsman's Row that he runs with a great big sista who's an ex-marine. Girl's got tits that won't quit. Name's Flora Jean Benson. Hear tell Floyd spends a lot of time these days dealin' antiques. What's he done?"

"Nothing I can prove. And that's the problem. I got a call from a couple whose front yard played host to a drive-by shooting over in Bonnie Brae the other night. They said a big black man, who turned out to be Floyd, was st-st-standin' at their front door asking questions. Turns out the guy who bought it in the drive-by is the same guy who found a bunch of body parts that our earthquake coughed up out of the Eisenhower Tunnel last week."

"Yeah, I heard all about that tunnel thing, and your drive-by too," said Billups. "How do you think Floyd's involved?"

"Don't know," said Cavalaris. "But you can damn sure bet he is. I was ho-ho-hopin' you could walk me into some kinda Floyd connection."

Billups shrugged. "Can you give me anything else to go on?"

Cavalaris stroked his chin thoughtfully. "Ever heard of a woman named Sheila Lucerne?"

"Nope."

"D-d-damn. I thought that might be the c-c-connection. How about the guy who bought it over in Bonnie Brae? Name was Cornelius McPherson. Any connection you know of between that name and Floyd?"

"Doesn't ring a bell."

"Shit," said Cavalaris, frustrated. "This is big, Otis. I know it, so I'm gonna toss you something that's t-t-top-drawer confidential. You're gonna have to be dead-man quiet about it. Turns out that McPherson and that dismembered guy they found up at the Eisenhower Tunnel both might have been linked to the JFK assassination. And the f-f-fuckin' bureau's involved. They even sent an agent out from LA to take a look. Now, does that info shed any new light on Floyd or any of his connections?"

"Sure does," said Billups, knocking the stack of papers he'd been studying onto the floor. "Sure in the hell does."

"Okay, okay!" Cavalaris broke into an eager smile. "So what's the c-c-connection?"

"My guess is that your Floyd connection is Mario Satoni."

"What? I th-th-thought he was long gone, out of the business."

"So they say, but it really don't matter. Satoni's your Floyd link, trust me. Word on the street down here in Five Points has had it for years that Floyd's uncle once saved Satoni's life. Shit, Satoni and Floyd are pretty much blood brothers."

"My, my, my. The th-th-things we learn when we kick over a few rocks."

"Want me to dig up any more on Floyd?" Billups asked, leaning over and straining to retrieve his toppled papers.

"No. I'll d-d-do the diggin' on my own. Th-th-thanks for the info, Otis. You're the man."

"Always think of myself that way," Billups said with a chuckle. "Watch yourself on this one, Greek. It has a hell of a mob smell to it, and from the way you're stutterin', I can see it's got you goin'. The JFK killin'! Damn! Now, that's somethin'!"

"You never heard me mention the initials JFK," said Cavalaris, aware that his longtime friend's take on the frequency of his stuttering was meant to be helpful.

"Never heard a word. Been too busy studyin'."

"You'll pass. Hell, they b-b-bumped a stutterer like me up to lieutenant, didn't they?" Cavalaris said with a chuckle as he hung up.

Ron Else liked to think of his job as more than third-level mop-up, but down deep he knew that for the last twenty years that was exactly what he'd been doing—mopping up conspiracy piss. And that was exactly what he'd been doing for the past half hour—mopping up, getting a third shot at the still unsettled Carl and Janet Watson—logging in time behind a nosy black bail bondsman and a stuttering cow-town homicide lieutenant.

The Watsons, familiar now with the interrogation drill, had been cooperative and even overly cordial, impressed by the fact that an FBI agent was taking the time to talk to them. Else, however, hadn't gotten any more out of the weary couple than he suspected Lieutenant Cavalaris had been able to dredge up. Janet Watson had been less talkative than her frank and forthcoming husband, who, despite his easygoing manner and classic blend-into-the-crowd looks, appeared to Else to be a man who had something brewing beneath his calm facade.

He left the Watsons' home, encouraging them to call him if the black man named Floyd reappeared or if they remembered anything they'd forgotten to tell him, and made a point of walking off the front yard crime scene. Tracking back and forth across the recently watered front yard and eyeing the direction from which the shots that had cut McPherson down had come, according to Carl Watson, Else tried to judge how expert a marksman the shooter would have to have been to pull off a dead-certain kill shot in the subdued evening light. Concluding that he was dealing with a professional, he continued toward his car, aware that there was something intriguingly eerie, even almost plausible, about the stories of everyone he'd spoken to since his arrival in Denver. The prideful, stuttering Lieutenant Cavalaris, the country load of a sheriff, Gunther Tolls, the put-upon, sad-faced former miner, Franklin Watts, and now the Watsons—they all seemed to be solid citizens. They appeared far different from the JFK conspiracy nutcases he was used to encountering.

For the first time in years, he had the sense that he'd run up against something that was more than just another piss-mopping detail. In the end, he figured he'd return to LA as he always did, reeking as usual of conspiracy piss. But for now he felt an exhilarating rush that had him assembling a list of investigative must-dos in his head. The most important one at the moment was to put an FBI face on the black man who'd beaten him to the Watsons' doorstep that evening: CJ Floyd.

Chapter 16

CJ had put the issue of a little police haranguing behind him as he floated on a sea of alcohol-intensified calm and postcoital bliss, angled across Mavis's bed, her warm, nude body curled against him. Suddenly his cell phone began ringing on the nightstand near his head, intruding on the lingering pleasure.

Mavis snuggled closer and said, "Don't answer it."

"Have to—got some things cookin'."

Mavis flashed her best childish pout and wagged an index finger at him. "Let it simmer."

"I won't be but a minute. Promise." Flipping the phone open, he said, "Hello."

Julie Madrid's response was filled with tension. "I've been trying to reach you all evening, CJ. We need to talk."

CJ eyed the antique school clock on the wall facing him, shook his head, and rose onto an elbow. "It's almost 11:30, Julie. Can it wait 'til tomorrow?"

"No! We need to talk right now, CJ. Our friendship depends on it."

CJ swallowed hard and sat up in bed; Mavis followed suit. There was no need to pretend he didn't know why Julie was calling. "Damion?" he asked softly.

"Yes," Julie said tersely. She wanted to say more, to ask why CJ had facilitated Damion's friendship with a onetime mobster—but she didn't, and she wouldn't. Not until she and CJ, the man who had rescued her from a life of playing the victim and had once threatened to beat her physically abusive, now dead ex-husband within an inch of his life if he ever again so much as looked at her funny, stood face to face.

"I'll be right there," said CJ, feeling the muscles in his chest tighten.

"I'll be waiting here with Damion," Julie said, cradling the phone.

"What's the matter?" asked Mavis, reaching across the bed to turn on the lamp on the opposite nightstand.

"I've run into a little problem with Julie and Damion."

"Are they in trouble?" Mavis asked, taking in the tortured look on CJ's face.

CJ paused to gather his thoughts before answering. "Not really."

"You didn't answer my question, CJ."

"It's a long story, babe. Bottom line is, somehow Damion's gotten himself tangled up in a problem that's linked to Mario."

"Mario the onetime mobster, or Mario the antiques dealer?"

"A little bit of both, I'm afraid." CJ moved to get out of bed. "I'll handle it."

"Don't be so blasé, CJ. It's not as if you're cataloging one of your antiques or bonding some lowlife out of jail." Mavis watched CJ walk dejectedly across the room toward the chair he'd draped his clothes over earlier. "What did Damion do?"

CJ shook his head and sighed. "This afternoon he took a couple of shots at someone who might've been trying to take Mario out. He just got around to mentioning it to Julie. Guess I should've told her myself."

"My God, CJ! The boy just turned twenty."

CJ slipped on his shirt and nodded, suppressing the urge to remind

Mavis that when he was Damion's age he had been in Vietnam manning a .50-caliber machine gun on the aft end of a navy gunboat. "Looks like I bought myself a problem hooking Damion up with Mario and that damn virtual store of ours." Eyeing Mavis and buttoning his shirt, he asked, "Got any advice?"

"Tread lightly, CJ. You're dealing with something that's way out of bounds for you."

"How's that?"

Mavis shook her head knowingly. As street-savvy and well-schooled in the ways of the world as the man she loved was, he never ceased to amaze her with his lack of understanding of certain fundamental things. Choosing her words carefully, she said, "Like it or not, you've made yourself a lightning rod between a mother and her son."

"But it's Julie and Damion."

"A mother and her son, CJ. Do I need to repeat it?"

"No." Fully dressed, CJ walked across the room and kissed Mavis softly on the forehead.

"Want me to come?" she asked, looking up at him.

"No. This is on me." CJ flashed her an uncertain smile and moved to leave the room. As his run-over Roper boots thumped across the bedroom's hardwood floor and then downstairs to the first floor, Mavis's words, *a mother and her son,* kept echoing in his head.

After two days of on-again, off-again rains, the humidity in New Orleans was in the energy-zapping 90s, and the murky gray sky had what Crescent City old-timers liked to call a dead man's cast. Carmine Cassias thought that things might never get back to normal after the city's devastating 2005 flood. He inhaled a sinusful of the sour, faintly musty odor that seemed now to be always present in the air, eyed the dozen corporate-league bowling trophies that his trucking company had won over the years, and switched the phone he'd had pressed to his right ear for the past ten minutes to his left side. Shaking his head and thinking more about what had happened to the city he loved than the conversation he was having, he said, his voice a low rumble, "She's fuckin' disappeared. Goddamn it, Ornasetti! That presents us with a problem. You and me and, most of all, the organization."

"So go find her," Rollie Ornasetti said, unperturbed.

Cassias, the reigning and increasingly rotund head of Louisiana's ambiguous and profitable organized crime family, gritted his teeth. "Go find her?" he said mockingly. "Listen up, you nitwit. Get fresh with me and I'll leave you out there swingin' in the breeze with nothin' but your nuts flappin'. I shoulda known when you called the other day about Ducane that somethin' more than what you were tellin' me was up, especially since your MO has always been to massage the dogshit outta the truth. Marcello, God rest his soul, always claimed that was how you wormed your way into the Mongoose thing in the first place—stretchin' the truth. Too bad he didn't have me around to warn him about your ass back then."

Cassias paused, eyed a man with a clean-shaven head and a pencil-thin mustache who was seated across the room from him, and popped a breath mint into his mouth. Savoring the burst of flavor, he flashed the man the barest hint of a nod. "Tell you what I'm gonna do," he said, turning his attention back to Ornasetti. "I'm gonna have one of my people, a little sharecroppin' colored boy I know, sweep Willette Ducane's parish one last time. I'll have him rattle a few cages and pinch a few nipples for me. And if we don't turn her up after that, I'm gonna push any problems I have up your way. Bottom line's this, Ornasetti. I'll sell your fuckin' ass for lunch money. Got it? I don't need anybody, especially the cops or the feds, lookin' into your shit and screwin' up my thing."

"It won't come to that," Ornasetti shot back defensively. "There's no way of tracin' anything about Mongoose back to me. Besides, I've got a real live scapegoat waiting in the wings. I made certain of that way back when Ducane forced my hand. Now that Ducane's remains have been discovered, sooner or later some eager beaver with a tin shield's bound to stumble across the little nugget of evidence that places the Ducane killin' on my sweet old uncle's doorstep. It's just a matter of time—trust me."

"Hope you're right. 'Cause if you're not, you're the one's gonna end up a scapegoat."

"I've got it handled," Rollie said smugly. "But if you find the Ducane woman, deal with her."

"Plug up your own shit, Ornasetti. Where the hell do you get off shoutin' orders at me?"

"It's plugged," said Ornasetti, aware that there was more than a little bit of Carlos Marcello's fire present in his second cousin.

"Better be," said Cassias, preparing to hang up. "Just remember what I said. It's your nuts that'll be swingin'." Slamming down the phone, Cassias shook his head and flashed Ornasetti a long-distance finger. Pausing to catch his breath, he glanced again at the man across the room. "Think you better make a call to Colorado."

The man nodded without answering.

"And tell him not to make a mess. Nice and clean. I don't wanna chance any comebacks."

The still-silent man rose, nodded, and turned to leave the room. He was almost to the door when Cassias mumbled, as if to assure himself that he was making the right decision, "Fuckin' dumbshit.

Does he actually think Marcello or Trafficante or even Handsome Johnny R. woulda given him a fuckin' free lifetime pass? Shit, no. He's a fuckin' fool—a fuckin' fool to the core."

Willette Ducane had scooted herself up to the hundred-year-old walnut table with the ugly gouge just after 9 p.m., making certain as she did that she had a view out of the room's only window. Word had filtered down to her that *folks* were looking for her, so she'd placed her .38 on the table along with a half-empty bottle of Jack Daniel's and spent the next two and a half hours sucking on sassafras jawbreakers, sipping JD on ice, and reexamining every item in the shoebox full of cards, letters, and papers that Antoine had sent between 1963 and his disappearance as well as the notes he'd jotted the day Kennedy had died. As always, she intermittently found herself eyeing the wood grain and the ugly gouge, and every once in a while she caught herself staring briefly out the kitchen window. But now, as she sifted through the last of Antoine's correspondence, her focus was on the three pages of notes that Antoine had jotted in a spiral-bound notebook the day of the JFK assassination. Those three sheets of paper, brown with age, had curled on themselves at the bottom. She tried not to cry as she flipped through the pages and studied them. Each sheet was filled with notes or sketches or Antoine's hastily printed queries to himself. The queries made a lot more sense to her now than they had when she'd first read them years earlier and cried like a baby.

Most of the first page contained sketches of what looked like rows of tenement houses, the kind of lower-working-class common-walled buildings her relatives up North had lived in a half century earlier. America now called them *townhouses*. The second page was filled with a series of times and October dates that ran down the page in two neat columns. Between the columns, near the middle of the page, Antoine had circled the word *Gary*. Beneath that he had drawn what appeared to be two ladders. One ladder extended from just beneath the G in Gary almost to the bottom of the page. The other started beneath the letter Y and also ran almost to the bottom of the page. Beneath the ladders was the bracketed word *Shore*. Between the two ladders Antoine had printed *NOV*.

For Willette, the third page, which she'd pored over more times than she could remember, remained the strangest. Written rather than printed on that page was a paragraph that was very obviously a description of someone. She took a sip of JD as she read the paragraph. *He was real dark. To me he looked almost colored. And he smelled like garlic and onions and something sort of sweet. Never got a good look at his hair because he was wearing a hat. But it was black. His shoes were dark brown and square toed. Never really seen anything like them before. He never said his name and I never said mine. He seemed okay with that, just like he seemed okay with our cab ride and with taking orders or at least pretending to take them from Ornasetti.* Beneath that paragraph, Antoine had written five words as if they were afterthoughts: *sunglasses* and *low post* and *high post*.

She stared at the handwritten paragraph for several more minutes, frowning and running two fingers along the edge of the long, deep gouge in the tabletop as she thought about her long-dead sister. She didn't know exactly what the three pages of notes meant, but she knew they were tied to the JFK assassination and that they likely said a lot about why Antoine had died.

She couldn't quite put her finger on what had come over her thirty-six hours earlier when she'd opened that trunk that contained Antoine's most precious things and realized she'd never before opened it without thinking that he might still be alive. She had cried briefly and asked her Lord and Savior to unburden her of her guilt, and for the next nineteen hours she'd done just about everything but sleep. She'd driven around the parish asking anyone she thought might have known anything, including the remaining few Marcello-connected people still alive, about the exact nature of the assignment Antoine had been on when he'd gone up North to Chicago in 1963. She'd screwed up the courage to ask a longtime perishable goods and liquor hijacker she'd known for over sixty years, a man who'd once supplied Carlos Marcello with the Creole women he preferred, "Do you know if my baby, Sugar Sweet, was in on the Kennedy killin'?" And the man had replied, "If I was you, I'd tread lightly, Willette. Word's come down that all of a sudden you're pushin' too hard. You may wanna think about a little time away from here."

After thinking it over, she'd taken the hijacking whiskey runner's advice to heart, but not before making a few other contacts and finding out that the corporate account number on the FedEx envelope she'd received with the newspaper clipping about Antoine had originally been scanned in Boulder, Colorado. A few hours before parking herself at the kitchen table and once again reading through Antoine's things, she'd packed a suitcase with clothes, nosed around the parish one last time, and bought a plane ticket to Denver on the Internet. Now that Antoine was officially dead to her, the same guilt that had weighed on her for over forty years was driving her to find out what had happened to him.

Tired and laden with guilt, she eyed the gouge in the tabletop one last time, muttered, "You've taken them both from me now," and poured herself a final glass of Jack Daniel's, knowing that now, instead of awakening to the painful, haunting memories of her long-dead sister, she'd forever awaken to the confirmed loss of her baby, Sugar Sweet.

Fortified with a double dose of her arthritis medication, no longer lying to herself, and no longer dreaming, she left her house just before midnight, nosing her Cadillac toward Baton Rouge and a twelve-unit, black-owned, mom-and-pop motel a few miles off Interstate 10. She'd stay the night there before catching a 7 a.m. flight from Baton Rouge to Dallas. A second flight would take her from there to Denver. Her long-barreled .38 and the shoebox full of Antoine's papers occupied the passenger's side of the Caddy's front seat. She knew she would have to leave the gun behind, but she'd find a replacement in Denver or Boulder, or wherever the account number on the FedEx envelope led her. After all, she'd been the one who'd taught Antoine to milk the information and illegal firearms pipelines.

Julie Madrid stood in front of the fireplace she had enlarged, rebricked, and remanteled before she and Damion had moved into the vintage Tudor-style house she'd bought in Denver's Washington Park neighborhood three years earlier. The 3,400-square-foot house was far more spacious than the two of them needed, and sometimes when she thought about growing up in a Jersey City tenement in one-third the space, she felt self-conscious, but she'd always dreamed of living in a sprawling Tudor like the ones she'd seen on grade school field trips to the New Jersey shore. When she'd spotted the "For Sale" sign in the front yard of the Washington Park house one day while jogging, she'd made a beeline for the empty house, gawking and peering through the windows for the next half hour. She'd put the house under contract without even setting foot inside.

Glancing briefly at the mantel, which was dotted with photo-graphs of Damion, CJ, and CJ's longtime friend Billy DeLong fly-fishing, trap-shooting, and branding cattle at the fifty-thousand-acre Wyoming cattle ranch where Billy had once been foreman, Julie tried to hide her displeasure. But when she turned her attention back to CJ and Damion, who were seated a few feet away from her, the hurt etched on her face told a different story.

"All I can say is, I'm disappointed," she said, eyes darting back and forth between them. "Terribly disappointed in you both," she added softly. She locked eyes with a grim-faced Damion. "I've moved past the point of being a terrified mother, Damion. Past the point of wringing my hands, and past the point of crying. Right now I'm sim-ply wondering when the police—or better yet, some hit man—will show up on our doorstep. What were you thinking? Has it sunk in yet that you tried to kill someone?"

When Damion answered with a downward glance and silence, she turned her attention to CJ. "Why didn't you immediately come and tell me what had happened, CJ? After all, it was you who put Damion's life at risk. You might have a mobster for a business partner, but Damion and I certainly don't. He's my only child, CJ."

CJ, who couldn't remember having had even a minor disagree-ment with Julie in all the years they'd known one another, paused thoughtfully before answering. "I made a mistake," he said hesitantly.

"I'll say. And you made an even bigger one when you hooked Damion up with a former mafia don. Look at the two of you, con-niving and lying and even trying to kill people—just like him."

"Mom, come on."

Julie flashed Damion the kind of steely eyed look she normally reserved for cross-examinations in the courtroom. "You might be twenty years old, Damion, and you might think you're a man, but you're not. I expect you to listen."

Having had his mother lash out at him in a way she never had and watched her tear into CJ, the person most responsible for turning their desperate lives around ten years earlier, Damion couldn't hide his feelings any longer. He knew he'd scared and disappointed her and forced her to do something she rarely did—cry—but he couldn't suffer through another round of accusations or hurtful words. Taking a deep breath, he said, "I've been listening, Mom, all my life. Listening to you tell me to do right, listening to you tell me to stay away from the wrong kind of people, listening to you talk about what the mob did to Grandpa back in New Jersey." Damion paused and locked eyes with Julie. "This isn't New Jersey, Mom, and I'm not my grandfather. I'm the one who made the decision to work for Mario, not CJ, and I'm the one this has happened to, not you. I know I should've told you what happened sooner, and I know you're pissed about us not calling the cops, but I'm the one who made that call, not CJ or Mario. Besides, siccing the cops on Mario would kill him."

Caught off guard by Damion's response and taken aback by his intimation in front of CJ that her father had suffered at the hands of the mob, Julie said, her voice booming with displeasure, "That's enough, Damion!"

"Maybe I should leave," said CJ as the words *a mother and her son* filled his head.

"No, don't, CJ. Please." Damion turned to face Julie. Trembling and with his voice quavering, he said, "CJ already knows about Grandpa, Mom."

Julie's jaw dropped. "Damion, how could you?"

Sounding more worldly than Julie would have expected he could,

Damion said, "Some burdens have to be shared with others, Mom, or they'll sink you."

After a moment of reflective silence, with the two people she cared most about in the world seemingly staring right through her, Julie looked at CJ and asked, "How long have you known about what happened to my father?"

"A couple of years."

"Have you ever mentioned it to anyone else? Flora Jean, Billy, Mavis?"

"Julie, please. Of course not."

Julie's eyes welled up with tears. "It's the biggest hurt I've ever had to deal with, CJ. Aside from my mother dying."

"I understand."

Julie flashed CJ a brief, insightful smile. "No, you don't. And I couldn't expect you to, really." Looking as if a lifetime of pent-up pressure had suddenly been released, Julie walked away from the fireplace and took a seat in a small wingback chair a few feet away from CJ. The only sounds in the high-ceilinged room were the ticking of a century-old grandfather clock in one corner and the soft, rhythmic wheeze of three people breathing. She eyed the floor and rubbed her hands together nervously as CJ and Damion sat motionless in their chairs. When she finally spoke, her words were measured. "But it's something I should've told you, especially in light of our relationship and your friendship with Mario. And it's a burden I never should've saddled Damion with."

Fighting back tears, Damion rose, walked over to his mother, and clasped her hand in his. "I'm sorry, Mom. I had to tell someone. I didn't want to have to carry all that hurt around with me the way you always have."

Julie slipped her hand out of Damion's and stroked a lock of hair off his forehead. "Are you okay, Damion? Really?" she asked, her voice cracking.

"Yeah. Yeah, I'm okay." He kissed Julie reassuringly on the forehead and looked up at CJ. The look on his face as much as said, *It's a new day now.* Again clutching Julie's hand tightly, Damion said, as if to test his new-day hypothesis, "I won't turn my back on Mario."

"I'm still trying to deal with all that's happened today, Damion. Let's delay that discussion."

Not wanting to force the issue, Damion nodded and said, "There's something else you should know."

Prepared for the worst, Julie said, "Go ahead."

Damion let out a barely perceptible sigh. "This afternoon, outside the courts over in Glendale, I think somebody might've been following me. Shandell spotted him."

Julie shook her head. "Damion, no."

"It was nothing, Mom," Damion said, wrapping an arm around his mother's shoulders.

Suspecting that Damion may have gotten himself involved in a kind of game he wasn't prepared for, CJ said, "The whole story, Damion. Now."

Frowning and taking in the look of concern on CJ's and Julie's faces, Damion considered just how to go about explaining Shandell's phantom man. Uncertain where to start, he said, "First let me get a glass of water." As he headed for the kitchen, he suddenly felt small and juvenile and unseasoned. But now wasn't the time to think about that, he told himself. He'd consider those shortcomings—how he'd betrayed his mother's trust and the issue of how best to deal with Mario—at a special place in the morning. A place where he could collect his thoughts and not be persuaded, disregarded, or interrupted.

Chapter 17

Randall Maxie latched on to CJ's Bel Air a block from Julie's house as CJ headed north on Downing Street toward home. Hugging the rear of an out-of-service RTD bus most of the way, Maxie told himself that Floyd and the Madrid kid had to be stink-on-shit tight if Floyd was at the kid's house holding his hand until after midnight.

He knew just about everything there was to know about Floyd and his reputation as a no-nonsense bounty hunter and bail bondsman. But he also knew that no one could live on rep forever. Floyd was pretty much past his prime, as far as he was concerned—a lot like Mario Satoni. Why Floyd was sniffing up the kid's shorts at midnight didn't matter. Maybe Floyd was priming the Madrid kid to be his replacement, or maybe he was banging the kid's mother. What mattered was that Maxie had a score to settle with Damion Madrid, and if some over-the-hill bounty hunter was stupid enough to toss himself into the mix, he'd end up paying a hefty price.

When CJ turned off Thirteenth Avenue onto Delaware Street and then quickly into his driveway, Maxie stopped for the light at Thirteenth Avenue and chuckled. He watched Floyd get out of the car, light up a cheroot, tip back his Stetson, and disappear into his house before continuing west on Thirteenth. Two blocks later he opened his glove box, reached inside, and extracted a CD. He slipped the disc into the car's CD player, turned up the volume on the $6,000 after-market stereo system, and prepared to enjoy the familiar and always energizing first melodic strains of *La Bohème*.

Deciding that he'd done enough reconnaissance for the evening and that he could deal with Floyd and the Madrid kid later, he eased his 310-pound girth back into his seat, primed to enjoy twenty minutes of his favorite opera on the crosstown drive home.

Carmine Cassias drifted into a fitful sleep a little after 12:30. An hour and a half later, with less than thirty minutes of what could be called real sleep under his belt, he woke up, slipped out of bed, and walked from his bedroom to his office at the opposite end of his sprawling, split-level, seven-thousand-square-foot Mediterranean-style house.

He normally turned the air conditioning up at night to keep his sensitive sinuses from drying out and giving him fits, but on this night, he'd cranked the system down a notch to combat the insufferable Louisiana heat and humidity. His house, forty minutes north of New Orleans, had escaped the ravages of Hurricane Katrina, and the only things he'd lost in the subsequent flooding were a couple of old cypress trees. At first blush, his post-Katrina world looked much the same as it had before the hurricane. In reality, the gaming, prostitution, and drug trafficking he controlled had taken a significant hit, and the cash flow had just recently started to come back from the enterprises that Carlos Marcello and the other men who had once controlled organized crime in Louisiana, Mississippi, and southeast Texas all the way down to Brownsville had entrusted to him.

Smiling and thinking that Marcello and the hard-knuckled boys of mid-twentieth-century America would've had a hard time imagining the dividends their efforts to grow the gaming industry had reaped, Cassias was reminded of something Marcello, his mentor, had been fond of saying: *Always view the glass half full, Carmine; that way you're halfway home to a horn of plenty.*

Angling across his office to the refrigerator behind his desk, he took out a half-gallon jug of lemonade and a chilled glass, filled the glass, and took a sip before walking over to the room's massive swinging French doors and opening them. Inhaling the warm, moist Louisiana air, he reveled in the soothing effect the air had on his sinuses. He stood in the open doorway for several minutes listening to the sounds of the crickets and cicadas and the hundreds of species of ambiguous swamp bugs that seemed wholly unaffected by Katrina. When he closed the doors a few minutes later, the aggravations that had stifled his sleep seemed to have abated. Walking back to his desk with a new sense of purpose, he picked up the receiver of one of three phones that occupied his desktop, sat down, and dialed a rarely used long-distance number.

The voice of the person who answered was groggy with sleep. "What's the problem, Carmine?"

"Did my number come up on your caller ID?"

"How else would I have known it was you who's waking me in the middle of the night?"

"Did you get a call from Jimmy earlier this evening?" asked Cassias.

"Yeah, that cue-ball-headed gofer of yours called me. He's a zombie, and he sounds like a fuckin' elf. I don't know why the hell you use him."

"Did he tell you to deal with Ornasetti?" asked Cassias, ignoring the commentary.

"Yeah."

"Well, I'm callin' to add a little cream to that coffee, and to give you a heads-up. This whole issue with Ornasetti is interferin' with my sleep. So here's the new deal. If you get any meltdown out there in the Rockies, any kind of fallout from the Mongoose thing that might send a spark of some kind flyin' down my way, I want you to extinguish it." Cassias paused before continuing. "You've got the green light to do Satoni as well."

"What?"

"You heard me."

"I thought Satoni was golden."

"He was. But since Jimmy called you about Ornasetti, I've talked to people in Chicago, Jersey, and Vegas. Satoni's become expendable. Things like that happen when all your cronies are dead and there's nobody left to speak up for you. Food for thought, don't you think?"

"Guess so," the man on the other end of the line offered as, easing up in bed, he eyed the outline of the woman sleeping next to him. "Wait a minute—I need to get to a place that's a little more secure," he said, slipping out of bed and walking to another room. "Okay, I'm set."

"You could've stayed put," said Cassias. "I'm done."

"That's it?"

"Yeah."

"Do I need to call you before I do Satoni?"

"No. Just use your judgment."

"Damn. Satoni's fallen that far outta grace?"

"It's a different time, Napper," said Cassias, calling the man by his code name.

"Guess so. Anything else?"

"Yes. Don't get sloppy. There's already been enough sloppiness."

"That was Ornasetti's doin'."

"I don't care whose doin' it was," Cassias said, slamming a fist down on the desktop. "I just don't wanna see any more of it."

"Got ya."

"Good. Now go back to your dreams," Cassias said, cradling the phone.

The man known as Napper tiptoed back toward his bedroom, stood in the bedroom doorway, and watched the chest of the woman in the bed rise and fall. Deciding that he wouldn't chance disturbing her, he turned, walked back down the hallway, grabbed a blanket from a hall closet, and headed for another bedroom to think over a game plan for taking out Ornasetti and Satoni.

Randall Maxie's massive belly undulated in a final wave of sexual delight as the smallish, dark-haired Latina from Denver's central motor-vehicle office, the woman who'd provided him with all the vitals he needed to locate Damion Madrid, wiped a stream of ejaculate off his belly with a steaming hot towel. The sounds of Beethoven's violin concerto echoed in the background. Smiling and watching the woman dry him off, Maxie sat up in the oversized leather chair where he seated himself on those nights when the woman either mounted him or stroked him to climax and asked, "Did you know that Beethoven only wrote one violin concerto?"

"No." The woman tossed her towels onto a nearby table.

"Well, he did." Realizing that he'd overshot the woman's frame of reference, Maxie slapped his belly. "A genius only needs one shot."

The woman flashed Maxie a subservient smile.

"You busy Thursday?" he asked, rising out of the chair.

"No."

"Good. I'll need you here again." He lumbered across the room, naked, and retrieved one of the half-dozen ankle-length silk robes he'd had made on a trip to Japan six months earlier. Slipping into the robe, he sidestepped his way over to a nearby scale and mounted it. The scale quickly registered 313 pounds. "Weight's holding steady," he said proudly as he turned to face the woman. "Now, go ahead and get dressed, and make sure I can see you. And try putting your fishnets back on slowly for a change."

The woman walked over to a closet that was just to the left of a wall-mounted sixty-inch plasma-screen TV, pulled back the accordion-style closet doors, and slipped a halter top, a pair of fishnet pantyhose, and a pair of faded shorts off the only hanger inside.

"Like I said, slowly," Maxie reiterated as he watched the woman slip the halter top over her head and slowly into place. She spent the next couple of minutes wiggling into her pantyhose and form-fitting shorts. Maxie smiled as she made a final adjustment to the halter top. "Good. I like it. Thursday at seven," he said as she moved away from the closet. "Think I'll have you ride me for a change." Maxie sidled up to her, drew two tightly rolled $100 bills out of the pocket of his robe, and slipped them into her palm. "See you Thursday."

"Thanks," the woman said sheepishly, turning to leave.

"And thanks for the info you gave me on that Madrid kid. It helped a lot."

"Anytime. I'll let myself out." The woman walked out of Maxie's study and rushed down a hallway toward the front door of his North Denver townhouse, praying for a breath of fresh air.

Maxie slapped his midsection and nodded. She'd done what she had been there for, and he'd paid her. He wasn't about to walk her to the door.

Fifty minutes later, after listening to the London Philharmonic's recently released rendition of Dvorak's *New World Symphony*, Maxie set aside an unfinished snifter of brandy and rose from his favorite chair to finally go to bed. He'd almost reached his bedroom when the call he'd been waiting for all night came in. It was 3:15 a.m. when he picked up the wall-mounted receiver and said, "Maxie here."

"You no longer report to Ornasetti," the man who called himself Napper said matter-of-factly.

Maxie grinned. "You got a money deal to go along with that order?"

"It's been discussed."

"And?"

"The deal's this. You walk away from what you've been doing for Ornasetti all these years and find yourself a new fish. That way you get to keep listenin' to those operas and symphonies you like so much."

"What?"

"You heard me, you big tub of lard. You make yourself scarce, and from now on you report to me."

Maxie erupted in laughter.

"Laugh all you want, friend. This has top-level clearance."

"Prove it," Maxie said, incensed. He slammed down the phone, muttered, "Fuck you, asshole," and continued into his bedroom.

He was sound asleep an hour later when a follow-up call came in. With his head abuzz from too much brandy, he answered, "Maxie here."

"Maxie, it's Cassias."

"How the hell do I know that?" Maxie shot back.

"Because what you told Napper got relayed back to me. I understand you wanted corroboration on an issue, so I'm obligin'. Ornasetti's no longer your problem—he's ours. And here's some advice. Stick with what you know, Maxie. Shakedowns are for sinners. And here's a final piece of advice. Keep what you know about the Ducane issue to yourself. It's a way to ensure that you can continue to enjoy Beethoven. Peace to you, my friend," Cassias said softly and hung up.

Realizing that he'd misjudged the gravity of the situation, Maxie sat straight up in bed. A personal call from Carmine Cassias meant that for once in his life, he'd better follow instructions. There'd be no more mopping up for Ornasetti. He'd come to the end of that road. It was time to forget everything Ornasetti had ever mentioned to him about the Kennedy assassination, but more importantly, it was time to completely erase from his mind the lengthy set of problems Ornasetti had had with Antoine Ducane.

Rivulets of sweat rolled down his face as he climbed out of bed, walked over to one of the two south-facing windows in his bedroom, and cranked the window open, hoping that the crisp 4 a.m. Rocky Mountain air would help him think. It wouldn't be hard to take a few steps back from Ornasetti. Ornasetti had as much as asked him to do that already. And it wouldn't be difficult to erase things from his memory, but he wouldn't run. Running would destroy his reputation, and reputation was all he had in his business. What he needed, he told himself, fanning fresh air against his face with his right hand, was something to take his mind off the fact that a steamroller could still roll up out of Louisiana and flatten him. Something that would allow him to tread water for a while. Something that would offer him a diversion. Suddenly he stopped fanning himself and smiled. He had just the thing. It had slipped his mind with all the phone calls. What he had was in fact a godsend—a little unfinished business with Damion Madrid.

He had no idea how long it would take Napper or whomever Cassias sent to settle up with Ornasetti—a few days, a week at the most, would be his best guess. What he did know was that he'd be settling up with the Madrid kid immediately.

Damion was already gone when Julie, who hadn't slept all night, rapped on his bedroom door just before 6 a.m. and called out, "Damion? I'm making waffles." With less than two hours of sleep under his belt, Damion had left the house an hour before daybreak to head for the one place where he knew he could think and clear his head. Under the guise of a 1:30 a.m. truce, he and his mother, who were barely communicating after he'd finished his story about the strange man in the car at the Glendale basketball courts, had gone to bed following a parting admonishment from CJ to call him in the morning.

Damion didn't respond to her second call for waffles, their customary Saturday-morning breakfast, so Julie knocked on the door a second time, telling herself that maybe he'd gone out for an early-morning run. When he didn't answer, she pushed the door open to find the room empty and his bed uncharacteristically unmade. Startled, she shouted, "Damion?" Rushing across the room, she flung back his closet door to see if the hiking boots and ankle and wrist weights that he normally wore on training runs were there. She let out a gasp when she saw the boots and weights arranged in a neat pile in the back corner of the closet. Suddenly the events of the previous night began playing themselves out once again.

Out of sync and trying her best to think in logical terms, she rushed from room to room calling out Damion's name. When she got to the garage and found his cell phone sitting on the top of the sprinkler-system timing box and his SUV gone, she panicked. She thought about calling CJ as she rushed back inside the house and down the Spanish-tiled hallway that led from the garage to the kitchen, but for some reason she felt too guilty to do so. Instead she raced to the phone in the kitchen and dialed Shandell Bird's number. When Shandell answered, his voice an early-morning foghorn, she asked, trying her best not to sound flustered, "Morning, Shandell, is Damion there?"

"No, ma'am," said Shandell, responding to Julie in the mannerly way he always used when speaking to a woman.

"You didn't go on a run with him, did you?" Julie asked, hoping against hope that Shandell's answer would be yes.

"Nope. We decided not to run 'til this afternoon."

"Did he tell you what he planned to do this morning?"

"No. Something wrong, Ms. Madrid?"

"No, no. I was just fixing breakfast, and Damion's not here."

"That's funny. Maybe he went for a jog on his own."

"Maybe. I'm sure he'll be back soon. Sorry to wake you up."

"No problem," said Shandell, sounding puzzled. "Can you have Damion call me when he gets in?"

"Sure will." Julie hung up without saying good-bye. She walked across the room, confused and concerned. Scooting a stool up to the cooktop island, she sighed and sat down. Her heart raced as she considered the fact that her only child, the treasure of her life, might be running from her. And all because she'd carried a volatile package of hate around inside her for far too long. She needed to fix that problem, find a remedy for it, in the jargon of the legal profession. But more than anything, she needed to reconnect with her son.

Rising from the stool, she walked back toward the room's wall phone. Halfway to the phone she stopped and paused to think about what she was going to say when CJ picked up the phone.

Chapter 18

Pinkie Niedemeyer got an early-morning, black-coffee-charged start out of Denver after being roused from a blissfully peaceful sleep by a 7 a.m. phone call from Mario telling him that CJ, motivated by a frenzied call from Julie, had called looking for Damion Madrid. When Pinkie had protested having to traipse off after a twenty-year-old who was probably simply out sowing his wild oats after Mario had asked him to go look for Damion, Mario had pointedly said, "Track down the boy, Pinkie. Your debt ain't fully paid up yet." Unhappy about the assignment but cognizant of the fact that he owed his life to Mario, Pinkie had taken off for the Pawnee National Grassland, the place where Damion's best friend, Shandell Bird, had suggested to CJ, who was running the traps in Denver, that if Damion were troubled, he'd probably head to to think things through.

Northeastern Colorado's Pawnee National Grassland is a two-hundred-thousand-acre expanse of short-grass prairie. The main entrance to the grasslands is marked by a simple weathered U.S. Forest Service marker thirty-six miles east of the Colorado State University dorm room that Damion Madrid and Shandell Bird had shared during their junior year.

Damion's daybreak pilgrimage to the grasslands had taken him north up I-25 to the outskirts of Fort Collins, where the interstate intersects Colorado state Highway 14. From there the drive to the grasslands, a drive he'd made more than a dozen times before, was a forty-minute trek east across rolling prairie and the South Platte River basin.

Damion had never heard of the wide expanse of prairie that before the 1930s Dust Bowl had once been productive farmland until he'd begun his stint at CSU. A foreign exchange student from Brazil had suggested that he visit the grasslands after CSU had suffered a devastating basketball loss to archrival Wyoming—a loss in which Damion, highly touted and starting as a freshman, had missed what would have been the final game-winning shot. That student, now his girlfriend, had claimed that according to Native American tradition, the grasslands were a place for reflection that had recuperative and regenerative powers. He'd shrugged off Niki Estaban's suggestion for months, skeptically agreeing to go see the Great Plains monument to peace and tranquillity on a cold, crystal-clear, ice-blue morning in early March, as long as she'd go with him.

The first time he saw the two rugged, imposing, forlorn-looking buttes towering over an endless sea of partially snow-covered grass, he knew he'd connected with a lost part of himself. His trips to the Pawnee, as he referred to what he now saw as a mystical place, had become common enough that his basketball teammates had jokingly taken to calling him *Blood Brother*, a nickname that Shandell simply shortened, whenever the situation called for it, to *Blood*.

Damion's two favorite grassland haunts had become Lips Bluff, the western butte, which rose majestically out of the pancake flatness, and the surprisingly lush Crow Valley campground with its shaded campsites and groves of cottonwoods. He loved trekking across the Pawnee's chalky, sandy soil toward the base of Lips Bluff in the early morning, always stopping at his favorite place along the way, a hardscrabble red-cedar break where geology had been beaten back by botany and a small thicket of the hardy evergreens that some claimed were no more than devil's weeds thrived.

He parked at the Crow Valley campground just before 7:30 a.m., to be greeted by air that was unseasonably crisp and a sky that was gem-stone blue. There were no other vehicles parked at the campground, and he'd encountered only one other vehicle, a mud-splattered step-side pickup, on his way into the Pawnee. He spent an hour at the campground, sitting around thinking and trying to accommodate to the fact that things might never be the same between him, his mother, and CJ. When he left the campground and headed east to begin the long hike to Lips Bluff, a healthy breeze had picked up. Out of the corner of his eye, he saw a white SUV lumber slowly past the camp-ground. It was only the second vehicle he'd seen on the property the entire time he'd been there.

Clad in Levi's, a faded blue chambray shirt, and a pair of run-over hiking boots that he kept in his SUV, he adjusted his sunglasses, tugged at the strap on his binoculars, and took a drink of water from the dented, navy-issue canteen that CJ had given him a few years earlier. CJ had carried it during his time in Vietnam.

Fifteen minutes later, as he closed in on what would be a brief rest stop, he watched two red-tailed hawks drift lazily overhead before soaring toward the cedars. When he reached the forlorn-looking cluster of cedar trees, he paused to drink in the overpowering ever-green smell, then wove his way along the outer margin of the iso-lated thicket. When he reached a familiar tree cluster, he kicked at a fallen tree to rout out any prairie rattlers and sat down.

He sat motionless for a while, gazing out at the sea of late-summer grasses, then watched a horned toad seemingly upset by, rather than fearful of, his intrusion hop slowly away from the uprooted end of the fallen cedar. His thoughts soon undulated back to the turmoil and tension of the previous evening. He still wasn't certain whether his mother's reluctance to show her full displeasure at his divulgence of a long-cloaked family secret was because someone had tried to kill him earlier in the day or because she was so shaken by the confluence of events that she was saving the wrath of her full disapproval for a more appropriate time and place.

Mindful of the possibility that someone could have followed him to the Pawnee, though it was a possibility that he pretty much discounted, he'd nonetheless kept a watchful eye on his surroundings from the moment he'd left his house. Sensing that he'd come to the right place to reflect on his problems, soothe the wounds to his psyche, wash away his guilt, and reenergize, he felt the tension finally begin to escape from his body.

Glancing toward Lips Bluff, he took a sip of water just as a gust of wind kicked up. In the distance he could see what looked like a wind-induced dust devil. He watched the dust cloud rise on the wind just west of the bluff, expecting it to dissipate quickly. When it didn't, he brought his binoculars up and focused them on what was now a straight arrow of dust rising from the trail that led from Lips Bluff.

His jaw dropped when he realized that someone on an ATV four-wheeler was headed across the parched terrain on a beeline toward him. Aware that motorized vehicles were forbidden in the grasslands, he sensed that he'd somehow locked on to trouble. There was no way anyone could have smuggled an ATV onto the grasslands without being noticed—unless, he told himself, they'd been bold enough to cross adjacent private lands to gain access to the back side of the buttes, the clear direction the ATV was headed from.

Recognizing that the ATV was still more than a mile away, he quickly ran down a list of who the driver might be. The possibility that the rider could be someone from the U.S. Forest Service, a joy-riding outdoorsman, or a rancher from an adjoining private ranch looking for strays came to mind first. He swallowed hard when he got to the possibility that the rider could be Mario's shooter. His hands trembled briefly as he struggled to keep his binoculars trained on the ATV, and he tried to fathom how anyone could possibly have known where he was unless they'd followed him from Denver, watched him leave the Crow Valley campground, and then out-flanked him. All of which were possible, he reluctantly admitted, especially since a vehicle with an ATV's maneuverability and speed could easily outpace someone on foot. Even so, he wondered why he hadn't heard the guttural sounds of a four-wheeler until he thought about the fact that the Pawnee was surrounded by tens of thousands of acres of private land. Anyone wanting to get around him while he was taking his time walking the only trail that led to and from Lips Bluff could've cut across any one of a half-dozen pieces of private land, and as absorbed as he'd been in his own thoughts, he likely wouldn't have heard the ATV until it was too late, thinking that the engine noise was coming from outside the bounds of the Pawnee.

The ATV was close enough now for him to see that the hatless, jacket-clad rider was a man with his own pair of binoculars looped around his neck. Damion's mouth went dry when he realized that a rifle case was strapped to the rear carriage of the ATV. He kicked himself for leaving Denver without his cell phone, something he hadn't discovered until he'd reached Fort Collins. Moistening his lips, he tried not to panic. There was still no guarantee that the man on the ATV was after him. Rifle case or not, the man could've been a Bureau of Land Management worker on a mission to thin out coyotes or thwart a growing rattlesnake population, or perhaps he was simply out there to check on one of the Cold War underground missile silos that were rumored to dot the Pawnee.

Damion's theories evaporated the instant the man brought the ATV to a halt, jumped off the vehicle, and trained his binoculars directly on the cedar break. Dropping to one knee, Damion muttered, "Shit!" as he scanned the cedar break for better protection. The largest of the trees in the entire cluster was twenty yards behind him. His back to the morning sun, he brought his binoculars up one last time to take a good look at the man on the ATV, aware that once he moved back toward the taller cedars for protection, his view would be obscured.

The man who now stood behind the ATV looked around slowly before slipping a rifle out of his gun case. Damion's eyes widened, and within seconds he was duck-walking his way toward the tallest protective stand of red cedars. Halfway to his destination, he stopped, scooped up several baseball-sized rocks, and tossed them toward the base of the largest of the cedar trees. He looked around for something else that he could use as a weapon and briefly thought about making a run for it. Realizing that there was no way he could possibly outrun an ATV across miles of wide-open terrain, he decided that his best option was to stay put and hope that someone, anyone, might come walking down the only trail that led to the buttes and scare off the ATV driver.

Scooting over to a pile of fallen trees, he rummaged through an assortment of tree limbs and extracted two branches. One was the size of a baseball bat. It was a club he could defend himself with. The other was an eight-foot-long, more willowy limb that could be used as a whip. Dragging the tree limbs behind him, he headed for the big red cedar.

He scooped up the rocks he'd tossed at the foot of the tall cedars into a pile and counted off each one: "Seven, eight, nine."

Aware that there was nothing to shield him from rifle fire except the trees themselves, he grabbed three rocks, wiggled his body up against the largest tree in the cluster, grabbed his baseball-bat-sized branch, and peeped out between the cedar's limbs.

Glancing down at the ground, he gauged how quickly he could grab additional rocks if he needed them. Convinced that he could retrieve the rocks within seconds, he muttered, "Good," and gritted his teeth, knowing that he had two things in his favor. Years of dribbling a basketball with equal facility with either hand meant that he could launch his rocks with equal accuracy using his right hand or his left. And he had the element of surprise on his side. He simply had to be letter-perfect with his aim. Breathing so hard now that it scared him and sweating like he'd just run a dozen wind sprints, he felt a sudden urge to run until he remembered what CJ had once told him about the element of surprise. *When someone comes up at you from the bottom of a sampan with nothing more than a pea shooter in their hand, don't matter that you're carrying an M-16. By the time you turn to fire, you're already dead.* Unfortunately, he was about to find out if that old war adage was true.

Randall Maxie had no idea what the Madrid kid would be up to at 5 a.m., but, unable to sleep after his chat with Cassias, he'd driven to Damion's house and staked it out, hoping to get a jump on the killing that was sure to come. When Damion's SUV had rolled out of the garage just before daybreak, Maxie had licked his chops and followed it. Everything else that had fallen his way had the stamp of good luck and serendipity on it.

He'd stumbled across the ATV only minutes after driving past the Crow Valley campground just as Damion had pulled in. It had been there for the taking, parked on private land next to a sagging barbed-wire fence. A set of shiny new barbed-wire stretchers rested on the four-wheeler's seat, and the keys had been left in the ignition. Country folks didn't think about having things stolen, he'd told himself, looking back to see Damion strike out on the lone trail that led to the Pawnee Buttes. He'd thought about going back to the campground and quickly dispensing with the kid, but he wasn't certain whether other people were there. Forced to design a plan for killing the kid on the fly, he'd run an end around Damion, cutting across private land on the ATV and snipping his way through barbed wire to arrive on the far west side of Lips Bluff well before Damion reached the cedar break. When he saw Damion disappear into the cedars, he brought the ATV to a stop thirty yards from the leaning edge of the trees, stepped off, retrieved his .30-06, checked the chamber to make certain he had the firepower he needed to complete his task, and walked slowly toward the line of trees, rifle in hand, knowing that Madrid had to be in the cluster of trees somewhere.

Slipping his right index finger onto the trigger of the .30-06, he eased his way around a large tree and worked his way south toward a clump of three smaller trees. It would be pretty much like getting pheasants to flush, he told himself, moving in for the kill—sooner or later the pressure always became too much. Moving methodically from tree to tree, the barest hint of a smile crossed Maxie's face. It was the incipient knowing smile that always came to him when he was about to enjoy a kill.

From the time Maxie slipped around the first lone red-cedar tree, Damion had had his eyes locked on him. He was surprised to see that his rotund would-be assassin was dressed not in a jacket but in a sport coat and expensive-looking slacks. The barrel of the man's rifle gleamed in the early-morning sun as Damion took a deep breath and felt a rivulet of sweat work its way down his neck. He watched as the huge man moved from tree to tree, huffing and puffing his way ever closer, beating back tree limbs and kicking at the underbrush.

Clutching two rocks tightly in his left hand and a third in his right, and eyeing the branch he'd grabbed earlier, which was now lying at his feet, Damion cocked his right arm and waited. The man was fifteen feet away and still blind to Damion's presence when, moist from sweat, the larger of the rocks in Damion's left hand slipped out of his grasp and thumped to the ground.

Startled, Maxie swung the barrel of his .30-06 in the direction of the thud and Damion's protective tree and fired off two rounds, splintering two branches.

Recocking his right arm, Damion let the first rock fly.

Maxie let out a howl as the rock slammed into the sweet spot above his right eyebrow and below his hairline. Blood gushed from his forehead as he raced toward where Damion, still partly camouflaged by tree branches, stood ready to let a second rock fly.

The second Damion cocked his arm, Maxie saw him and dropped his rifle. Their eyes met briefly as Maxie slipped a 9-mm Glock out of the right pocket of his sport coat. As he moved in for the kill, Damion let his rock fly and turned to run. He'd barely taken a step when a shot rang out and a screaming Randall Maxie dropped to his knees, clutching his right shoulder.

Uncertain what had happened, Damion turned to see another

man racing toward them. The tall, slender man stopped short and then walked slowly toward Damion's shooter, all the while keeping a stainless steel P94 Ruger 9-mm aimed at the larger man's head. When the man with the Ruger yelled, "Run for cover, Damion— run!" Damion took off running, confused and uncertain who the man who'd saved his life was. He stopped to look back over his shoulder and saw that the shoulder of the downed shooter's sport coat was soaked with blood. When the skinny gunman looked up and realized that Damion had stopped, he screamed, "Head for cover, Damion, goddamn it! Mario sent me. Now run!"

Damion raced for two cedar trees thirty yards away. He was too frightened to look back and too pumped with adrenaline to realize that the two men, who were now staring each other down, knew one another. He was gasping for air and well out of earshot when Pinkie Niedemeyer walked up to Randall Maxie, aimed his 9-mm at Maxie's head, and said, "A penny for your thoughts, Maxie. And that's a penny more than they're worth."

Since 6 a.m. Ron Else had been talking on the phone and intermittently pacing back and forth across the badly stained cigarette-damaged carpet of his stale-smelling motel room that overlooked I-25. He had talked to informants in three cities, and superiors in Los Angeles and New Orleans. The conversations had been punctuated with innuendoes, threats, thoughtful pauses, laughter, and in some cases clear disbelief. Disbelief that Else had stumbled onto a viable new lead in the Kennedy assassination.

When Lieutenant Gus Cavalaris called from his office a little after 9:30 as Else stood on the balcony of the third-floor motel room, drinking bitter coffee and watching Denver's early-morning rush hour fade, Else smiled to himself, content that his phone conversations had finally worked themselves full circle and back to Denver. "What have you got for me, Cavalaris?" Else asked, a hint of playfulness in his voice.

Reluctant to tell the condescending FBI agent that he'd just received new information about the Ducane and McPherson murder cases but feeling duty-bound to do so, Cavalaris said, "Got a heads-up for you in the Ducane murder. Last night up at the Eisenhower Tunnel, Sh-Sh-Sheriff Tolls's people found a twenty-dollar gold piece with an S stamped on the coin's reverse side tucked inside a fragment of what they suspect was a pocket torn from Ducane's shirt."

"So?" Else said smugly.

"So that coin's a Satoni family trademark. Their brand, more or less. The coins have been floating around Denver for years. I th-th-think it's time we had a talk with Satoni about any connection he might have had to Ducane. But for the record, as f-f-far as the McPherson case is concerned, that's still mine."

"I see," said Else, trying to maintain his composure in light of the more significant conversations he'd already had that morning. Taking a sip of coffee, he smiled and shook his head. "Suppose I told you the McPherson murder could turn out to be a whole lot bigger than some over-the-hill miner buying the farm? What would you say to that, Lieutenant?"

Cavalaris stood his ground. "The law and the courts are on my side, Else. Do whatever you want with the Ducane murder. B-b-but, like I said, the McPherson case is still mine."

"What?" Else tossed what was left of his coffee over the balcony railing and slammed the empty cup down onto the glass top of a rickety outdoor table.

"The Mc-Mc-McPherson case is mine."

"Mine, your ass! You listen to me, my stuttering cow-town friend. Those cases belong to whoever I say they belong to, and right now, unless you can somehow trump me on the issue—and I can assure you, there are federal laws that say you can't—those cases belong to me."

Cavalaris, who hadn't been forced to suffer the indignity of another law enforcement officer making fun of his speech impediment since his police academy days, frowned and gritted his teeth. In an attempt to defuse his anger, he walked around his chair, dropped to one knee, and opened the door to the minirefrigerator that was nestled below the battle-scarred credenza behind his desk.

"You still there, Cavalaris?"

Tightening his jaw muscles and squinting back his anger, he slipped a soda out of the refrigerator and unscrewed the cap. "Yeah."

"We're on the same page, then?"

"Same page," Cavalaris said robotically, taking a swig of ginger ale and standing.

"Good. Because with that twenty-dollar gold piece in hand, we've got a legitimate reason to go after Satoni. You wanna run him down, or do you want me to do it?"

"I'll locate him," said Cavalaris, sounding winded.

"Do that," said Else. "Just remember, I want to be there when you take him."

"I-I-I'll let you know when I've pinned him down."

"I'll talk to you later."

"Yeah, later." Cavalaris cradled the phone and eyed the bulletin board that hung on the wall behind his desk. Reaching nearly to the top of the memo-laden bulletin board, he pulled a yellow-headed pushpin out of a faded three-by-five black-and-white photograph, brought the photo to within inches of his nose, and stared at it. The photograph had been pinned to the bulletin board in the same position for so long that he'd almost forgotten about it. He was glad he hadn't because the photo represented an important trail to his past. A broad-faced, thick-necked man with a crew cut filled the whole of the photograph. As he focused on the face of the man in the photo—the last of his colleagues to overtly make light of his stuttering, an overbearing, beer-swilling, poor excuse for a human being and a Denver Police Academy classmate who'd ultimately punched out of the class—Cavalaris, who'd spent a lifetime subduing his affliction, reflected on a cold, hard fact of life. A fact that would drive him to make certain that Ron Else would eventually eat his words. A fact that he'd be forced to think about each and every day of his life. *Human beings, by their nature, can be exceptionally cruel.*

Chapter 19

Light-headed from blood loss, and in fear for his life, Randall Maxie had moments earlier admitted to Pinkie Niedemeyer that he'd been stalking Damion on his own, not at Rollie Ornasetti's behest. Maxie had come clean because he knew that Pinkie, a man cut from the same cloth as he, might just let him bleed to death out in the middle of the Pawnee grasslands.

He also knew that Pinkie was there on orders from Mario, and because of that, the Madrid kid would be his salvation. Pinkie wouldn't risk blowing a hole in his head or letting him bleed to death with the kid looking on.

With Pinkie's 9-mm still aimed squarely at his head, Maxie said, "Got a bargaining chip for you, Pink. Something you and that kid standing over there shaking like a leaf should consider."

Niedemeyer, who detested being called "Pink," glanced at Damion. "Better spit it out, Maxie, 'cause if it was up to me, I'd ride outta here on that four-wheeler right now and let your fuckin' ass bleed to death."

"But it's not up to you, is it, Pink?" Down on his knees and gasping for air, Maxie forced a smile. "So here's my ticket out of this dust bowl. I know all about that guy Ducane, the one whose body got coughed up out of the Eisenhower Tunnel last week. And what I know lets Mario off the hook."

"The hook for what?"

"Don't play coy with me, Niedemeyer. I'm bleeding to death, damn you. You know what I'm talking about. The JFK assassination."

"So?"

"So I can tell you a story that proves Mario wasn't involved."

"He's already got proof," Pinkie protested, watching Maxie fall forward onto his belly.

"You can't let him die! You can't let him die!" Damion screamed, racing toward the two hit men.

Pinkie dropped to one knee and, with his gun still aimed at the base of Maxie's skull, lifted Maxie's head by a hank of hair. "You got enough wind left in you to sing your song if I drag your ass outta here?"

"Yeah." Maxie's answer was barely a wheeze.

Pinkie, who'd had more than one occasion to tie a makeshift tourniquet around the bleeding limb of a Vietnam buddy, took in the pleading look on Damion's face. "Okay. Let me take a look at that arm." He grabbed the seam of Maxie's sport coat and ripped the sleeve off with one quick jerk to find a bloody shirt sleeve and a jagged through-and-through wound in the fleshy part of Maxie's upper arm. A bloody pendulum of flesh swung from a thread of tissue just below Maxie's armpit. "You sure as hell ain't gonna bleed to death from this." Turning to face Damion, he said, "Get over here, kid. Gonna need you for a bit."

Damion approached, looking wary, as Pinkie ripped Maxie's shirt sleeve off at the seam. Pinkie's gun never wavered. Shoving the blood-soaked sleeve at Damion, he said, "Roll it into a rope and tie it tight around his arm just above his armpit."

Without answering, Damion squeezed the blood out of the shirt sleeve, knelt, and slipped it around Maxie's arm.

"Knot it up, kid," Pinkie ordered as Maxie let out a relieved sigh.

Damion's hands shook as he tightened the improvised tourniquet around the 310-pound hit man's arm. Satisfied that the tourniquet wouldn't slip and that his knot would hold, Damion looked up at Pinkie and said, "Done."

Admiring Damion's handiwork and flashing him a wink of approval, Pinkie said, "Not quite. I want you to fill him up with as much water as you can. We've still gotta haul his lard ass outta here, and we need to keep his blood pressure up." Glancing back toward the ATV, Pinkie shook his head. "Shit! The three of us on that fuckin' dune buggy's gonna be tight."

"I can walk out." Damion slipped his canteen strap from around his neck, knelt, lifted Maxie's head, and forced him to take a drink of water. As he coaxed Maxie to drink, he had the strange, sudden feeling that he'd dropped through some *Alice in Wonderland* hole in the universe and into combat.

"The hell you will. The three of us roll outta here together, or we don't roll at all."

Maxie took a long sip of water, looked up at Damion, and said with a smirk, "Your friend needs the three of us to leave here together for a very good reason, son. If I croak, he's going to need somebody to say he didn't pop me. You're his insurance policy, kid."

Ignoring Maxie and wondering why he was on his knees tending to someone who'd just tried to kill him, Damion looked up at Pinkie for guidance.

Pinkie flashed Maxie a glance that said, *I'll leave you here, damn it.* "You wanna be trucked outta here, asshole, you best shut up. The only words I wanna hear outta your fat ass from now on are words tellin' me all about that dead man, Ducane." Turning to Damion, he said, "Okay, kid, time for you to help me lift him up." Maxie let out a howl as they each slipped an arm under his. "No pain, no gain," said Pinkie as the burly hit man grimaced in pain. "Let's move it," he added as they wobbled their way toward the ATV.

Realizing he was about to make it out of the grasslands alive, Maxie said, "You must owe Satoni one hell of a debt, Pink. Out here on a mission like this."

Pinkie grinned knowingly. "And with your Ducane story to pass along, I'd say I've pretty much chipped away at most everything I owe."

Now barely able to stand, Maxie remained silent, but Damion, struggling to make sense out of all that had happened to him in the past hour, eyed Pinkie inquisitively and asked, "How do you know Mario?"

"It's a long story, kid," said Pinkie, as they struggled to prop Maxie up on the front seat of the ATV. "As long a story as the one Mr. Maxie here is about to tell us, I suspect." Pinkie climbed behind the wheel of the ATV. "And since he's our special guest, I'm gonna let him go first. You're on, Maxie." Pinkie tapped Maxie in the stomach with the barrel of his 9-mm and nosed the ATV in the direction of the trailhead. "And this better be good for all our sakes. 'Cause if it ain't, I just might decide to cruise right on past Poudre Valley Hospital on the way home."

When Pinkie and Damion walked through the door of CJ's office a few minutes before noon, dressed in bloodstained clothes and looking for all the world like transients in need of a meal, CJ knew he was in for trouble. After waving them to sit down and offering them coffee, which Pinkie refused in favor of a shot of vodka, CJ listened intently to Damion's version of what had happened at the Pawnee, capping off his tale with a description of how they'd literally rolled

Randall Maxie out of Pinkie's SUV onto the emergency-room driveway of Poudre Valley Hospital near Fort Collins, leaving the barely coherent Maxie to fend for himself. After Pinkie offered a few final embellishments, CJ let out a sigh, shoved the telephone on his desk toward Damion, and said, "Call your mother. She's worried to death. She's called here four times."

As Damion picked up the receiver, Pinkie whispered to CJ, "I need to make a call too." CJ nodded toward Flora Jean's vacant office. Pinkie stepped across the room and quickly disappeared into the adjoining office, prepared to bring Mario up to speed on what Maxie had told him.

"What should I tell her?" Damion asked as CJ turned back to face him.

"Tell her where you are and that you're all right."

"Should I tell her what happened?"

"That's up to you."

Damion glanced toward the open doorway to Flora Jean's office, where Pinkie, who'd heard CJ's directive, was dialing Mario's number. As he dialed his home number, Damion asked Pinkie, "Should I tell her?"

Pinkie shrugged. "Don't ask me, kid. I never had a mother."

At a loss what to do, Damion swallowed hard as Julie answered with an expectant "Hello" on the second ring.

Trying his best to sound normal, Damion said, "It's me, Mom."

"Damion! Where are you? I've been frightened to death. Are you okay?"

"I'm fine. I'm down at CJ's office."

"Where've you been?"

"Up at the Pawnee, thinking." He glanced at CJ, and then at

Pinkie, aware that his words were the foundation for the half-truth. "After what happened last night I went up there to think. I'm sorry I blurted out what I did about Grandpa."

"That's okay, Damion. I've had some time to think too." For the first time in hours, her heart seemed to have stopped racing. "It's probably best that it came out now. How soon will you be home?"

"In an hour or so. I need to finish up some things here with CJ. Talk to him about whether or not I should continue working for him and Mario."

"It's okay—to work for them, I mean."

In a tone meant to let her know that he was capable of making that decision on his own, Damion said, "I know it is, Mom. I'll be home in a little bit."

"Fine." Overjoyed that Damion was all right, Julie decided not to press the issue.

"We'll talk some more then. Love you." Damion cradled the phone, looked up at CJ, and said, "Decided not to tell her what happened at the Pawnee."

"Reasonable decision—for the moment. Just remember, if what really happened ever comes up for discussion, don't lie."

Damion nodded and glanced toward the doorway of Flora Jean's office. Pinkie, who'd just hung up from talking to Mario, dusted off the front of his trousers as if he expected the ground-in dirt and blood to disappear. "Did you tell her everything, kid?"

"No, but what I told her was the truth."

"Good. 'Cause we're both gonna have to be real truthful here in a little bit. Mario's on his way down here, and he's madder than shit. Wants to hear about what happened at the grasslands firsthand, especially the Antoine Ducane part. Had to convince him to get his butt down here instead of gettin' a gun and chasin' after Rollie himself. Shit, the man's eighty-two."

CJ frowned and shook his head. "Damn it, Pinkie. That's just what I need. An eighty-two-year-old former mafia don rolling in here armed and with a bad attitude."

The words had barely left CJ's mouth when Flora Jean walked through the front door, returning from lunch. When she glanced across the foyer to see Pinkie standing in the doorway to her office, disheveled, haggard, and with bloodstained clothes, she said, "Uh-oh." Fixing her gaze on an equally grungy Damion, she asked, "Where the hell the two of you been, sugar?"

"To the Pawnee grasslands," Damion said, sheepishly, aware that the bare-bones truth that he'd told his mother would be quickly deconstructed by the former marine intelligence operative. "And we had a little trouble," he added, deciding to tell the truth. "Some guy tried to kill me."

Mario arrived twenty minutes later, looking as agitated as CJ had ever seen him, and for the next half hour Damion watched in amazement as the street-smart, war-hardened four-person assemblage of Mario, Pinkie, CJ, and Flora Jean dissected every facet of what they knew about the Cornelius McPherson and Antoine Ducane murders as they tried to determine how those murders might possibly be tied to the assassination of America's thirty-fifth president.

CJ and Flora Jean were on their third cups of coffee and an impatient Pinkie Niedemeyer was gnawing at the fingernail of his remaining pinkie when CJ, who'd been pushing Mario to let Flora Jean bring her fiancé, Alden Grace, in on what was clearly a defensive investigative strategy, said, "Like it or not, Mario, you're gonna have to let Flora Jean unleash Alden. We need info at his kind of level if you don't wanna end up riding down to FBI headquarters once a week."

"He's frickin' CIA, Calvin. No way."

"He's not," Flora Jean shot back.

"Well, he's former military intelligence. Same damn thing in my book," Mario countered, fingering the swollen gash in his forehead.

"And so am I." Flora Jean slammed her fist into her right palm, causing the half-dozen silver African bracelets that encircled each of her wrists to erupt in a loud jingle.

"Would the two of you stop?" CJ walked over to Mario and rested a hand on the old man's shoulder. "I need to know about how Antoine Ducane fit into the JFK assassination plan, Mario, if you expect me to help you, and I don't think we'll find that information anywhere in the halls of Congress, the National Archives, the Warren Commission report, or the Internet." CJ forced back a chuckle. "I'm gonna need somebody with a little bit of cred inside the intelligence community if I wanna get a leg up. Alden's all we got."

"Why? I've already told you there's no question Rollie was in on the JFK hit. And didn't Pinkie say just a few minutes ago that Maxie told him and Damion pretty much the same damn thing? Ain't that enough?"

"That's plenty. But it still doesn't tell us what we need to know about Ducane. Why and how he got killed, or what his connection to the Kennedy assassination plot actually was. All we've got is Maxie claiming—while he's bleeding to death on the way to the hospital, mind you—that Ducane showed up on Ornasetti's doorstep right after the JFK assassination, and that for at least five years after that Ducane milked Rollie for lots of coin."

"Hell, Calvin. What the shit do I care that Ducane was squeezing my dumb-ass nephew?" Mario eyed CJ sternly. "Damn. You're startin' to sound like you're more interested in solvin' the JFK killin' than in helpin' me."

"Come on, Mario. Get real. And you should the hell care, especially if you expect to be kept out of the assassination mix. Who's to say that you weren't the one giving Ducane orders to milk Ornasetti dry, or that maybe you even called some of the shots on the JFK assassination yourself?"

"Everyone knows that's bullshit!"

"Yeah. Everybody here. But what about the cops and the feds? If I'm gonna keep your butt out of their meat grinder, I'll need to find out why Ducane was blackmailing Rollie. Seems as though on his life-saving ride out of the Pawnee grasslands, sweet old Randall Maxie forgot to mention anything to Pinkie or Damion about that." CJ flashed Damion a wink.

"Well, you're gonna have to ask Rollie that."

"I plan to." CJ glanced across the room at Pinkie. "Your turn, Pinkie. Why would Ornasetti let someone like Ducane, your basic small-time Louisiana thug, from all I've been able to gather, hold him up for money on a regular basis when he easily could've eliminated the problem?"

Pinkie stroked his chin thoughtfully, looked at Damion, who was drinking in every word as if he expected to be quizzed on the conversation later, and said, "Can't be certain, but my guess would be that Rollie was takin' orders from somebody else."

"Mine too," said CJ, watching every head in the room, including Damion's, nod in agreement. "Question is, who?"

"Carlos Marcello would be my guess. You've got a Louisiana connection drippin' all over the place," Mario said sternly. "Or maybe Handsome Johnny Rosselli outta Chicago. He hated Kennedy."

"What about Santo Trafficante?" Pinkie added.

"Maybe," Mario said with a shrug. "None of 'em loved our boy from Boston. But they're all dead." Mario suddenly sounded nervous.

"And you're just about the last man standing," CJ said, relieved that Mario seemed to have finally grasped the point. "But fortunately the beat, as they say, goes on. The same way Rollie stepped into your seat here in Denver, somebody sure as hell took over Marcello's and Rosselli's and Trafficante's seats too. Could be that with the right incentives, those people might want to help us out."

Mario snickered. "Are you crazy, Calvin? If anybody inside the organization had a hint that I was sittin' here tellin' tales outta school, I'd pay one hefty and very permanent price. So don't expect to go diggin' into the lives of people or places or things that don't concern us. 'Cause if you do, trust me, everyone in this room'll end up payin'."

Pinkie offered an affirmative nod before asking, "But just for the record, Mario, who do you think carries the most power of persuasion these days?"

"Depends on the kind of persuasion you're talkin' about."

"The kind that could get a president killed," CJ said.

Eyeing the ceiling thoughtfully, Mario said, "My guess would be that nowadays that kinda heat could only come outta Jersey, Vegas, Miami, or New Orleans."

"New Orleans? Even after Katrina?" CJ asked, looking surprised.

"You bet. It's not where the seat of power happens to be but who's sittin' in it. I'd sure as hell put money on New Orleans bein' in the mix 'cause of Carmine Cassias. He took over from Marcello, and unlike my fuckin' blockhead of a nephew, Cassias knows what he's doin'."

"Bad mother, I take it."

"Badder," Mario countered.

"And Jersey, Vegas, and Miami? What about them?"

"Don't know much about who's sittin' in those seats right now. Been outta the loop too long. Cassias I know 'cause of some off-track bettin' deals he set up with kin of Angie's."

Feeling a bit more satisfied than he thought he had a right to be, CJ said, "Then that takes us full circle back to Antoine Ducane, a dead little Louisiana damsel named Sheila Lucerne, and an authentic slice of American white bread, Carl Watson."

"Who the hell's Watson?" asked Pinkie.

"Watson and Lucerne are a couple of people who I think can put us on track to who killed Ducane," CJ said thoughtfully, massaging his chin.

"But didn't you just say that the Lucerne woman was dead?" asked Mario.

"Yep, but sometimes dead folk have a lot to say. You just have to listen. There's a reason that McPherson guy—the one who initially discovered Ducane, or what was left of him, up at the Eisenhower Tunnel—turned up dead in Bonnie Brae the other night, and I'm betting the reason's somehow tied to our mystery lady, Sheila Lucerne. Let me ask you something, Pinkie. When you came charging down into Mario's basement the other day, how'd you know Mario was in trouble?"

"Word on the street," Pinkie said softly.

"Come off it, Pinkie. I'm not buying it." Pivoting to face Mario, CJ said, "It's your ass in the sling, Mario. I need Pinkie to tell me the truth."

Mario paused and looked around the room until his eyes met

Damion's. Suddenly lying seemed to be the wrong choice. "Okay, okay. So Pinkie and I knew that Rollie and Ducane once had a connection. But that's it. Honest. We just didn't want their connection to all of a sudden end up puttin' me on the hot seat."

"Good to know we're all on the same page," said CJ, turning his attention back to Pinkie. "So here's the next question. Think Maxie was leveling with you out there at the grasslands, or do you think there's a chance he could have been holding something back?"

"Wouldn't put it past him," said Pinkie. "You'd think he'd know more about Ducane's murder than he told me and Damion, especially after wipin' up after Rollie all these years."

"Sure would. Problem is, we've got a time-sequence problem here. According to what Maxie told you and Damion, Ducane's Ornasetti-funded gravy train derailed long before they finished constructing that Eisenhower Tunnel wall that Ducane's body ended up trapped behind. That tells me that for a time, at least, the money to buy Ducane's silence about the JFK killing had to be coming from somewhere other than Ornasetti. But according to McPherson's story in the paper, Ducane didn't disappear until 1972. Apparently Ducane's second source of money wasn't enough to keep him from having to keep his tunnel-mucking day job."

"Can't believe Ducane was that much of a miner anyway," said Mario. "I never met him but once over at Richie's Diner, but I heard he was more of a riverboat dandy than any kind of miner."

"Good thing to know," said CJ. "Especially since Maxie probably hedged on the truth in his little talk to Pinkie and Damion. I'd say Maxie needs another talking-to. In my book, at least, he's the prime suspect in the McPherson murder. Could be Maxie had long-distance orders to shut McPherson up."

"From Louisiana?" asked Pinkie.

"I'm not sure. Think maybe you can find out?"

Pinkie smiled. "If that fat-ass SOB is still alive, I sure can."

"Then do it, 'cause I'm guessing we've got very little time before cops and feds start falling out of the sky." Turning to Mario, CJ said, "We're gonna need Alden Grace, Mario. I need your okay."

Uncertain where else to turn in order to keep from being sucked into a gathering investigation that was likely to eventually place him at both the front and back ends of the JFK assassination, Mario offered a reluctant "Okay."

"Fine. That's two bases covered. There's a third. Carl Watson. Since he's the one who ended up with McPherson's body on his front lawn, my guess is he's gotta be in the mix somewhere. I'll see if I can get Julie to have one of her law clerks sniff out all they can about Watson, his wife, and our mystery woman, Sheila Lucerne."

"What about Ornasetti?" Damion called out from his seat in the far corner of the conference room.

Smiling and realizing that Damion had taken in every word, CJ said, "He'll keep for the moment, especially since he doesn't know that Maxie's pretty much sold him out. Once I finish with Watson, I'll have a talk with him."

"Be careful, CJ," warned Mario. "He's a fuckin' snake."

"So I've heard," CJ said with a smile, clearly unintimidated. He was about to tell Damion to head for home when Julie, looking annoyed and slightly guilty, walked through the open doors of the old Victorian's drawing room. Frustrated at waiting and still worried to death about Damion, she'd been unwilling to sit at home waiting for him any longer. Two stern-faced men followed in her wake. Seeing his mother standing there looking peeved gave Damion a start, but it was the presence of Lieutenant Gus Cavalaris and the man to Julie's left—a man with a badly pockmarked face who was holding a wallet containing an FBI shield out in front of him—that grabbed CJ's attention.

Chapter 20

Ron Else stood in the doorway of CJ's conference room, staring at the surprised collection of people inside, feeling as if he'd just struck Klondike gold. He'd spent a career sifting through JFK assassination investigative trash and conspiracy swill. He'd bumped across most of the western United States on assassination-related boondoggles, tracking down bullshit and wannabe bravado, all kept afloat by healthy doses of innuendo, coincidence, and flat-out nonsense. But now he told himself, he might have stumbled across the mother lode. Nudging aside the startled Julie, who hadn't realized that she had two men on her coattails until they'd followed her up CJ's steps and into the building, Else said, "Sorry, Miss, but I'm afraid I'm going to have to ask everybody here to drop what they're doing and answer a few questions." Glancing at Julie, assured that he was doing her a favor, he added, "I'm afraid this is official FBI business you've stumbled into, Miss. I'm going to have to ask you to step into the room with everyone else or leave."

Julie fixed a penetrating stare on Else and then on Cavalaris. It was a go-for-the-jugular cross-examination stare that caused Flora Jean, aware that Julie's mission to simply come get Damion had been derailed, to mouth, "Oh, shit."

"In or out," Else demanded. "If you're here to get someone's bond made, I suggest you come back later."

Julie's jaw muscles twitched in anger as she stepped into the conference room. Surprised by the move, Else said, "Your call," motioning for Julie to move farther into the room. Turning to face Cavalaris, he said, "The man to my left is Lieutenant Gus Cavalaris of one of your Denver Police Department's homicide units. I'm Agent Ron Else of the FBI." Else flashed his FBI shield again for effect. "Some of you already know Lieutenant Cavalaris—Floyd, Benson, Satoni." The hint of a smile formed at the corner of Else's mouth. He'd done his homework, and in the process he'd dredged up not only a driver's license and old military ID photographs of Flora Jean and CJ but a forty-year-old FBI file photo of a much-younger-looking Mario.

He'd gotten word a half hour earlier from the two-man stakeout team that he'd sicced on Mario that they'd followed Satoni from his house to a bail-bonding office on Denver's Bail Bondsman's Row. Else had decided to pounce, realizing that if he played his cards right, he'd have a chance to confront not only Satoni but also the black man who'd put such a scare into the Watsons. His voice boomed as Else said, "Lieutenant Cavalaris is here to help me ask a few questions." Pausing to take a breath, he said, "Now that you all know who the lieutenant is and who I am, why don't those of you I don't know respond in kind? Young man over there in the corner, your name, please."

"Damion Ma—"

"His name is Damion Madrid," Julie said authoritatively. "And I'm Julie Madrid. His mother."

"I see," Else said dismissively, turning his attention to Pinkie Niedemeyer, the other person in the room whose face he couldn't put a name to. "And you are?"

"Andrus Niedemeyer."

A fleeting look of recognition flashed across Cavalaris's face. He was about to ask Pinkie if they'd ever met when the steamrolling Else said, "Fine. Now that everyone's accounted for, here's our game plan."

"No, here's the game plan, Agent Else," Julie said, spitting Else's words back at him. "First, you're going to stop barking orders. Then you're going to explain to me in great detail exactly why you're here. And finally, if you don't have one hell of a good reason for being here—a warrant, a writ, a court order, or some other handy-dandy document that our courts recognize as reasonable cause for charging onto these premises and engaging any one of my clients in conversation, and a birth-certificate valid reason for detaining them—I am going to ask you and Lieutenant Cavalaris to leave."

Else eyed Julie in disbelief.

Julie reached into her purse, took out her wallet, extracted one of her business cards, and handed it to the suddenly crestfallen agent. "And for the record, Agent Else, I much prefer the term 'Counselor' to 'Miss.'" She flashed Damion, who could hardly believe his ears, a quick wink. "So, gentlemen, before you interrogate any of my clients, I'll expect you to dot a few I's and cross a few T's for me. In case you've forgotten, we all tend to have to do those kinds of things when it comes to carrying out the intent of our laws."

Kicking himself for forgetting bureau protocol and his manners—Else slipped his wallet out of his back pocket, extracted a business card from it, and handed it to Julie. "Certainly, Counselor."

Scrutinizing the card, Julie said in a voice filled with sweetness, sarcasm, and theatrical courtroom charm, "So, Agent Else, you're a long way from home. Tell me, how can my clients be of help to you?"

"You don't expect me to believe that your son is a client, do you, Counselor?"

Julie smiled. "He is until he says he isn't, Agent Else."

"Okay. In order to save time, we'll go there for the moment." Addressing Julie but looking point-blank at Mario, he said, "Lieutenant Cavalaris has had a couple of recent homicides served up onto his plate. Turns out those murders are linked to a very old investigation of mine."

"The Kennedy assassination?" Julie asked matter-of-factly, catching Else off guard.

"Yes," said Else, trying to guess just how much the petite, curvaceous, feisty green-eyed attorney who'd caught him with his shorts hovering around his knees knew about his career association with the Kennedy killing, and whether she might in fact be a mob-connected attorney. The fact that he'd been getting noise from contacts and informants on the East, West, and Gulf Coasts the entire time he'd been in Colorado told him that people in very high places were suddenly nervous about the possibility of someone uncovering some dirty little assassination secret. It was possible that Ms. Madrid was part of a modern-day crime leadership organization that was far less sexist than the old.

Stroking his chin thoughtfully and trying his best to think three steps ahead of Julie, Else said, "I really only need to have one conversation, and that's with Mr. Satoni."

"Okay with you, Mario?" Julie asked, looking Mario squarely in the eye.

"I've got nothin' to hide," Mario said, looking at Damion, well aware of why Julie had so aggressively come to his rescue.

"Then by all means let's talk, Mr. Else," said Julie.

"I'd prefer to move the discussion to somewhere more private," Else said, hoping to stake out a logistical advantage.

Mario eyed Julie for direction.

"Fine with us." She gave Mario a thumbs-up sign. "Are my other clients free to go?"

Pleased that he'd closed the deal, Else, who'd landed the fish he wanted—the man most likely in his eyes to have insight into the Ducane and McPherson murders—glanced at Cavalaris, who nodded his okay. Looking back at Julie, Else said, "They are for now." He knew he could always come back and put pressure on Floyd and Benson. All in all, he told himself, things had worked out to his advantage. "Ready to leave whenever you are, Counselor. My car's parked out front."

"Fine." Julie walked over to Mario, hoping to usher him out the front door before Cavalaris, who kept eyeing Pinkie, scored a recognition hit that would, at least temporarily, have her representing a hit man. Clamping Mario's right hand in hers, she asked, "Ready to go?"

Mario simply nodded.

As they moved to leave, she cast a parting glance Damion's way. Noting his bloody clothes, while at the same time maintaining her seasoned lawyer's cool, she asked, "You okay?"

"Sure."

"Stay here with CJ until I get back," Julie said. Leading Mario by the hand and thinking about everything that had happened in the past fourteen hours, she followed Cavalaris and Else toward the front door, recognizing as she descended CJ's front steps that, of all things, she now found herself representing the kind of man who had caused her father's death.

The clerk manning the FedEx service counter inside the dimly lit front lobby of an old cinder-block building in an aging Boulder, Colorado, industrial park eyed Willette Ducane with the frustrated look he generally reserved for the Christmas rush season. The only reason he hadn't handed off the tired-looking old woman to his supervisor and called it a day was the fact that during the month of August, FedEx employees nationwide were being evaluated on how well they handled customer service issues, and calling in his supervisor to arbitrate a problem like the one he was facing would likely cost him valuable customer-satisfaction bonus points and a possible year-end raise. Cocking an eyebrow and tapping the business end of a ballpoint pen on the countertop, the man said, "I've told you, ma'am. I can't give you that information."

Exasperated, Willette said, "But the package was mailed from here in Boulder. The tracking number proves it." She drummed three fingers across the address label affixed to the envelope she'd received with the *Denver Post* article about Antoine.

"I know that, ma'am," the clerk said, struggling to control his temper. "But it's the age of identity theft. I can't give you the information you're asking for. I've told you, the information's confidential."

Gritting her teeth, Willette shifted her weight onto the cane in her right hand. Thirty years earlier she never would have taken such guff off a woolly-headed, earring-wearing clerk, and if she were back home in Louisiana, even now, she might've grabbed the man by his collar, pulled him face to face with her, and demanded the information she was after. But she was in Colorado, not Louisiana. After two bumpy, exhausting flights from hell—flights on which she'd been served only flat-tasting soda and rock-hard pretzels—and a nerve-racking drive from Denver International Airport to Boulder, her arthritic knees were screaming bloody murder. Recognizing that she was too rest-broken to come to blows with some Neanderthal, she asked sharply, "What time do you close?"

"7 p.m."

"Ummm." Eyeing the clerk as if she expected him to make a run for it, she checked her watch. She'd booked a room at a motel just off the Boulder Turnpike, a room that the clerk had earlier told her was less than five minutes away. After a couple of hours' rest, she'd have enough energy to come back and go another round with this clerk or a different one, but it might be less aggravating to simply speak right then with his supervisor. She was on the verge of asking the clerk to get his manager when a burly, freckled-faced FedEx driver with a receding hairline and a rosy-cheeked, cherubic face strolled into the room carrying a couple of boxes under his arm. Looking up at the clerk, he said, "How's it going, Marty?"

When the clerk didn't answer, the man walked over to the counter, placed one of his packages on a scale, and checked the weight of the package on the scale's digital readout.

Willette glanced briefly at the man before again fixing her gaze on the clerk. "Can you get your supervisor for me?" she said finally.

Surprised by the woman's tenacity and concerned that he might end up losing customer-satisfaction points, the clerk shoved Willette's envelope, which was lying next to the scale, toward the driver and asked him, "Is the account number on that envelope one you recognize?"

"Not off the top of my head," said the driver. "Let me scan it." The driver extracted a bar-code scanner from a leather pouch that hung from his belt, scanned the nine-digit account number, and said, "Number's for a place near Bellvue. Peak to Peak Bed and Breakfast up north, outside of Fort Collins in Poudre Canyon. Pick up and deliver there three, four times a week." He quickly turned to leave.

"Thanks." Pleased with himself for being so quick on his feet, the clerk grinned from ear to ear. The breach of protocol hadn't been his but the driver's, and to top it off, the driver was none the wiser. As soon as the driver walked through the front door, the clerk said to Willette, "Your envelope came from one of those bed-and-breakfast places. It's a good hour-and-a-half drive from here."

"Can you write the name down for me?" Willette asked softly, aware that the clerk had gotten the unsuspecting driver to do his dirty work. As the clerk wrote the name of the bed and breakfast on a scrap of paper, she teased her envelope back toward her, folded it, and slipped it into her purse. Taking the scrap from the clerk in one hand and gripping the head of her cane tightly with the other, she turned to leave. She was halfway to the exit when she looked back over her shoulder at the woolly-headed clerk. "Slick never beats savvy, son. Trust me. I've been around the block." Her voice boomed with authority as the suddenly wide-eyed clerk's supervisor walked up behind him and asked, "What was that all about?"

Willette left the FedEx office exhausted but buoyed by the fact that she now had an important part of the information she had flown and driven more than a thousand miles to get. The envelope that had resurrected so much pain for her and caused her to cry for nearly two whole nights had come from a place in some obscure Rocky Mountain canyon. She'd find that place, she told herself, if it killed her.

By the time she drove her rental car into the parking lot of the Harvest Hotel, every cell in her body seemed to hurt. A chipper-looking blond woman, whom Willette pegged as a college student, greeted her from behind the front desk as Willette limped, suitcase in tow, across the lobby. Noting Willette's obvious pain, the receptionist said, "Let me help you with that."

"No need," said Willette, struggling with a suitcase filled with medications, cosmetics, three changes of clothes, Antoine's notes and sketches from the day of the Kennedy killing, and every card, letter, and note that Antoine had sent to her after his move to Colorado. Parking the suitcase directly in front of the reception counter as if daring it to move, she said, "Need to check in."

When the woman and Willette finished talking fifteen minutes later, Willette had directions on how to get to Poudre Canyon, the address and phone number of the Peak to Peak Bed and Breakfast, and the name of a good place to eat in Boulder that evening. Thanking the clerk, she struggled with one last gasp of energy to the first-floor room she'd requested, limped across the room, her purse tugging at her shoulder, let out a sigh, and sprawled across the bed.

Twenty minutes later she sat up on the edge of the bed, a little less tired but still in pain, and took a piece of paper from her purse. She dialed a phone number slowly, and when the person on the other end of the line answered, "Peak to Peak Bed and Breakfast; this is Lydia," in a voice that sounded recorded, Willette responded carefully, "I need to make a reservation."

"For when?"

"Tomorrow. And I need to check in early," said Willette. She knew that should her visit to the bed and breakfast, which the hotel clerk had told her was in pretty remote country, turn out to be productive, she'd need as many daylight hours as possible, given her failing eyesight, to try to get at the heart of what had happened to her precious Sugar Sweet.

"I'm afraid our check-in time is 1 p.m."

"That's okay. I'll just leave my bag and check out the area."

"That'll work just fine," said the woman. "It's a wonderful time of year for that. We have six rooms, all with baths. Prices range from eighty-five to one twenty-five. Any preference?"

Pausing to consider what she was sure was a Southern richness in the woman's voice, Willette said, "I'm on a pretty tight budget."

"I'd suggest the Longmont room. It's eighty-five plus tax and lodging fees. You'll love it. I'll need a credit-card number and a name to hold the room."

Willette paused before offering a response. "Ann Reed. And I'm gonna pay cash."

"I'm afraid I can't guarantee the room without a credit card."

"That's all right. I'll be there by 8 a.m."

"The room could be gone, Ms. Reed."

"I'll chance it."

"Okay, but can I get a phone number from you in case we fill up? I'd hate for you to show up and there not be a room available."

"Sure." Willette eyed the number on the hotel's phone and read it off to the woman.

"Got it. Is there anything else I can help you with?"

"Yes. Yes, there is. I'm gonna need to send out something by FedEx while I'm there. Can you handle that for me? Fill out the paperwork, expedite the mailing?"

"Surely. I handle most of those requests myself. I'm the manager."

"That's great."

"And if you arrive early enough in the morning, we'll still be serving breakfast. You're welcome to join our other guests."

"Well, thank you so much. I may just do that."

"We'll see you tomorrow morning, then."

"You certainly will," said Willette, cradling the receiver and thinking there was something hauntingly familiar about the woman's voice. Something she was going to have to think long and hard about.

Chapter 21

The man known to his Gulf Coast contacts simply as Napper kept reminding himself that things were unfolding too easily. On Carmine Cassias's orders, he had traced Willette Ducane's junket from Baton Rouge to Dallas and ultimately to Denver simply by having a friend who worked for American Airlines, check travel itineraries out of New Orleans and Baton Rouge for her name. It had been far too simple, and that bothered him. In his business, simple on the front end almost always translated into problems on the back end. And since he was dealing with a house of cards that could easily collapse under the right kind of pressure, he knew he would have to use special precautions and exacting measures when it came to dealing with Ornasetti, Satoni, and the Ducane woman.

Now, as he sat at a coffee shop at the corner of Colorado Boulevard and Eighth Avenue, sipping hot chocolate in 90-degree heat, reading the *Denver Post* sports pages, and running through a series of killing plans, he had the feeling that just too many things were coming up roses.

Pausing to clear his head, he eyed the woman at the serving counter, who'd looked at him with surprise when he'd placed his order for hot chocolate. When he'd smiled at her and said, "Habit from a former life," the woman had failed to return his smile, so he'd palmed a $3 tip as he'd headed for an empty table.

Earlier in the day he'd followed Mario Satoni from his house in North Denver to a Delaware Street bail-bonding office on the western perimeter of downtown Denver. After staking the office out for close to an hour and a half, he'd watched two men who couldn't be mistaken for anything but cops cart off in an unmarked police car Satoni and the hot little exotic-looking number they'd followed into the building earlier. He'd followed that car to a building in downtown Denver, then called Cassias to give him a heads-up. After a follow-up conversation with his groggy, spaced-out-sounding Denver contact, Randall Maxie, who'd told him to watch out for Satoni's lapdog, Floyd, he'd called Cassias back and been given the green light to handle everyone on his list, including the bail bondsman, Floyd.

When Cassias had warned him in closing that it might be prudent to observe for a while rather than act, he'd countered, "I was doing this kind of work long before you took over the reins down there in Louisiana, friend. My job is to handle messes. Yours is to make sure I get my money."

Asserting his authority, Cassias had ended the conversation with a stern warning: "I know your pedigree. Just don't allow your past success to fuck with my current well-being."

Eyeing his empty cup, Napper pushed aside the sports pages, reminding himself as he did that well-being was the order of the day—his, Cassias's, and the organization's. He stopped short of ordering another cup of hot chocolate after deciding that a second jolt of sugar and caffeine wasn't worth the risk of having someone at the counter remember the color of his hair or how tall he was or that he was sitting around drinking hot chocolate on a 90-degree day.

Perhaps, after having things fall into place so easily, he just might need a healthy dose of what twenty years earlier he would have called *case hardening*. Life had become too mundane, too fucking ordinary and everyday pleasant, he told himself as he left the coffee shop in a rush and walked north along Colorado Boulevard toward his car. He'd been given the okay to kill at least two people, maybe as many as four. It was time to forget the ordinariness of his life and reflect on the iron will and attention to detail it would take to pull off the killings.

After ten initial shaky minutes, Mario Satoni reverted to his former self, enduring two hours of interrogation by an FBI tag team that included Ron Else and a seriously overweight man with busy eyebrows and mottled yellow teeth.

With Julie running interference, even though he realized that her thoughts were still clearly with Damion, he went toe-to-toe with the seasoned agents, never acquiescing, never admitting for one moment that he'd in any way been involved in the JFK assassination or the Ducane or McPherson murders, and never cracking in the face of their rapid-fire questions. Julie intervened the half-dozen times that Else brought up Mario's late wife, Angie, but Mario wavered, admitting finally, under the weight of his long-suffering grief, that Angie's family had indeed had a tradition of handing out twenty-dollar gold pieces with a boxed "S" stamped on the reverse to loyal friends, family, and associates.

When Else intimated that such a gold piece had been found among Antoine Ducane's remains and that the coin's presence linked Mario to Ducane's murder, Julie stepped in with a vengeance, forcing Else to admit that the gold piece could have come from any one of a hundred sources, including long-dead family members, Rollie Ornasetti, or any number of Ornasetti's flunkies.

Just before the two-hour mark of the interrogation, which was taking place, to Julie's surprise, not in Denver's FBI offices, but in another downtown building, Julie forced the agents to admit that they couldn't continue to browbeat Mario and hold him without pressing charges based only on the fact that some coin had been found with a dead man. Else and the other agent reluctantly huddled briefly outside the room along with Cavalaris. Ten minutes later she and Mario left, Julie with a newfound appreciation for the eighty-two-year-old former don's guile, facility with words, and impenetrable iron-clad will.

They hailed a cab to head back to CJ's office, with Julie's thoughts focused on Damion's well-being and Mario's centered on Else's parting salvo to Julie: "Make sure your client's available for further questioning, Counselor. I'm sure we'll talk again."

As they got out of the foul-smelling cab in front of CJ's office, Julie looking relieved, Mario looking exhausted, Julie's cell phone rang. "Go on inside. I'll take care of the fare," Julie insisted, waving for Mario to go ahead. Recognizing the phone number on her caller ID, she flipped open her cell phone with one hand as she fumbled in her purse for a $10 bill with the other. "Julie," she said, watching Mario head up the sidewalk to CJ's office. Her eyebrows arched when the eager-sounding law clerk on the other end of the line said, "Becky here, and have I got news!"

Julie stood on the curb listening, her eyes getting wider by the second as she drank in her law clerk's words. When the cab driver called out, "Hey, lady, I'm holdin' up traffic here; you need change?" she waved for him to take off.

Continuing the conversation as she headed into CJ's office, she broke into a wide grin. "Hell of a twist," she said, mounting the front steps. "Stay on it, Becky. This could get better. Be sure and call me if it does." She flipped the cell phone closed, shook her head, and pushed open CJ's front door.

As she stepped past Mario and into the small foyer that had once been her secretarial alcove to see Damion sitting in an overstuffed chair looking bored, the muscles in her throat tightened as she rushed across the foyer to embrace him. Her purse strap slipped off her shoulder and she dropped her phone. Bending down and hugging him harder than she had in years, she said, "Damion, baby, are you okay?"

"Sure, Mom. Sure, I'm fine."

Teary-eyed, she stepped back, retrieved her cell phone, and said, "You should've left me a note this morning. Something to let me know you were going up to Pawnee Buttes. You've had me scared to death."

"Yeah, I know," Damion said, shaking his head and looking guilty as charged. "I was going to call you, but I forgot my cell phone. After what happened last night I needed to go somewhere I could think. I know I shouldn't have said what I did about Grandpa, and I feel terrible about getting you and CJ crosswise with each other." Damion locked his eyes to the floor. "I never slept a wink all night."

Julie let out a relieved sigh and eyed Mario briefly before turning her attention back to Damion. "Neither did I. I felt a little betrayed at first, but now that I've had time to think things over, I know that what I was really suffering from was guilt and a healthy dose of fear. Guilt that by coming within fifty miles of someone like Mario, I might end up losing my hard-earned privilege. Fear that someone might see, if they looked close enough, who I really am: Julie Romero Madrid, the mob-connected trucker's daughter, instead of Julie Madrid, the lawyer."

"But Mom, you *are* a lawyer," Damion said, eyeing Julie quizzically, surprised that she'd just referred to her father as something other than a saint.

Julie forced a wry smile. "So I am, Damion. So I am." Looking at Damion and hoping that she wasn't about to forever tarnish a relationship that had been built on honesty and trust, she spoke slowly. "There's a reason your grandfather lost his trucking company, Damion. A reason he got steamrolled and back-stabbed by the people I've always pledged myself to hate. The story I've told you all these years is only partially true. Your grandfather lost everything, all right, but not because of being so upstanding and virtuous. The truth is, he was in lockstep with, not at odds with, the mob, and they tossed him aside when he was no longer needed." Julie's eyes welled up with tears as Damion rose from his chair and hugged her.

The sound of CJ thundering back down the stairs from his apartment, where he'd rushed to get a couple of aspirin for Mario, and the squeaking noise of the first-floor conference room's heavy mahogany doors sliding open, caused Damion and Julie to look up.

Realizing that Julie was crying, CJ stopped on the bottom stair, eyed Mario and Flora Jean, who stood looking dismayed in the conference-room doorway, and said softly to Julie, "You all right?"

Blinking back tears, Julie forced a smile. It was the self-assured, never-intimidated smile that CJ had come to know so well. A smile that let him know that the petite, tough-as-nails woman who stood facing him had somehow navigated another mine field.

"I'm fine, CJ. As fine as Cuban sugarcane and just as sweet," she said with a wink. A wink offered to let everyone standing there know that in spite of her tears and whatever had caused them, Julie Madrid would be moving ahead.

"Anything I can help with?" Flora Jean asked.

"No. Not really. Damion and I have just been blowing a little truth into the sails of an old wife's tale."

CJ eyed Damion, uncertain whether he'd told his mother about what had happened at Pawnee Buttes. Damion had sworn earlier, against both CJ's and Mario's advice, that he'd take the story to the grave. Damion's barely perceptible head shake told CJ that Julie's tears hadn't been about Pawnee Buttes. Sensing something very personal and private that even he couldn't be privy to, CJ eyed Julie, uncertain what to say. When she flashed him a reassuring look that said, *Let's move on,* he took the hint and said, "Mario tells me you scored a knockout downtown."

"Sure did. But it was a technical one at best," Julie said, inching her way back on point.

Perceiving that after Pawnee Buttes and a confrontation with the FBI, he'd earned the right to offer his take, Damion said, "You sure threw that FBI guy for a loop, Mom, when you said all of us were your clients."

"I had to do something, especially with you sitting there in the room. Besides, that FBI snob rubbed me the wrong way." Julie smiled. "Think he may have a problem with women. Truth be told, though, if we don't watch it, I could very well end up representing everyone who was here when he and that homicide lieutenant came barging in. Bottom line is, if we don't want that happening, we need to find out a few things."

"Which are?" Flora Jean and Damion asked in near unison.

"First off, in order to keep Mario out of the hot seat we need to find out who killed Antoine Ducane and that Eisenhower Tunnel maintenance worker, Cornelius McPherson." Julie paused and let what she was about to say next gather a full head of steam. Staring directly at Mario, she said, "And that likely will mean that we'll need to peg who really killed JFK. Not that I'm a skeptic, mind you," she added with a smile, "but Lee Harvey Oswald, come on!"

"Mom, get serious."

"I am serious," she said, recognizing that Damion, by virtue of involving himself with Mario, had stepped into life's fast track, unintentionally dragging her along. "In for a penny, in for a pound, sweet son of mine. Time you learned that." Her tone was deadly earnest. "For now, I'd simply like for you to sit there and listen." She turned her attention to CJ. "On my way in I got a phone call from one of my law clerks. The clerk I asked to find out about the woman who once owned the house over in Bonnie Brae where McPherson was killed."

"Yeah, Sheila Lucerne," CJ said, recognizing from Julie's tone that her law clerk had uncovered something important.

Julie nodded. "Well, it turns out that Ms. Lucerne may not have died in that accident her onetime boyfriend, Carl Watson, told you about after all. Seems she may have simply disappeared. My law clerk says she had no trouble digging up a couple of newspaper accounts that describe a fatal head-on crash Lucerne supposedly had with a semi on the Boulder Turnpike back in 1973."

"Yeah. That's how Watson said she died." CJ glanced around the room and realized that everyone, especially Damion, was hanging on Julie's every word.

"Well, if she did, the details surrounding Ms. Lucerne's death sure got buried awful fast. My law clerk, whose undergrad degree is in journalism, mind you, couldn't find a single follow-up newspaper account of what was supposedly a fiery crash. She also couldn't find a second source for the information, and she couldn't find a byline on either of the two original stories." Julie stopped and took a deep breath. "Here's what else she couldn't find. There was never a newspaper obit for anyone named Sheila Lucerne. And my law clerk says she searched the *Post* and the *Rocky* obits for a month before and after Lucerne's supposed death. Now, here's the topper. There's apparently no record of a police investigation into the accident. Seems like Watson's story, except for the two newspaper accounts I mentioned, materialized out of thin air."

"Anything else?" asked CJ, his voice rough with suspicion.

"Just this. Vital statistics couldn't dig up a death certificate on Lucerne, the cops can't confirm her death, or even that she was in a wreck, there's no record of her being taken to Denver General, the only Front Range Level III trauma center at the time, and my law clerk couldn't sniff out one piece of information about next of kin."

"Plant," Mario boomed. "We're dealin' with a frickin' plant."

Every head in the room nodded except Damion's. "A what?" Damion asked, looking confused.

Mario eyed Julie and asked, "Can I school him?"

"Better now than later."

Turning to Damion, Mario said, "A plant. It's what folks in high places and people with power do to get their way when they wanna get rid of a danglin' participle. More or less, it's the last-ditch handiwork of lyin' politicians and desperate criminals so they can have their way."

When Damion nodded as if to say, *Oh, I see*, Mario looked over at CJ and said, "I'd say the Lucerne woman was either paid to take a hike, she was taken out of circulation permanently by onetime associates of mine, or, if she really did know something about the JFK assassination or the Ducane killin', she's livin' out her life on the government's payroll."

"Witness protection?" asked CJ.

"You betcha," Mario shot back.

Nodding and slipping a partially crushed carton of cheroots out of the pocket of his riverboat gambler's vest, CJ tapped out his last cheroot. He moistened the end, slipped the cheroot between his lips, and looked at Flora Jean. "I'm thinking that if we're ever gonna get down to bedrock on this thing, we'll need to dig a couple of levels deeper, and that means sooner or later we're gonna have to talk to Alden Grace. Think if he tweaked a few of his intelligence sources he'd be able to come up with the names of some people who wanted Kennedy out of the way besides Lee Harvey Oswald? Serious names, I mean. Not the kind you hear mentioned on late-night talk shows, *Oprah*, or in the movies."

"That's a tall order, sugar. Besides, if you asked 'em straight up who shot JFK, half the people on the planet would be willin' to provide you with a name other than Oswald's. And remember, now, Alden's retired military intelligence, not CIA. But I'll see what I can do."

CJ eyed Mario to see if he'd again nix the use of the retired two-star general. When Mario, still numb from his FBI grilling, didn't so much as flinch at the mention of Grace, CJ said, "Great. The fact that Alden's not CIA could turn out to be a blessing, especially since lots of folks think it was really the CIA who did Kennedy in."

"I wouldn't discount the possibility," said Mario. "Especially since the CIA was and still is made up of the kind of I-own-the-world types who woulda been just egotistical enough to hook up with similar-minded associates of mine."

"Marcello and Trafficante?" asked CJ.

"Or even Rosselli," Mario responded. "What I can't figure out is why any one of 'em woulda cast their lot with a dumbshit like Rollie." Mario suddenly found himself smiling. "Unless, of course, they needed a patsy. That could be it! Hell, before we go traipsin' off lookin' for skeletons in the CIA's closet, I think we should lean on Rollie."

"I will," said CJ. "But for now, he's on my list behind Carl Watson."

"Why second?" asked Flora Jean, watching Mario and Julie nod in agreement.

"Because of Sheila Lucerne. I've got a feeling she may be the key not only to the Ducane murder but to the whole JFK thing. And if she is, her old boyfriend Watson's a lot more likely to give her up than Rollie."

"One thing's for sure, Watson will be easy enough to tap," said Julie. "We know where he lives and works. According to my law clerk, he's been playing moon-rocket engineer, climbing the corporate ladder over at Lockheed Martin for the past thirty years."

"Who'd'a thunk it?" said CJ. "Lucerne, Watson, the mob, the CIA. Hell, could be we've got ourselves a real live presidential hit man living right here in Denver masquerading as a moon-rocket engineer."

"Or a don," said Mario, making certain to include Rollie Ornasetti on CJ's list.

Salivating at the thought of bringing ultimate closure to the JFK assassination, CJ nodded in concurrence before turning to Flora Jean. "Think it's time to call Alden."

"No need to, sugar. I'm gonna see him in less than an hour. I'm guessin' he won't have a lot for us off the top of his head, but once he touches base with a few of his contacts, trust me, he'll come up with somethin'."

"Stay on it, and both of you be careful," CJ said. "Could be we've latched on to the tip of an iceberg," he added, checking his watch. "Shit. It's almost five. If I've got any chance of catching up with Watson at work, I'll have to head for Lockheed Martin right now." Flashing Julie a grin, he said, "I know you're a big-time attorney these days, Ms. Madrid." The grin broadened. "But I was sorta hoping I could get you to play at being a secretary for just a few minutes. I need someone who can sound real 'executive secretary' official to call over to Lockheed Martin and see if one of their top engineers is at work, and if he's not, when he'll be in."

Julie broke into an ear-to-ear grin, recalling how often, during her years as CJ's secretary, she and CJ had worked a similar bait-and-switch in order to get some unsuspecting family member to divulge the whereabouts of some bond skipper. "Like we used to do in the old days, Mr. Floyd?"

"Exactly," said CJ, watching Damion's eyes widen as Julie, looking suddenly energized and stepping into a role that Damion had never seen her in, walked over to a nearby phone, dialed information, and said to the operator in the most official-sounding of voices, "The number for Lockheed Martin, please."

Part V

The Solution

The day Gus Cavalaris had turned thirteen, his great-uncle, a wine-maker from the island of Sardinia, had given the sensitive, stuttering teenager thirteen shiny silver dollars and two important hard-and-fast rules to live by: *Never sulk over a bad grape harvest—prepare instead for next season* and *Always follow your instincts, never convention. You'll be a better man for it.*

Forty-one now, Cavalaris had spent most of his life subconsciously following his uncle's advice. Advice that had enabled him, for the most part, to ignore the discouraging utterances of men such as FBI Agent Ron Else.

Else's shortcomings were his own to wrestle with, and the McPherson killing, not the Kennedy assassination, was what Cavalaris realized he was being paid to investigate. As things stood, he told himself, tagging along after Floyd and Mario Satoni was probably his best option for bringing resolution to that case.

Earlier in the day he'd ordered a stakeout detail for Satoni's house, done some homework on the Satoni family's affinity for defacing twenty-dollar gold pieces, and had a brief conversation with McPher-son's friend and coworker, Franklin Watts, to see if Watts might recall whether McPherson had ever carried a twenty-dollar gold piece with an "S" stamped on it. He'd forced back a chuckle when Watts had said, "Hell, if Cornelius had a coin like that, it would've been in the bank earning interest. Cornelius was a man who liked to keep real close to his money. Why are you asking anyway, Lieutenant? Something to do with the issues that FBI agent was so keen on?"

When he'd told Watts he wasn't at liberty to say, Watts, raising his voice in defense of his dead friend, had said, "You can take this to the bank, Lieutenant. Cornelius wouldn't have had anything to do with killing anyone."

Surprised by Watts's adamant, loud defense of his friend, he'd made a mental note to check into the world of Franklin Watts.

After finishing up some late-day paperwork, he'd gotten a haircut, grabbed an early dinner at a twenty-four-hour diner near the Denver Performing Arts Center, and finally settled into the task that he had assigned himself—staking out CJ Floyd's Victorian. He'd been parked on Bail Bondsman's Row, four houses down the street from Floyd's place, watching rush-hour traffic stream down Thirteenth Avenue and out of the city for about half an hour when CJ came rushing out of his office, Stetson in hand.

When Floyd jumped into his Bel Air and backed out of his driveway in such a rush that he nearly scraped the car's pristine right-rear hubcap on the curb, Cavalaris had the feeling that not only was Floyd about to lead him to water but that he would finally get the opportunity to drink.

Nosing his unmarked car south on Delaware Street as Floyd turned west onto Thirteenth Avenue, he allowed Floyd a five-car-lengths lead before slipping in behind a dump truck, prepared to follow the Bel Air and his instincts.

The Lockheed Martin Astronautics division's futuristic-looking campus, home to the U.S. space program's Titan and Atlas rockets, sits twenty miles west of downtown Denver, nestled into the foothills. The metallic silver headquarters building, the architectural high-light of the Jefferson County complex, sits against the backdrop of red sandstone rock formations and the Rocky Mountains and has the splendidly low, wide feeling of a space temple.

Carl Watson had gone to work for the aerospace giant thirty years earlier, armed with a newly earned PhD in both mechanical and aeronautical engineering. Over the years he had gained a sterling reputation as a mechanical systems troubleshooter, working his way up to the point that his opinions were now powerful enough to gar-ner boardroom attention.

Considered by colleagues to be calculating and brilliant but a bit eccentric, Watson had been known to wear the same suit every work-day for a week and eat mustard-smothered fried-bologna sandwiches and dill pickles for breakfast. When a project he was in charge of lagged because of a systems design glitch, he would stay at work and sleep in his office, gnawing at the design problem, often for weeks, until it was solved. He was known to take frequent trips abroad, ostensibly to check on the quality assurance programs of some of Lockheed Martin's business partners, and he enjoyed the reputation of being that annoying fly on the wall that project partners, collab-orators, and associates hated to see coming.

Watson left his office in the headquarters building, whistling to himself, a little before 6, as was his custom, expecting to make it home in time to shave, change clothes, and take in a 7:30 play with his wife at the Denver Performing Arts Center. His face became a mask of irritation and his whistling stopped as he prepared to crank his Volvo's engine to exit the top terrace of the headquarters building's oddly configured parking area, only to see CJ Floyd in his rearview mirror.

Watson tapped his horn as CJ stepped from behind the rear bumper and walked toward him. Only a half-dozen cars remained on the terrace, and CJ had pegged his chances of being interrupted by a Watson coworker—or shooed off by the security guard he'd avoided when he'd slipped into the elevated lot by driving up a ramp the wrong way just after another car had come down it—at less than 10 percent.

"Evening," CJ said as a perplexed Carl Watson tried his best not to look intimidated.

"What on earth are you doing here, Floyd?" Watson said through the rolled-down window.

CJ smiled. "Following the scent of the number on your license plate. It's a scent that has a way of betraying you."

"I'll call security."

"Why don't you do that? And while you're at it, I'll call the cops. Might as well explain to everybody wearing a badge why the hell you been lying about Sheila Lucerne being dead."

Caught off guard, Watson asked, "How'd you know I'd be here? And how'd you get past security?"

"A real smart lawyer friend of mine sniffed you out. Here's a little piece of advice. If you wanna avoid people, you need to learn to alter your schedule. As for security, I'd say that considering what it is your company does, somebody here oughta consider sending that job out for another bid. I'd check the timing on your exit gates if I were you, and maybe get your rent-a-cops to understand that traffic on a one-way street can always flow the other way, no matter what the signage says. Now that I've shared all of my little secrets, how about us getting back to Sheila Lucerne?" CJ poked his head through the open window. "Why the charade, Mr. Watson?"

Eyes locked on the dashboard, Watson adjusted himself in his seat. "That's personal."

"I see. Personal enough that I'm guessing you wouldn't dare share the information with the cops, and certainly personal enough to have never mentioned it to your security-minded employer. Of course not," CJ said, smiling. "Why the hell would you tell Lockheed Martin that you once faked an old girlfriend's death? Especially when it might start them thinking there could be other things you've faked."

"I don't know what you're talking about, Floyd."

CJ straightened up, rested his right arm on the car's roof, and flashed Watson an intimidating downward stare. "Then let me spell it out for you. Remember that lawyer I mentioned to you earlier? Turns out she's a lot more than just smart; she's resourceful to boot. Has to be. Her firm's got lots of mouths to feed. Secretaries, law clerks, wannabe partners, the partners themselves. So just to check out her resourcefulness, I asked her to have one of her real hungry law clerks do some digging and see what she could come up with about Sheila Lucerne. Guess what she found?" When CJ slammed his palm down on the roof, Watson flinched and rose six inches out of his seat. "Just this. That accident you told me about? The one you claimed your old girlfriend Sheila died in? My friend the lawyer and I think it was staged. Turns out that law clerk of hers couldn't find but two brief old *Denver Post* articles describing the accident. No police reports, no death certificate, no hospital admission, and lo and behold, no follow-up stories. All she could find was one amazingly well-placed and very brief story about a Boulder Turnpike crash and the car's driver, a woman named Sheila Lucerne who died at the scene. It was a story that led to nothing but a dead end."

CJ stroked his chin thoughtfully. "Wonder how much you'd have to pay somebody to plant a story like that? A lot, I'm guessing. I'm also guessing you probably couldn't get it done unless you were connected to people with a whole lot of clout. Mobsters, politicians, people like that." CJ stuck his head back into the car until he was nearly cheek to cheek with Watson. "I'd vote for the mob, myself. Wonder how finding out that one of your employees was linked to the mob would sit with a big-time government-contract-rich company like Lockheed Martin?"

Watson inched his face away from CJ's. Drumming his fingers on the dashboard and desperately looking around the car's interior, he finally said, "What do you want, Floyd?"

"Answers. Just a few simple answers. Like what really happened to Sheila Lucerne, and what was she running from?"

"And if I tell you?"

"You've done your good deed for the day, and you've held on to your job."

Gripping the steering wheel with both hands, Watson eyed the vintage Bel Air that blocked his exit and let out a sigh. "I don't know why I should tell you. I'd do better telling this to Lieutenant Cavalaris."

"Because, Mr. Watson, I'm standing here prepared to make your tidy little life 100 percent miserable."

"Could be you're bluffing."

CJ slipped his cell phone off his belt and flipped it open. "You're free to talk to my friend the lawyer and find out. Be happy to dial the number for you."

"Okay, okay. So Sheila and I faked her death. Who did it harm?"

"That dead man they found on your front lawn the other night is one likely person."

Pondering how on earth an old girlfriend he hadn't seen in decades could possibly have brought him so much trouble, Watson took a deep breath and stared straight ahead. "I was just a kid at the time. In my midtwenties. Sheila was older than me, and she had me by the nose. You would have to have seen her to understand why. Beautiful, 100 percent curves and cleavage, and with a set of legs on her that wouldn't quit. And she had one of those throaty, come-hither kind of voices that just seemed to paralyze me. I would've jumped off a bridge if she'd told me to back then."

"So instead you helped her stage her own death?"

Watson smiled knowingly, as if the thought of what he and Sheila had pulled off somehow served to forever unite them. "It wasn't hard. Sheila knew people who could get things done. The kind of people I didn't think existed except in the movies. One of the people she knew was that guy whose remains they found up at the Eisenhower Tunnel after our recent earthquake."

"Antoine Ducane."

"Yes. He and Sheila had a thing going years before I met her. Something I could never quite put my finger on. Love, larceny, lust? I don't exactly know which. Could have had something to do with the fact that they were connected in ways that she and I weren't. They were both Creole and from god-awful Louisiana. I never met Ducane, and I only saw his picture once. Sheila kept it in a dresser drawer. She mentioned him a few times in passing, and whenever she did, her eyes would glaze over. I can tell you this, though. They could've passed for brother and sister—they had the exact same cinnamon-toned skin, aquamarine eyes, and curly jet-black hair."

"I see," said CJ, noting the similarities. "So what triggered the fake car crash?" He scanned the parking lot, keeping an eye out for security.

"Ducane—I'm certain of it. One night after Sheila had sent me to the kind of sexual heights a man could only dream of, she told me she was going to have to disappear. Said someone she'd known several years back had resurfaced and brought her a world of difficulties. I begged her not to run, told her I'd stand by her no matter what. She laughed at me, called me a foolish white boy, and told me if I didn't help her stage that accident, both of us would be sorry. I thought if I helped her, there'd be a chance that I'd be able to get her to stick around, and that even if I couldn't right then, someway, someday, she'd come back." Watson's voice became a whisper. "That was a mistake."

"So you pulled off a plant?"

"That's exactly what Sheila called it—a plant. And just so you know, she's the one who lined everything up. The newspaper photographer, the writer, the semi, the driver, even the ambulance and the tow truck. I was never quite sure how she did it, but she did. And until right now, I thought she'd pulled it off without a glitch."

"She did one hell of a job. It took an earthquake to out her. So where'd she go after the phony crash?"

"I don't know. All I know is this." Watson swallowed with such force that his Adam's apple quivered. "When it was all said and done, she told me she was going to disappear into another world. One like mine. A world that would be lost and lonely and lily-white. And that if I ever came after her, she'd see to it that I only made that mistake once."

"And you never saw her again after that?"

"No. I took her at her word. I'd seen her handiwork, watched her make her own life disappear. I had no question that she could do the same thing for mine. She was connected to someone or something with enough juice to fuel a rocket." Watson cleared his throat, as if to clear a bad taste from his mouth, looked straight ahead, and said, "I did see her one other time, long after the wreck. Not in person, though, just her photograph. It must've been fifteen years ago now. I spotted her photograph in one of those weekly newspaper throwaways. The kind they fill with advertisements for carpet cleaning, trash hauling, and dentures on the cheap. I was in Boulder when I picked it up. I'd flipped through most of the paper while waiting for my wife to come out of a shoe store on the Pearl Street mall. A few pages from the end of the tabloid, I swore I saw a photograph of someone resembling Sheila. When I looked closer, I realized that without a doubt it was her. She looked older, of course, but there was no mistaking that face. She had a come-hither smile and was wearing a low-cut dress. When my wife came walking out of the store, my nose was within an inch of the newsprint—I could've licked the photo off the page. But as we walked to the car, I remembered Sheila's parting admonition to me all those years ago, and I thought, *Been there, done that.* I threw the paper in a trash can and never looked back."

CJ took a step back from the car. "So why was her picture in that weekly?"

"She was advertising for a bed and breakfast up in Poudre Canyon. The ad identified her as the place's manager. There's no way I could ever forget the name of the place—Peak to Peak Bed and Breakfast. She was using the name Lydia Krebs."

"So why didn't you go after her? She was only two and a half hours away by car."

"I've told you already. The lady could've made me disappear. Besides, I'm an aerospace engineer, Mr. Floyd, not some street tough or, God forbid, James Bond. When I err, it tends to be on the conservative side of things. The side that makes sense to an engineer, like putting a half-dozen backup systems into a moon rocket. Bottom line's this: I didn't want the pleasure boat that had become my life to get rocked, possibly even destroyed. What about you? Which side of the fence would you have come down on?"

"I don't know. But I can tell you this—I've never responded real well to threats, and that would've included one from Sheila Lucerne."

"So you would've gone after her?"

"I am going after her," CJ said with a confident smile.

Watson shook his head. "Bad choice. The better choice in my book would be to call Lieutenant Cavalaris."

"Could be you're right. But if I did, there's a chance I'd end up letting down a friend. And like you just pointed out, we live in a world where backup systems are important. Turns out I'm pretty much the only one my friend's got."

"Sheila's connected to people who could kill you, I'm certain of that."

"Think you're probably right."

"Then why go after her? That's why we pay the police."

CJ stepped farther away from the car and looked down at Watson. "The problem with the police, Mr. Watson, is that they move too slow, they posture too much, and they've never been real supporters of that friend I mentioned."

"Have it your way."

"Oh, I will," CJ said, turning to leave. "Like you, I'm afraid I'm a little too entrenched in my ways to have it any other." He touched the brim of his Stetson. "Thanks for the info. I'll see which side of the fence I land on." His footsteps echoed off the concrete as he walked away.

By the time he reached I-25 to head north for Poudre Canyon, CJ had used his cell phone to reserve a room at Peak to Peak Bed and Breakfast and a very nervous Carl Watson had called Lieutenant Gus Cavalaris to tell him about his parking-lot conversation with Floyd. Neither CJ nor Watson was aware that Cavalaris had been parked less than fifty yards away from them during their conversation, and CJ remained unaware that Cavalaris was now the same five car lengths behind the Bel Air that he'd been when they'd left CJ's Delaware Street office an hour and a half earlier.

Neither CJ nor Cavalaris had any idea that the man calling himself Napper had also latched on to the Bel Air, thinking as they all left Lockheed Martin that since the money was right and the opportunity ripe, he should probably take out Mario Satoni's boy before dispensing with Rollie Ornasetti.

A light drizzle was falling in Denver when the Rockies-Dodgers game—in which the Rockies had squeaked in a 2-1 win over Mario's beloved Dodgers on a bases-loaded tenth-inning pinch-hit homer—ended. Frustrated by the game's outcome, Mario found himself fidgeting with a photograph he kept on an end table next to the La-Z-Boy recliner in his TV room. The photograph, a favorite, had been taken at his wedding just as Mario, clad in a tux and looking dapper, and Angie, radiant as an angel, raised their arms to fend off a shower of rice as they ran from the doors of Denver's St. Catherine's Church toward a waiting limousine.

Mario eased back in the recliner and brought the photograph to his heart. Glancing across the dimly lit room, he said softly, "It's down to me and them, Angie. Got no choice in the matter. Sorry." Shaking his head, he picked up a cordless phone from a nearby TV tray and dialed Pinkie Niedemeyer. The conversation was at first informative, with Mario giving Pinkie a blow-by-blow on what had gone down during his FBI grilling, and Pinkie assuring Mario that he still had Damion Madrid's back.

Mario grunted, sat back in his chair, and said, "Stay on Maxie, Pinkie, and in a way he can understand. He knows more about what happened to Antoine Ducane than he's lettin' on."

"How hard you want me to lean on him?"

"As hard as you have to." Mario raised the photo from his chest and glanced at it.

Surprised by the order, Pinkie asked, "You hear what you're sayin' to me, Dominico?"

"Yeah."

"This ain't like you, Dominico. Callin' for a settlement. You sure you okay?"

"I'm fine."

"Okay. But mind tellin' me what's got your motor runnin'?"

"Fear, Pinkie—fear. That and maybe a little too much pride. I don't like bein' grilled by the FBI 'bout somethin' I didn't have nothin' to do with. I don't like folks dredgin' up a life I put behind me forty years ago, and I don't like people sayin' derogatory things 'bout my Angie. But most of all, I don't like havin' to ask you and CJ and Julie Madrid for help. Makes me feel tired and dried up. I don't have a lot of time left, Pinkie. And what I've got left, I wanna enjoy in peace. Before I let somebody take that away from me, I'll take a lot more than that back from them." He stroked the glass that covered the wedding photo. "So do what you have to to get Maxie to tell the truth about Ducane, and while you're at it, try and find out if he's the one that did in that old miner, McPherson. He'd damn sure be at the top of my list."

"All right, but I got a few needs to be met as well."

"Shoot."

"If I get Maxie to sing a tune that's to your likin', what's my take?"

"That debt you owe me becomes null and void."

"Sounds good to me. What about CJ and his people? They gonna know you called me on this?"

"No. I don't want them to ever have a glimpse of this side of me."

"So I can take Maxie out if need be?"

"That's what I said," Mario whispered, eyeing the wedding photo a final time before rising from his chair.

"I'll be in touch," said Pinkie.

"I'm here." Mario cradled the phone and headed toward the kitchen. His heart was thumping in his chest as if it were fifty years earlier, and his stomach began to churn as his body reacted to the fact that he'd just given Pinkie approval to kill a man.

Chapter 23

Ted's Place, a northern Colorado landmark and way station for travelers, sits at the junction of U.S. Highway 287 and Colorado Highway 14, where it has served as a convenience store, gathering place, and gateway to the wild and scenic Cache la Poudre River and rugged Poudre Canyon for more than eighty-five years.

CJ had made the drive from Lockheed Martin to Ted's Place in an hour and a half, clocking speeds in excess of ninety miles an hour. His rush to get to the Peak to Peak Bed and Breakfast was fueled by the knowledge that at nine o'clock the place closed. Julie, whom CJ had called for a little research help on Lucerne, had called back forty minutes into the drive to tell him that her quick computer check of tax records showed that Lucerne had quit-claimed a house in Denver's Bonnie Brae neighborhood to Carl Watson in late 1972. The only other information she'd been able to dig up on Lucerne was that she was originally from Monroe, Louisiana, and that before her vanishing act, she'd worked briefly as an office manager for a Denver trucking company.

By the time CJ pulled into Ted's Place for gas, what had been just a drizzle when he'd left Lockheed Martin was a hard, steady rain. In less than three minutes he refueled the Bel Air and headed for the barn-like convenience store to pay for his gas.

The lump that had settled in Gus Cavalaris's throat when he'd hit the northern outskirts of Denver four car lengths behind Floyd's Bel Air and realized that Floyd wasn't about to slow down had worked its way down into the pit of the veteran homicide lieutenant's stomach by the time he followed the Bel Air into Ted's Place. He had no idea where Floyd was headed, but he figured they wouldn't be traveling much longer because there wasn't much in the Poudre Canyon that CJ could be aiming for—the cattle-ranching community of Walden was the farthest likely point.

Realizing that he had sweated through his shirt, Cavalaris shook his head in amazement, surprised that he and Floyd hadn't been pulled over by the state highway patrol. As he parked his car at the gas-pump island farthest from the way station's convenience store, he suddenly found himself wondering what the stakeout team he'd assigned to Mario Satoni had come up with. Still queasy from the drive, he had the feeling that the team back in Denver had drawn the cushier assignment. When Floyd, who'd raced up the highway like a bat out of hell, had failed to return after five minutes inside the store, he decided he'd better go inside and have a look.

Napper pulled into the parking lot of Ted's Place with a smirk on his face and coasted to a stop one pump island away from Floyd's now unoccupied car and the other car that had been glued to Floyd's ass all the way up I-25 and 287. He stepped out of his vehicle into a gust of wind and rain and quickly jammed an ice pick into Cavalaris's right rear tire. "Cop rocket," he mumbled, slipping back into his vehicle and driving over to Floyd's car. Stepping out again into the wind and darkness, he looked around to make sure no one was watching, took a homing device out of his jacket pocket, knelt, and slapped the device onto the Bel Air's frame.

A barrel-chested man wearing coveralls greeted Cavalaris from behind a cash register that sat precariously on a U-shaped, linoleum-covered countertop. "Windy enough for you?"

Ignoring the question and looking around to see if Floyd had given him the slip, Cavalaris said, "N-n-need to use your restroom."

The man shrugged. "At the top of the steps, to the left."

As he headed for the restroom, Floyd rounded the corner. Cavalaris quickly turned his back and stepped into an aisle whose shelves were overflowing with fuel additives, candy, and videotapes. Out of the corner of his eye and thinking, *That was close*, he watched Floyd leave in a rush.

His vehicle now hidden from view by gas pumps, Napper watched Floyd get into his car and make a beeline for the parking lot's western exit. When he was certain that Floyd was headed up Poudre Canyon, he smiled, glanced back at the astonished-looking driver of the now flat-tired, unmarked police cruiser, and retook the road.

Satisfied that when the time came he'd be able to handle Floyd, he ran a probable timetable for doing just that through his head: thirty minutes for Floyd to drive up the canyon, forty-five minutes or so to handle his business, and thirty minutes to drive back down. An hour and forty-five minutes in all—two hours tops. That would give him plenty of time to work his magic and set up for the man who was running interference for Mario Satoni. He didn't give a rat's ass about snuffing some minor-league bail bondsman. Ornasetti and Satoni were the two people he'd been instructed to handle. But since he got paid by the body, and he'd been advised that it would be smart in the short run to ride herd on the man who'd in effect become Satoni's eyes and ears, he'd decided it was what he should do. Especially since Floyd was quite obviously headed for a rendezvous with Sheila Lucerne. A meeting that suggested that Floyd in all likelihood knew more than he should about Antoine Ducane.

State Highway 14 switchbacks its way from five thousand feet up a steep slope of Poudre Canyon piedmont to temporarily open up in the Laramie foothills, about twelve miles northwest of Ted's Place. The highway had been undergoing a recent facelift, and repaving and widening had taken place in several of the canyon's narrows.

In what was now a heavy downpour, CJ could see heavy construction equipment parked along the road. The heaviest concentration of equipment was parked in a staging area south of the Hewlett Gulch, where there was a trailhead that ultimately snaked its way to the river below.

Dropping into second gear and banking into a curve, CJ checked his watch. It was 8:35. Congratulating himself on making a record run—and in a rainstorm, no less—he felt a sudden sense of relief. There was no question now. He would reach Peak to Peak Bed and Breakfast well ahead of Sheila Lucerne's scheduled nine o'clock departure.

He wasn't quite certain how he would approach Lucerne—or Krebs—or whatever she was calling herself, and he realized he had only minutes to come up with a game plan. But as the Bel Air cut through darkness and rain, he told himself that was all the time he would need.

The downpour had slackened to a misty drizzle by the time he pulled into the empty parking lot that flanked the two-story, hand-hewn log-and-clapboard structure that was Peak to Peak Bed and Breakfast. Forced by the wind to hold his Stetson in place, he walked across the parking lot and through a blanket of fog. He mounted the isolated inn's four-inch-thick Douglas-fir steps at exactly a quarter to 9. A framed needlepoint sign tacked to the front door read, *Don't Mind Your Waders—We're Fly-Fisher Friendly*. Unable to find a door-bell, he simply knocked. Moments later, a cheerful-looking woman swung back the front door. "Mr. Floyd, I hope. I've been expecting you," she said without the barest hint of surprise at seeing a large black man sporting a Stetson at her front door.

"Sure am." CJ removed his Stetson and stomped the moisture off his boots.

"Welcome to Peak to Peak. I'm Lydia Krebs. Come in." There was a noticeable air of Southern hospitality in the woman's voice. When she said, "Let's get you registered," drawing out the word and rolling its r's in a way that matched Mavis Sundee's Baton Rouge–bred father's, CJ knew the woman calling herself Lydia Krebs had spent her share of time in Louisiana.

He followed the tall, stately Krebs down a narrow hallway to a desk at the end. When she turned back to face him, pen in hand, he could see why she'd been able to make the switch from being Cre-ole to being white. Her ivory-colored skin was flawless, with hardly a wrinkle, and although he suspected she had to be pushing seventy, she looked much closer to a woman of fifty-five. A flattering swath of silver hair highlighted her face, and her keen features and aquama-rine eyes signaled to anyone who might ponder her ethnicity, *White lady here, white lady here*.

Looking up at CJ, she said, "You didn't mention whether you'd be paying with a credit card or cash, Mr. Floyd."

"Neither one, I'm afraid."

Looking puzzled, Krebs said, "Those are the only forms of payment we accept. I'm afraid we don't take checks."

CJ cleared his throat and listened for the sounds that would indicate that other guests were in the house. Hearing nothing but the distant ticking of a grandfather clock and convinced by the empty parking lot that he and Krebs were alone, he said, "I'm afraid I'm here for more than fly fishing."

"I'm afraid I don't understand."

"I'm looking for a murderer, Ms. Krebs—or perhaps it's Ms. Lucerne," CJ said boldly. "And I have a feeling you're the key."

"I don't think I can help you in that department. To my knowledge, we've never had a murder up here. And for the record, the name is Krebs."

"I'll take your word for that, Ms. Krebs. But the murder I'm talking about happened a long way from here. The victim's name was Antoine Ducane." CJ eyed Krebs for a reaction. Her response was simply a stoic, dug-in look.

"Didn't know him."

"Funny. A former boyfriend of yours, Carl Watson, claims you did."

"He's mistaken."

"Hmmm. And I guess he's mistaken about you being Creole, and about your quit-claiming your house to him, faking your own death, and disappearing into the bowels of this canyon to turn up nice, right, and white." CJ paused and took a deep breath. "Watson says you threatened him when you ran. Now, why on earth would you do that?"

"You should probably leave, Mr. Floyd."

"Afraid I can't do that. At least, not until I have some answers."

"Answers to what?"

"Answers to what really happened to Antoine Ducane, and maybe even to why a friend of his, a man named Cornelius McPherson, was recently murdered."

"Never heard of McPherson. You sound like a cop, Mr. Floyd. Sure you aren't one?"

"Furthest thing from it. All I am is somebody trying to help out a friend."

"Must be some friend."

"His name's Mario Satoni."

"Don't know that name either."

CJ smiled. "Gotta hand it to you—you're tough. But maybe not as tough as you'll need to be for the problem at hand. Here's the bottom line, Ms. Lucerne, and some of this I'm sure you already know. Your boyfriend Ducane was more than likely tied to the JFK assassination, and he's probably dead because of that connection. Now, here's your problem. Denver's finest and the FBI have latched on to that fact. And so, perhaps, have other people. Count on this, Ms. Lucerne. Sooner or later somebody besides me will find you. If I were you, I'd think about picking my poison—the cops, the mob, or the FBI. I don't know which one you're running from—maybe all three— but if a half-petered-out old bail bondsman like me can track you up here, can those other folks be far behind?"

"I don't think you're nearly as petered-out as you claim, Mr. Floyd. But petered-out or not, you're free to leave. If you don't, I'm afraid I'll have to call the police."

Uncertain whether she was bluffing, CJ decided he'd made his point. He was alone with someone he'd just accused of being linked to at least two murders. He was unfamiliar with the layout of the building, and he was unarmed. For all he knew, Krebs might decide to drop him on the spot, leaving the cops nothing to investigate but the shooting of a late-night intruder. Donning his Stetson, he reached into his vest pocket, took out one of his business cards, and handed it to Lucerne. "I'm easy to contact. In case you change your mind, call me."

"I won't. And I won't. Change my mind or call you, that is." She tossed the card aside.

"Your choice," said CJ, pivoting to leave and thinking as he did that he would have to find another way to crack the protective armor of the recalcitrant Sheila Lucerne.

"Have a safe drive back down the canyon, Mr. Floyd, and please don't come back."

CJ walked back down the hall to leave Sheila Lucerne standing in the glare of an overhead light. As CJ closed the door behind him, she tried her best to look unconcerned, but she couldn't. After more than thirty years of disappearing into the rock face of a canyon and changing the very essence of who she was, she realized she might have to reinvent herself again.

The cell-phone reception in Poudre Canyon was episodic, but after a dozen speed-dial calls to Flora Jean while navigating the canyon in fog so thick he could barely see fifteen feet in front of him, CJ finally got through. "I'm headed down Poudre Canyon," he said in response to Flora Jean's "Where the hell are you?" "Can't see a damn thing up here. It's as bad as the morning mist off the Mekong River we used to get back in 'Nam. Hope it's better once I get to Ted's Place."

Realizing that CJ, a man prone to understatement, must have his hands full, Flora Jean said, "If it's that bad, maybe you should call me back, sugar."

"Nah, I'm talking on a hands-free. This won't take but a second anyway. I ran into a dead end with that woman I told you about, Sheila Lucerne. She stonewalled me. I need some ammo that'll give me a second shot at her, and soon. I wouldn't put it past her to run."

"I'm listening."

"Can you add a look-see at Lucerne to that laundry list of things you've got Alden checking into?"

"Don't see why not. When I left his place about an hour ago, the man woulda done anything I asked him." Flora Jean suppressed a snicker.

Aware that the torrid love affair between former marine Sergeant Flora Jean Benson and onetime General Alden Grace continued to boil—an affair that had started, against all the rules of military conduct, when they'd served together during Desert Storm—CJ simply chuckled. "What did Alden have to say about a possible new take on the JFK assassination? Did he know anything about Ducane? What about Marcello and Trafficante? Had he ever heard of Cassias?"

"Would you cool your jets, CJ, and slow down for a minute?"

"Sorry, Flora Jean, but I think we might have stumbled across something that could put a new twist on history." He drew a deep, reflective breath. "I wasn't but nine years old when JFK was killed, but I can recall nearly everything about the shooting and the death shroud that killing draped over the country back then. The assassination seemed to hit a little heavier in the black community than most. I'm afraid way too many black folks saw JFK as their salvation. I was in school when it happened, and I can still remember my gym teacher, a bowlegged former Florida A&M linebacker and World War II veteran, crying.

"They let us out of school early that day to go home, and as I turned onto Delaware Street on my bicycle, I realized my Uncle Ike had draped a black tablecloth across the front-porch banister. When I dropped my bike in the driveway and walked up the front steps of the house, Ike met me. Eyeing the tablecloth, he announced in a voice as sad as I'd ever heard, 'It's the biggest thing I had in the house that was black.' He walked back inside without saying another word, and like most of America he spent the next week in mourning."

"Sounds like that assassination had a hell of an effect on him."

"And me too, I suspect," said CJ, peering into a new fog bank and slowing down to less than ten miles an hour. "In less than eight years Martin Luther King and Bobby Kennedy would be dead, and I'd be on my way to Vietnam. Somehow it always seemed to me that the JFK killing opened the floodgates on America, and we're still trying to dog-paddle our way back upstream. Maybe if I can shed just a little bit of truth on that killing, those waters might calm down, temporarily at least." Forcing back a sigh, CJ said, "So anyway, what's Alden's take?"

"It's an interestin' one, I can tell you that. While I was whippin' him up that pepper steak he likes so much and lubricatin' us both with enough wine to cut our cholesterol in half for the year, Alden made half-a-dozen calls to old intelligence contacts. Folks he knew before I ever met him. And except for one lead, he came up with nothin'. Said his friends all got real nervous when he brought up the JFK assassination. Almost to a man, he said they told him that everything concernin' the JFK killin' has already been dealt with, and most of the info's either already out in the public domain, like CIA documents, police documents, the House Select Committee on Assassinations' report, the Church Committee report, and the Warren Commission report, or it's locked down tighter than a drum for the next fifty years."

"So what's the one thread he found?" CJ slowed the Bel Air to a near stop as a rolling bank of fog enveloped the car.

"Carlos Marcello. Seems the long-deceased Louisiana don had his paws into our sweet state in a couple of the strangest ways. Back in the 1960s, before César Chávez got the United Farm Workers movement rollin', the farsighted Mr. Marcello, seein' an opportunity to line up an army of workers whose wages he could tap for union dues and whose votes he could count on to swing elections, tried his best to get farm workers here in the good old Centennial State to line up under the Teamsters' umbrella."

"What?"

"You heard me. The Teamsters."

"Now, that's a stretch."

"I said the same thing. But Alden didn't think it was all that unusual. Especially since the Teamsters and our nation's truckers move the lion's share of America's goods, including Colorado's Western Slope peaches and its Arkansas Valley cantaloupes."

"I damn sure would've missed the connection. Did Marcello succeed?"

"Nope. Chávez was too nimble for him, and on top of that, Chávez spoke the right language. But here's a bone for you. Alden claims that if Marcello was stretchin' his tentacles this far west, it's possible that Ducane just mighta been runnin' interference for him. Servin' as sort of a forward guard for whatever kinda graft and corruption opportunities might open up in Colorado down the road. Ducane was a mine worker, after all, and if memory serves me right, John L. Lewis's boys always had more than a tinge of mob-connected corruption tagged to them. That means to me that Ducane havin' a link to the Teamsters wouldn't be such a stretch."

"Makes sense. Can Alden get us any more info?"

"What was that? I can hardly hear you."

"Can Alden get us more information?"

"Oh. Gotcha. He's tryin'. But he says that in order to loosen up his contact's lips, we're gonna need to provide him somethin' more concrete."

"Tell him I'm trying, and to stay on it. And if he finds out anything else that might help us figure out what really happened to Ducane, or for that matter JFK, have him pass it along." Tapping his brakes, CJ hollered, "Damn!"

"What's the matter?"

"Can't really tell. Somethin's blockin' the road up ahead. Looks like either a tree or a telephone pole. I'll call you back when I'm around it."

"Okay, but take it slow, sugar."

"Can't go any slower; I'm stopped. Talk to you later." Flipping his cell phone closed, CJ turned up his jacket collar, opened the car door, and stepped out into blackness.

Chapter 24

The wind was gusting at close to forty miles an hour, and it was raining sideways when CJ stepped away from the Bel Air. He could barely see the shoulder as he walked in the glare of the idling car's headlights and down a 5 percent grade, hoping to see what was blocking the road. All he could really make out were the undulating shapes of heavy equipment parked along the Poudre River side of the highway. The sight let him know that he was back to Hewlett Gulch, and that Ted's Place was only a few minutes away. When he realized what was blocking the highway, he mumbled, "Shit." A tree trunk, three feet in diameter, rested all the way across the highway. It extended beyond the shoulder over the fifty-foot drop-off to the river below like some bizarre diving platform.

As he walked along the length of the trunk, wondering where it had come from, he heard a diesel motor rev. He turned to see a road grader bearing down on him.

Recognizing he'd been set up, CJ sprinted for the Bel Air, hoping to get to the glove compartment and his .44. A couple of strides later he heard the report of a pistol and the thud of bullets slamming into the canyon wall. The grader's blade was almost on top of him when he dove headfirst along the rain-slicked highway and beneath the front bumper of the Bel Air.

As he crawled beneath the undercarriage toward the rear of the car, the road grader's engine slipped to idle. The grader's headlights had the roadway around the Bel Air lit up like daylight, and he had no idea why the grader had stopped instead of simply plowing him and the Bel Air into the canyon wall. Feeling strangely reflective, as if somehow he'd dropped through a hole in the universe and was somehow back in Vietnam on one more river-patrol mission, CJ was having second thoughts about going for his .44 when it hit him that there was another, more accessible gun in the Bel Air.

When his shoulder grazed the sizzling-hot muffler, he jerked his arm away and mumbled, "Shit!" A pocket-calculator-sized object fell from the undercarriage as he lowered his shoulder. He fumbled with it for a second before he realized that it was a homing device. Aware now of how the road grader's operator had been able to pinpoint where he would be and when, he shook his head disgustedly.

The weapon he was after was in the Bel Air's trunk. Grasping the rear bumper, he slid from beneath the car and peered around a rear taillight. The grader's operator, caught in the glare of the massive machine's headlights, was on foot, and headed for the Bel Air, a gun in each hand. He was dressed in black, wearing a hooded sweatshirt, Levi's, and muddy high-topped sneakers. The hood was pulled tightly around his head, and all CJ could make out was that the man was white.

Aware that he couldn't wait much longer or the killer would be on top of him, CJ popped the trunk and patted along the floor of the trunk for one of the flare guns inside. As he grabbed the first one, several shots rang out, and a bullet pierced the trunk lid. Rising from his squat just enough to be able to see his hooded assailant, he waited. The man was ten feet away when CJ took aim and pulled the flare gun's trigger.

The flare caught the man in the neck, knocking him off balance as CJ prepared to charge him. CJ had barely taken a step when a shot rang out, and the Bel Air's left front headlight exploded. Startled, he heard someone scream, "Floyd! Stay down!"

He dropped to his knees and hunched against the Bel Air's rear bumper. Half-a-dozen gunshots exploded around him, and then, except for the loud hum of the road grader's engine, there was silence. An eerie silence that was finally broken by the sound of footfalls on the pavement and the rushing sound of dirt sliding.

Deciding it was now or never, CJ duck-walked his way along the canyon wall, reached the Bel Air's front door, swung the door open far enough to wedge his shoulders inside, opened the glove compartment, and grabbed his .44. He poked his head above the hood to see someone with their back turned to him standing next to the fallen tree and peering down over the drop-off toward the river below. There was a gun in the person's right hand.

"Stay fuckin' put!" CJ screamed. Stretching both arms out across the Bel Air's hood, he aimed the .44's muzzle squarely at the person's back. "I've got somethin' here that'll take you right over the edge of that cliff if you so much as shiver. Now, drop that piece you're holding and turn around."

The man dropped the 9-mm he was holding into the dirt.

"Turn!" CJ yelled. The muscles in his face went slack when CJ realized the man he had his .44 trained on—the man who had obviously screamed for him to stay down when it counted—was a very puzzled-looking Gus Cavalaris.

It's a wise rabbit with more than one hole, Napper kept telling himself as, flashlight in hand, he worked his way along a rock ledge twenty-

five feet above the Poudre River. Without hesitation, he'd jumped
in near darkness onto a ledge that was fifteen feet below the shoulder of Highway 14 and doused his flashlight. The ledge would take
him back to where he'd parked his SUV in a thicket of sagebrush
and thistle half an hour earlier. It was there that he'd run across a
cache of heavy equipment and the backhoe he'd used to move the
tree that had stopped Floyd in his tracks. He'd originally planned to
take his shots at the nosy bail bondsman when he came out of a series
of S-curves just above Hewlett Gulch, or to jam the bondsman's car
into the south canyon wall using a road grader. That, however, would
have required shooting at a moving target in the dark, or sifting
through wreckage and very likely a mangled body to see if the bondsman was carrying anything of importance that he might have gotten from Sheila Lucerne. Blocking the highway with a tree in order
to get a better shot and an intact body had seemed like a better idea,
but unfortunately, the plan hadn't panned out.

Concerned now about taking a misstep that would send him plunging to certain death, he could still hear voices from above him on
the highway.

"I don't see him anywhere," he heard someone call out. Uncertain
whether it was the voice of the bail bondsman or the person who'd
come to Floyd's aid, Napper continued sidestepping his way toward
safety in the darkness. "Son of a bitch just vanished," he heard someone yell. He had the urge to scream, *I jumped*, but instead continued
maneuvering his way along the ledge until he reached the end. As
he started uphill toward his SUV, aware that the half-cocked young
people who now played the game he'd been playing for decades never
would've considered a back-door plan, he couldn't help but smile.

As he worked his way up a twenty-foot embankment toward level ground and his vehicle, his flashlight went out. "Low bid," he mumbled, shaking his head. Stumbling along in darkness, he heard the wail of a siren in the distance. Moments later, winded and soaking wet, he reached his SUV, slipped inside, cranked the engine, and, running with his lights out, eased down the path the SUV had cut in the canyon plateau's native grasses on his drive in from the highway. Glancing in the direction of the siren, he said, "Too late," as he turned onto the highway. Snapping on his headlights, he yelled, "I'm gone!"

Ron Else stood at the corner of Glenarm Place on downtown Denver's Sixteenth Street Mall, just across the street from the city's famed Paramount Theatre, trying to decide whether the information he'd just paid an informant $500 for had been worth the price. He'd chosen the location to meet the blockheaded man with massive clumps of hair missing from his head for no other reason than the fact that it was 100 percent public. The informant had appeared out of the 11:30 darkness to inform Else that the Antoine Ducane investigation had certain people in New Orleans and Miami very nervous.

That news alone wouldn't have been worth a dime to him. He already knew that any investigation with the potential for shedding new light on the JFK assassination would cause more than a few ripples.

What, however, was worth something, he reminded himself as he watched a group of six teenage goths, dressed head to toe in black, stroll across the Sixteenth Street Mall's shuttle-bus lanes toward the Paramount, giggling and whispering obscenities, was that the informant had told him that if he wanted to strike pay dirt on the Ducane killing, he should spend more time looking at Rollie Ornasetti and less time jamming up Mario Satoni. Uncertain how the informant knew he'd been leaning on Satoni, he'd asked the man, "Why Ornasetti?"

The informant's response had been, "Because way back when, Ducane cost Ornasetti a long stretch of money." It was that response that suddenly had him worried.

Before he could ask any more questions, the man had said, "Don't ask me no more, 'cause I don't know no more, and if I did, it wouldn't be worth the money. Always preferred livin' to dyin'."

Deciding that he'd gotten what he'd come for, Else had given the man five $100 bills and watched him disappear into what had grown to a throng of more than two dozen mall-walking goths.

Glancing at his watch and realizing that it was almost midnight, he decided he might as well cruise by Ornasetti's townhouse and office complex in Denver's trendy LoDo district and familiarize himself with its stakeout and take down possibilities. As he headed to where he'd parked his car, he knew he'd now be able to better point his efforts in the right direction.

CJ and Gus Cavalaris sat eye to eye across the table from one another, drinking coffee in a cramped booth near the front door of Ted's Place. Both men were well aware that any chance they might have of putting a face on CJ's shooter was being washed away by the rain. There had been crime-scene evidence for Cavalaris or the Larimer County sheriff to inspect: two bullet holes in the Bel Air's trunk lid, two slugs from a .38 Magnum, the Bel Air's shattered front headlight, a maze of footprints—CJ's, the shooter's, and Cavalaris's—an idling road grader, and the homing device CJ had found. But that didn't tell them who CJ's would-be assassin had been.

Even though a half-dozen people had run up against the barricade on Highway 14 and had reported the fallen-tree hazard with a 911 call before turning around to head back down the canyon, none had reported seeing anything else out of the ordinary. Even so, CJ understood very well that his shooter had to be knowledgeable enough about heavy equipment to have maneuvered a fallen tree across the highway, especially in the poor weather conditions. Knowing that fact but unable to capitalize on it, the sheriff had wrapped up his preliminary investigation of the crime scene with a promise to come back in the morning at first light, but neither CJ nor Cavalaris was expecting much to come of that visit.

"You w-w-want another hit of coffee?" Cavalaris asked, glancing down at the notes he'd jotted into a waterlogged notebook.

"Nope. I'm done," said CJ, still trying to make sense of the evening's events.

"Hope you're also done with s-s-sticking your n-n-nose into police business." Cavalaris slipped a pen out of his shirt pocket and tapped it on the crinkled page of his notebook. Surprising CJ, he said, "S-s-so this is what we've got. A woman named Sheila Lucerne, who you claim very likely knows why D-d-ducane died, and m-m-maybe even more. A pr-pr-professional killer who probably murdered McPherson, and from the looks of it has now decided to latch on to you, and one otherwise small-time mafia don named Rollie Ornasetti who's been in over his head in this th-th-thing from the beginning. Have I covered everything?"

Puzzled as to why Cavalaris had suddenly opened up to him, CJ nodded and said, "Yeah."

"Y-y-you look confused, Floyd."

"I am."

"Why?"

CJ shrugged. "Never had a cop—one who was thinking right, at least—include me in their strategizing."

Cavalaris smiled. "And you wouldn't n-n-now if it weren't for a couple of real p-p-pertinent things."

"Which are?"

"First off, the McPherson killing took place on my b-b-beat. It's my case, and I take all my cases personally. Besides, there's a l-l-lot more to the Ducane and McPherson killings than a couple of onetime miners buying the farm. This thing's gonna turn out to be a whole universe bigger than y-y-you and m-m-me, Floyd."

"And your second reason?"

The muscles in Cavalaris's face tightened. "You ever been made fun of, Floyd?"

"Who hasn't?"

"How'd you d-d-deal with it?"

"Shrugged it off, for the most part."

"G-g-good answer, because that's just what I've been d-d-doing all my life. Easy enough of course to f-f-figure out why." Cavalaris looked directly into CJ's eyes. "Any idea what it took for me to make police lieutenant?"

"A lot of hard work, no doubt."

"I wish." Cavalaris looked away and stared into space. "H-h-hard work was only a tiny fraction of the d-d-drill. I had to pass a psychological p-p-profile and reasoning test, not just once or twice but a h-h-half-dozen times. And reading comprehension and simulated situation tests out the g-g-gazoo just to prove that I wouldn't screw up a case and let some mass murderer with a bloody ax in his hand and a dead man at his feet walk because the ax man's lawyer claimed his client couldn't understand what I was s-s-saying when I read him his rights."

"You obviously jumped through the hoops."

Cavalaris nodded and smiled. "I d-d-did just that. Mostly with the help of a police academy classmate of mine who happened to under-stand the problem of r-r-running a race where the other guy's got half a football field head start. Problem is, all that hoop jumping has t-t-taken its toll on me. So in between jumps, I've m-m-made myself a few promises. One of those promises has been to never help the a-a-arrogant self-absorbed assholes I know lack the c-c-capacity to walk a mile in another man's shoes. And in my world that includes l-l-lots of folks with shiny b-b-badges and fancy titles."

CJ took a long, slow sip of coffee. "Agent Else, for instance?"

Cavalaris simply nodded.

"I understand your take, Lieutenant, and believe me, I know what it's like to be on the outside looking in. But if you're looking for somebody outside that boys-in-blue club you belong to to help you out, why pick me?"

"D-d-don't really know. B-b-been asking myself that all evening. Let's just say I like your tenacity. It's a lot like that classmate of mine. But to be truthful, right now I've got n-n-nowhere else to turn. It's you or an FBI agent who cuts against my grain. Else could have me out of his hair in the blink of an eye. All he has to do is turn the right screw. I either go with him or I go with you, and g-g-going with him's not an option."

"It's your career, man. But I'd think a decision like that over long and hard."

"Oh, I h-h-have. Over and o-o-over, and every time I get to the point that I'm about to play ball with Else, I end up with this i-i-image of him staring down at me and laughing."

"Fine by me. Like I said, it's your career. But I need to get some-thing outta this arrangement too."

"Shoot."

"Lay off Mario," CJ said bluntly. "He's eighty-two years old, and he's wearing down. He didn't kill Ducane or McPherson, and he damn sure didn't have anything to do with the JFK assassination."

"You're p-p-positive about that?"

"As positive as you are that that police academy classmate of yours is the one big reason you made it over the hump. Mario did the same thing for me once, helped me over the hump. Just after I'd lost almost everything I owned in a business venture that went south. I owe him."

"Like I said, sometimes enlightenment requires walking in another man's shoes. I'll do my b-b-best."

There was a long silence as the two men took long sips of coffee. "So where do we go from here?" CJ asked finally.

Cavalaris, who seemed to have already thought through at least a rudimentary strategy, said, "Since b-b-both you and the sheriff here confirmed that Lucerne has left that bed and breakfast she manages for the night, I'll have to wait and have my talk with her tomorrow. After that I go see Ornasetti."

"And my job is?"

"Your j-j-job is to talk to Satoni. F-f-find out if he knows or remembers anything special about Ducane. And while you're at it, ask him if he's aware of any, uh, h-h-hit men who happen to know their way around heavy equipment. In other words, scratch the dirt for anything we might've overlooked."

"And Mario gets a pass," said CJ, determined to pin Cavalaris down on the issue.

"He does from me. I can't s-s-speak for Else or his FBI crew."

"Okay," said CJ, feeling a twinge of guilt over withholding information about Sheila Lucerne from Cavalaris.

"We're set, then," said Cavalaris, reaching for his wallet. "I-I-I've got the coffee."

"Thanks," CJ said. Wondering as they rose to leave whether he could really trust a cop, CJ was convinced that Cavalaris was wondering the same thing about him.

Proud that he and his attorney had stonewalled Mr. Ronald T. Else, the insipid FBI agent who'd hauled him in for a two-hour midday interrogation, Rollie Ornasetti had spent the rest of the day gloating, smoothing things over with Carmine Cassias, and trying unsuccessfully to locate Randall Maxie. As a last resort, he'd called the sexy little Latina he knew Maxie was poking. All he'd gotten was a cheerful message on her answering machine saying that she wasn't in. When he'd mentioned Else's escalating probe into the JFK assassination during the second of two calls to Cassias, he'd been told to keep his mouth shut.

It was close to 1:30 a.m. when Ornasetti pulled his BMW into the parking lot beneath his Lower Downtown Denver townhouse and office. After enjoying an evening at his favorite jazz club, Dazzle, he was drifting along on a margarita-induced buzz and feeling no pain. Easing into his parking stall, he shut down the engine and opened the door to get out. He'd barely taken a step toward the elevator when, still dressed head to toe in black, Napper stepped out from behind a concrete support beam, looped a choke wire around Ornasetti's neck, and tightened it until, gasping for air and with his fingers clawing at the wire, Ornasetti dropped to his knees, unconscious. A few droplets of blood, the result of his clawing and the noose breaking skin, splattered onto the floor as Ornasetti slumped to the concrete.

Looking around to make certain he hadn't been seen, Napper slipped a syringe and a set of handcuffs out of his pocket. He jammed the needle into Ornasetti's forearm and muttered, "Pleasant dreams," before handcuffing the now slobbering mobster. Reaching into his pocket, Napper pressed the trunk-lid remote button on his car keys, checked to make certain Ornasetti was still breathing, slipped his hands under Ornasetti's arms, and began dragging him toward his own vehicle.

He hadn't exactly followed Cassias's orders to kill Ornasetti. But what did that matter? Cassias's orders had been preempted, and pre-emps were a way of life in his world. Lifting Ornasetti by his belt and shirt collar, he bulldogged the Denver don up onto the car bumper and into the trunk. In a final effort, he looped Ornasetti's legs into the trunk, took a short breather, closed the trunk lid, and called it a day.

"So, who's the group?" Damion asked, swaying to the beat as the Coasters broke into their classic 1950s hit "Yakety Yak." Damion and his girlfriend, Niki Estaban, had been listening to old R&B tunes, Damion's musical passion, and playing a game of name-that-record-artist to the point that Niki was bored.

"I don't know, Damion. It was before my time."

"It's the Coasters. You've gotta try harder, Niki."

"Okay, okay. But I'm pooped, just like your mother. In case you missed it, she waved the white flag and headed for bed an hour ago. Game's over, Damion. You win."

Realizing he'd driven both his mother and Niki to the point of frustration, Damion frowned, shook his head as if to say, *I've done it again,* and said, "All right."

Recognizing that she'd offended him, Niki jumped out of her chair, rushed to Damion's side, kissed him on the cheek, and whispered, "Just try being a little less competitive. It'll do you good, Blood."

Damion smiled and mulled over the fact that it was as much his competitiveness as anything else that had saved his life at the Pawnee grasslands. Even so, he knew Niki was right. He needed to strap a governor on his overwhelming need to win. "Let's call it a night." He slipped an arm around Niki's waist and eyed her quizzically.

"Something wrong?"

"Nope. Just thinking about the future."

Niki smiled. "Ours, I hope."

"Ours, mine, yours, my mother's. I wonder if I'm really cut out to be a doctor."

"Come on, Damion. Shandell says that's all you've ever talked about becoming since the third grade."

"People change."

Looking him squarely in the eye, Niki said, "You're tired, Damion. I can see it in your eyes. People's thoughts turn crooked when they're tired. Let's call it a night."

Damion winked and slipped his hand down onto Niki's hip.

"No, you don't, Damion Madrid," she said, her response clearly meant to tease. "Your mother's a criminal lawyer. I don't want her coming after me for orchestrating a late-night seduction of her son. Besides, I'm tired, babe. You all right with that?"

Damion nodded and kissed Niki softly on the lips. "And she's a hell of a good one at that. Who knows, maybe I should give the legal profession some thought."

Niki smiled and squeezed Damion's hand supportively. "Wouldn't hurt, Blood. Wouldn't hurt one bit."

"I made a bad choice. You ever done that?" Napper said to Carmine Cassias. Frowning and shaking his head, he shifted his weight to the back of the unstable toilet seat he was seated on and switched his cell phone from his right hand to his left. Fifteen minutes earlier he had checked into a $29-a-night motel on the outskirts of Denver. The bathroom had turned out to be the most livable space in the filthy, foul-smelling room he'd been given.

"A real bad choice," Cassias said, disapproval ringing in his voice.

"You should've dealt with Lucerne first. Why the shit would you go after some bail bondsman who's peripheral to every fuckin' thing?"

"I thought Lucerne might've told him somethin'. Spilled her guts to him about what she may have known about the Ducane killing. I knew I could always come back and deal with her. I wasn't so certain about him."

"Well, you fucked up, Einstein. Now we've got ourselves three loose cannons to deal with—Willette Ducane, Ornasetti, and your bail bondsman."

Napper, dressed in a white T-shirt and baggy, coffee-stained boxers, glanced across the narrow strip of carpet that separated him from the bathtub. Inside the tub, and looking like a corpse, a thoroughly drugged Rollie Ornasetti sat propped up. "I'll deal with them," Napper said, eyes locked on Ornasetti.

"You bet you will, and fast. Have you been able to get a line on Willette Ducane?"

"No, but she's here. Got confirmation that she came in on a flight out of Dallas yesterday. I'll find her."

"What about Ornasetti?"

"No problem there," Napper said, smiling.

"You sound awful sure of yourself for someone who just bought himself a whole set of problems. Just remember, I'm one of the few people around who can still yank your chain, my friend. Tell people your whole foggy history, let 'em in on who the hell you really are."

"You wouldn't want to do that," said Napper, his tone meant to be searing.

Cassias laughed. "You threatenin' me, smartass?"

"No."

"Good. 'Cause I've got shit on you that's a whole shit-stained roll of toilet paper long."

With his eyes still locked on Ornasetti and his jaw muscles twitching, Napper held the phone out in front of him at arm's length and shook his head as he tried to calm himself. Speaking in a whisper, he said, "Wouldn't be smart."

"What was that?"

"Nothin'."

"Didn't think I heard anything," said Cassias, sitting up in bed, and eyeing the wall-mounted antique school clock in front of him. "Just do what we agreed on. You got that?"

"That's what you're payin' me for."

"You're right," Cassias said authoritatively. "Call me back when you've got better news. Later." He cradled the phone, let out a sigh, slipped out of bed, and headed for the kitchen, hoping a glass of orange juice would help settle his nerves.

Rubbing his hands together as if to warm them, Napper remained seated. He stared at Ornasetti, who'd begun to drool and wheeze. "Hope you're a good negotiator," Napper said, as if he somehow expected Ornasetti to respond. "'Cause you're sure as hell are gonna need to be one."

Rising from the toilet seat, he dusted off the back of his boxers and walked back into the darkened motel room, clutching his cell phone. He could hear the sound of eighteen-wheelers thumping along the industrial highway outside. By his calculation, he had twenty-four hours, maybe thirty-six tops, to handle his problems. If he didn't settle them in that time, he'd have more than Cassias, Willette Ducane, some jig of a bail bondsman, and third-tier mafia don Rollie Ornasetti to deal with. He'd have his own life to worry about.

As he stretched out on the bed to think, a mournful groan erupted from the bathroom. The sound told him Ornasetti was drifting back into the real world. Shaking his head and mumbling, "Shit," he reached down, slipped a large, cumbersome phone out of a tooled leather case that sat on the floor next to the bed, and dialed ten quick numbers. The response he got was a busy signal, the signal that the rest of the world recognized as a reason to hang up. His response, however, was to steady his nerves and immediately begin talking.

CJ and Pinkie Niedemeyer met at the same place they usually did when they had business to discuss—Denver's High Line Canal. It was close to 2 a.m. and drizzling when Pinkie, speaking in a whisper as they stood on the earthen shoulder of the sixty-six-mile-long artificial waterway that snaked through the Mile High City, said, "I'm tellin' you, I don't think it was Maxie who took out that guy McPherson. Mario's had me checkin' on who mighta popped the guy, just to make certain fingers don't start pointin' his way, and you know what? My contacts say it wasn't Maxie. And I gotta agree. Drive-bys ain't Maxie's style. He's always been more inventive, less in-your-face, if you know what I mean. Like that stunt he tried to pull off up at the Pawnee grasslands. Now, that's Maxie."

"Then who the heck killed McPherson?" asked CJ.

"Beats me."

CJ stared out into the misty haze, slipped a cheroot out of his pocket, lit up, and took a long drag. "Think maybe that Watson guy I told you about could've dialed up the McPherson killing? Nobody saw the shooter's car but him. Maybe Watson lied."

"Possibly. But if he did, he woulda more than likely pulled some gang-banger off the street to pop McPherson. And from what the cops and everybody else is sayin', the job went down way too professional for that."

"Then I'm stumped." CJ tapped a bullet of ash from his cheroot.

"Makes two of us," said Pinkie. "Let's forget about McPherson for a sec. What's your game plan for dealin' with that Lucerne woman you mentioned and the shooter somebody's got doggin' your ass?"

"I think I'll give Lucerne a little more time to think things over before I contact her again. My guess is, right now she's busy trying to decide whether to run or not. I'm thinking she'll stay put because this time around, I don't think she's got anybody to help her disappear. Whoever helped her out before would more than likely kill her on a second go-round."

Pinkie nodded. "That's the way they do it in my neighborhood."

CJ dropped his half-smoked cheroot onto the canal's equestrian path and stubbed it out with the heel of his boot. "You got Mario covered?"

"Got somebody watchin' him right now. He'd be real unhappy with me if he knew that, though. Thinks he's twenty-two instead of eighty-two. Better fill you in on somethin'."

"What's that?"

"Mario gave me the okay to settle up with Maxie if need be."

"*What?*"

"He told me I could settle. He ain't Santa Claus, for God's sake, CJ. In case you forgot, he was head of a family once. And he's nervous. Thinks maybe Maxie has orders from Rollie to take him out. He's gotta protect himself."

"How the hell does he expect me and Julie to keep him out of jail if he's out there acting like it's fifty years ago?"

"He's a proud man, CJ. And believe me, he ain't never forgot what it's like to give orders."

"Well, would you please ask him to bank those smoldering coals?"

"I'll do what I can."

"Afraid you'll have to do more, Pinkie. Otherwise Mario's gonna turn the clock back. We both know he's that stubborn. I've been thinking about how Maxie's tangled up in this Ducane, McPherson, JFK mess all day long. That story he told you and Damion about Ducane extorting money from Ornasetti for all those years after the JFK assassination is only the tip of the iceberg. I'm sure of it. Right now we need to see the whole damn thing. You're gonna have to have a talk with him, Pinkie. There's no other way."

Pinkie smiled. He was a dog with a bone.

"I know what you're thinking, Pinkie, but whatever you do, and regardless of Mario's okay, don't push it to the point of no return."

"I'll be gentle."

"You do that," said CJ, suppressing the strange urge to remind someone who was a hit man that there was a fine line between a kill and a near kill.

"You got any more business for me to attend to?"

"No. Just keep me up to speed on Maxie."

"Will do," Pinkie flashed a confident smile. It was the kind of smile CJ remembered seeing on the faces of more than a few American soldiers and sailors who'd lost their humanity in Vietnam, and the lead-in to CJ's fitful night of sleep.

Ashen-faced, Willette Ducane arrived at the Peak to Peak Bed and Breakfast a little after 8 a.m. She'd never had occasion to drive in the mountains, and the trip up Poudre Canyon along a road rife with hairpin curves and storm-generated rock slides had her palms sweating and her heart beating full bore.

As she stepped out of her rental car into the crisp mountain air, she thought about whether or not to carry the .38 police special she'd purchased at a gun shop in Boulder the previous afternoon. Deciding that's what she would do under the circumstances if she were back in New Iberia, she leaned back into the car, swept the .38 off the front seat into her oversized purse, and headed for the front door of the bed and breakfast.

Entering the building without knocking, she stood briefly in the entryway listening to the sounds of people talking and silverware clanking. Tightening her purse strap on her shoulder, she limped down the hallway until she reached an open archway. Beyond the archway was a room filled with five linen-draped tables and nearly a dozen people.

When Sheila Lucerne looked up, coffee pot in hand, to see Willette enter the room, she smiled confidently. "Can I help you?"

"Sorry to interrupt," said Willette, as every eye in the room gravitated to her. "I have a reservation."

"For breakfast or lodging?"

"Lodging. I called yesterday for a reservation. It should be under the name Ann Reed."

"Certainly. I'm Lydia." The name rolled off Sheila's tongue as if she'd been born with it. "I'll be with you shortly," she said, filling a balding man's cup with coffee. "Why don't you sign the guest book up by the front door and take your key out of one of the slots above the book? You're in number eight."

"Thanks. I'll settle on in, then." Willette turned to head for the guest register as a pimple-faced teenage girl clutching plates in both hands rushed past her.

As the girl entered the dining room, Willette heard Lydia say,

"Right on time," stringing out the words in a drawl that had unquestionably been honed in her neck of the woods.

Except for a couple from Iowa standing in the hallway, getting directions to Fort Collins from Sheila, the bed and breakfast had cleared out by the time Willette reappeared after settling into her room.

"You can't miss it; it's a red-brick building on the right just before you get to the downtown bypass," Sheila said to the bearded Iowan. "There'll be saddles and tack in the window."

The man thanked her and headed for the door with his wife in tow.

Wiping her brow and exhaling, Sheila turned to face Willette. "Morning rush. Thank God it's over. You'd think people wouldn't be able to find us up in this canyon, but my, my, how they do."

"Means you must offer somethin' real special."

"I'd like to think so. Sorry I couldn't really help you when you came in," Sheila said apologetically. "But I had my hands full. Are you all settled?"

"Yep. Your young helper took my money, signed me in, and showed me to my room."

"Emily's a gem." Sheila dusted off her hands and removed the apron she was wearing. "So what's your agenda for the day, Ms. Reed?"

Willette, who'd thought long and hard about how to broach the subject of why she was there, reached into her purse, slipped out the now badly dog-eared FedEx envelope that had contained the *Denver Post* press clipping about Damion's remains being found, and, looking Sheila squarely in the eye, said, "Need to know if you sent this." She handed the envelope to Sheila. "It's got your FedEx account number on it."

Caught off guard and looking every bit of it, Sheila took the envelope. "I'm not sure."

"Well, take a good look, sweetie. Especially since you told me on the phone just yesterday that you handle every bit of the FedEx business for this place."

Sheila scanned the address label. "New Iberia, Louisiana—that's a long way from here. There's a chance Emily could've sent it."

"Eleven hundred air miles and one hellacious drive up a canyon," Willette said, nodding and moving a half step closer to Sheila. "That envelope you're holdin' contains a newspaper story about an earthquake you had here in Colorado just recently. A highway maintenance worker found the remains of a man up at your Eisenhower Tunnel in the quake's aftermath. Now, I'm gonna ask you again. Did you send the envelope?"

"No." Sheila's response was emphatic.

"I see. Well, at least you're givin' the same answer." There was a moment's hesitation before Willette reached into her purse, extracted the .38, and aimed the barrel squarely at Sheila. "There's nobody here, Lydia, if that's really your name. I've checked. No sweet little Emily, and no good folks from Iowa left to run interference for you. Just you and me. So, my dear, I'm thinkin' we might as well let down our hair and share some secrets. For starters, my name's not Reed, it's Willette Ducane. And those remains they found up at the Eisenhower Tunnel were my son Antoine's. Now, we can keep playin' ring-around-the-rosy if you wanna, and dance around the issue of whether you knew my Sugar Sweet all day, but before I leave here, you're gonna tell me everything I should know about you and my son."

"You've got the wrong person, Mrs. Ducane."

"Don't think so." Willette forced a smile. "And wouldn't you know it, your eyes are dartin', sweetie. I've got the right person, all right. And the right FedEx account number. And most importantly, you're the right kinda woman." Willette shook her head. "Antoine was always partial to you crossover types. And you're like my sister—his real mama—pure-D crossover. I'm from where women like you do what they have to, sweetie. Believe me, I understand. Antoine preferred the types who could walk both sides of the street. One day you're white. Next day you're black, just like his mama, Monique. Sorta gave both of 'em a bigger box of toys to choose from, I guess. Never saw no percentage in passin', myself. Always figured you had the same chance of runnin' into good or evil, or maybe even sweetness and light, no matter which side of the street you walked."

Surprised to hear that Willette wasn't Antoine's mother, Sheila took a half step forward.

"Stay where you are, sweetie. This piece I'm holdin' ain't no friggin' piece of costume jewelry."

Confused and out of sorts, Sheila thought about the fact that in a span of twelve hours, two people had been able to invade a world that she'd spent nearly thirty-five years crafting. She was angry with herself for sending the newspaper story about the earthquake and Antoine to the New Iberia address she'd kept all those years. In a moment of weakness, guilt, arrogance, and all-out stupidity, thinking she was free of the past, she'd made a terrible mistake. A mistake that had exposed her. Years earlier, when she'd staged her disappearance, she could've chosen to go to Montana or Idaho, or even the Everglades. But she hadn't. She was in love with Colorado. That too had been a mistake. But the biggest mistake she'd made, the one that had her struggling to maintain her composure as she stared down the barrel of a .38, was falling in love with Antoine Ducane. With a hint of nervousness in her voice, she said, "I can call the sheriff. He's a friend of mine."

"Do that, my little passing-for-white princess, and I'll shoot you right here on the spot. I'm eighty-eight years old, and I've pretty much already run my race. Won't faze me one bit to plug you, honey."

Sheila stared past Willette as if searching for some magical way out of her predicament. Suddenly she remembered the bail bondsman. "Then let me make a phone call to someone else. It could help us both out."

"Why? Is somebody else out there ready to put a hole in you too?"

"No. I'm afraid that would be way too simple."

"Well, pick your poison, hon. I don't know how serious whoever you're itchin' to call is about helpin' you, but like they say down my way, I'm here, and I'm as serious as a heart attack."

"Okay, okay! I'll tell you our story, mine and Antoine's. Then you decide if I should make that phone call."

"I'm listenin'."

Eyeing the .38, Sheila said, "Can we go into the living room and sit down?"

"Lead the way." Willette motioned Sheila toward the living room with a wave of the gun. "What's your real name, by the way? I'm guessin' it ain't Lydia."

"I'm Sheila Lucerne."

"Nice name. Innocent and kinda biblical," said Willette as they stepped into the living room. "The kinda name I know my Sugar Sweet woulda loved."

Twenty minutes later Willette had a better understanding of Antoine's years in Colorado and an appreciation for Antoine and Sheila's strange love story. According to Sheila, the two had met at a Denver social mixer thrown by a New Orleans acquaintance whom each had known separately. The mixer had been an affair at which fair- and dark-skinned blacks with a Louisiana connection got together to choose opposite-skin-toned partners for the evening. She and Antoine, both light-skinned enough to pass for white, had ended up together because, perhaps intimidated by their good looks, no one else had stepped forward to choose either of them. In the wake of that gathering, first a friendship and then a five-year romance had blossomed. The love affair had ended abruptly in 1972. Sheila was just about to tell Willette why when there was a knock at the door.

"Let 'em knock," said Willette. There were three more knocks as Sheila sat looking drained, and then silence. "So what happened in 1972?" Willette asked finally.

Sheila looked around the room helplessly. "First off, you should know that by then I knew Antoine was connected. We'd been going together for over five years. I knew most of his Denver associates— even some of the people he worked with up at the Eisenhower Tunnel."

"What happened?" Willette asked impatiently.

"Hale Boggs died in a plane crash up in Alaska." Sheila blurted the words out.

"The Louisiana congressman?" Willette asked, looking perplexed.

"Yes. That plane crash sent Antoine into orbit. I'd never seen him so upset."

Still looking puzzled, Willette asked, "Why would Antoine care about what happened to Boggs?"

"Believe me, I asked myself the very same thing back then. When I put the question to Antoine, asked him point-blank why he cared about what had happened to some mealy-mouthed politician, he danced around the issue. For three weeks after that crash, Antoine was at odds with himself, juggling his work schedule up at the Eisenhower Tunnel, working twelve-hour shifts with three days on and one day off. On his off days he came down from the tunnel to Denver like always, but not to see me. He spent that time with other people. It wasn't until the end of those three weeks that I learned why the Hale Boggs plane crash had him so shaken. He told me Boggs had been a member of the Warren Commission that had investigated the JFK assassination, and that in the months leading up to the plane crash and his death, Boggs had been making noises about being unhappy with the commission's finding that Lee Harvey Oswald had killed the president. According to Antoine, Boggs had been pushing for the investigation into the assassination to be reopened. Three weeks to the day after that Alaskan plane crash, Antoine told me he'd been in on the plot to kill Kennedy himself. I was scared to death for both of us every second after that. Two weeks later Antoine disappeared."

Willette took a deep breath and very slowly ran her tongue around the inside of her mouth. She'd always known deep down that Antoine had probably been in on the JFK killing, but she'd told herself that he'd been a minor cog in a much larger wheel. A runner, a driver, a drop-off man, a utility infielder of sorts. She'd purposely lied to herself. She'd never pushed him to tell her what had happened up in Chicago all those years ago, weeks before the assassination, and she'd never asked him why he'd run off to Colorado afterward. She'd never asked about the doodles and sketches he'd made on the day of the assassination or the day afterward while they'd sat at her kitchen table, glued to the TV. And there'd been reason. In spite of her reputation for toughness, she'd been afraid too. Afraid to talk or speak or ask for fear that she'd somehow end up like Antoine's mother, her gullible baby sister. Monique had gotten herself involved with the mob as a teenager and eventually worked her way all the way up to having an affair with Carlos Marcello. Suddenly, as she thought about Monique, she found herself fighting back tears. Finally she asked, "Did Antoine tell anybody else about his involvement in the Kennedy assassination?"

"I'm not sure, but I have a feeling he told a friend of his, a man named Cornelius McPherson who worked with him up at the Eisenhower Tunnel bore." Sheila drew a deep breath. "McPherson's the miner mentioned in that article I sent you. He ended up getting murdered down in Denver just the other day."

Still unable to envision Antoine as a miner, Willette asked, "What exactly did Antoine do up at that tunnel? And what about other mining friends of his besides McPherson?"

"He operated a crane for a bit, but mostly he drove a truck. As for his mining friends, as far as I ever knew, McPherson was it. Most of the people he hung out with were in Denver."

"Not a lot to go on, I'm afraid."

"There is one other thing," Sheila said sheepishly. "It's related to that phone call I wanted to make earlier."

"Spit it out, child."

"Last night a man came by here asking all kinds of questions about Antoine. A linebacker-sized brother dressed head to toe in black and sporting a Stetson. I stonewalled him—told him I'd never heard of anyone named Antoine Ducane."

"A cop, maybe?"

"No way. I can sniff out a cop a mile away. He claimed to be a bail bondsman. I've got his card."

Willette eyed the .38 she'd placed on the coffee table between them and thoughtfully stroked her chin. "Since we're confessin' here, I might as well too. I'm pretty sure there're some connected kinda folks from back down in Louisiana who're up here in Colorado after me. And if what you're tellin' me is true, it's a lead-pipe cinch that sooner or later they'll be after you." She broke into a half grin. "Looks like the two of us are stuck between what people like to refer to as a rock and a hard place. We can sit tight, call the cops, contact your mystery man in black, or run. It's your choice, honey. As for me, I'm too old to run."

"Makes two of us."

"The bail bondsman, then?" asked Willette.

"Unless you trust the cops, he's the best thing we've got. I'll go get his card." Sheila rose from her chair. "But what if we're wrong and he's somehow connected to people from Louisiana who'd like to make us both disappear?"

"Then we'll just have to disconnect him," said Willette, reaching forward and tapping the butt of her .38. "But before we give him a jingle, maybe you can tell me a little more about how the whole Hale Boggs thing unfolded and how it is that, unlike my Sugar Sweet, you managed to keep on breathin' and vanish up here into these canyon walls."

"You ever heard of something called *a plant?*" asked Sheila, certain Willette's answer would be no.

"Sure have," said Willette, smiling. "It's mob parlance for facilitatin' somebody's disappearance instead of killin' 'em."

Sheila looked at once surprised and guilty. "Turns out that money to get by on, and my move up here the following year, was my reward for never saying anything about what I thought might have happened to Antoine. I spent some time in Denver after he disappeared, setting myself up as a living, breathing white woman. Even hooked up with a real nice white boy, an aerospace engineer, before I was told to move up here."

"Bet the new boyfriend didn't like you buggin' out on him."

"He didn't. But like me, he liked living, and since he'd gotten himself all tangled in my life, he had no choice but to go along with the long-term consequences of the plant. How about I tell you the whole story after we talk to that bail bondsman?"

"Time's a-wastin'," said Willette. "And by the way, we got one other good reason for goin' with the bail bondsman."

"What's that?"

"He's black," said Willette reaching for the .38 and stowing it back in her purse.

Chapter 26

Droplets of dried blood spotted the parking stripe just to the left of Rollie Ornasetti's BMW. Hours earlier Denver police had cordoned off a fifty-square-foot area around the late-model BMW, and crime-scene technicians were now busy dusting the car for prints.

Gus Cavalaris stood inside the ribbon of crime-scene tape talking to a stubby fireplug of a cop with a bulbous nose and bushy sideburns that were on the verge of being dress-code noncompliant.

"So what've you g-g-got for me, Toby?" Eager to head for Poudre Canyon, Cavalaris eyed his watch.

The husky cop looked at notes he had jotted on a folded sheet of paper. "Not much more than I had when I called you earlier. And for the record, Lieutenant, I know you're in a hurry, but you're the one who put the word out to be called about anything that went down concerning Ornasetti."

"S-s-sorry, Toby. Got too many irons in the fire right now. If I d-d-don't get up north in a hurry, I'm afraid a little chicken I'm after is gonna fly the coop. Should've dealt with the issue last night."

"No question we've got ourselves a missing chicken here. It's a cinch Ornasetti's gotten himself either killed and planted, or abducted. And considering the minimal amounts of blood the crime-scene boys have found, I'd vote for the latter."

"Who called it in?"

"Ornasetti's secretary. She flagged down a passing patrol car after she got to work this morning and found Ornasetti's car sitting here with a door wide open." The cop eyed his notes. "Told me Ornasetti normally walks into the office like clockwork with a box of LaMar's donuts and his thermos of coffee between eight and eight-thirty every morning. He's got a five-thousand-square-foot townhouse-office combo just above us. I've checked the place and the secretary out. She's a 42D, with the curves to match, but she wasn't much help." The cop folded up his notes, shoved the piece of paper into a shirt pocket, and glanced at the BMW. "No real signs of a struggle, and there's nothing missing from the car, at least on first blush. A cell phone and a fancy voice-activated tape recorder were sitting on the front seat. Nothing on the recorder; I checked. For right now that's about it, Lieutenant."

Cavalaris walked over to the car. The cop stayed glued to his side. "N-n-nice car," he said, running a finger along the rear bumper.

"This year's model," said the cop. "A hundred and thirty grand if you want one." Eyeing Cavalaris quizzically, he asked, "Why the interest in Ornasetti? Never knew you were into small-time, old-school North Denver mobsters, Lieutenant. Always thought our city's more upscale homicides were your beat."

Cavalaris smiled. "Normally, you'd probably be r-r-right, b-b-but your missing mobster's linked to one of my cases." Peering into the shiny black BMW and thinking about the car Carl Watson had described in the McPherson drive-by, he said, "Real plush."

"A whole lot plusher than the sled dogs we get to mush around all day."

"You can say that again." Cavalaris stroked his chin thoughtfully. "Think this car might be linked to my case. Can I get you to do something for me, Toby?"

"As long as it don't involve pissin' into the wind or underaged women."

Cavalaris slipped his wallet out of his back pocket, fished out the business card on which he'd jotted Carl Watson's home and work numbers, and handed it to Toby. "Call either of the numbers on the card and ask for Carl Watson. Tell him you want him to have a look at a car—see if there's any chance he recognizes it."

Toby Sanchez eyed the car longingly. "So you're thinking this baby was involved in the murder case you're working?"

"It's better than an even bet. G-g-gotta run. I'll get back with you this afternoon."

"What if I can't hook up with Watson?"

"Then let me know, and I'll d-d-deliver him to the car."

"Think your guy Watson might've swept in here and done Ornasetti?"

"Don't know. B-b-but it's a sure bet that if Watson balks at coming to s-s-see the car, he and I will need to have a serious heart-to-heart. I'm outta here, Toby."

"Watch those twists and turns goin' up the canyon, Lieutenant. They can be murder."

"Oh, I know," said Cavalaris, breaking into a grin. "I kn-kn-know."

After a restless night's sleep and an early morning spent asking himself whether he'd made a deal with the devil by agreeing to, in effect, partner with a police lieutenant, CJ wasn't sure he wasn't going soft. He'd had a talk with Flora Jean, who'd told him moments after she'd arrived at work that Alden Grace still hadn't come up with anything that could help Mario or move their investigation of the Ducane killing and its possible link to the JFK assassination forward. "Alden says he needs some physical evidence, or at least somethin' more concrete than what we've given him, in order to get the tongues he knows waggin' about the JFK killin'. The folks he deals with don't talk to nobody on the basis of hearsay, sugar. It could get 'em killed," had been Flora Jean's exact words.

Following that conversation, CJ disappointedly left the office, cheroot and coffee cup in hand, and headed for Rosie's Garage in Five Points to have his best friend since childhood, Roosevelt Weeks, check on the damage to the Bel Air. Rosie had just replaced the car's headlight and was in the midst of reminding CJ that he was getting too old to run the streets he still insisted on running when CJ's cell phone rang. Surprised to hear Sheila Lucerne announce herself on the other end, CJ crossed his lips with a finger to let Rosie know he had to deal with something in private, slipped into the Bel Air, and took a seat behind the wheel.

Sheila was coy at first, failing to mention the reason for the call, and CJ knew she was sizing him up. When he pushed for her to get to the point, she dropped a bombshell. "Antoine Ducane's mother's here with me, and we need to talk. How soon can you get here?"

CJ wondered if he'd heard her right. "Why me?"

Sheila said without hesitation, "Two very good reasons, Mr. Floyd. You're not a cop, and you're black."

"I can be at your place in less than two hours," said CJ, checking his watch.

"Let's cut that time in half. How about I meet you at Barbour Ponds State Park in an hour. I know a place where we can get lost in the trees."

"Is being lost that important?" CJ asked as Rosie signaled for him to turn on the Bel Air's headlights.

"You can bet your life on it, Mr. Floyd. One hour. I'll be in a white Chevy wagon," she said, abruptly ending the conversation.

CJ was twenty-five minutes south of Barbour Ponds State Park, speeding along at eighty-five, when Pinkie Niedemeyer called. His greeting was curt, his message to the point. "We got problems, CJ. That FBI agent who barged in on us the other day is leanin' on Mario again."

"Else? Damn! Sure is a persistent cuss."

"Like a dog with a bone. Mario called me a little bit ago to tell me that Else came by his place while he was still in his PJs. Wanted to talk to him about Rollie Ornasetti disappearin'. Seems like somebody either snatched Rollie or popped him last night."

"And Mario's a prime suspect. Did they haul him in?"

"Nope." Pinkie snickered. "Mario was too quick on the draw. Soon as he saw Else headin' for his front door, he called Julie. Told me she was there in no time flat. Mario says Else got nothin', unless of course you count the fifteen-minute verbal ass-stompin' he got from Julie."

"Where's Mario now?"

"At home."

"Call him and tell him to keep his butt right there. All damn day if he has to. I'm onto something with Ducane, and if it pans out, I may need to talk to Mario in a real hurry."

"Okay. And by the way, I'm on my way right now to find out how much of that line Maxie fed me and Damion the other day was a lie."

"How'd you find him?"

"It's easy to run down three hundred–plus pounds of blubber when you're passin' out hundreds."

"Real generous of you, Pinkie," CJ said, laughing.

"Come on, CJ. You know better than that. The generosity's all Mario's."

"Guess Mario still knows how to loosen tongues."

"Yeah," said Pinkie.

"Let me know how you do with Maxie."

"I'll do fine. Just fine. Talk to you later," Pinkie said confidently.

Neither Gus Cavalaris's stuttering, which seemed at the moment to be worsening, nor the fact that Cavalaris remained glued to him like a bluetick heeler on a stray seemed to bother the Larimer County sheriff, who continued his task of policing the previous evening's washed-out crime scene. "I should've impounded that guy Floyd's car instead of simply dusting it for prints, Lieutenant."

"And w-w-what would you have found in a rainstorm?" Cavalaris asked.

"Not much. Just like I didn't find anything when I drove up to that bed and breakfast Floyd claims he was coming from last night. There was nobody there but a couple from Iowa. The lady who runs the place was gone for the evening. Wonder why Floyd was up there in the first place."

"Beats me," said Cavalaris, feeling not one bit guilty about holding information back from the sheriff.

"Well, he was coming from there, and the shooter knew it. Why else would he have strapped a homing device to the underbelly of Floyd's car?"

"Makes sense," said Cavalaris. "Think I'll drive up the canyon a bit and see if I can spot anything that m-m-might've been overlooked." He made a half turn toward his car.

"I've already done that," the sheriff said defensively. "Nothing.

After I'm done here I'm gonna head up the canyon and go house to house. See if I can't come up with something. Why's this guy Floyd so important to you, anyway?"

"He's k-k-key to a murder case I'm working back in Denver."

"Must be some case."

"It is," said Cavalaris, cutting off the discussion. He headed for his car, trying his best to reconcile himself to the fact that he'd decided to cast in his lot with a bail bondsman he hardly knew, and to pinpoint why he'd become so interested in what had happened to Antoine Ducane. The answer, he told himself as he got into his car, was simple when you came right down to it. He was a cop, he was on the trail of the crime of the twentieth century, and he had a chance to not only overturn history but stick it to an overbearing, full-of-himself, pompous FBI agent. Why not use somebody like Floyd? Somebody who'd keep the trail hot.

Pulling onto the highway and kicking up a contrail of mud as he headed up the canyon, he had the sense that things would soon start to warm up.

Forty minutes later Cavalaris barreled back down the canyon, having learned from a young girl named Emily who worked at the Peak to Peak Bed and Breakfast that for the first time since she'd worked there, her boss, Lydia Krebs, had shown up late that morning. The girl had also informed him that sometime after breakfast Krebs had left her a note saying that she'd left with one of the guests. The trip hadn't been a total loss, however. When he'd asked the girl whom her boss had left with, she'd walked him to a guest register in the hallway and pointed to the name "Ann Reed" three lines up from the bottom of the page.

Pinkie Niedemeyer stood outside the apartment where the sad-faced woman from Chihuahua lived. He was tempted to kick the flimsy door off its hinges, rush in, grab Randall Maxie by the throat, and choke at least a little bit of truth out of him. But since he was certain that even if Maxie were at death's door, he'd still have a gun close at hand, Pinkie decided to try a less gung-ho but equally effective approach. He knocked.

The woman's response was a faint "Who is it?"

"A friend of Maxie's."

"Who?" the woman said, sounding as if she were being coached.

"Andrus Niedemeyer."

"He can't see you right now. He's resting."

"Gotcha." Taking a step back from the door, Pinkie slipped his 9-mm out of his leg holster, cocked his right leg, and with a single engineer-booted thrust kicked the door open, sending the doorknob and the chain lock flying into the room.

The woman screamed as the doorknob rebounded off the wall. Lunging into the room, Pinkie grabbed the woman by the arm, and by the time a startled Randall Maxie appeared in the doorway of a nearby bedroom, the woman, kicking and screaming and shielding Pinkie from Maxie's gun, was firmly in Pinkie's grasp.

Smiling at Maxie, Pinkie said, "Didn't figure you'd talk to me without me havin' some kinda bargainin' chip. So I decided to grab myself one." Pinkie let out an "Ummph" as the woman elbowed him in the gut. Squeezing her until she could barely breathe, Pinkie yelled, "I'll cold-cock her, Maxie. Better tell her to stop!" Pinkie's 9-mm was aimed squarely at Maxie's chest.

Maxie, his right arm supported by a sling, said, "What the fuck do you want, Pinkie?"

"Some straight answers. The ones you gave me and the Madrid kid the other day seem to run a little crooked." The terror-stricken woman, barely able to breathe and worn out from kicking, said in a near whisper, "Tell him, Randy. Tell him."

"And if I don't?"

"I'll drop the both of you on the spot and call it a day."

"Think you can do that before I get off a couple of rounds of my own?" asked Maxie.

"We'll see."

Tears streamed down the woman's face as she gasped for air. The two men stood facing one another down for the next thirty seconds until Maxie finally said, "Let her go."

"I'll do that just as soon as you pop the clip on that piece of yours and kick it over here to me."

Shaking his head and looking disgusted with himself for letting Pinkie get the drop on him, Maxie dutifully removed the clip, dropped it on the floor, and kicked it over to Pinkie.

Pinkie released the terrified woman, retrieved the clip, and said, "Tell her to have a seat. Right there in the chair next to you. And do the same yourself." Pinkie smiled. "Two people, two guns, two chairs. Damn, my stars must be in alignment."

The woman and Maxie took seats in two pressed-back chairs that hugged a half wall that separated the apartment's living room from a small kitchen.

"Good. And by the way, love your sling," Pinkie said, snickering. "Always heard they had real good doctors up there at Poudre Valley Hospital." Pinkie stepped back to the door and slammed it shut. "Think you're probably gonna have to spring for a new doorknob, Max." Moving back into the living room and with his gun still trained on Maxie, he said, "So, let's get down to business. I need the whole nine yards on your role in the Ducane killin'."

Maxie eyed the woman. "Not in front of her."

Pinkie shrugged. "She's free to leave the room as long as she's not goin' to get a gun. I'll send you both on the road to glory if she goes after one." Pinkie smiled at the woman. "I'll kill you, sweetheart, if I so much as smell a weapon."

"She knows better than that, right, Margarite? Why don't you go in the bedroom and lie down, sweetie. I can handle things out here," said Maxie.

Shivering in fear, the woman offered an obedient nod and rose from her chair.

"Compliant," said Pinkie, watching the woman disappear into the bedroom.

"I prefer them that way."

Pinkie smiled and shook his head. "Pigs and men with tiny little dicks usually do. Let's forget about your preferences for the moment and get back to Ducane."

"And if I set the record straight for you, what's in it for me?"

"Let's see." Pinkie pretended to stroke his chin. "How about I let you see sunset tonight and sunrise tomorrow."

Not the least bit flustered, Maxie asked, "What's your angle in all this, Andrus? Is Mario going to let you off the hook for that job you were supposed to do for him a few years back and didn't? I'm in the know more than you think, Pinkie."

"That ain't your worry, asshole."

"Okay," said Maxie, his eyes never wavering from the barrel of Pinkie's 9-mm. "I don't know why I held back telling you this in the first place. It's no skin off my nose. Ornasetti's the big loser." Maxie eyed the ceiling pensively. "Ducane came up from Louisiana in late 1963, full of sugarcane swagger and Karo syrup and fresh on the heels of the JFK assassination. I always suspected he and Ornasetti were involved in that hit, but neither one of them ever let on just how. Ducane dropped out of the sky and onto Rollie's back like an eight-hundred-pound gorilla. The word back then was that if Rollie didn't dance to his tune, he'd sing a song about the JFK assassination to the whole damn country, starting with the feds and the press. He had Rollie scared shitless. In order to keep Ducane from peddling what he knew about the assassination, Rollie decided to pay him off for his silence."

"The fucker was that stupid? Why didn't he just get rid of Ducane?"

"You have to remember the times we were in back then. Rollie was a nobody trying to be a somebody in a top-heavy organization. A moldy piece of Limburger smelling up a world that belonged to his uncle. He couldn't afford to make a misstep, much less have anybody focus their microscope on him. I'm told there were lots of people around the country who didn't want to see a miscue on his part either."

"So how long did Rollie end up stroking Ducane off?"

"For a long time—from '63 to '72. And paying him off wasn't all Rollie did. He got Ducane a job up at the Straight Creek tunnel dig, a cushy, high-paying job as a trucker. Easy enough for Rollie. He and his people controlled most of the trucking from eastern Montana to the Colorado Continental Divide back then. Ducane's job was hauling rock out of the dig that would eventually become the Eisenhower Tunnel. The Creole son of a bitch liked to brag that he was a miner, but all he ever did as far as I know was nursemaid a Dumpster."

"So what happened in '72?"

"I don't know exactly. All I know is that one day in mid-November, Rollie came to me and told me Ducane needed to take a permanent rest. He said Ducane was not only getting overly expensive but also troublesome to keep. I never knew where the pressure was coming from to take him out, but a week after Rollie came to me that first time, I know Ducane's ass got planted."

"Up at the tunnel?"

"No."

Pinkie looked surprised. "Then where?"

"Out at an old sugar-beet factory in Brighton would be my guess. Can't believe you've never heard about the place."

"I've heard of it. Even used it in a roundabout way. Just wanted your honest take on Ducane's fate for a change. So how did Rollie get a pass to the factory? Last I heard, he was a don, not a handler. Rule is nobody but handlers has access out there."

"Easy. Back then Rollie had a trucking contract to haul sugar beets all over Colorado, Wyoming, and Montana. That was his in, as far as I know. Rollie somehow got Ducane to come out to the place one night, and he did him."

"How in the hell did he get Ducane to come out there?"

"Beats me," said Maxie. "Maybe he offered Ducane a chance to get out of the freezing tunnel-digging cold up in the mountains and promised him a job hauling sugar beets down where it was warmer. Your guess is as good as mine."

"So what about the specifics?"

"Supposedly Ducane got pickaxed, right in the back of his head, and ended up with his butt planted in with the sugar beets in a storage locker." Maxie broke into a toothy grin. "A permanent siesta at a frosty 34 degrees."

"But a short stay, since his body eventually ended up at the Eisenhower Tunnel," said Pinkie. "How long did the body stay out at the sugar-beet factory?"

"I don't know. Three days, three weeks, a year. All I know is that just like the rest of the world, I was surprised as hell when I read about Ducane resurfacing at the Eisenhower Tunnel after that earthquake."

"Think Rollie planted him behind that tunnel wall?"

Maxie shrugged. "Beats me. I'm not even sure Rollie did him out at the factory. That would've been a very unusual job for Rollie. He never liked to get his hands dirty—still doesn't."

"You tellin' the truth for a change?" asked Pinkie, aiming the 9-mm's barrel at Maxie's head.

"Why would I lie? You and that Madrid kid damn nearly drained all the blood out of me. My arm's pretty much useless. You scared my sweet little piece of Mexico shitless, and you've got a fucking gun aimed at my head."

"Because it's your nature, Maxie. And people like you don't change their nature real easy." Pinkie smiled and stepped back toward the door, his 9-mm still trained on Maxie. "I'll find out if you're lyin'. Trust me. In the meantime, I'll leave you with a message that Mario asked me to pass along. Go after the Madrid kid again, and I get to kill your big fat ass, no questions asked. And if by chance you're lyin' to me again, I get to make sure that somehow, somewhere, sometime before that damaged wing of yours has a chance to heal, I get to disable your lard-ass permanently. And don't you think that would be one hell of a disability for a man in your profession to overcome?"

"Mario wouldn't okay that," said a very surprised-looking Maxie.

"Don't fool yourself, Maxie. Mario's been on the hot seat lately.

Ain't nothin' he hates worse than lookin' in the rearview mirror for cops. Just remember, I get to toy with your ass, however I like, if you fuck up again." Pinkie swung the door open, stepped out into the hallway, and, still backing away, said, "To a speedy recovery, Max. Later."

Chapter 27

CJ turned off I-25 into the eastern glare of the midmorning sun and headed for Barbour Ponds State Park. As he drove into the prairie-like setting with its panoramic view of 14,259-foot Longs Peak, he was still thinking about Pinkie Niedemeyer's second call, in which Pinkie had relayed everything Randall Maxie had told him about Ducane.

Still not convinced that Maxie had told Pinkie the whole truth, CJ had told Pinkie he'd get back to him as soon as he talked to Sheila Lucerne and Antoine Ducane's mother, who'd appeared out of the blue.

As CJ followed a winding gravel road into the park past two small lakes and dozens of campsites, looking for a third, larger lake where Sheila Lucerne had said she'd meet him, he had the sense that he was finally closing in on a very large truth. A truth he wasn't certain he really wanted to know.

Squinting into the sun, he found himself thinking about the Vietnam War, truth, and a farm boy from Pennsylvania he'd served with named Gerald Shadden. Shadden had, like him, babysat a .50-caliber machine gun on the aft of a 125-foot patrol boat. It was 1972, and back in the United States bad politics and failed policies had supplanted news about the actual grunt work of war. Two of CJ and Shadden's 42nd River Patrol Group's 125-footers had been assigned the task of ferrying CIA operatives up and down the Mekong River delta so that they could carry out covert hit-and-run missions that included taking out U.S. allies and duly elected South Vietnamese officials who'd been fingered as potential Vietcong sympathizers.

Shadden, who'd come to know some of the South Vietnamese officials, thought helping the CIA eliminate one's own allies was idiotic, and he made a written point of that fact, not only to his own boat's captain but to the patrol group's commander. Three days later, when Shadden's patrol boat returned from a hastily ordered search-and-rescue mission to supposedly pull a downed F-111 pilot out of the drink—a task normally assigned to the U.S. Coast Guard boats—Shadden was dead. Word soon circulated that he'd been killed by a sniper. But everyone from newly made third-class petty officers to career four-stripers understood that Shadden had been taken out not by the enemy but by the CIA. The morale-crushing fallout after Shadden's death generated a terse command directive that stated that in the future, and as deemed necessary, patrol-group command would have the ultimate responsibility for assigning the appropriate naval personnel and boats to search-and-rescue missions. The hidden meaning behind that communication, which soon became known to the troops as "Gerry's Deal," was lost on no one: *Go against the grain, sailor, and we can send you out and have you shot.*

CJ, therefore, understood quite well that by delving into the murder of someone who very likely had been linked to the JFK assassination, he ran the risk of becoming Gerry Shadden's latter-day equivalent. But for him, just as it had for Shadden, doing the right thing still mattered. Perspiring and trying not to second-guess himself, he left memories of Vietnam and Gerald Shadden behind as he shaded his eyes and spotted the tree-lined shore where he was to meet Sheila Lucerne.

Uncertain whether he was walking into a setup like the one he'd experienced in Poudre Canyon, he popped the Bel Air's glove compartment and checked for his .44. "Okay," he muttered, eyeing the gun butt and bumping along the rocky lakeshore until he spotted the white Chevy station wagon that Sheila Lucerne had told him she'd be driving. He pulled the Bel Air to a stop twenty yards from the station wagon, slipped the .44 under his belt, and got out. Moments later he heard a thud a few yards away. He looked toward where the noise had come from and spotted a baseball-sized rock. Twenty feet beyond the rock, Sheila and another woman sat at a picnic table that was all but obscured from view by two massive Colorado blue spruce trees.

When Sheila waved for him to join them, he slammed the Bel Air's door and headed for the picnic table. With his Stetson tipped forward to shade his eyes, he made the walk slowly, finally stopping a few feet from the table. The sun's unflattering glare made Sheila Lucerne look less attractive than she had the previous evening, but the woman seated next to her, elderly and bent over, seemed surprisingly radiant.

"Morning," CJ said, standing his ground.

"Hi," said Sheila, looking past CJ toward the Bel Air. She scanned the terrain in every direction slowly and carefully until her eyes came back to meet CJ's. "You weren't followed, were you?"

"Don't think so." CJ nodded at the other woman and touched the brim of his Stetson.

"Good. And Mr. Floyd, you won't need that gun." Turning to Willette, she said, "Willette Ducane, CJ Floyd."

"My pleasure," said CJ, reaching out and shaking Willette's misshapen arthritic right hand.

Willette smiled and patted the top of CJ's hand. "Thanks for comin'."

Continuing to look around, Sheila said, "Willette has come all the way from New Iberia, Louisiana. She's hoping to find out what happened to her son, Antoine."

"I see." CJ's response had a clear ring of skepticism. "Mind me asking just what after all these years prompted you to wanna do that?"

"I, aahh . . ."

"It was at my prompting, I'm afraid," Sheila said supportively. "I sent her a newspaper clipping about them finding Antoine's remains up at the Eisenhower Tunnel."

"Strange behavior for someone hiding behind a new identity, don't you think?"

"I felt guilty."

"Awful late to start showing it."

Willette cleared her throat. "Would you two stop? This ain't no time for finger-pointin', Mr. Floyd. As a matter of fact, neither one of us is certain we can even trust you. Bottom line is, we're here talkin' to you 'cause we got nowhere else to turn. I don't know what made Sheila decide to send me that newspaper clippin'. Maybe she thought a mother needed to know after all these years what had happened to her son. Could be she figured that with Antoine officially dead, and decades of water under the bridge, she could finally act, if not talk, freely. Don't really matter. What matters is what happened to Antoine. I've spent more than forty years tryin' to outrun the fact that I shoulda never let Antoine get caught up in a mess that ended up costin' him his life, tellin' myself that I never shoulda let him leave New Iberia for Colorado, and askin' myself why I didn't come after him. I understand guilt, Mr. Floyd. So, even if you ain't, I'm willin' to give Sheila a little bit of slack."

"So why didn't you come after him?" asked CJ, his tone now less accusatory.

"I was scared. Scared to death, in fact. And believe me, fear ain't somethin' that comes natural to me. Let me start you at the beginnin', and maybe you'll understand. I've already told Sheila most of this. Maybe it'll be easier the second time around. First off, Antoine wasn't really my son. Truth is, he was my baby sister's boy. My sweet, naive, beauty-contest-winnin', insecure baby sister." Willette let out a mournful sigh. "Monique wasn't but sixteen when she had Antoine. Sixteen and thinkin' she owned the world. She was supposed to go to LSU to become a nurse, but she got to runnin' with the wrong crowd. A white crowd who told her that for a colored girl she was beautiful and sexy and smart. A pack of connivin', manipulatin' folks who unfortunately filled her full of what she'd always been wantin' to hear. Let her know that she could cross the color line if need be."

"Who'd she fall in with?" CJ asked.

Willette swallowed hard and frowned. "I doubt you'd know the name, but she fell in with Carlos Marcello and his lowlife bunch of mobster swamp rats."

"Oh, I know the name, all right."

"Then you know Marcello was Louisiana's top crime boss at the time. Thankfully, the SOB's long since dead." Looking hurt, Willette said, "I suppose when you come right down to it, it was my fault Monique fell in with him. I was four years older than her, and I knew better. Especially since I'd walked almost the same damn road a few years ahead of her—listened to Marcello's people's bullshit, sucked down their promises to turn me into a recording star. I compromised cops and businessmen and unsuspecting politicians for Carlos Marcello and his crew. Even helped him rig elections while his henchmen were out threatening would-be voters' lives. But unlike Monique, I was lucky enough to get out from under their pull. More importantly, I wasn't foolish enough to get hooked on the man's dope."

Willette took a deep breath and stared out toward the Rockies. "Maybe I should've made Monique leave Louisiana and its dirty politicians and criminals and through-and-through corruption for a place like Colorado. But, to tell you the truth, back then I didn't know places like this existed. Anyway, one thing led to another, and next thing I knew, Monique was not only strung out and doin' the mob's biddin', she was pregnant. Fifteen, Catholic, unmarried, and pregnant by a white man. You know what it was like to have all those things goin' against you back then, Mr. Floyd?" Before CJ could answer, Willette looked at Sheila, shook her head, and said, "Course not. Only a woman would understand. In the end it didn't really matter. Turned out Monique wasn't gonna give up that baby. No way—nohow. Said she'd die before she'd have an abortion or give up her child. I tried to get her to tell me who the baby's father was, but she never would. Three weeks before Antoine was born, she disappeared. To this day I don't know where she went. All I know is she showed up on my doorstep, lookin' like hell, with Antoine in her arms at the end of them three weeks.

"A few weeks later, just before midnight, a limo showed up at my house, and two white men came inside to talk to me and Monique. The driver and another man stayed in the car. The two men, who Monique obviously knew, were dressed in stingy brim hats and trench coats, and they were nice enough at first. But after they asked Monique several times to see the baby, and Monique refused each time to let 'em, things took a turn 'til finally one of 'em grabbed me in a bear hug while the other one snatched Monique by her hair. He dragged her over to the kitchen table, slammed her face down on the table, and jammed the barrel of a gun into her right ear. As I kicked and screamed, the man holding Monique took a hatchet outta his coat pocket, the kind they use down our way for choppin' chicken necks. With Monique's head still pressed against the table, he swung the business end of that hatchet down full force. The blade ended up buried in the tabletop, no more than an inch or so from Monique's head, and Monique let out a scream I can still hear to this day. The man with the hatchet laughed, looked at me, and said, 'She's coming with us. Next time I'll do her for real—and then the baby.' Monique's legs gave way, and she slumped to the floor. They ended up havin' to drag her to the front door on her knees. A few feet from the door she looked back at me and said, 'Stay with Antoine, Sis. No matter what.'"

Willette's eyes glazed over, and her voice became a wheeze. "I never saw Monique alive again. I looked all over three states for her, and off and on she wrote me sayin' she was okay, the same way Antoine did after he came up here to Colorado, but I could never be sure the words in those letters were hers. People I knew told me they thought they'd saw her in Baton Rouge, or Macon, or Augusta—even Houston. But they were never really sure it was her, and most of 'em said whoever it was they'd seen was all skin and bones. Word circulated around the state for years that Antoine was Carlos Marcello's Creole woman's baby. Thought so myself—just couldn't prove it. But when Antoine won an art contest in junior high school and a chance at a college

scholarship, and one of Marcello's men, a shriveled-up, bug-eyed little Cajun I'd known over the years, showed up at the judgin' and
bought the paintin', I knew I was right. After that, Marcello, by way
of the Cajun, became a patron of sorts—buyin' up almost anything
Antoine sketched. By the time Antoine was seventeen, the mob had
him under their spell. I don't think Antoine ever knew for sure that
Marcello was his father, but I think he suspected it." Wringing her
hands, Willette let out a long, sorrowful sigh. "There, now, I'm done
with it. Have you heard enough, Mr. Floyd?"

"Some story," said CJ.

"And every word's true."

"I'm not doubting you. Just thinking. Do you think Marcello could've
talked Antoine into taking part in the Kennedy assassination?"

"No question about it. He'd already turned my Sugar Sweet into
a criminal. And I brought something with me that'll cinch it." Willette reached down and lifted the shoebox full of correspondence
that Antoine had sent her between 1963 and 1972 from the picnic
table's bench seat. "Might as well have yourself a seat," she said, plac-
ing the shoebox in the middle of the table. "It's gonna take us a while
to sort through what's in this box."

The table rocked as CJ seated himself across from the two women.
As Willette lifted the top off the box, she said just above a whisper,
"There's a lifetime of pain inside this shoebox, Mr. Floyd, believe
me."

"Can you tell me what happened to Monique?" CJ asked sympathetically.

Glassy-eyed, Willette said, "She died in 1957, when Antoine was
a teenager. I'm told she OD'd. Some of her effects turned up just
before Christmas that year. A watch I knew was hers. A cheap, gold-

plated bracelet and a couple pairs of silver earrings. They came in a padded envelope that Antoine found by our front door." Willette paused, fighting to regain her composure. "I shoulda gone after Monique harder than I did after they took her, or got my .44 and shot the fuckers on the spot that night. And when you come right down to it, I shoulda come up here to Colorado after Antoine. But I didn't. I was too scared, or at least pretendin' to be. But I'm here now, crippled, half blind, and with a foot in the grave, and come hell or high water I'm gonna find out what happened to my Antoine. I'm hopin' you'll help me, Mr. Floyd."

"I'll try. Why don't we have a look through your papers and chart ourselves a course?" said CJ.

Willette took a handful of papers out of the shoebox and glanced over at Sheila. "You might as well tell Mr. Floyd the whole nine yards about you and Antoine, same as you told it to me. And don't hold nothin' back, sweetie. We're dealin' with the last chance I got of takin' a little piece of my life back and keepin' my sanity." Looking back at CJ, she said, "Anything else you wanna know, Mr. Floyd?"

"Not right now, and by the way, I prefer CJ."

"CJ it is, then," Willette said, forcing a smile as she dug deeper into the shoebox.

Thirty minutes later, after sifting through close to half the papers in the shoebox and listening to Sheila Lucerne's rueful tale, CJ understood why Sheila had staged her death. Friends of Antoine's, she told him—people she'd known only casually—had come to her back in 1972 and told her that if she didn't disappear, they'd kill her. With tears in her eyes, she admitted that she'd known that Antoine was mob-connected, that his mining job at the Eisenhower Tunnel was pretty much pancake makeup and fluff, and that his income was really extorted from a well-known Denver mobster. CJ surprised both women when, before Sheila had a chance to mention the mobster's name, he said, "Rollie Ornasetti."

"Yeah," said Sheila. "Want me to give you a thumbnail sketch of the man?"

"No need," said CJ. "I've already got a full-blown picture."

It was almost noon when they began sorting through the rest of the papers in the shoebox. A few minutes into the task, CJ mentioned that he'd been told that in early 1972 Louisiana Congressman Hale Boggs had tried to distance himself from the findings of the Warren Commission's report on the JFK assassination. He glanced at Willette and asked, "Think that could've had anything to do with Antoine's disappearance?"

Willette shrugged. "Don't know, but Sheila and I were just talking about that yesterday. Why?"

"Because in October of '72, Boggs died in a mysterious plane crash in Alaska."

Sheila said, "First the congressman died, and Antoine got all jumpy. Then Antoine disappeared, and then I was told to disappear or be killed. Who the heck's pulling the strings here, CJ?"

"Who knows? Mobsters, the CIA, maybe even a pack of wacko Cuban dissidents. At one time or another, every one of those groups has been brought up as the power behind the Kennedy assassination. One thing for sure," CJ said, smiling, "we know it wasn't Oswald. And whoever they were, or are, they also may have eliminated Rollie Ornasetti last night."

"How's that?" Willette asked, looking puzzled.

"This morning Ornasetti turned up missing."

"So whoever killed Antoine, and maybe even JFK, is still at it?" Sheila asked.

"Real likely. Did Antoine have any friends, mobster or otherwise, that he was particularly tight with?"

"Not really."

"Does the name Cornelius McPherson ring a bell?"

"Yeah. He's that miner who got killed."

CJ stroked his chin thoughtfully. "Did Antoine know Carl Watson?"

"Of course not."

Looking up from a collated stack of papers, CJ said, "Well, I think Watson might've known him. I talked to your old boyfriend yesterday evening, and he mentioned to me that you and Antoine could've passed for brother and sister, you looked so much alike."

"Why would he have said that?"

"He saw a photo of Antoine once at your house."

Sheila looked perplexed. "Possible, but unlikely. Antoine hated having his photograph taken. And I don't remember having any around the house."

"Strange. Looks like I may have to check back in with our Mr. Watson."

"When you do, don't you dare tell him where I am," said Sheila.

"I won't," said CJ, thumbing Antoine's papers and spreading them out on the table. "Here's the top seven," he said, looking at Willette for guidance. "At least from what you've said. Let's try to make sense out of what we've got here and decide which way to go."

"You can discard the two in the middle and the two at the ends," said Willette. CJ teased four sheets out, nudged them aside, and looked intently at the remaining three sheets. The first sheet was filled with a handwritten description of a dark-haired man Antoine had met in Chicago. "When did Antoine write this?" CJ asked, handing the sheet of paper to Willette.

"The day of the assassination or the day after. I'm pretty sure."

CJ read the page several times, paying particular attention to Antoine's description of the man's hat and strange-looking shoes and his comment that the man had been wearing sunglasses. But it was a seeming afterthought, the words *low post* and *high post*, near the bottom of the page, that garnered most of CJ's attention. *Low post*—benign words when you were referring to a player's position on the basketball court, CJ thought, but more evocative when used in reference to warfare. During his years in Vietnam, the four words had had but one meaning: they'd always been used to refer to the position of a sniper. Suddenly he had a sense that he was looking at a piece of an assassination trial run. He had no idea who would have been assigned those low-post or high-post positions—Antoine, the dark-haired man, or someone else entirely—but he had the feeling that Antoine Ducane was clearly describing a shooter's role in the JFK assassination.

CJ set the first sheet of paper aside and read the second sheet, taking note of the word *Gary* and the list of dates in October that Antoine had jotted down. Earlier Willette had confirmed that the October dates coincided with when Antoine had been up North in Chicago in 1963. *Gary*, CJ reasoned, was a reference either to someone named Gary or perhaps to the bustling nearby steel town of Gary, Indiana. He couldn't be sure. Uncertain which possibility to pursue, he decided to come back to the issue later.

What made the least sense to CJ remained Antoine's drawings of what appeared to be a bank of row houses on the third sheet of paper and a string of strange ladder-like objects and the word *Shore* on the second sheet. He was also stumped by the fact that Antoine had abbreviated the word *November* between the ladders.

Realizing they could spend the rest of the day trying to guess the hidden meanings, CJ said, "Still don't know what it all means, but I know somebody who might be able to tell us."

"Who?" Willette asked, eagerly.

"My business partner's boyfriend."

"Your partner's a woman?" she asked with surprise.

"Absolutely."

"Is her boyfriend a mobster?" Willette asked.

"Nope. A long way from it. He's former military intelligence. The marines."

"Might as well use him," said Sheila. "I don't want to keep running the rest of my life."

"This guy got any credentials besides bein' in the military?" asked Willette.

CJ smiled. "Sure does. But I don't think they show up on his résumé." CJ was aware that since his retirement from the U.S. Marine Corps, Alden Grace had continued to take intelligence assignments around the world.

"Then go for it," said Willette.

"I'll need copies of Antoine's drawings and notes."

"Take the originals," said Willette. "Might as well show your friend the real thing."

"I'll have to fax them to him. He lives down in Colorado Springs."

"Fine by me," said Willette, looking as if a long-present weight had just been lifted from her shoulders. "So whatta we do next?"

"Next I get the two of you to somewhere that's safe. I don't want you going back up to that bed and breakfast. You just might run into the same person I ran into last night."

"What?" said Sheila, looking puzzled.

"It's a long story. I'll tell you later. Bottom line is, you need a safe house. And I've got one for you."

"You got another friend who's a marine?" asked Willette.

"Sure do. That partner I mentioned. But that's not where you're going. You're going to visit a friend of mine who's a lawyer. You'll be safe at her place."

"If she'll have us," said Sheila.

"Oh, she'll have you." CJ slipped his cell phone off his belt, prepared to call Julie. "And for backup, she has a very protective six-foot-five, 240-pound son."

"Tough kid?" asked Willette, blinking back tears as her thoughts suddenly drifted back to Antoine.

CJ scooted the papers he'd laid on the table back into a pile and rose from his seat. "And getting tougher by the day," he said with a wry smile, tapping the papers together until they were perfectly aligned.

Chapter 28

CJ stood in his office, looking at Antoine Ducane's notes and sketches. The sheet with the ladders continued to baffle him. He'd faxed the three pages to Alden Grace an hour and a half earlier, but so far there'd been no response from the former general. Flora Jean, to whom he'd just finished telling the whole convoluted Antoine Ducane story, stood a few feet away looking nearly as baffled as CJ. "What do you expect Alden to tell you, CJ? That Oswald didn't really shoot Kennedy?"

"No. I'm not looking for a home run, just a single. Maybe he'll recognize something in these sketches or Antoine's notes that'll tell us who killed JFK, or maybe one of Alden's intelligence cronies will see something. It's not like I'm dropping this on Alden out of the clear blue sky; he's been in the loop for a week."

"You're hopin' for a lot, sugar. Alden ain't no magician."

Winking at Flora Jean, CJ said, "Damn, and you always had me believing he was."

"Can we stay locked on serious for the moment, CJ?" said Flora Jean, trying not to snicker. "When I asked Alden to help us out last week, I didn't know we were gonna step into shit quite this deep. I can see why you're hot to track down Ducane's killer, now that the woman who raised him is all of a sudden payin' us to find out what happened to him. And I can understand your loyalty to Mario—and not wantin' him, at his age, to get sucked under by the system. But we could find ourselves hangin' out there, sugar, if we stick our noses too far into the Kennedy mess. We got a sayin' in the corps—you probably had your own version of it in the navy. 'Poke your nose in enough foxholes, and sooner or later you're bound to run across somethin' that's bigger and badder than you.'"

"I understand, Flora Jean, but I'm afraid I'm in a little too far to back out now."

"Yeah, and that's what's got me bothered. You're like a dog with that proverbial bone. And it's a bone that could end up explodin' in your face."

When the familiar squeak of the front door opening interrupted the conversation, CJ asked, "Expecting somebody?"

Flora Jean shrugged. "Nope."

Before either of them could head for the front door, Gus Cavalaris stepped into CJ's office, smiling and looking altogether pleased with himself. "Floyd, Benson. Must be my l-l-lucky day."

"Lieutenant?" CJ forced back a frown.

"I've been h-h-hoping to catch up with you. H-h-how are your nerves holding up after last night?"

"Just fine," said CJ, eyeing Flora Jean, who'd only in the past hour heard CJ's version of his Poudre Canyon adventure.

"G-g-get your headlight repaired?"

"Sure did. But you didn't drop by to talk about repairs to my car, Lieutenant."

"N-n-no. Afraid I didn't. I'm here about s-s-something else, in fact. Don't know if you're aware of it, b-b-but Rollie Ornasetti's disappeared."

"I heard."

Feigning surprise, Cavalaris said, "Now how'd y-y-you hear that? Oh, Ms. Madrid, of course. Somehow I keep f-f-forgetting about all the connections you've got. Satoni, Ornasetti, Ms. Benson here, your counselor, Ms. Madrid, and, oh, almost forgot the Lucerne woman you visited last night."

The muscles in CJ's face stiffened as he watched Cavalaris break into a toothy grin. "I know more about Lucerne than you think. We all have our sources, Floyd. I'm sort of p-p-partial to Carl Watson, myself. Trust me, I would've been right there d-d-during the visit I'm sure you had with Lucerne if it hadn't been for a flat tire that shooter of yours likely provided me. All's well that ends w-w-well, don't you think? Probably should've mentioned this all to you when we had our little chat at Ted's Place, but I figured it c-c-could wait. At least until I g-g-got a chance to go up to the Peak to Peak and talk to Lucerne myself. So I went up there early this morning, and you know w-w-what? I ended up missing Lucerne. A young lady who works there told me she'd just left with an elderly woman named Ann Reed. You wouldn't happen to kn-kn-know who the Reed woman is, or where she and Lucerne might be off to, would you, Floyd?"

"Afraid not, Lieutenant."

"Ms. Benson?"

"Don't know either of 'em," said Flora Jean.

Looking Flora Jean and then CJ up and down, Cavalaris said, "I th-th-thought we had an understanding, Floyd. But I guess we don't. Just remember, the n-n-next time you find yourself weaponless and in a firefight, I might not be there to save your butt."

Unmoved, CJ reminded himself that he wasn't the only one who'd held back information. Cavalaris, by means of his Carl Watson connection, had done the very same thing. "I appreciate you saving my bacon, Lieutenant, and maybe I should've been a little more straight with you about the Lucerne woman, but since you've already talked to Carl Watson, you know as much about her as I do."

"I do for a fact," said Cavalaris, still hoping to draw CJ out. "I know she staged her own death—something you t-t-typically don't do in my experience unless you've got yourself an insurance policy to cash in on, or the devil on your trail. I also know Lucerne was p-p-probably mobbed up, at least according to Watson. The obvious connection, I think we both know, was Antoine Ducane. Hope you're not holding anything else out on me," said Cavalaris. "Because we're heading for a t-t-train wreck here, trust me. The kind that could grind all three of us standing here, and who knows how many other people, into the dirt. Got a heads-up for you, Floyd. Agent Else has his nose stuck into the Ducane and McPherson murders just as deep as we do. I've even heard tell there're people s-s-sitting around in high places talking about taking a new look into the Kennedy assassination. Any idea where that p-p-puts you, Floyd? In the crosshairs of the kind of people who'd just as soon stick a shunt in your jugular and bleed you out as see you live."

"I get your drift, Lieutenant."

"I'm certain you do. L-l-let's just hope I've made my point, there's no undertow associated with that drift, and you end up sucked out to sea. C-c-call me if the water rises." Smiling, Cavalaris turned, walked out of CJ's office, and disappeared out the building's front door.

"Heady advice," said Flora Jean, hearing the front door slam shut.

"And I don't think for a second he's bluffing," CJ countered.

"Then maybe you should give your investigation a break, give the Ducane woman her money back, and exit gracefully."

"I'll give it some thought, but for right now I'm sticking."

"Why?"

"Guess I'm just too far along with fitting all the pieces of the puzzle together."

"Suit yourself," said Flora Jean.

They stared at one another for several eerily quiet seconds before CJ's phone rang.

"Hope it's not Else," CJ said, shaking his head. "All we need is for that whiffle ball to come down here and add his two cents." He picked up the phone and said gruffly, "Floyd here."

"It's Alden, CJ."

"Hey, what's up?"

"Plenty. Is Flora Jean there with you?"

"Sure is."

"Put me on speaker phone." The former general's tone had the unmistakable ring of an order. "You'll both need to hear what I have to say."

"It's Alden," CJ said to Flora Jean. "He wants us on speaker phone."

"What's up, sugar?" said Flora Jean, pushing a button on CJ's phone and patching everyone in.

"Serious consequences, I'm afraid, if what CJ faxed me isn't some hoax," said Alden.

"They're genuine," said CJ. "All three sheets came from the woman who raised Ducane. She always claimed to be his mother. Turns out she's really his aunt."

"Where's she from?" asked Alden Grace, his tone brimming with suspicion.

"New Iberia, Louisiana."

"Makes sense. Louisiana, and New Orleans in particular, has always been touted as the crucible for the JFK assassination plot. Problem is, half the jokers in Hollywood and every conspiracy buff on the planet have beamed up their own private take on the planning. It's hard to put any credence in one more take on that killing."

"So I'm off base, then, thinking Ducane was in on the plot?"

"No, to the contrary. I think you're on to something deadly serious. I called a few of my domestic intelligence sources. Even faxed a couple of them copies of what you sent me. They were back to me chirping like sparrows within fifteen minutes." The former general paused and cleared his throat. "You're into something that could be real risky for you, CJ."

"How risky?"

"Risky enough to get you permanently eliminated from the game," Alden said, drifting into intelligence speak. "Get off the bus, CJ."

"You're the second person to pass on that advice in the past half hour. And believe me, I'm considering it real hard. But I'd sure like a few questions answered before I go riding off into the sunset. First off, who's up to bat here, Alden? The CIA, the mafia, international conspirators, disgruntled Bay of Pigs Cubans? Just what the hell gives?"

"Can't tell for sure. Maybe none of those groups you mentioned, maybe all four. I can tell you this, though. Antoine Ducane was in on the Kennedy assassination, no doubt about it."

"You mean Ducane was in Dallas?"

"Hold on a minute, CJ. You're getting ahead of me. Let me offer you a little intelligence insight. The plot to kill JFK didn't just happen; it evolved. People in my line of work have known that for years. The take-out scenario involved shoring up plans to kill the president in two other cities besides Dallas: Chicago and Tampa. Conspiracy nuts, the press, and certain people in government have known this for a very long time. You could fill Dumpsters with the unclassified documents that are out there to support the fact. But let me just straighten out the wrinkles for you. I had one of my sources confirm what he knows about the details of the proposed hits in all three cities. Here's the sequence of events according to him. You listening, Flora Jean?"

"Sure am, sugar."

"Fine." They heard paper rustling as Alden consulted a sheet of hastily jotted notes. "The Chicago assassination was planned for November 2, 1963. No question that's where Ducane was stationed. The October dates that Ducane jotted on the one document you sent me, and his abbreviated reference to the month of November, circumstantially at least, substantiate that."

"So what the hell happened in Chicago a full three weeks before Dallas? And how can your source be so sure he's right?" CJ asked.

"He's paid to be right, CJ. Just like me. Now, here's the filler. JFK was supposed to get into Chicago's O'Hare Airport on Air Force One around 11 a.m. and be the centerpiece of a November 2 motorcade that would take a sixteen-mile trip from O'Hare and down what back then was called the Northwest Expressway before swinging into the city's famous downtown Loop. My source claims that once the motorcade got to the Loop, it was to have taken the Jackson Boulevard exit off the expressway. The whole shebang would have to have slowed down to make a hard-to-negotiate left turn onto Jackson Boulevard before heading over to Soldier Field stadium, where Kennedy was supposed to hook up with Chicago Mayor Richard Daley and other dignitaries to watch the Army-Air Force football game. Now, if I were a betting man ..."

"Which you ain't," Flora Jean chimed in.

"But if I were, I'd say that that turn onto Jackson Boulevard, which I was told was a flat-out 90 degrees, is the one place where Kennedy's limo would've been forced to basically stop. And that's one of the places where Ducane, if he'd been assigned to be an actual shooter, could've taken his shot at the president."

"What about other places?" asked CJ.

"I was told the motorcade also had to pass through one of Chicago's scores of warehouse districts. Warehouse canyons, really. Canyons of buildings that were pretty much akin to the Texas School Book Depository in Dallas in terms of their height, accessibility, and shooting access points. Bottom line is, they were mirror images of the place where Oswald supposedly took his shots."

"Supposedly? You don't sound real convinced that Oswald was the man, Alden, and that's real worrisome coming from someone in the intelligence community."

"Never have been convinced Oswald shot Kennedy," said Grace. "Always knew somebody out there was blowing smoke."

"So we've got two good locations in Chicago where Ducane could've been a shooter," CJ said, sounding almost euphoric.

"No question. Problem is, somewhere around 9 a.m. on the day of the motorcade, JFK canceled. Speculation has always been that he canceled the motorcade because of pressing issues with Castro and Cuba and he had to get back to Washington, and there's probably some truth to that. But there's also more than likely a little truth to the fact that his people picked up on the assassination vibes that had worked their way around the Windy City. The FBI did in fact have reports of a carful of Cubans who were speeding around town threatening the president. Could be there actually was a car like that. Could be the bureau boys were lying. They do that, you know. Could be the story was a newspaper plant. Who knows? What we do know is that JFK was saved by the bell in Chicago."

"What about Tampa?"

"According to my source, the Tampa assassination attempt was set for November 18, 1963."

Astonished by the revelation, CJ exclaimed, "Damn! Where the hell are your contacts getting all this?"

Grace laughed. "Contrary to what you might think, it's public record. Given enough time, you could've dug it out for yourself. That's if you had the patience to sift through tens of thousands of unclassified CIA, Department of Justice, State Department, and Warren Commission documents. Strange you ask, though, because I asked my contact the same question. He said most of the Tampa plot info bubbled right off the pages of the House Select Committee on Assassinations' report— a document schoolkids can access right off the Internet."

"So why hasn't somebody ferreted all this out before?"

"Because you're talking about something that happened almost a half century ago, CJ. Time passes, people forget, the world moves on, and pretty soon nobody but conspiracy-theory nuts, operatives like my sources, and history buffs care about what happened."

CJ glanced at Flora Jean and winked. "I've never really seen myself in any of those camps. Go ahead with what happened in Tampa, Alden; we're all ears."

"I'm told it went down like this. Kennedy rolled into Tampa on November 18. He had a motorcade in an open-topped car scheduled for that day. And this time, unlike Chicago, he didn't call off the motorcade. For almost forty minutes, Kennedy stood up in the limo waving. It's well-documented that someone threw a candy bar at the limo along the route. The candy bar thumped down on the hood of the car behind him, and even though the thud supposedly sounded like a gunshot, word is, and photos document it, that Kennedy remained standing. I was told that there were lots of possible places for an assassin to take his shot, but that the two most likely spots were as the motorcade made a left-hand turn in front of the Floridian Hotel before heading over a bridge to an armory where Kennedy was to speak, or from a warehouse along the route. Interesting, don't you think? A 90-degree turn and warehouses, just like Chicago."

"Eerie," said CJ. "The whole setup sounds awfully cookie-cutter."

"It gets even eerier. Turns out, I was told, that in all three cities there was a lawman or an equivalent involved in the plot who was connected to the mob. That person's job was to monitor any plot leaks that sprang up and squelch anything that popped up on the radar that might suggest that there would be an assassination attempt on Kennedy. And like everything else I've told you, the information on the rogue lawmen is both well-documented and readily available. The mafia's man in Chicago was a guy named Richard Cain, who it turns out was not only a mobster but the chief investigator for the Cook County sheriff's office. Records show that Cain had also worked on CIA- and mob-initiated plots to take out Castro. In Tampa, the name that surfaces, although his involvement in the assassination attempt there was never confirmed, was another law enforcement type, Frank Fiorini. The Dallas connection turned out not to be a cop at all—Jack Ruby served that function."

Barely able to digest what he was hearing, CJ asked, "So why didn't things go off in Tampa?"

"My people say the hit was called off by a local Tampa don, Santo Trafficante Jr., because he thought it would bring down too much heat on him."

CJ shook his head. "We're into the soup now, General."

"And it's boiling. Now, here's the final piece of the puzzle, and I think it's the key to your Antoine Ducane connection. For most of the time between November 1 and the assassination on November 22, Carlos Marcello, always considered to be a key player, if not *the* key player, in the assassination plot, was involved in his own deportation trial in New Orleans. Turns out the government was trying to slide Marcello the hell out of here. Because of that, he didn't have the chance to be as active in the plot to kill Kennedy as he probably would've liked. The word I have is that he convinced two other key mobsters, Trafficante and Chicago's Johnny Rosselli, to stand in for him. During the course of his trial, Marcello was reportedly only out of New Orleans for one three-day weekend. A weekend, it turns out, that just happened to coincide with the timetable for the hit in Chicago. Now, here's the beef. Because of the timing of his trial, Marcello supposedly had to enlist the help of a small-time would-be don out of Denver. Someone who'd been licking his boots for years. Wanna take a crack at who that might've been?"

"Not Rollie Ornasetti?"

"None other."

"Damn! Where'd that information spring up from?"

"Two of my sources, and they're both golden," said Alden.

"I believe you, Alden, but why haven't your sources said anything in all these years?"

"Want to tell him, Flora Jean?" Alden asked.

Flora Jean smiled and faced CJ. "Fraternity rules, sugar. In the world of intelligence and espionage, the rule of thumb is to never swing at balls outside your strike zone. The folks who gave Alden the information he's passin' on to us are in another orbit. They got no problem seein' the moon from where they're standin', but they're obligated not to ever take any trips there. Bottom line is, these guys, just like everyone else in the intelligence community, are in the business of keepin' secrets. Why else do you think they wouldn't give Alden so much as a hiccup until those papers you got from Willette Ducane turned up? Wouldn't surprise me if they didn't talk for another fifty years."

"But in all these years, don't you think somebody would've said something?" CJ asked.

"In the world you and I live in, sugar, but never, ever in theirs. We're lucky Alden's in theirs."

Shaking his head, CJ leaned toward the speaker. "So you think Rollie Ornasetti was in on the JFK assassination?"

"He sure was," Alden said matter-of-factly. "Just like Ducane. But I don't think Ducane was pegged to be a shooter anywhere but in Chicago, and in all likelihood Ornasetti was also probably slotted for Chicago and Chicago only. Ducane would've been way too green and too far outside the sphere of the kinds of shooters mafia kingpins like Marcello, or Johnny Rosselli, would've brought in for a hit of that magnitude. My guess is that in Chicago, Ducane, just like Oswald, was brought in to play the role of a patsy, and there's no question in my mind that he would have been if things had gone down as planned. The lingering problem for the assassination planners was that, unlike Oswald, Ducane got a chance to see the big picture."

"And when he saw what happened to Oswald live and on national TV, he couldn't have felt all warm and fuzzy."

"That's my take," said Alden. "Especially since Ducane's notes and sketches support the fact that he was to have been a shooter in

Chicago, especially his note about *low post* and *high post*. He was probably part of a team of two shooters, maybe even three, and unfortunately, like Oswald, his fate in Chicago would've certainly been to play the patsy in the catbird's seat upstairs. More than likely from a warehouse along the canceled parade route. By the way, those sketches of what you thought were two ladders on one of the pages of Ducane's notes gave me fits, but I think I've figured out what they really are."

"Clue me in," said CJ.

"I don't think they're ladders at all. My guess is they're doodles of railroad tracks. South Shore train-line tracks. Tracks for trains that still run around Lake Michigan to this day, shuttling people between, get this, the Windy City and Gary, Indiana."

"So Ducane was jotting subliminal travel notes to himself, then."

"More than likely. Because if he was a shooter, fall guy or not, he would've been warehoused somewhere a safe distance from Chicago."

"So if Ducane, like Oswald, was a patsy, who was the real shooter?"

"That's where, unlike everything I've told you up to now, speculation starts to seep in. Ducane's notes provide clues, but they don't spell out everything. The page where he describes a man he shared a cab ride with in Chicago gives us the best hint."

"Yeah, the dark-skinned guy wearing strange-looking shoes, a hat, and sunglasses."

"That description could fit a lot of people," said Alden. "But it also describes a couple of top-rung hired assassins the mob used back then. I'd say Ducane was very likely sharing his ride with the person who probably shot Kennedy. There might very well have been a different patsy in each of the three target cities—Ducane, Oswald, and God knows who else—but I'd bet my bottom dollar there was only one actual shooter hired to cover all three cities. It would've been too risky to the plot's secrecy to have had more."

"There you go bettin' again," said Flora Jean, watching CJ's eyebrows arc in anticipation. "Would you just tell us who?"

"My guess is that it was either James Files, a hit man from the Chicago family who once confessed to the JFK assassination and was later mysteriously exonerated, or Lucien Sarti, a hired assassin and drug pusher out of Corsica. I'd take Sarti myself. He's dead, by the way. Killed in a shoot-out in Mexico City in 1972. He fits Ducane's description almost to a T, right down to the strange-looking more-than-likely-Italian shoes and trademark fedora. Even better, according to one of my sources, a guy who's paid to know, several weeks before the assassination, Sarti was known to have flown from France to Mexico City. Word is he stayed there a day or so and was eventually brought into the U.S., crossing the border at Brownsville, Texas."

"Who do you think brought Sarti in for the hit?"

"Marcello or Trafficante, more than likely. They were the two American mobsters with the closest connections to the mafia in Marseilles."

CJ shook his head and sighed. "So, bottom line is, we've got ourselves a hit man and a patsy that nobody else in the world seems to know about but us."

"You're only half right there, CJ. The whole world knows about Sarti, and for that matter Files. Books, TV shows, and even documentaries have showcased them. The person the world doesn't know about is Antoine Ducane, Oswald's mirror image and a man who, in the end, knew way too much for his own good."

"Then why didn't they kill him way back when?"

"I've thought about that long and hard," said Alden. "And the only good reason I can come up with is that the "New York City syndrome" bit somebody involved in the assassination plot squarely in the ass."

Flora Jean giggled and shook her head as she watched a look of puzzlement spread across CJ's face. "You've slipped into intelligence speak again, sugar," she said to Alden. "Afraid you're gonna have to translate for CJ."

"Easy enough," said Alden. "Fortunately or unfortunately, a lot of folks in New York City seem to think the sun rises and sets on Gotham. They're too damn myopic to realize that there's a whole great-big rest of the world out there. I'm thinking that with a touch of the syndrome clouding their judgment, Marcello, Trafficante, and Rosselli saw Ducane's, and maybe even Oswald's, role as unimportant and secondary. Because of that, I'm thinking they came down with the New York City syndrome in a real bad way. The symptoms probably intensified after Marcello was acquitted in his deportation trial and Kennedy was dead. And why not? To their way of thinking, with Kennedy out of the way, why worry about some small-time New Iberia, Louisiana, 'Creole boy' who nobody in the world would've believed in the first place if he ever came forward to claim that he'd been involved in the plot to kill JFK. On top of that, who would've believed some Mile High City wannabe don like Rollie Ornasetti, looking to work his way up in the organization? Especially in the light of the fact that nothing ever went down in Chicago. New York City syndrome to a T, don't you think, Flora Jean?"

"Absolutely, sugar. Kingpins—governmental, mafia, or otherwise—sometimes forget to clean off their plates after they've been feasting. They seem to expect somebody to do that for 'em. Sometimes you wait a little too long for your dishwasher, and don't forget Ducane was supposedly Marcello's little Creole love child."

"I don't know," said CJ, sounding unconvinced. "Marcello was ready to sacrifice Ducane in Chicago."

"Maybe Marcello's guilt got the better of him," Flora Jean countered.

"Seems like way too many loose ends hanging for me," said CJ.

"Possibly, but for more than forty years it's worked," said Alden.

"No argument there," said CJ. "That leaves us with one unanswered question: How'd they actually kill JFK?"

"Can't be sure, but here's my guess," Alden said. "And it's based on a feeling in my gut, twenty-five years as a marine intelligence officer, and what my sources say are the cold, hard facts about the physical evidence in the case. Since Oswald certainly didn't shoot JFK, there had to have been at least a second gunman. Someone who was more than likely shooting from what's now commonly known as the grassy-knoll area of Dallas's Dealey Plaza. That would have been Sarti, in my judgment.

"As for the physical evidence, we've had decades of speculation about a possible botched Kennedy autopsy, incompetent pathologists, cover-ups, brain stealing, and flat-out prevarication on the part of doctors, the Secret Service, LBJ, and the Warren Commission. But there's no question from all the photos we have of the events in Dallas that day and the testimony of doctors who treated Kennedy at Parkland Hospital after he was shot that there was an entrance bullet wound in the front of Kennedy's neck. Which means there had to have been a shot that came at Kennedy from the front. And that brings us to a hard, cold fact. The Warren Commission report, with all its single-magic-bullet theory claiming that JFK was shot in the back of the head with a bullet that also hit Texas Governor John Connally, is pure, unadulterated hogwash."

Alden drew a deep breath. "That said, here's your problem, CJ, and it's probably a life-and-death issue to consider. You're sitting on documents that could help cement the fact that there was unquestionably a second shooter in the JFK assassination. And that's a place, quite frankly, where I wouldn't want to be sitting right now. Moreover, it's a place I don't want Flora Jean anywhere near. Here's my advice. Drop the whole thing. It could get you killed. As we like to say in my business, whether you're a spook, spy, or private eye, it always pays to know who the other bogeymen are—and in this case, CJ, you flat-out don't."

"Want to translate again for me?" CJ asked.

"Sure. Back in 1963 the CIA had a bunch of agents assigned to a program called Operation Mongoose. Mongoose was the code name for ongoing initiatives that President Kennedy set up inside the State Department, the CIA, and the Defense Department following our disastrous Bay of Pigs attempt to overthrow Castro. The operation's mission was to coordinate anti-Castro activities, up to and including a Castro assassination, if necessary. Some people have suggested that after Dallas, the mob, if indeed it did orchestrate the JFK killing, tried to deflect suspicion from itself by channeling it in the direction of Operation Mongoose. In doing so, however, the mafia found out it had more in common with the Mongoose people than it expected."

"Like what?"

"Like greed for power and money, or desire for the ability to control the populace, just to name a few. In the end, some people have argued, including a couple of my own sources, that the two parties became hard-and-fast allies instead of enemies."

"And my problem with that linkage would be . . . ?"

"Your problem would be that you'd have not one but two groups of people with a bevy of trained assassins trying to clean your clock if you insist on trying to find out who killed Antoine Ducane. Like I said before, drop it, CJ."

CJ stroked his chin thoughtfully. "I'm thinking about it."

"Think long and hard because you're not dealing with gang-bangers and bond skippers or your normal complement of wife beaters, thieves, rapists, and arsonists. And this isn't Vietnam, where at least you had a .50-caliber machine gun to speak for you. You're dealing with a whole different animal. These are the people who would kill a president. They won't hesitate to kill you. One final word. If you're determined to keep charging ahead, don't include Flora Jean."

Glancing at Flora Jean, CJ said, "Gotcha."

"I'll talk to you later," said Alden. "Hopefully by then you'll have decided to drop the issue. It will be a lot better for your health; trust me." He cradled the phone, leaving CJ and Flora Jean to stare at one another in disbelief.

Chapter 29

Successful police work, like anything else, Gus Cavalaris had learned, involved making the right choices, and sticking to Floyd, the veteran homicide lieutenant had kept telling himself since leaving Floyd's office, was the right choice. Especially if he ever expected to find out who had killed Cornelius McPherson.

Solving the McPherson murder might represent no more than a modest success when viewed against the backdrop of the Ducane murder and the JFK assassination, but modest successes, he'd also learned long ago, often opened the door to greater ones. He had the feeling that when all was said and done, Floyd would take him where he needed to be. He didn't expect to turn out to be Floyd's rabbit's foot again, but from the look of things, Floyd was desperately in need of one. Somebody wanted the nosy bail bondsman dead, no question.

As he peered out through one of the bay windows of Dozens, a breakfast and lunch eatery that sat catty-corner from the Denver police administrative offices and Bail Bondsman's Row, he could see Floyd's Delaware Street Victorian. Eyes locked on that building, he wondered how long it would be before Floyd led him to pay dirt.

He'd just taken a healthy sip of coffee when his waitress appeared. "No rush, sir, but we closed at two."

"Oh, sorry." He eyed his watch and realized it was 2:10. "L-l-lost myself in a problem."

The waitress smiled. "Happens to me all the time."

"Do you g-g-get most of yours solved?" Cavalaris rose to leave.

"Only about half the time," the waitress lamented, shaking her head.

"That's better than me." Cavalaris chuckled and headed for the cash register to settle his bill. He looked back at the waitress as he handed the restaurant's manager a $10 bill. Smiling back at the waitress as he waited for his change, he said, "Guess I'll just have to try a little harder."

After ending his phone conversation with Alden Grace, CJ spent a good part of the next two hours in his office trying to come up with a good reason for continuing to pursue something that Alden Grace had assured him could get him killed. He knew he wasn't sticking with the Ducane case because of the $1,000 retainer Willette Ducane had paid him to find out who'd killed Antoine. And although he had to admit that the JFK assassination angle fascinated him, that wasn't the reason he was staying with it either.

What had his investigative senses heightened flowed from an altogether different wellspring. The very same thing that he knew kept Damion Madrid glued to the basketball court and Julie buried up to her eyebrows in a legal case. The persuasive force that pushed him to drive thousands of miles in search of a rare antique license plate to add to his collection or risk his life chasing a bond skipper across three states. In the end, what had him in dogged pursuit of Antoine Ducane's murderer, in spite of the risks, was his competitive nature. Surprisingly, Mavis may have summed it up best, calling whatever it was that drove him and people like him to do what they did an "elixir," the tenuous cure-all that made life worth living.

In many ways, he knew Mavis was right. Perhaps chasing down Antoine Ducane's killer would be his last thrill ride. The one he was meant to take before he settled for good into a life of peddling antiques and collectibles on the Internet.

Weary of trying to analyze what made him tick, he spun his desk chair around, took a Coke out of the minirefrigerator behind his desk, popped the top, and looked up at the wall of photographs in front of him. The wall, a virtual rogue's gallery, was filled with photos of more than a hundred bond skippers he'd brought back to face justice during his more than thirty years as a bounty hunter and bail bondsman. Staring at the photos, he nursed his Coke for a couple more minutes in silence. When he'd finished his drink, he called Mario to find out if he had any idea what might have happened to the conveniently missing Rollie Ornasetti and to see if Mario might have an inkling of how Ornasetti might have handled his Ducane problem years earlier.

Mario endorsed Pinkie Niedemeyer's take, confirming that Ornasetti probably would have used his Teamsters connections to help him get rid of Ducane, just as Randall Maxie had suggested. He wasn't certain that Rollie would have disposed of Ducane at the abandoned sugar-beet factory in Brighton, as was mob practice back then, he told CJ. But it was a safe bet. What neither man could figure out, however, was how Ducane's body had ended up at the Eisenhower Tunnel.

They talked briefly about whether Ornasetti had been snatched by higher-ups in order to muzzle him or whether he'd been hit, agreeing in the end that he'd probably been abducted.

When CJ told Mario he was going to run out to the old sugar-beet factory and have a look around, Mario offered a stern warning: "Don't go out there by yourself, CJ. It's a special kind of dumpin' ground, if you know what I mean. Special enough for you to have somebody ridin' shotgun if you insist on takin' your ass out there."

Recalling the promise he'd made to Alden Grace about not putting Flora Jean in harm's way, CJ asked, "Who am I gonna get to go out there with me on such short notice?"

Pinkie Niedemeyer, who'd been listening in on the conversation on Mario's kitchen phone, spoke up: "Guess I'm it."

"Pinkie?"

"Nobody else but."

"How come you're on the line?"

"'Cause I asked him," said Mario. "Figured you mighta been the FBI callin'."

"Wire tapping's more up their alley," CJ said, smiling. "I don't think they'd call."

"Well, if it's tapped, I got somethin' for the powder-puff-carryin', sissified assholes. Kiss my ass!" Mario said loudly.

Clearing his throat, CJ said, "About as good an answer as any, I guess. Pinkie, you still there?"

"Yeah."

"Sure you wanna go out to that sugar-beet factory with me?" CJ asked. "I've been told by Alden Grace, no less, that I'm cutting things too close to the bone with this Ducane thing already."

"So what was your response?" asked Pinkie.

"Didn't have one really."

"Then we go out to the factory and have a look. What else you got to live for, your old-age pension?"

"Problem solved," said CJ. "Meet me at my place, in twenty minutes. I wanna get to Brighton by sunset," he added, thinking that he'd inadvertently left Pinkie Niedemeyer's name off his list of diehard competitors.

"I'll be there," Pinkie said, cradling the phone and walking from the kitchen to where Mario sat in the TV room. "CJ's got some serious business he needs help with, Dominico."

Mario simply nodded. "There ain't never been anything but serious business takin' place out there where you two are headed. Don't let it snap back and bite you."

"Oh, we won't," Pinkie said with a grin. "In case you forgot, your government once paid both me and CJ to kill people."

CJ reacted with a start as his garage door swung open. "Damn it, Pinkie! You looking to get shot? Close that door."

CJ was kneeling twenty feet across the garage from Pinkie in front of a workbench that ran the width of the garage. Standing, he dusted off his hands. The battered navy footlocker he'd carried through two tours of Vietnam sat with its top raised just in front of him.

"No way. You're too damn old, and your aim's too bad," Pinkie said, smiling. He swung the garage door shut and walked across the uneven concrete floor that CJ's Uncle Ike had laid fifty years earlier.

"When did you become a comedian?" CJ asked, glancing up from the footlocker.

"I didn't." Pinkie's smile melted. "Just thought a little levity might help the situation. Here's a heads-up. We're headin' across the DMZ and into hostile territory if we go out to Brighton, CJ. Take my word for it. You up for that?" The look on Pinkie's face had turned deadly serious.

Surprised by Pinkie's use of the term for the demilitarized zone that had separated North and South Vietnam during the war, CJ turned his attention to the contents of the footlocker. "You think we could run into that much resistance?" he asked, reaching into the footlocker and taking out the M-16 he'd brought back from Vietnam and Ike's nickel-plated .45. He laid the two weapons on the floor.

"Depends," said Pinkie.

"On what?"

"On whether or not there's been any activity out at the old sugar-beet factory lately. Trust me, neither one of us wants to go muckin' around out there if there has been."

"Anybody able to clue us in on the activity level?" CJ asked as he stared down at the eyeglasses-sized box that contained the Navy Cross he'd earned during Vietnam.

"The half-senile, slope-headed old bag of bones who's been de facto caretaker out there for years."

"Caretaker? Who the hell owns the property?"

Pinkie smiled. "People, CJ, people. No worries, though. I already called the old cuss. Told him I'd be out there this evenin'."

"You told somebody we're coming?"

"Had to. Otherwise the old geezer woulda shot us, no question. Told him I was comin' to check the place out—consider reusin' his place after years of bein' away."

CJ shook his head. "Don't think I really wanna know a lot more, Pinkie." He took a half-dozen clips of ammo for the M-16 and a half-empty box of ammo for the .45 out of the footlocker.

Pinkie shook his head. "I'd take more firepower if I was you."

"You've gotta be bullshitting."

"Wish I was," Pinkie said, frowning. "Here's the deal, CJ. Ornasetti's more than likely been snatched. Here we are stickin' our noses into a couple of killin's that trail back to the assassination of JFK.

The FBI's got their noses up our asses, yours more than mine, thank God, and some stutterin' Denver homicide cop's got his up theirs. I've even heard that people in certain kinds of business and ah . . . fraternal organizations as far away as New Orleans are gettin' antsy. So if we go anywhere, stickin' our noses where they don't belong, we go prepared."

CJ scooped up a handful of additional ammo clips and set them on the floor before teasing a Kevlar vest out from beneath a clear plastic box filled with marbles.

"Whatta you got there?" asked Pinkie, staring at the box of marbles.

"My collection of jumbo shooters. Started collecting 'em when I was six. Every one's a proven sticker."

Pinkie smiled. "You know, I had a few of them once myself. How come you keep 'em out here?"

"Because I don't want them to mistakenly get mixed in with the antique store's inventory and sold."

"They're that valuable?"

"Nope. Just that important."

"That why you keep your Navy Cross out here too?" Pinkie asked, eyeing the box that contained the medal.

"Nope. I keep it and the M-16 out here to remind me that life can always turn more insane than it is."

Pinkie shrugged. "Everybody's gotta dance to their demons, I guess."

CJ nodded, closed the top of the footlocker, snapped the combination lock shut, and slipped the footlocker back beneath the workbench. Looking at Pinkie, he asked, "What about the old guy out at the plant? Can we trust him?"

"Have for years."

"But what about now?"

"We'll just have to see."

"You got a vest?" CJ asked, tucking his Kevlar vest under his arm.

"Got it on," said Pinkie. "And an Uzi and a .44 Mag out in the car. The only thing we'll need to pick up on our way out there are some potatoes."

"What?" CJ asked, looking puzzled.

"Taters," Pinkie said with a grin. "I'll explain on the way."

"Okay," said CJ. "And by the way, I never figured you for a Boy Scout, Pinkie."

It was Pinkie's turn to look puzzled. "I wasn't."

"Well, if you weren't, you sure as hell usurped their motto." Smiling, he eyed the bulge of Pinkie's protective vest.

"Oh, yeah? So what's their motto?"

"'Be prepared.'"

"Good one. Bein' prepared is a damn sight better than bein' dead. Let's get the hell outta here," said Pinkie, wondering what CJ would have to say about his preparation when he explained the reason for the potatoes.

As they headed for the door, CJ glanced back at the footlocker, hoping things weren't about to turn Vietnam-style insane.

Chapter 30

Napper enjoyed sitting on a park bench and feeding the geese along the lakeshore in Denver's City Park. It gave him the opportunity to enjoy a part of the Queen City he rarely had the chance to—and, of course, to play his special game with the geese. He'd watched the sun slow-dance its way west for better than an hour, and he'd almost emptied the bag of croutons he'd brought along to feed the geese.

He'd dealt with Ornasetti, who'd reluctantly, after twelve long hours, taken him up on his offer to start a new life, the only option the small-time Denver don had aside from a bullet to the head or a lethal injection. As soon as he was finished with the geese, Napper planned to drop in on Mario Satoni and offer him a similar deal. Pleased that he was set to tie up so many loose ends in less than thirty-six hours, it galled him, nonetheless, that he hadn't been able to settle up with Satoni's friend, the bail bondsman. When he'd asked for some additional time to deal with Floyd, however, he'd been told to stick with his primary objectives, Ornasetti and Satoni.

Disappointed that his respite in the park would soon end, he glanced around at the half-dozen geese that remained from what had once been a gaggle of close to twenty. He checked his stash of croutons and tried to determine which of the geese was the fattest and the least deserving of a snack. He'd just made his choice when his cell phone rang.

"Napper?" the caller asked hesitantly.

"Yeah."

"It's Arnie. I got a problem out here at the plant."

"Spell it out, Arnie."

"You know Pinkie Niedemeyer?"

"No, but I've heard of him."

"He's headed out here to take a look around."

"He got a dump?"

"Nope. That's why I called. He ain't used us in years."

Napper watched the geese start to walk away toward a boy who was tossing a Frisbee. "Wait a second, Arnie." He flung all but the very last of his croutons at the geese, who made a U-turn and headed back toward him. "Okay."

"So what should I do?"

"Let him look around. He knows the place, doesn't he?"

"Yeah. But he's got no reason to come out, and he's gonna have somebody with him. I don't like the idea of him bringin' no guest out here, Napper."

"Who's he bringin'?" Napper's eyes narrowed to a determined squint.

"He didn't say."

"How soon's he comin'?"

"He said he'd be out before dark."

Aware that no matter what the reason for Niedemeyer's visit, it was more than likely Mario Satoni's interest the skinny hit man truly had at heart, Napper said, "Wanna make a quick five hundred, Arnie?"

"How?"

"Help me set up Niedemeyer and that guest of his. Things are a little scrambled for me at the moment, and I don't need anybody scramblin' them up any more."

"I don't know, Napper. On whose orders?"

"Mine."

"I might need clearance."

"Then get it and call me right back." Napper snapped his cell phone closed and mumbled, "Shit." He hated waiting for clearance. It magnified the fact that he had to answer to someone. Clearances were for bureaucrats—courage for soldiers, he thought as he watched the boy who had distracted the geese walk away. Relieved that he'd be able to finish his game, he sprinkled his final half-dozen croutons down at his feet. As the geese encircled him, he shooed all but the fattest goose away. When that goose lumbered into range, he glanced around to make certain no one was looking, grabbed the goose by the neck, and wrung the forty-five-pound bird around so fast that anyone spotting the move would have realized it wasn't a first-time maneuver. The goose kicked a few times before going limp.

He nudged the dead bird under the bench, retrieved a black trash-can liner bag from his pocket, snapped it open with a flip of his wrist, knelt, and rolled the goose into the bag. He looked around once again to make certain no one had seen him and smiled. As he tightened the drawstring on the trash bag, his cell phone rang. "Napper here," he said, knotting the drawstring.

"We've got clearance," Arnie said, his voice wavering.

"Good. I'm headed your way. I'm just finishing up with somethin' right now. I'll call you back to work out the logistics on my way there."

"And don't forget my money," said Arnie, taking a swig from the bottle of Jim Beam in his quivering right hand.

"No chance." Napper gripped the trash bag with one hand and snapped his cell phone closed with the other. As he walked toward his vehicle, he broke into a satisfied smile. He loved playing games that ended in death. Always had, even as a kid. It invariably gave him an erection, and sometimes his skin tingled for as long as five minutes after a kill. At that very second, in fact, he had the sense that hundreds of feathers were tickling every inch of his skin.

The goose felt a lot heavier to him than was typical, but it wasn't until he weighed it on the scale in the bed of his truck that he realized it was seven pounds heavier than he'd guessed. As he left the park and headed for Brighton, he had the sense that he would be rewarded with another kill or two that evening. The human kind—and that kind of kill always elevated his excitement to the ejaculatory level.

Uncomfortable with the fact that Pinkie Niedemeyer had brought someone along with him, and even more upset that the man was black, Arnie DeVentis, following Napper's directive, took fifteen minutes longer than was his custom in getting the particulars on CJ, whom Pinkie described as a "settlement agent" out of LA. He finally waved Pinkie's SUV onto the abandoned sugar-beet factory's thirty-acre grounds and closed the entry gate a half hour before twilight.

The abandoned plant had once been the largest and most productive of the Great Western Sugar Company's Colorado, Nebraska, Wyoming, and Montana sugar-beet factories. During the 1920s, the plants were said to have produced more sugar during their annual eighty-five-day fall refining season than the cane fields of Louisiana. The Brighton, Colorado, plant, originally built in 1916, just twenty-nine miles from downtown Denver, had ceased operations in 1967. In the

years since, its once impressive six-story-tall red-brick main manufac-
turing building and adjacent massive filtering annex had gone to seed.
All that remained behind the crumbling shell of the main building
and annex, where ten cold-storage sugar-beet sheds with a storage
capacity of eighty thousand tons, six pulp silos, and a mill pond fed by
natural springs had once stood, was a four-story-tall silo, the dilapi-
dated remains of three cold-storage sheds, and a dried-up pond.

Pinkie and CJ followed Arnie from the abandoned plant's entry
off state Highway 7 along the rutted road that led to what was left
of the remaining structures in the burnt-orange glow of the impend-
ing sunset. As they pulled to a stop a mile from the highway in front
of the four-foot-high remains of the brick-walled northeast corner
of the main building, CJ leaned toward Pinkie and said, "Reminds
you of what we left behind in 'Nam, don't you think?"

"Does at that," said Pinkie, drinking in the isolated landscape. He
waited for Arnie, who'd parked his pickup five yards or so behind
them, to walk up to his SUV before he rolled down his window.

"What do you wanna see?" Arnie asked, bending down and peering into the SUV to get a better look at CJ. His right arm shook as
if he were a little bit nervous, and the smell of alcohol was evident on
his breath.

"Thought we'd just take a look around the place," said Pinkie.
"Wanna introduce my friend to its possibilities."

"Might as well start right here at the main building," said Arnie.
"Not much to it, as you can see. Then we can have a look at the silo,
the storage sheds, and finally the slicer, if you're up for it." Arnie
turned to CJ and smiled. "It's a beet slicer left over from the factory's
production days. Got it set up in one of the sheds."

"What do you use it for now?" asked CJ.

"For cuttin' through anything the consistency of a sugar beet—taters, fruit—that sorta thing. Guess you could even get it to slice up human flesh, if you had a mind to." Arnie snickered. The snicker quickly escalated to a raucous laugh. Taking a deep breath and exhaling a stale alcoholic fog in CJ's face, Arnie said, "So do we take a look at things the way I suggested?"

"Sounds like a reasonable enough agenda to me," said Pinkie. CJ nodded approvingly.

The two men got out of the SUV, and Pinkie stepped to a rear door, opened it, and slipped the Colorado State University gym bag that Damion Madrid had given him off the back seat. "Whattaya got there?" Arnie asked, looking puzzled.

"Taters," said Pinkie. "I figured you'd show us the slicer, so I brought along something to slice." He set the gym bag on the ground and unzipped one of its two zippers. When he squeezed the sides of the bag, a half-dozen russet potatoes rolled out onto the ground. Scooping the potatoes up, Pinkie said, "I've got two or three dozen more in here—catch." He tossed a potato to Arnie.

Arnie grabbed for the potato, but the pint of Jim Beam he'd polished off a half hour earlier wouldn't let him catch it. Kneeling, he scooped the potato up off the ground and, in an attempt to demonstrate his sobriety, tossed it from hand to hand. "Still got my reflexes. And at seventy-six." He looked toward the darkening sky. "We better get movin'; daylight ain't gonna be with us much longer."

"It's your show," said Pinkie, winking at CJ and hefting the gym bag. "Wouldn't wanna get off our agenda."

By the time they'd finished inspecting two of the three sugar-beet storage sheds, the compound was aglow in the magenta haze of twilight. CJ had scrutinized the two sheds, which were each the size of a small two-story house, looking for any evidence that Antoine Ducane, or anyone else for that matter, might've been sliced and diced, pulverized, or even laid out for a permanent beauty rest. Both sheds, however, were in the throes of final collapse. He had barely been able to walk around inside them without hitting his head on something, much less determine whether anyone had ever been killed inside.

Now, as CJ stood inside the surprisingly pristine-looking third shed scrutinizing Arnie's beet slicer while Pinkie inspected an inoperative Humvee-sized refrigeration unit, a look of disappointment spread across CJ's face. He'd hoped to stumble across some link to the Ducane murder at the abandoned factory. Something that would help him determine how Antoine Ducane had been killed there and then transported to the Eisenhower Tunnel. A hospital gurney, a stretcher, a pine box, some gunnysacks—anything suggesting a method of transport and transfer. Instead he'd toured two ramshackle sheds, had a look at a silo, and was now standing a few feet from a sugar-beet slicer that, although operable, certainly wasn't the kind of machine anyone would use to slice up a human being.

"Wanna see anything else?" Arnie asked, inching his way toward the shed's door, and taking in the look of disappointment on CJ's face.

"Nope. We've seen enough," said CJ, aware that sometimes you end up shooting a blank. Shrugging off the apparent miscalculation, he turned to Pinkie, who still stood across the room. CJ had barely uttered, "Let's shove off," when the lights in the shed went out. Seconds later the only door swung open, and Arnie DeVentis was out the door. "Hey!" Pinkie called out. "Shoulda been watchin' the fucker closer." He raced to the door, gym bag draped over his shoulder.

When he stuck his head outside, three rounds from a semiautomatic handgun sent him diving back inside. "Son of a bitch set us up. Shit!" Pinkie slipped the gym bag off his shoulder, letting it drop to the floor. "Still any good at puttin' an M-16 together in the dark?" he called out to CJ.

"Like ridin' a bike."

"Then you better get over here and start. I'm already half done with my Uzi."

CJ walked across the floor and knelt next to the gym bag. A minute and a half later, he was holding a loaded, fully assembled M-16. "So what's our exit strategy?" he said to Pinkie, moving the rifle from hand to hand, regaining its feel.

"Since there's only one way outta here, I say we wait for it to get a little darker and hope that whoever's bound to be out there waitin' for us has less firepower than we do."

"And if they don't?"

"Then it looks like we got ourselves stuck back to the future, Petty Officer Floyd."

Gus Cavalaris, congratulating himself for having had the sense to stick with Floyd, had scaled the rickety fence that surrounded the sugar-beet factory grounds a half hour earlier and slowly worked his way across the wide-open grounds until he now stood behind the crumbling four-foot-high remains of the northwest corner of the headquarters building, trying to determine where the three shots he'd heard had come from. When Arnie DeVentis appeared out of nowhere, headed toward him at a dead run, Cavalaris, his right hand on the butt of his 9-mm, yelled, "Hey! Stop!"

Arnie reached for the semiautomatic in his jacket pocket, but Cavalaris was quicker. The second of three shots he fired at the slightly inebriated old caretaker hit him in the right thigh, and he crumbled to the ground. Seconds later Cavalaris stood over Arnie with the barrel of his 9-mm aimed squarely at the old man's chest. When he reached for his cell phone to call for backup, he found that the phone wasn't clipped to his belt. Realizing that he'd probably lost it sometime between scaling the compound's fence and working his way to the main building, he said, "Shit!" As he watched the circle of blood on Arnie's pants leg grow, he said, "Should've s-s-stayed put."

"Who the hell are you?" Arnie said, trembling.

Cavalaris reached into his pants pocket, slipped out a wallet containing his police badge, and flipped it open. "Lieutenant Gus Cavalaris, Denver Homicide. More important thing, though, is w-w-who are you?" When Arnie didn't respond, Cavalaris slipped his handcuffs off his belt, turned the now moaning old man over onto his belly, and slapped the cuffs onto his wrists. As he turned to retrace his steps to look for his cell phone, machine-gun fire strafed the ground in front of him. A second strafing splintered several bricks at the top of the building's remnant of wall. He looked toward where the gunfire seemed to be coming from to realize that someone was shooting at him from the compound's remaining silo. A third strafing sent him leaping to the ground, spread-eagled next to Arnie. Looking more agitated than afraid, he said, "Nice f-f-fuckin' place you've got here, old man."

"Let's move it!" CJ yelled at Pinkie in the wake of the third round of machine-gun fire.

"Why now? It's not dark."

"Because we don't wanna be sitting here where Arnie deposited us when whoever's out there gets around to dusting us. There's a reason Arnie left us here. Let's go." CJ duck-walked his way to the shed's door, opened it just enough to slip out into the fading twilight, hoping he hadn't been seen, and began crawling, M-16 cradled across his arms, toward the first shed they'd visited.

Pinkie stayed glued to CJ's heels. They were a few feet from the shed when a string of bullets danced across the dirt in front of them.

CJ glanced skyward toward where he thought the gunfire was coming from, rolled onto his side, and squeezed off a full M-16 clip at the top of the silo.

Pinkie followed CJ's lead, uncertain what he was shooting at. The response they got as CJ nudged open the crumbling shed's door with his rifle muzzle and they both crawled inside was the unmistakable return fire from a submachine gun. "Somebody else out there with an Uzi," CJ said, panting.

"Or an AK-47," Pinkie said, nearly crawling over him. As Pinkie kicked the door to the shed closed, a round of shots from an automatic handgun rang out. "Shit! How many people are out there?"

"I'm guessin' two," said CJ. "That machine-gun fire came from the top of the silo, but those pistol shots came from ground level and from an automatic. I don't think the pistol shots were meant for us."

"You sure?"

CJ smiled. "As sure as I am that after babysittin' that .50-caliber of mine for two tours, I swore I could hear the son of a bitch breathing."

"What about the other shooter, then? Arnie?"

"I'm not sure," said CJ. "I could've sworn Arnie's shots came from a semiautomatic before."

"Wonder who the guy with the automatic's shootin' at? Us or them?"

"One way to find out. Hey, Arnie, you out there?" CJ yelled, as loudly as he could.

A round of machine-gun fire peppered the side of the shed. A few seconds of silence followed before Cavalaris yelled, "Floyd, y-y-you out there? It's Cavalaris."

"Yeah," CJ yelled, happy to hear the familiar stutter.

"I'm pinned down over here inside a corner of what's left of some building," Cavalaris called out. "Fifteen yards or so from the s-s-shed that just got strafed. You in there?"

"Yeah."

"Our shooter's on t-t-top of the silo."

A volley of machine-gun fire sent Cavalaris sprawling to the ground.

"And he can hear us yelling," CJ said, shaking his head. Looking at Pinkie, he asked, "Think you can keep our shooter occupied while I slip out of here and around to the exit-stair side of that silo?"

"Are you crazy, CJ? Let Cavalaris call for backup."

"I'm hoping he already has."

"Then let's wait."

"I don't think that would be smart," said CJ. "There's no telling what our friend out there has cooked up for us. Could be he's got grenades."

"Shit! So what's your plan?" asked Pinkie, well aware of the damage a grenade could do to the rickety shed.

"I'm gonna crawl outta here and head for the back side of that silo with this relic of mine from Vietnam burping." CJ patted his M-16. "There's a ground level access door to that silo somewhere and I'm gonna use it to our advantage. Keep an eye on me once I get to the silo. In the meantime, keep the guy on the roof occupied and let's hope that somebody shows up."

"And if nobody does?" Pinkie asked.

"Oh, they will. Sooner or later somebody's bound to hear that there's a war goin' on out here."

"Why don't we just sit tight?"

"How many ways do I have to say it, Pinkie? We were set up. And we may still be," CJ said, not bothering to mention that in all likelihood Ducane's killer had stepped out of the closet and he planned to bag him.

"Listen for my shots," said CJ, crawling back toward the door. As he slipped out of the shed and worked his way across the ground toward the exit-stair side of the silo, all he could hear was his own labored breathing and the wind.

Trying his best to think three steps ahead of the bail bondsman and Niedemeyer, Napper was beside himself. He'd been prepared to dispose of the two of them. What he hadn't counted on was a third man gumming up the works. Realizing that he had very little time to work out a solution, he weighed his options. He could stand his ground and hope to finish off the bail bondsman and Niedemeyer while there was still a glimmer of daylight. He could move down to ground level and use his grenades. Or, as a last resort, he could make a phone call on the special phone he'd brought and extricate himself from his predicament. But he realized that once he made that phone call, he'd end up just like Ornasetti, or worse. He'd spent decades straddling two fences, and he'd made it work. He'd molded himself into a perfect chameleon and served two masters. And now he found himself a hair's breadth away from falling off his perch. As he saw it, he'd even helped a few people out. He'd been Sheila Lucerne's beacon to safety, although she'd never realized it. At Antoine Ducane's request, and for a mere $10,000, he had come up with a safety net for her. He'd even shown Ornasetti how to keep breathing.

Scanning the darkening landscape, upset that he'd left his night-vision goggles in his truck, he muttered, "Damn." He'd never expected Floyd and Niedemeyer to arrive with an arsenal, and never in his wildest dreams had he expected a stray dog like Cavalaris to come tagging along. No matter. All he could do now was play out his hand.

A hint of a breeze kicked up as CJ crawled along the south rim of the silo in the last glimmer of light. Reaching a recessed access door on the silo's south side, a door he'd suspected had to be there, he rose to a crouch and wedged all of his 240 pounds into the eight-inch-deep recess. He patted his stomach and considered a plan to take out the machine gunner. Convinced as he glanced skyward that he could work his way clockwise around the base of the silo and fire up at the gunman from 12, 3, 6, and 9 o'clock positions before jumping back to the safety of the door access as he drew return fire, he nodded and thought, *Why not?* It wasn't a bad course of action if his ammo held out and if he played the game of cat and mouse just right. Hopefully the gunman, uncertain where the next round of M-16 fire might come from, would respond by exposing himself briefly, but long enough for Pinkie to pick him off as he leaned over the edge of the silo to fire down on an ever-moving target. The success of the plan depended, however, on an experienced former infantryman like Pinkie recognizing his role in a maneuver that couldn't be communicated to him.

Taking a deep breath, CJ patted the bulge of ammo in his pockets and thought, *Now or never,* as he stepped out of the doorway and fired up at the gunman. The gunman's return fire kicked up a spray of dirt and rock that made CJ wonder, as he jumped back into the protection of the doorway, if he hadn't chosen the wrong plan.

After two more sets of serve and volley and an interim round of machine-gun fire meant to keep Lieutenant Cavalaris pinned down, Pinkie had caught on to CJ's strategy. Hoping the machine gunner hadn't as well, and anticipating a fourth exchange, Pinkie sighted in on the top of the silo at 9 o'clock. Barely breathing now, he waited for CJ to let loose with his M-16.

Seconds after CJ opened fire, Napper leaned over the side of the silo to fire downward. Pinkie emptied thirty-two rounds into the top of the silo, splintering the top edges of a protective three-foot-high stem wall and sending concrete flying. When Napper let out a wail, CJ and Pinkie yelled, "Hit!" in near unison.

Bleeding from a nicked shoulder artery, his right arm limp from a fractured collarbone, and his shoulder blade shattered, Napper lost his grip on the AK-47 and fell to his knees. The submachine gun dropped into a pool of blood near his knees. Realizing that his choices for survival had suddenly narrowed down to either bleeding to death on the spot or taking his chances on an uncertain future, Napper scooted over to the silo's protective concrete stem wall and, back to the wall, propped himself up.

Laboring to breathe, he reached for the phone case at his feet, snapped the front of it open, and entered a ten-digit number. When he heard the busy signal on the other end of the line, he said, in barely a whisper, "It's Napper. I've got a Code 3."

Chapter 31

Gus Cavalaris's call from his vehicle for backup turned out a virtual army of cops from eight jurisdictions, including an incident command unit and a SWAT team from Adams County. An ambulance, its roof-mounted lights flashing red and yellow in the early-evening darkness, sat in front of the crumbling headquarters building, awaiting delivery of a semiconscious Arnie DeVentis. Cavalaris stood a few feet from the ambulance talking to the Adams County sheriff. Ten yards away, Pinkie and CJ sat on the ground, back to back, handcuffed to a badly rusted standpipe.

DeVentis, mumbling barely intelligible threats and obscenities, lifted his head off the stretcher as two paramedics rolled him toward the ambulance. "I'll settle wif you cocksuckers. I—I—I'll settle . . ."

As the paramedic pushing the back end of the stretcher passed Cavalaris, the frustrated homicide lieutenant grabbed him by the arm. "Need to talk to your patient. Won't take but a sec."

The paramedic shook his head. "Sorry, Lieutenant. His blood pressure's barely pegging seventy over fifty, and he's headed for the kind of shock that can't be reversed if we don't get him some help real quick." Slipping out of Cavalaris's grasp, he nodded to the paramedic leading the stretcher to keep moving.

Looking disgusted, Cavalaris turned back to Sheriff Vickers, a tall, silver-haired man sporting a crew cut, and mumbled, "Shit."

Recognizing Cavalaris's frustration but beset with problems of his own, the sheriff said, "We don't get many wars out here, Lieutenant. Mind telling me what the hell started this one?"

"Can't t-t-tell you for sure," Cavalaris yelled, trying to be heard above a roar of background noise. "Not 'til I t-t-talk to whoever's m-m-manning the submachine gun up there on top of that silo." Cavalaris eyed the silo, thinking how deceitfully peaceful it looked in the moonlight.

"Don't hold your breath, Lieutenant. I don't think he'll say much more than the guy those paramedics just carted out of here. And that's if we can get him off that rooftop." Vickers glanced at CJ and Pinkie. "Your two Rambos over there saw to that. According to them, our shooter's hit pretty bad, and you saw what happened when I tried to coax him down from his perch. Could be he wants to die up there."

"Yeah," said Cavalaris, recalling the three rounds of machine-gun fire that had sent him and the sheriff scurrying for cover in the ruins of the headquarters building after Vickers's failed attempts with a bullhorn to persuade the shooter off the rooftop.

"Could be he's finally passed out," said Vickers.

"Or he's d-d-dead."

"Don't think so. The pilot of that chopper I called in to spot him reported that when he punched up his spotlights, our shooter made a move to take cover. But we'll know for sure in a little bit. I've got a couple of my SWAT boys headed up the back side of that silo to take a closer look."

Looking puzzled, Cavalaris said, "You know, it's almost like he's trying to h-h-hold out up there for as long as he can for s-s-some reason."

"Yeah. He probably doesn't want to end up staring at half-a-dozen counts of attempted murder."

"Maybe." Cavalaris sounded unconvinced. "Think I'll g-g-go see how your SWAT boys are doing."

The sheriff bristled. "No, you won't, Lieutenant. I don't know how you hotshots in Denver handle situations like this, but you're out in the country now. You're staying put."

Cavalaris frowned. "This situation's a lot m-m-more explosive than you th-th-think, Sheriff."

"I expect it is, seeing as how I've had the tranquillity of my peaceful little corner of the country shattered by some bozo on a silo armed with a submachine gun. A man who, it ends up, was trying his best to take out the Rocky Mountain region's top hit man and an M-16-toting bail bondsman. Like I said, Lieutenant, you're not moving."

"How about I t-t-talk to Niedemeyer and Floyd again, then?" asked Cavalaris, certain CJ and Pinkie had heard bits and pieces of their conversation.

"You've talked to them already, and they barely said a thing."

"Could be they're feeling more talkative by now."

Vickers shook his head and shrugged. "Go ahead. Got nothing to lose from it. I've gotta go see what's taking that Flight for Life helicopter so long to get here." He eyed the top of the silo. "If they don't hurry up, it's a sure bet our shooter's gonna be dead." As he pivoted to head for the command post he'd set up, the sheriff glanced back over his shoulder at Cavalaris. "Stay put, Lieutenant. That's an order."

As soon as he was certain the sheriff was out of earshot, Cavalaris walked over to CJ and Pinkie. "You two ready to talk yet?" When he didn't get an answer, he knelt and said, "W-w-well you'd better get your tongues lubricated. Something's not r-r-right here. No way it should take a Flight for Life chopper an hour to get out here. Not when a police-spotter helicopter was here in twenty minutes.

I n-n-need some straight answers, and quick. I'm starting to get a w-w-whiff of something that smells an awful lot like somebody besides the sheriff is orchestrating things out here. So, I'm gonna ask you the s-s-same questions I asked you half an hour ago. Why'd you two c-c-come out here, and who's up there on that roof?"

Neither CJ nor Pinkie responded.

Cavalaris said, "Okay. H-h-have it your way. The sheriff may not know what he's s-s-stumbled into, but I do, and trust me, the sh-sh-shit's gonna hit the fan again real quick. And when it does, I've got a f-f-feeling the three of us just might end up in the same lifeboat paddling for shore. So sooner or later b-b-both of you are g-g-gonna have to decide who to cast your lot with. Me, the sheriff, or who-ever else happens to eventually sh-sh-show up at this tea party. L-l-like they say, better the devil you know than the ten who w-w-want to cut your nuts off. Think about it." Cavalaris rose and called over his shoulder, "Think hard," as he jogged toward the silo.

"He's got a point," CJ said to Pinkie, watching Cavalaris disappear into the darkness.

"Screw him; he's a cop," Pinkie countered.

"Okay," said CJ. "But he's right about one thing. Sooner or later the shit will hit the fan."

Cavalaris checked to make certain he had a full clip in his 9-mm, patted the three additional clips in his pocket, and started up the silo's back stairs. When he reached the first-story landing, one of the two SWAT members who were three-quarters of the way to the rooftop shouted, "Hey! Get the shit off of these stairs!"

"The sheriff sent me," Cavalaris shouted up to them. "Lieutenant Gus Cavalaris, Denver Homicide."

"Not likely," one of the men hollered back. He leaned over the stair railing and trained his weapon on Cavalaris. "Stay put!"

Undaunted, Cavalaris yelled, "Shoot me and you'll be e-e-explaining why for a lifetime."

"I will if I have to. There's a guy up there with a submachine gun." The burlier of the two cops adjusted a communication earpiece as he watched Cavalaris continue up the stairs to stop a few steps below the third-floor landing. "Sheriff, this is Silo One. We've got a problem on the stairs."

Shaking his head in disbelief, the smaller of the two, a bug-eyed man with buck teeth, trained his 9-mm on Cavalaris. "Let's see your badge!"

Cavalaris slipped his badge wallet out of his shirt pocket and handed it up to the shorter cop as the cop's partner yelled into his lapel mike, "Sheriff, come in. This is Silo One. We've got an emergency."

The bug-eyed cop brought Cavalaris's badge up to his eyes and said, "Hm." He handed the wallet back to Cavalaris. "So you're a cop. Now turn around and get your ass off these damn stairs."

Responding to a rush of static and Sheriff Vickers's voice in his ear, the other cop barked, "We've got a Denver homicide lieutenant up here on the stairs with us, Sheriff. Said you sent him. He legit?"

Vickers slammed a fist into the palm of his right hand. "He's legit. But I didn't send him. Get him off those stairs any way you have to."

The cop readjusted his earpiece, glanced down at Cavalaris, and then looked skyward, startled by the sound of an approaching helicopter. "The sheriff just gave me the okay to toss you over the stair rails if need be, Lieutenant. It would be a lot easier on all of us if you'd just turn around and walk back down."

"I d-d-don't—"

Cavalaris's protest was interrupted by the sound of the helicopter closing in rapidly. Seconds later, the top of the silo was awash in light.

"What the shit? Did you call in another spotter, Sheriff?" the burly cop yelled into his mike.

"Hell, no," said Vickers. "I asked for a Flight for Life chopper."

"Well, that's sure not what's hovering over our heads. It's a casualty-evac gunship, the kind we had in Desert Storm."

Before the sheriff could respond, a military medevac helicopter descended to within thirty feet of the silo's roof. Seconds later a battlefield-style casualty-evacuation basket, suspended by ropes, dropped out of the open door of the chopper. When the basket reached the rooftop, two men with submachine guns slung over their shoulders and dressed head to toe in black started snaking their way down two ropes that had been dropped from the opposite door.

"What the fuck?" yelled the burly cop. "Sheriff, you seein' what I'm seein'?"

"Sure am. The damn place is lit up as bright as day. I'm headed your way. Get up to the top of that silo and see what the hell's goin' on."

The two SWAT cops started up the stairs as the two men who'd dropped from the helicopter disappeared from view behind a rooftop stem wall. Cavalaris had become an afterthought.

Barely conscious and bleeding badly from his right shoulder, Napper had crawled to within a few feet of the silo's back stairway. When he had reached the metal hand rail that looped over the stem wall and tried to pull himself up, he had fallen onto his side and passed out. He was still lying there, drifting in and out of consciousness, when the two men from the chopper—one a former combat medic, the other a onetime army sharpshooter—reached the rooftop. The two men were standing over Napper when the stockier of Sheriff Vickers's two SWAT cops reached the top of the stairs. As he poked his head over the stem wall, a volley from the sharpshooter's MP5 nearly took his head off.

Screaming, "Shit!" he leaped down three stairs, looked down at his partner, and yelled, "Don't know who the hell's up there, but they're armed for a damn war." Glancing up at four cones of light streaming from the belly of the helicopter, he barked into his lapel mike, "We're outgunned up here, Sheriff. Got two shooters armed with submachine guns."

"Then get the hell out of there!" the sheriff yelled. "I'll see if I can't get some heavier artillery out here."

Sounding relieved, the burly cop said, "Roger," as he and his partner started descending the stairs. "Time to head off this tube of concrete," the bug-eyed cop called out to Cavalaris when they reached the third-floor landing.

"I heard the reception you got," said Cavalaris.

"Yeah—now, down the stairs, Lieutenant! Sheriff's orders!"

Cavalaris eyed the two SWAT cops, gritted his teeth, and clambered up the stairs as the burly cop fumbled with his earpiece. He kicked his ankle out of the grasp of the smaller cop as his partner yelled into his mike, "Sheriff, Cavalaris just slipped us. He's headed back up the stairs. Should we go after him?"

"Shit, no! I don't need you two getting killed because of some nitwit. Get the hell off those stairs. Now!"

As the two SWAT cops retreated, Cavalaris, clutching his 9-mm in his right hand, worked his way slowly up the stairs. Uncertain what he'd do once he reached the top, he realized his head was spinning. But not so much that he failed to recognize that he might have just flushed his career, or that there was someone on the roof of that silo who was important enough to rate having the men and machinery of war dispatched to rescue him. Telling himself that no matter what the cost, he intended to see who the hell that person was, he continued climbing.

The noise and wind whip from the chopper intensified as he got closer. Realizing that he needed to play it smarter than the lead SWAT cop had when he'd breached the stem wall, Cavalaris decided he'd have a look over the wall from somewhere other than the center of the stairs. Perhaps three feet to the left or three feet to the right of center. It didn't really matter as long as it wasn't the spot where a man with a submachine gun would be aiming at him point-blank.

He recognized that he had one other thing going for him. Since the machine gunner hadn't come after the SWAT cop, he didn't expect the man to come after him, and that gave him an advantage—the advantage of knowing that the two men who'd dropped out of the chopper were on a rescue mission, not a search-and-destroy mission. A mission that seemed to also mandate that no one see who it was who was being rescued, and that offered him another advantage. The men on the rooftop would have their hands full.

A few steps from the top of the stairs, he slipped his 9-mm into his pocket, knowing it would take two hands to maintain a grip on the stair railing and all the strength he could muster to pull himself up by the hand rail, peek over the stem wall, and hopefully duck back down behind it before any shooting started. His hands were moist with sweat as he slipped over the hand rail and onto the edge of the step. As he adjusted his footing, preparing to pull himself up, he heard voices.

"I think I've got him stabilized," someone called out over the noise of the chopper. The man's words ran together as if they were one.

"Good, 'cause we need to get the hell outta here," a second person said. "We only had a six-minute window, and it's closing in on five." The man's words were fluid and self-assured.

"I'm gonna need a hand getting him in the basket," the first man said.

"Now?"

"Yeah."

The word *now* seemed to set everything in motion. At almost the same instant that the sharpshooter shouldered his MP5 to help the paramedic lift Napper into the basket, Cavalaris poked his head above the stem wall. In the few seconds it took the precariously balanced Cavalaris to see who it was that the two men were transferring into the basket, the sharpshooter caught a glimpse of Cavalaris's forehead.

The sharpshooter released his grip on Napper, aimed the barrel of his MP5 at the stem wall, and squeezed off fifteen rounds at the spot where Cavalaris's head had been. With bullets and concrete chips flying everywhere, Cavalaris, mumbling to himself, "No w-w-way, no f-f-fuckin' way," was already scurrying back down the stairs. By the time he reached the second-story landing, the paramedic and the sharpshooter were being hoisted back up into the chopper, and the basket containing the severely wounded former miner, Franklin Watts—a man known in the clandestine world he'd navigated for more than four decades simply as Napper—was being swung into the belly of the chopper. Fifty seconds later, the helicopter's spotlights went out as the pilot nosed it north. In the span of less than a minute, rescue mission complete, the chopper disappeared into the darkness.

On the ground now and racing toward Sheriff Vickers's command post, Gus Cavalaris, his heart thumping as hard as it had the day he'd made lieutenant, was certain he now knew who'd killed Antoine Ducane. All that was left to determine was at whose request Ducane had been killed—and why.

Chapter 32

An hour and a half after the helicopter carrying Franklin Watts had disappeared into the eastern Colorado sky, Sheriff Vickers and a regiment of law enforcement officers from six jurisdictions remained on the crime scene while reporters and crews from three local TV stations milled around behind a police barricade scratching for information.

Gus Cavalaris had been detained at the sheriff's central command post for over half an hour and had been assured by the angry Vickers that by sunup he'd have a misconduct letter as long as the Declaration of Independence in his file, and that more than likely he'd soon have a new rank of sergeant. Cavalaris now stood in the moonlit brightness several yards from where CJ and Pinkie remained handcuffed. All three men were being guarded by a youthful Adams County deputy sheriff who normally worked the department's evidence locker. But since all hands had been called on deck, the deputy had drawn the assignment of standing watch over CJ and Pinkie and keeping an eye on Cavalaris until the sheriff found time to interrogate the three men again.

When an unmarked police cruiser pulled to a stop behind a SWAT van twenty yards away, the deputy barely looked up. The car's two occupants got out quickly and walked toward the deputy, moving in unison. The taller of the two men sported a mustache. His wispy thin eyebrows were barely evident, and he was wearing a baseball cap emblazoned with the initials "FBI." His capless shorter partner was nearly bald and midwinter pale. An ugly six-inch-long scar ran from just below his right earlobe to the top of his shirt collar. The taller man walked directly up to the deputy, flashed an FBI badge, and said, "I'm looking for Lieutenant Cavalaris. I was told I could find him and a couple of other men we need to talk to over here."

The deputy nodded toward Cavalaris. "That's him over there, but you'll have to get permission to talk to him from the incident commander, Sheriff Vickers." The deputy smiled. "The lieutenant—well, he's sorta under house arrest."

"We've already talked to Vickers, son. Who do you think sent us over here?" the man in the cap said.

"I'll have to check," the suddenly nervous-looking deputy said, watching Cavalaris walk toward him. Speaking into his lapel mike, the deputy said, "Sheriff, it's Potter. I've got a couple of FBI types over here wanting to talk to Lieutenant Cavalaris and the two guys in handcuffs. Is it okay?"

"Yeah," came the sheriff's response, loud and harried.

"We need to talk to Cavalaris and the other two men in private," the taller of the two FBI agents said to the deputy. "Why don't you take a five-minute break?"

"Sorry; I've got orders not to budge from here." He eyed the two men circumspectly as Cavalaris, who was now standing beside him, asked, "You l-l-looking for me?"

"We sure are, if you're Lieutenant Gus Cavalaris."

"I am."

The man in the cap pulled out an ID wallet and flashed his FBI shield. "Agent Ron Demming, Lieutenant." Nodding at his partner, he said, "Agent Hogan." Introductions completed, Demming turned quickly back to the deputy. "We've got it from here, son. Why don't you take a stroll?"

"Can't," said the deputy, eyeing CJ and Pinkie.

"I told you we'll watch them," said Demming. "This won't take but a few minutes."

"The sheriff'll have my hide."

"We're FBI, son," Demming said with a scowl. "I'm afraid *we'll* have your hide if we don't get a couple of minutes alone here with these men."

The deputy looked at Cavalaris. "Think it's okay, Lieutenant?"

"It's okay," said Cavalaris. "Go on."

The deputy looked briefly at Pinkie and CJ, checked his watch, and announced authoritatively to Demming, "Three minutes; that's it." He walked away toward a throng of other cops.

"Three minutes it is," said Demming. "We need to talk, Lieutenant," he added when he was sure the deputy was out of earshot.

"About what?" asked Cavalaris.

Demming slipped a 9-mm automatic out of his shoulder holster, glanced around into the moonlit darkness, and aimed the gun directly at Cavalaris. "I hate to have to pull rank on you, Lieutenant, but we've got a national security issue to deal with here. Don't make a ruckus. I want you to listen to my instructions and follow them to a T. You're going to walk over to the two men in handcuffs, uncuff them, and then walk back with Agent Hogan and me to our vehicle." He handed Cavalaris a handcuff key. "This should work. Once we reach the vehicle, you'll find three sets of handcuffs on the back seat. I want each of you to slip on a pair of cuffs, take a seat, and stay quiet. Now, you wanna hand me your weapon?"

"And if I d-d-don't?"

"Then I'll have to shoot you. Them too," Demming said, nodding toward CJ and Pinkie.

Cavalaris laughed. "Here, in the middle of three dozen cops?"

"Like I said, we're dealing with a national security issue here, Lieutenant. I shoot you; they shoot me. Bottom line's the same either way. Security doesn't get breached."

"You're serious," Cavalaris said in disbelief.

"Absolutely. Now, why don't you trot over to the men in handcuffs, pass along my instructions, uncuff them, and walk with me and my partner back to our vehicle?" Demming looked around to make certain the nervous deputy wasn't on his way back yet and that there was nothing but open space between where he stood and the car. "And Lieutenant, we're on the clock. That deputy's going to return any second, so move it. Oh, one last instruction. Once the three of you are in the vehicle, look down at the floor. You'll see several spring loaded U-bolts sticking up out of the floor. Slip your handcuff's chain under the lip of one of those bolts and clamp the bolt down until it locks. You'll be a tad uncomfortable anchored to the floor and bent over like pretzels, but that's okay. The ride'll be a short one. Now, get going. And make sure you tell those other two that if they so much as walk anything but a straight line on our way to the car or lift a head up once you're all in the back seat and anchored down, I'll shoot every one of you point-blank. You with me?"

Cavalaris nodded and walked with Agent Hogan over to CJ and Pinkie. During the walk, Hogan kept the barrel of his 9-mm aimed at Cavalaris's side. Cavalaris's instructions to CJ and Pinkie were exacting and brief, and soon all five men were headed for the unmarked cruiser. A minute later, CJ, Cavalaris, and Pinkie sat in the back seat, locked down and jackknifed in semifetal positions. Demming, on his knees and facing them from the front seat, kept his gun barrel trained on the back seat as Hogan threaded the vehicle through a maze of police cars, past a second SWAT van, and finally past a glum-looking line of news reporters. It was another three minutes before the nervous deputy from the evidence locker raced up to Sheriff Vickers to report that the five men were missing.

On a deserted Adams County road three miles from the sugar-beet factory, CJ, Cavalaris, and Pinkie were transferred to an armored car, where their mouths were taped shut and they were handcuffed to bench-style metal seats with their ankles also shackled. For the next half hour they rode along in silence. When the armored car finally pulled to a stop, they were unloaded and led across the pristine-looking concrete floor of what at first appeared to be a warehouse.

Demming and Hogan, now armed with submachine guns, escorted them to a walled-off area the size of a spacious living room that was tucked into a corner of what CJ suddenly realized was a huge World War II–style Quonset hut. When Demming swung open a door in the center of the walled room, CJ was the first to see Ron Else seated at a metal 1950s-style teacher's desk in the middle of a room. They were ushered to a long metal bench that was bolted to the floor. "Everybody have a seat," Demming said. Once they were seated their feet were shackled to U-bolts in the floor. Demming checked each man's handcuffs to make sure they were secure before taking three steps back, aiming his submachine gun at CJ, and announcing, "All set."

Else nodded and watched Demming strip the tape off all three men's mouths. Able once again to breathe normally, CJ and Pinkie gulped fresh air as Cavalaris began coughing violently.

"You about done there, Lieutenant?" Else asked after watching Cavalaris cough and gasp for air for the better part of a minute.

Red-faced, Cavalaris looked up and squeaked out, "Yeah."

"Hope so, because we've got a lot to discuss here, and in a very short time." Else glanced down at a sheet of paper on his desk. "So what have we got here?" he said, tapping the paper with an index finger. "Hmmm ... Cavalaris, Augustas, homicide lieutenant, Denver Police Department, seventeen-year vet, twice decorated for bravery. A lifelong stutterer. Not bad, Lieutenant, overcoming the odds like that." He turned his attention to Pinkie and smiled. "Niedemeyer, Andrus, known to friends and associates as Pinkie. Professional hit man. One tour of Vietnam, one Purple Heart. Just couldn't get the killing out of your system, huh, Niedemeyer?" His gaze finally fell on CJ. "Floyd, Calvin J., bail bondsman, bounty hunter." Else chuckled. "And latter-day antique merchant. Two tours of Vietnam and, oh my, a Navy Cross." Else drummed his fingers on the paper. "Tough hombres, it would seem." He eyed the other two agents before locking eyes with Cavalaris. "So, I've got a question for you, Lieutenant. Why were you out at the sugar-beet factory tonight?"

Cavalaris leaned back against the wall, took a deep breath, and said, "Investigating the m-m-murder of a man named Antoine Ducane. But y-y-you already know that, don't you, Agent Else?"

Else turned to CJ and Pinkie without responding. "And you two? Why were you out there?"

"Same reason," said CJ.

"But you're not a cop, Mr. Floyd. So you must've been investigating Ducane's death for somebody other than the taxpaying citizens of the city and county of Denver."

"I was, for a client."

"Your client have a name?"

"Yeah, but I'm afraid that's privileged information."

Else laughed. "What if I told you that your client's name's Willette Ducane?"

"I'd say the same thing. Privileged information."

"Okay, Floyd. Play it tough. Just remember, in the end it might cost you."

Realizing that CJ was stalling for time, Cavalaris interrupted. "Almost forgot, Agent Else, but I'm a-a-afraid I'm gonna have to a-a-ask you to have Agents Demming and Hogan show me their FBI badges again. I sort of missed getting a good look at them in the dark." Cavalaris's tone was unmistakably condescending.

Ignoring the remark, Else said, "Tell me what you know about Sheila Lucerne, Floyd."

"Afraid I'm gonna have to ask for some additional ID too," said CJ, smiling and following Cavalaris's lead.

"Niedemeyer?" Else asked, turning red. "Wanna tell me why you were out at that sugar-beet factory?"

"ID first," Pinkie said, flashing Else a spiteful grin.

The veins in Else's forehead pulsated as he forced a wry smile. "Okay. You want identification? Fine, I'll give you some." He reached into a desk drawer, fished out several ID wallets, spread them out on the desktop, and flipped the one closest to him open. The wallet contained an FBI shield. He eased it across the desktop for all three men to see. He then shoved a wallet with an LAPD shield inside across the desktop, followed by a third wallet with a U.S. Secret Service badge, and finally a wallet with a U.S. Customs shield. Smiling as he watched each man's eyes dart from wallet to wallet, he said, "The bottom line's this, gentlemen. I'm whoever I want to be, which, unfortunately for the three of you, means I can also pretty much do anything I want to. You can appreciate that kind of leeway, can't you?"

When no one spoke up, Else said, "You three strays have been rooting around in a hole you never should've stuck your inquisitive noses into, and you need to ease back out on your haunches, turn tail, and haul ass back down the road. Clear enough?"

"And if we don't?" CJ asked, continuing to stall but less certain now whether the tactic could help them.

"Then I'll have to deliver the same message to you, Mr. Navy Cross recipient, that I was forced to deliver to Cornelius McPherson."

"I see," said CJ, wondering how forthcoming Else would continue to be in his obvious attempt to let the three of them know that he meant business. "And I'm betting your friend you rescued from the silo rooftop is the one who delivered that message to McPherson?"

Else flashed CJ the sly, knowing smile of someone well-schooled in the art of interrogation. "That's your take, Floyd. Perhaps you need to stop confusing fact and fiction. Rooftop rescues, intimidating messages, even this meeting we're having right now. Did any of them happen for real? And if they did, and you told somebody about them, who would believe you? I'm simply suggesting what could happen if you stick your nose any deeper into that hole I mentioned. Of course some people prefer to step away from those kinds of treacherous holes and find themselves a whole new life."

"Like Rollie Ornasetti and Sheila Lucerne," said CJ. "Sorry, but I like the life I've got. Don't need you or anyone else inventing a new one for me." When Else didn't respond, CJ said, "Doesn't sound to me like any part of what you're offering here is in the FBI policy manual. Midnight helicopter rescues, contract hits, new identities—hell, they all seem more like a page from a CIA handbook."

"There you go, Floyd, rooting around where you shouldn't once again. Here's some advice. In order to put together a puzzle, you first need to make sure you have all the pieces. Otherwise, in the end all you have is an unfinished puzzle. If I were you, that's where I'd leave things—unfinished."

There was a moment of silence before Cavalaris spoke up. "We seem to be dancing around some issue here, Else. W-w-wanna spell it out?"

"Cut the con, Lieutenant. You know exactly what the issue is. And I'm telling all three of you to back the hell away from it!"

"Why not just kill us and be done with it?" CJ asked matter-of-factly.

"That's your problem to figure out, Floyd. Just like it'll be your problem to keep from making missteps in the future. The kind of missteps that could get you run over by a bus, or maybe even a road grader," Else said, flashing CJ a toothy grin. "What I'm saying to you is, the three of you are going to get to spend the rest of your lives walking around on eggshells. We'll see if you like it."

"Won't bother me," said Pinkie. "I don't scare that easy." He leaned forward on the bench and locked eyes with Else. "You're just a flunky, Else. You ain't poppin' us 'cause somebody told you not to. Somebody who can't afford the publicity. It would be tough to explain takin' out the three of us after what happened tonight. And shit! That could start people to, uh ... how do you keep puttin' it? Rootin'. I don't know what infected pussy you crawled out of, Else. The FBI's or the CIA's, or whether your orders are comin' from the people I usually get my assignments from, which I doubt. But I don't run scared. Can't afford to. You'll have to kill my ass first, fucker."

Else smiled. "I had the feeling that would be the kind of response I'd get from you, Niedemeyer. So here's a little food for thought. There's a homicide committed every nine minutes in this country, and if I choose to I can peg you as the killer in just about every new one. Arrange to have your DNA found at a murder scene in a dozen different cities on a moment's notice. Get my drift, hit man?"

Pinkie's eyes narrowed into a determined squint. "Fuck you, asshole."

Hoping to get Pinkie under control, Cavalaris spoke up. He was certain Else had no idea that he'd caught a glimpse of Franklin Watts during the silo rescue, and that, he reasoned, gave them a leg up on Else. A leg up that he couldn't afford to get chopped off because of Pinkie. "And if we s-s-stop rooting? What happens then?"

"Like I've already said. You walk. Then all you have to do is get used to your eggshells. I'd forget about Ducane and McPherson and whatever else it is you think Ducane might've once been party to and go back to my mundane little life if I were you, Lieutenant."

Cavalaris sat back on the bench. Eyeing CJ and then Pinkie and giving each a subtle nod he hoped they understood, he said, "You've g-g-got me convinced."

"Floyd? Niedemeyer?"

Uncertain why Cavalaris had suddenly decided to change their strategy from stalling to caving in but realizing there had to be a reason for the switch, CJ said, "Yeah, I'm okay with it."

"Me too," said Pinkie, reluctantly following suit.

"Good choice," said Else. "But just to make sure you all keep playing the game the right way, I've got a final piece of advice. First off, Floyd. Go back to rooting around in things that don't concern you and some people real close to you could get hurt, maybe even killed. The Madrids, the Benson woman—and of course Satoni." Else chuckled and turned to Cavalaris. "And Lieutenant, got no problem at all with you. I can have you off the force and bagging groceries in a split second. An easy enough thing to do considering your a-a-affliction. Some rookie cop misinterprets an order of yours during some intense situation, he shoots the wrong person, maybe even a politician, and you're thin-blue-line history. As I'm sure you know, life can be a tough row to hoe for stutterers."

Suppressing the urge to lunge at Else, Cavalaris thought about the piece of the Antoine Ducane puzzle he had tucked away for safe-keeping: the leg up that just might keep him and CJ and Pinkie from spending the rest of their lives looking over their shoulders. Controlling his rage, he simply smiled.

Else drew a deep breath and turned to Pinkie. "I've already said my piece to you, Niedemeyer. Think about it." He swept the ID wallets on the tabletop into a pile and dropped them one by one back into a desk drawer. "So, gentlemen, I'd say that's about it."

Drinking in the look of consternation on the three men's faces, he laughed. "Yep, I'm whoever and absolutely whatever I want to be. Remember that." He glanced briefly toward the two men with the submachine guns, nodded, and said, "Think it's time we take an armored-car ride in the country."

Chapter 33

The predawn sky was low and dark when CJ, with Gus Cavalaris and Pinkie standing at his side, rang Julie Madrid's front doorbell.

Hours earlier they'd been left in a corn field a hundred miles from Denver at the remote eastern edge of Elbert County. They zigzagged their way across miles of farmland in the dark before finally stumbling onto a creek and following it downstream until they reached a farmhouse. Cavalaris banged on the back door of the farmhouse until a rail-thin, weary-looking, barefoot man wearing coveralls appeared at the door. After Cavalaris announced that he was a police officer, the man reached to his right, grabbed a shotgun, snapped the weapon's twin barrels shut, and aimed them at Cavalaris's Adam's apple. When the man demanded to see some ID, Cavalaris, calmly and without a single stutter, asked him to call his captain back in Denver. Cavalaris had to repeat his captain's cell-phone number four times backward and forward before the shotgun-toting farmer agreed to make the call. After talking to Cavalaris's captain for over fifteen minutes while his pimple-faced fifteen-year-old son stood pointing the shotgun at the three men, the farmer finally let the exhausted trio into the house. When he put Cavalaris on the line with his captain, it was another five minutes before Cavalaris turned to CJ and said, "Settled, at least temporarily, but don't expect a warm reception in Denver." And when the farmer finally asked why the three of them were out in the middle of nowhere stumbling around in the dark, Cavalaris said, "We're w-w-working undercover, sir."

"Drugs!" the farmer said, glancing knowingly at his son.

Cavalaris smiled and said, "Nope. N-n-no drugs. But if you can help us get back to Denver, I'll give you some of the particulars."

A few minutes later the farmer and his son, both of them listening wide-eyed to Cavalaris, agreed to drive the three men back to Denver. For the entire two-hour trip, they listened in amazement as Cavalaris recounted what had happened at the sugar-beet factory. Every word of it was the truth up to the point of Ron Else's arrival. Everything after that, Cavalaris made up on the fly.

Moments after CJ rang Julie's doorbell a second time, Julie, who'd already been awake for an hour, appeared at the door, dressed in a full-length Vietnamese silk robe and looking as fresh as if it were midday. Only mildly surprised to see the disheveled trio on her doorstep, she ushered them into the house. Shaking her head, she said, "No need to explain. I watched your Broadway opening last night on the TV. No doubt there're still reporters out there at the sugar-beet plant waiting for you to surface. News, you know. They had your names still crawling across the bottom of my screen last night at 1 a.m."

"Figures," CJ said with a shrug, his voice noticeably hoarse.

"I've already been on the phone with Flora Jean, Mavis, and Alden this morning. Alden drove up from Colorado Springs last night. He's at Flora Jean's," Julie said as they walked down the hallway that led to her living room. "Mavis is beside herself. Better call her, CJ."

Barefoot and dressed in CSU basketball warmups, Damion appeared in the kitchen doorway near the end of the hall. Relieved to see that CJ, Pinkie, and Cavalaris were all in one piece, he said, "You've been all over the news."

"So I've heard," said CJ.

"No cops here yet, but we're expecting 'em. What happened?"

"Damion, please." Wagging a finger at Damion but looking directly at CJ, Julie said, "Call Mavis. I'll get Flora Jean, Alden, and Mario headed this way. Willette and Sheila are upstairs, asleep. I'll get them up in a sec." Turning to the weary-looking Pinkie and Cavalaris, she asked, "Up for some coffee?"

"Yes," said Cavalaris. "I'm th-th-thinking we've got a long day ahead of us."

"Sure thing," Pinkie added. "As long as I can have a shot of whiskey in mine."

"CJ, coffee?" Julie asked.

"Yeah, and I'm calling Mavis right now," he said, punching in Mavis's number on the kitchen's cordless phone.

Turning back to Pinkie, Julie asked, "Any brand preference?"

"Nope. As long as it's alcohol."

"How do you like your coffee, Lieutenant?"

"B-b-black, if you don't mind. And strong," said Cavalaris, surprised by the graciousness of the woman he'd up until then thought of only as simply one more shark.

Smiling, Julie said, "Sounds like a civil rights slogan," as she watched CJ walk, phone in hand, toward a far corner of the room.

Looking exhausted, CJ took a seat on a metal kitchen stool. With his back turned to everyone, he spoke softly into the receiver. "Mavis, it's me." There was a pause before, in response to Mavis's rapid-fire questions—"Where are you? Are you okay? And should I get right there?"—CJ answered, "Julie's. Yes. Yes. And hurry up."

An hour and twenty minutes and three pots of coffee later, Julie, CJ, Cavalaris, Pinkie, Flora Jean, and Alden Grace sat at Julie's dining-room table, thoughtfully dissecting everything that had occurred from the moment Antoine Ducane's body had been found at the Eisenhower Tunnel until CJ, Pinkie, and Cavalaris had been dropped in the corn field outside Limon. Sheila Lucerne, Damion, Mavis, Mario, and Willette Ducane sat in the adjacent kitchen, doing a lot more listening than talking. On the heels of Alden's deconstruction of the three-city JFK assassination plot, the discussion, opinionated and vocal, had moved to the issue of what Antoine Ducane's role had been in the assassination and what exactly had happened to Ducane back in 1972.

Mavis, sounding subdued, startled everyone by leaning forward on a kitchen stool and asking, "So how did they get Antoine's body up to the tunnel?"

Surprised that the question had come from Mavis, Pinkie, who'd been waiting for an opening, said, "I'm tellin' you, they froze the body. I'm sure of it. Just before all hell broke loose last night, I was in the process of inspectin' a refrigeration unit in that old sugar-beet storage shed CJ and I had been escorted to." Pinkie shook his head. "We shoulda known better. Anyway, I remembered seein' a couple of similar units when I was ... ah ... out at the ... ah ... place on business before. I think that sugar-beet-slicing show that old care-taker put on for us was just PT Barnum bullshit, made up to keep the old fart amused. The real way I think old Arnie and the folks tellin' him what to do handled the ... uh ... kinds of problems that came up out there was to freeze the problem away and then move it." Pinkie looked at Cavalaris and shrugged. "Never thought I'd be talkin' like this in front of a cop."

"Like I told you last night, you never know who you might end up sharing a lifeboat with, Pinkie." Cavalaris glanced across the table at Alden Grace. "What's your take, General?"

"Pinkie's assessment makes sense to me. With his Teamsters Union trucking connections, Ornasetti, if you believe he called for the hit on Antoine, would've had the resources to move a frozen body anywhere he wanted, no questions asked. And the time frame certainly fits. I've checked. Antoine disappeared about the time the interior Eisenhower Tunnel mechanicals and the tile support walls were being constructed in late 1972. The exact same time that Congressman Hale Boggs's plane disappeared in Alaska, just to reiterate."

"So they s-s-stuck Antoine's body in with the tunnel wall concrete, and nobody was the wiser?" Cavalaris asked.

"Not they," said Alden, shaking his head. "From what you and Pinkie have said, that was more than likely Franklin Watts's responsibility. Since Ornasetti's gofer, Randall Maxie, told Pinkie yesterday morning that Ornasetti wouldn't have dirtied his hands with the matter, and you've said yourself that Watts was the man on the silo rooftop last night, Watts certainly gets my vote."

"And I'd stuff the ballot box," said Cavalaris. "Last night I was n-n-nearly as close to Watts as I am to everyone sitting at this table." Cavalaris looked at Pinkie and then CJ, whom he was having a harder time convincing. "Watts was your machine gunner all right. How many times do I have to tell you?"

"Okay," said CJ, still sounding unconvinced. "So thirty-five years ago this guy Watts, who nobody here but you has ever seen, killed Ducane out at the sugar-beet factory. He then trucked the body up a mountain, deposited Ducane's remains behind a wall of concrete at eleven thousand feet, and shuffled off to Buffalo." CJ shook his head.

"Sounds a little iffy. But if Alden's buying in, I will too. One thing for sure—somebody schooled in handling heavy equipment was up there dancing around with me in Poudre Canyon." Moving quickly to cover the fact that he hadn't mentioned his Poudre Canyon encounter to Mavis, CJ said, "What I wanna know is this. If Watts did kill Antoine, who gave him the order?"

"Rollie Ornasetti; who else?" said Pinkie, taking a sip of tepid coffee that was now more bourbon than brew.

Once again CJ looked less than convinced. "Do you think Rollie actually ever had that kind of juice?" He glanced toward the kitchen. "Mario?"

"No way." Mario's response was emphatic.

"Then who called for the hit on Ducane?" Pinkie asked Mario, looking puzzled.

CJ responded instead, sensing Mario's reluctance to talk in front of Cavalaris. "My guess is that it would have to have been Carlos Marcello."

"You think Carlos called for a hit on his own son?" Willette asked from the kitchen.

"Why not?" asked Cavalaris. "We already know that Marcello probably set Antoine up to be Oswald-style cannon fodder in Chicago, and that he was lucky enough to get Antoine, a huge potential liability, out of his hair and glommed on to Rollie Ornasetti up here in Colorado. Maybe when Hale Boggs started making noises about taking a new look at the JFK assassination, Marcello decided to get rid of all his problems at once. Eliminate one with a plane crash and bury the other one up here in the Rockies."

"Okay, let's say that's what happened," said CJ. "That Marcello, not Ornasetti, was controlling Franklin Watts from down in Louisiana, and that Marcello gave Watts the go-ahead to kill Antoine. That provides us with a solution to one problem and leaves us with a whole lot of unanswered questions. Like, was somebody pulling Marcello's strings, where has Ornasetti disappeared to, and is somebody down in Louisiana still controlling what's going on up here in Colorado? Marcello's been dead for years, and I don't think his ghost is in charge of things."

Sheila Lucerne responded quickly. "I can't tell you if anybody was pulling Marcello's strings but I can tell you where Ornasetti probably is right now. He's either dead or in the process of getting a new identity. I've traveled that road."

"That sound reasonable to you, Mario?" asked CJ.

Still uncomfortable about sharing his opinion in front of a cop, Mario said, "Guess so."

"S-s-so, who do you think would be in charge of arranging th-th-things for Ornasetti at this stage?" asked Cavalaris.

When Mario didn't answer, Cavalaris stood and walked into the kitchen. Stopping short of Mario and looking him squarely in the eye, he said, "I know you don't t-t-trust me, Satoni. Figures. I-I-I'm a cop. But there're some things that went down l-l-last night out at that sugar-beet plant that haven't been touched on yet. Real important th-th-things that affect everyone sitting here. So how about h-h-holding off on passing final judgment on me until we've aired everything out?"

Mario looked past Cavalaris toward CJ and Pinkie. Watching them both nod, he said reluctantly, "I'm listening."

"Appreciate it." Cavalaris pivoted and returned to his seat. Mario said softly, "Nowadays the person in charge of arrangin' the kinds of things we've been talkin' about would be Carmine Cassias."

"And what about Franklin Watts?" CJ asked, aware that Cavalaris had squeezed as much information out of Mario as he was going to get. "If Watts survived last night's shoot-out, would Cassias be the one in charge of lining him up with a new identity?"

"More than likely," said Mario.

"So the bottom line here is that over the years Watts probably passed from Marcello's control to Cassias's?"

Mario's response was barely a whisper. "Probably."

Before CJ could follow up, Alden Grace cleared his throat and glanced around the room until his eyes met Flora Jean's. "What do you think, babe?"

Flora Jean shook her head. "Probably not, sugar."

"Yeah. That's what I'm thinking too," said Alden.

"Okay, Mr. and Mrs. Cloak-and-Dagger. Wanna dial us common folk in on what you're thinking?" CJ asked.

"We're thinking Cassias isn't Carlos Marcello," Alden said. "Probably not even half the man."

When everyone looked at Mario for confirmation. Mario said, "You're right there."

"What we're thinking," said Alden, nodding in agreement, "is that Cassias was probably having his strings pulled by somebody too. More than likely the same somebody who's in charge of Mr. Covert Chameleon Ron Else."

CJ and Cavalaris eyed one another sheepishly, aware that in their haste to get their arms around the crime of the twentieth century, they hadn't taken the time to check out Else the way they should have. Cavalaris had received verification that Else was who he claimed to be when he'd sent an initial inquiry to the Los Angeles FBI office. Now he realized he could have been talking to just about anyone—a plant, a cohort, a fictitious supervisor, even some out-of-work actor. "The s-s-son of a bitch played me," Cavalaris said angrily.

"That he did," said Alden, understanding the dangerous game Else was playing. "But don't be too hard on yourself. He's probably been FBI and CIA and a bunch of other things in between for a long, long time. He's had time to get good at it."

CJ's mistake had been to simply dismiss Else as a pompous FBI windbag. "Okay, Alden. We blew it," said CJ. "But if somebody was pulling Cassias's strings, mind letting us all in on who it was?"

Alden smiled. "More than likely that would have been, and probably still is, what we call a *combo platter* in the trade."

"Uh-oh," said CJ. "I feel a case of intelligence speak coming on."

"And you're right. But you've got Flora Jean here to translate. Just remember, this may all sound awfully implausible."

"We're listening," CJ said eagerly.

"Here's my take in a nutshell. Everybody gets their strings pulled in this life. And everybody's puppeteer has reasons for pulling those strings." Alden winked at Flora Jean. "Whoever was controlling Cassias likely had a set of reasons that stretched all the way back to the JFK assassination. Reasons that could only have served to benefit them. Here's a quick list of possible beneficiaries. First off, the CIA. No secret there. Prior to Kennedy taking office, the CIA had carte blanche to pursue its operations worldwide. But as every historian on the globe now knows, JFK was about to put an end to that freedom. He planned to end the war in Vietnam, no question, but more importantly, he was going to end the private little war that the CIA had going on in Laos. A war that the CIA, working hand in hand with the mafia, had set up in order to facilitate its astoundingly profitable drug-trafficking operations."

Alden glanced at Mario, who offered no response. "Both groups were also making money from their connections inside America's military-industrial complex. You make war, and somebody makes money. That's always been the case. By ridding themselves of JFK, the mafia would get an extra plum in its drug-trade pudding. It would also rid itself of JFK's brother Bobby and put an end to Bobby's anti-mafia crusade, and its partner the CIA would be able to go back to doing business as usual."

Alden took a deep breath as every eye remained focused on him. Looking ever more serious, he said, "So there's your anti-JFK CIA and mafia connection. But you also had scores of politicians, corporations, and top-level government bureaucrats, like FBI Director J. Edgar Hoover, wanting Kennedy out of their hair. Not to mention the anti-Castro Cuban community who Kennedy had let down with his mishandling of the Bay of Pigs invasion of Cuba."

"Sounds like half the world stood to gain from a Kennedy assassination," said CJ.

Alden shook his head. "Not quite. But what counts is that the American power elite I just mentioned—greedy politicians and industrialists, the CIA acting on behalf of the military-industrial complex, and the mob—certainly did, and that's a coalition capable of killing anyone."

"Strange bedfellows," said CJ.

"Not really." Alden smiled and glanced around the two rooms. "Look at the group assembled here. And you have to keep this in mind. Whenever and wherever there's money to be made—whether it's Las Vegas, pre-Castro Cuba, or Vietnam—organized crime, governments, and financiers will wheedle their way into the action. During the Vietnam War years, the most lucrative action was in the defense industry. In effect, the way to make money back then, especially if you were the mob, was to extract it from the war machine itself. Kennedy knew that, and he wanted the mob out of that business. They wanted to stay in and voilà—no more Kennedy."

CJ stroked his chin thoughtfully, realizing that Alden, a man who'd spent a career in the military and espionage game, had everyone spellbound except Mario and Flora Jean, who looked as if they were a page ahead of him in the sermon.

"So here's the bottom line," Alden said, his gaze locked on CJ. "As strange as it may sound, the factions I just mentioned—the CIA, the mob, corrupt politicians and bankers and industrialists—were the ones telling Carlos Marcello what to do. Marcello simply hired someone to pull the trigger."

"Think they're still telling Carmine Cassias what to do today?" asked CJ.

"They sure are, but not in the way you think—not in a one-on-one sense. Nowadays they operate more like America's new post-9-11 bogeyman terrorist. But the only thing they're interested in blowing up is their wallets. Like terrorists, there are select cells and personnel inside our own intelligence community: Ron Else, for instance, whose job it is to maneuver his way around the law and do whatever that combined power elite I keep mentioning instructs him to do. Else and people like him usually carry out their assignments under the trumped-up umbrella of 'national security.' You said yourself that one of Else's machine-gun-toting escorts coughed up that old bromide last night."

CJ nodded. "Sure did. So, let's sum up what we've got—start to finish. You're still sticking with the Corsican hit man, Lucien Sarti, as Kennedy's actual assassin and with Carlos Marcello as the man who was pulling Sarti's strings on orders from some invisible American power elite."

"Exactly."

"Hell of a premise," said Cavalaris, looking more than a bit dumbfounded. "Any chance you can put a more personal face on that so-called power elite for us?"

"Not really. All I can tell you for sure after swimming around in the intelligence and espionage soup for more than twenty-five years is, excluding the mob, they're the kind of people who've had seats of power in our government since the Revolutionary War. The very same people whose sound bites you hear on the nightly news screaming for the enactment of a one-world monetary system and a global military police force that would supplant monetary systems and police forces that are currently national."

"And JFK refused to play ball with them?" asked Julie, uttering her first words in over half an hour. As the consummate trial lawyer, she'd learned long ago that you could learn more from listening than talking. And once again, she had.

"That's it," said Alden. "And by refusing, he sealed his fate."

"Quite a postulate," Julie said thoughtfully. "And not exactly a new one, I'd add. I remember taking an economics law course in law school where the professor claimed that there was a social elite in America and Europe that's been able to control the destiny of nations around the world for more than two hundred years. I thought he was just blowing smoke."

"He wasn't," Alden said. "What your professor was probably alluding to was the Rothschild plan. A plan built on the premise that wars are fought so that the combatants end up benefiting the international banking community's social elite by borrowing money from them to fund their wars. The plan's not a myth—it's frighteningly real. Thought up by a money-grubbing nutcase named Mayer Amschel Bauer in 1773, a man who made no bones about wanting to control the banking resources of the world."

"Damn," said CJ. "Sounds like he wanted to rule the world."

"He probably did," said Alden, shaking his head disgustedly. "Problem is, there are people like him born every day."

"No argument there," said CJ. "The question for us right now is, where do we go from here?"

"Besides duck and cover, you mean?" asked Alden, flashing CJ the deadly serious look of a commanding general. "Where we all go from here is to drop the issue. We know that Franklin Watts probably killed Antoine Ducane." Alden glanced sympathetically at Willette. "I've told everyone why I think Lucien Sarti was probably JFK's assassin, and we know that Rollie Ornasetti's dead or out there waiting in line for either the mob or representatives of my so-called power elite like Ron Else to furnish him with a new identity. We can't take things much further."

"Fine. I'm ready to back off." CJ glanced knowingly toward Pinkie and Cavalaris as he mulled over the threats Else had issued to each of them the previous night. "But here's a final question. What if Else and his band of rogue FBI brothers or CIA brothers, or whatever they're calling themselves that day, decide to come back?"

"First off, they're not rogues," said Alden. "They're far deadlier. They can switch identities in an instant, and they're agency-approved and real. All I can say is that if they come back, we deal with them. Everyone sitting here has to understand that." He looked around the two rooms. His gaze stopped briefly on each of the ten people. "We're all going to be living with a secret now, and if Else and his cronies ever decide to raise their ugly heads again, then just like the twelve people who originally made a pact with Mayer Bauer to be participants in his Rothschild plan, the eleven of us will have to make a pact to protect one another and persevere."

The room fell silent as suddenly all eyes were on Alden and CJ. "Are we of one mind?" asked Alden.

"One," came CJ's response as slowly, one by one, each and every head in the room began nodding.

Epilogue

The story that CJ and Pinkie told Sheriff Vickers when they surprised him by walking into his office several hours after the meeting at Julie's, in the custody of Gus Cavalaris and with Julie Madrid at their side, sounded as convoluted and improbable as the story Vickers's deputy had recounted about their disappearance the previous evening.

Reluctant to alarm Julie, CJ hadn't told her about Ron Else's threats until they were on their way to meet with Vickers. Focused on the issue at hand and sounding unintimidated, Julie announced that she'd deal with that issue later. She then reminded all three men of two things they had agreed on earlier: there could be no secrets from her if she was to be their lawyer, and when they met with Vickers, she would do the talking.

Their meeting began on a down note with Vickers announcing that Arnie DeVentis had died that morning, and he would therefore unfortunately have to rely on CJ's, Pinkie's, and Cavalaris's accounts of what had occurred at the sugar-beet factory before the sheriff's arrival. Looking directly at Cavalaris, Vickers said, "So give me the specifics, Lieutenant."

Cavalaris glanced at Julie, who nodded for him to go ahead. Side-stepping any mention of Antoine Ducane, Cavalaris described the gist of his Cornelius McPherson investigation, including why he believed the man who'd been rescued from the silo rooftop—whom it turned out CJ and Pinkie had also been after—had probably been

McPherson's killer. As he told the story, he glanced back and forth between Julie and the sheriff, thinking all the time about the possibility of a lost career and the single word *eggshells*.

Leery of Cavalaris's account, Vickers and a deputy, in spite of frequent objections from Julie, spent the next hour interrogating the three men about everything from who had hired CJ and Pinkie to look into the McPherson killing to a question the sheriff posed at least a half-dozen times: Why had the FBI intervened the previous night, and why was the FBI now saying that the mysterious agent in charge of whisking CJ, Pinkie, and Cavalaris off almost to Kansas had been dead for almost four years?

When no one came up with an answer to his question, the sheriff said, "We're gonna need some more time with this case, gentlemen, Ms. Madrid. We still need to clear up the issue of the DeVentis shooting, the lieutenant's interference in my SWAT operation, and of course the ghost of that FBI agent, Else." The sheriff eyed Cavalaris. "In the meantime, Captain Patterson's waiting to see you in the room next door. I'm sure you'll have a lot to say to your boss. Afraid your other clients are gonna be guests here with me in Adams County for a while, Ms. Madrid. For the moment, all I can charge them with is trespassing, inciting a disturbance that led to loss of life, and possession of illegal firearms. But depending on what we find out about the DeVentis shooting, things could easily be stepped up to a murder charge. You better hope we don't find out that the old caretaker took a bullet from one of their weapons, counselor."

Cavalaris was about to tell the sheriff that it was his shot that took out DeVentis when Julie raised her hand and cut him off. "I'll handle this, Lieutenant." Smiling at the sheriff, she said, "Do what you have to, Sheriff; just remember that in many ways the law's nothing more than a competitive sport. Hope your team's up to the competition."

The twenty-eight hours that CJ and Pinkie spent in the Adams County jail paled in comparison to the time Julie put in during the next six weeks preparing a defense for them—a defense that, as she'd fully expected, never saw the light of a courtroom. After a rash of newspaper stories about the Brighton shoot-out served Cavalaris up to the public as a dogged cop trying to do his job and CJ and Pinkie as vigilante heroes, the case against the three men fizzled out. Cavalaris, it soon came out, had actually shot Arnie DeVentis, a known mobster who'd bled to death from a leg wound after setting CJ and Pinkie up to be killed by the silo rooftop shooter. Behind-the-scenes political maneuvering initiated by Denver's police chief and mayor also served to help their case. Neither man had a desire to have a Denver cop, much less one who was being hailed as a hero, hauled into court and painted as an obstructer of justice—especially with a purported hit man and a bail bondsman, as their lawyer kept reminding reporters, as his character witnesses. Ultimately the case against CJ and Pinkie was plea-bargained down to a trespassing and minor illegal-weapons-possession charge. They were each fined $2,000, which Mario Satoni gladly paid, and Cavalaris was exonerated. What was never revealed about those offstage negotiations was that the mayors of both Denver and Brighton, along with their chiefs of police, had been lobbied by Colorado's governor, a man with political aspirations that some said included the White House, to make the sugar-beet shoot-out go away.

In order to appease Sheriff Vickers, Cavalaris did receive a letter of reprimand, but the citation for valor he received a month later in

Denver, and his continued media-darling coverage by the press, embarrassing as it was for him, served to mitigate the sting.

During the six weeks that Julie was busy preparing her defense, Cavalaris and CJ were able to put a better, but still incomplete, face on Franklin Watts, although they never uncovered his CIA code name, Napper. They learned that the small house that Watts had rented for decades in the mountain community of Silverthorne, just west of I-70's four-mile ascent to the Eisenhower Tunnel, had burned to the ground in the early-morning hours on the night following Watts's helicopter rescue. The burned-out hulk of a late-model BMW, the car that Cavalaris suspected Watts had used in his drive-by shooting of Cornelius McPherson, was found in the charred remains of that home's garage. The house, they found out from neighbors, had been emptied the afternoon before the fire by three men dressed in brown uniforms who had pulled up to the house in a moving van. One woman who described the movers as polite and efficient also recalled that one of the movers, a chunky, balding man, had an ugly scar running down the side of his neck.

Watts's personnel records at the Colorado Department of Transportation, thirty-nine years' worth all told, had also somehow disappeared by the time CJ and Cavalaris went to retrieve them. The only thing the baby-faced twenty-year-old who had released the records prior to their arrival could recall about what he continually called "an official records transfer" was that a tall, impressive-looking FBI agent had requested the records and that the agent had dropped by the DOT offices and picked them up in person.

CJ and Cavalaris were able to unearth one gold nugget, however— a nugget surreptitiously obtained from a copy of Franklin Watts's phone records. Watts, it turned out, in the days leading up to the Brighton shoot-out, had made an inordinate number of calls to two phone numbers in Louisiana and Washington, D.C. The Louisiana phone number belonged to Carmine Cassias. The Washington, D.C., number, however, showed up as disconnected.

Convinced from their investigation that Watts had killed both Ducane and McPherson, and that if Watts hadn't died that night at the sugar-beet factory, he was more than likely now living a CIA-, FBI-, or mob-initiated new life, CJ and Cavalaris left the Colorado mountains satisfied that the McPherson and Ducane murder cases had been solved. For them, however, the JFK killing and the thirty-fifth president's assassin would always remain yet another matter, although both men remained reluctantly convinced that Corsican hit man Lucien Sarti, as Alden Grace had asserted, had killed the president.

The roar of the partisan Colorado State University Moby Arena crowd was so loud that a jubilant CJ and Julie Madrid could barely hear themselves talk. They'd just watched the CSU basketball team, in only its third game of the season, not simply nudge or squeak out a win over UNLV—a bitter Mountain West Conference rival and a team that had come into the game ranked sixth nationally—but crush them 88-62.

Damion and Shandell Bird, now college seniors, had scored a total of 48 points, and Damion had finished the game with his second triple-double of the season: 23 points, 11 rebounds, and 10 assists. Televised nationally as the Saturday game of the week, thanks in large part to UNLV's lofty ranking and the presence of Colorado State's two preseason-consensus All-Americans, the game had garnered enough early-season national attention to warrant one of CBS's top announcing crews.

The stands remained full of euphoric fans holding their index fingers in the air and shouting, "We're number one," as CJ and Julie began weaving their way courtside to take in the postgame star-of-the-game TV interview set to feature the CSU coach and his two young stars. A few rows up from the court, CJ turned to Julie and said, "Not bad for a kid who's gonna cut this all loose after this season and head off to medical school."

Julie smiled. "It's what he's always wanted to do, CJ. You know that. There's not enough money in the world to get him to change his mind."

CJ nodded understandingly. "That's for sure."

On the floor now, they watched a TV technician adjust the lighting for the interview. Looking around at the crowd, surprised that Aretha Bird hadn't joined them by now, CJ asked, "Have you seen Shandell's mom?"

"I saw her for a couple of minutes before the game," said Julie. "She didn't say much, and frankly she looked a little worried. But she always looks that way before a game. Said she'd see me after the game."

"Maybe Shandell's having problems with his grades," CJ said.

"Not according to Damion."

"Girls, then," CJ said, smiling.

"That would be my guess. Hey, here they come," Julie said excitedly as she watched the CSU coach, flanked by Damion and Shandell, walk up and shake hands with TV commentator Clark Kellogg.

The four men stood in a semicircle inside a roped-off area as Kellogg, who'd been the game's courtside analyst, stepped between the coach and the players. "Everybody ready?" he asked as Damion, spotting CJ and Julie, smiled and raised an index finger skyward.

Shandell repeated the gesture, but only after Damion prodded him with an elbow.

"Okay," said the lighting technician. "Ten seconds. Four, three, two, one." He nodded and cued Kellogg.

Smiling at Coach Haroldson and offering him a lead-in, Kellogg said, "Big win, Coach."

"Don't think they come much bigger this early in the season. But when you're at home, you have the crowd behind you, and you have a team with our kind of resolve, good things happen."

"Three games, three wins, and you've just knocked off the nation's sixth-ranked team. Some people are saying this could be your year."

"If it is, I can tell you why." Looking at Shandell and Damion and beaming, Haroldson said, "Four years ago the two guys standing beside me decided to stay here in Colorado instead of taking off for California or North Carolina or Indiana to play ball. And you see what it's given us here at CSU." Looking straight into the camera, he said, "We do play basketball here, folks. Colorado's not just for skiers."

Turning quickly to Damion, and cutting the coach's recruitment message short, Kellogg said, "And here's one player who stayed, Damion Madrid. You had your second triple-double tonight, Damion. Must have felt real good in front of the home crowd."

"Absolutely." Damion draped an arm over Shandell's shoulder and pulled his best friend to his side. "But we couldn't have done it without the Blackbird here. Like everyone says, the man soars."

"So what does the great Larry Bird say about you turning his name into a nickname, Shandell? Blackbird certainly seems to have stuck," said Kellogg.

"Haven't talked to him, but I think he's probably okay with it."

"Think you'll be able to keep these two clicking the rest of the year?" Kellogg said, turning to the coach.

"I hope so."

Kellogg turned his mike to Damion. "You're an academic All-American, headed for med school, I'm told. No NBA in your future?"

"No." Damion glanced out into the crowded court and spotted Julie. "It's medicine for me, like I've always said. But lately I have given some thought to an additional career."

"And what's that?" said Kellogg, looking surprised.

"Law school, maybe."

Hardly believing her ears and with a look of amazement on her face, Julie turned to CJ and whispered, "What?"

"Got me," said CJ, shrugging.

"Quite a switch. What brought that on?" asked Kellogg, watching his floor director signal for him to wrap it up.

"A few things happened over the summer," said Damion. "Got me to thinking about combining a career in law and medicine."

Looking straight into the camera, Kellogg said, "You heard it here first on CBS, folks. Sounds like it'll not only be a full four years here at CSU for Madrid and Bird but a couple more degrees for Damion Madrid as well. Four years of suiting up these two should make you happy," Kellogg said to Coach Haroldson.

"Always great to coach student athletes."

"Well, from the start of things this season, it looks like you're on a roll." Watching the floor director spin his finger winding-clock fashion, Kellogg said, "Our final score from Moby Arena tonight, Colorado State, 88; UNLV, 62. For CBS Sports, and all the CBS crew here in Fort Collins, Colorado, thanks for joining us."

After a round of handshakes and some parting comments, Kellogg walked away, leaving Damion, Shandell, and Coach Haroldson waving to fans. "Let's go hit the showers," Haroldson said finally. Winking, he added, "Good game."

Blowing Julie a kiss and flashing CJ a thumbs-up, Damion hollered, "See you after I shower, and don't forget Niki's coming with us to eat." He and Shandell started across the court as CJ turned to Julie and said, "Med school and law school—kinda pricey."

Julie shook her head. "I'll say. That's the first time I've heard any of it. Looks like we'll have a lot to discuss at dinner."

"Sure looks ..." CJ stopped midsentence as he caught sight of a thick-bodied balding man with his right hand jammed into his jacket pocket running across the court toward Damion and Shandell. Pivoting and leaving Julie speechless, CJ raced across the court and threw a cross-body block into the man just as Damion was about to disappear into the home-team tunnel exit. The man crumpled to the floor, and the box of popcorn in his left hand went flying.

When Damion looked around, CJ, who'd quickly scanned the man's neck for a scar only to find to his dismay that there wasn't one, was helping the man up. "Sorry," said CJ. "You okay?" Looking at the man head-on, CJ could now see clearly that the man's only real resemblance to the mysterious machine-gun-toting Agent Hogan was his build and his baldness. CJ shook his head and again said, "Sorry."

The visibly shaken man dusted himself off and, trying his best to look macho in front of Damion, eyed CJ and said, "You want Madrid's autograph that bad? Go for it." He waved CJ ahead of him. "I'll go second." He slipped an autograph book out of the pocket he'd had his hand jammed into and mumbled, "Jerk!"

Looking confused, Damion said, "Somethin' wrong, CJ?"

"No," said a thoroughly embarrassed CJ. "I was just running to tell you to take your time showering. We've still gotta find Niki." He eyed the man he'd tackled, offered one last apology, lowered his head, and walked back across the court toward a startled-looking Julie, thinking with every step he took, *Eggshells. You'll be walking on eggshells, Floyd, for the rest of your life.*

Even with Sheila there now to comfort her, the time just before sunset remained painful for Willette Ducane. That was the time when she always thought about Antoine. As she looked out toward the bog from her rocking chair and watched bog mist rise and blend in with the humid air, she listened to the bog's rhythmic, mysterious aquatic noises and realized that for her, the race was almost over.

Word had circulated around the parish as soon as she'd come back from Colorado with Sheila Lucerne in tow that the reason Antoine had left Louisiana all those years ago and had gone up North was because of a woman. A woman who had now come to New Iberia to care for Willette. Neither woman had encouraged any talk that would reveal the real story, and Willette knew that half the people who were whispering about them realized there was a deeper truth. But in the six weeks since they'd been home, the two women who'd cared the most about Antoine Ducane had settled into the symbiotic routine of comforting one another, let the truth be damned.

Word had come down from Carmine Cassias to his people to leave both women alone, but only after Cassias himself had been told that any hint of action against Willette and Sheila that might draw attention to the chaos that had recently occurred in Colorado, or resurrect the long-buried story of plans to rid a country of a president, would be his undoing.

There were people above Cassias. People with the kind of power and status that he could never attain, much less understand. And he listened to them. Those people, like their ancestors, had given Cassias his orders: *Revive the JFK assassination issue in any way, shape, or form, and you will assuredly go the same way.*

When Cassias had sent an emissary to tell Willette and Sheila that if they kept their mouths shut about anything they suspected might have happened almost forty-five years ago, no harm would come to them, the emotionally and physically drained women—one tired of hurting, the other tired of hiding—had accepted the offer with barely a comment.

Continuing to rock and eye the bog, Willette reminded herself that all she wanted out of life in the time she had remaining was to be left in peace. As she watched the last rays of sunlight meld into the bog's foggy mist, Sheila stepped out onto the porch. "You wanna come in now?" Sheila asked softly. When Willette didn't answer, she said, "Did you hear me?"

"I heard you, Monique," said Willette. "I'll be in in a sec." Willette, who'd taken to calling Sheila Monique in the past two weeks, eyed the bog and the mist and the final glimmering rays of sunlight one last time before scooting forward in her chair to get up. Struggling to rise as Sheila rushed to her aid, she said softly, "Monique's here with me, Sugar Sweet. No worry. Everything's gonna be okay 'til you come back home from up North, baby."